The Profile Picture

Chrissy Ward

Published by Clink Street Publishing 2023

Copyright © 2023

First edition.

ISBN:
978-1-915229-92-2 - paperback
978-1-915229-93-9 - ebook

Introduction

The story unfolds as Maria, an independent determined woman now in her mid-fifties, is on the verge of attending an important occasion which will inevitably change the course of her life forever. The sequence of events preceding this day, sees her follow a tumultuous journey between her past and the present, where many mistakes and errors of judgement are laid bare.

Following the sale of her beloved business, which has occupied her life for the past eighteen years, Maria returns to her home county, where she immediately embarks on a rather ambitious refurbishment programme to transform her new home to its former glory.

Never one to miss an opportunity, it's not very long before Maria, quite unexpectedly, finds herself involved in a completely new business venture, which in turn leads her to experience many more of life's challenges. At the same time, actively pursued and encouraged by her young niece, Maria reluctantly becomes drawn into the world of social media where she finds herself reunited and face to face with many characters from her past.

Struggling to deal with the aftermath of emotion, caused by her own memories which have been kept locked away for many years, Maria eventually uncovers the key to so many unanswered questions and now, finally, she can make sense of so much, she could previously never understand.

With the missing pieces of her life revealed and the puzzle of her past now complete, it is time for Maria to make her final decision and decide once and for all which path to follow.

The Prelude

Realistically, I suppose I should have envisaged a restless night, but I most certainly hadn't anticipated feeling such incredible tension and nervous anxiety, which, despite my best efforts, stubbornly remained present and active all morning. As a result, nothing so far had quite gone to plan, which didn't bode well for any occasion, let alone one of this magnitude. In the last 24 hours I'd scrutinised every aspect of the day ahead and there was only one thing I wasn't concerned about and that, believe it or not, was the cake.

A cursory glance in the hall mirror as I reached the bottom of the stairs did nothing to provide the reassurance I was looking for; in fact, it was quite the opposite. Maybe, with the benefit of hindsight, it would have been a sensible idea to purchase an alternative outfit or would that have caused more confusion and uncertainty? Anyway, in all honesty I'd struggled to find one that I liked, let alone two.

I could remember clearly the hours I'd spent one Saturday, frantically running from one store to another, and at first it seemed I was searching for the impossible, until a kindly assistant recommended somewhere she thought I might like to try. It was a tiny little shop, just outside the main shopping centre and one which I would normally have instantly dismissed, but surprisingly it was here that eventually I found an outfit I considered at the time to be perfect.

Initially, it was the colour that caught my eye, a beautiful, delicate shade of powder blue. The outfit itself, a two piece in the most exquisite Italian lace, fitted like a glove; the skirt with a flared, fluted hemline provided elegance, and the top with its beautifully draped neckline added just the right amount of style. Admittedly it wasn't anything like I'd originally set out to buy, but I'd fallen in love with it, and I thought, at the time, it was ideal.

But that was then, and this was now, and any confidence I might have experienced in the shop, while being praised and admired by the enthusiastic assistant wasn't anywhere to be seen today. As I continued to criticise my reflection, the unmistakable sound of tyres crunching over gravel sent a refreshed surge of panic through my whole body. With a deep breath and a trembling hand, I reached for my keys, there was no time for further deliberation, it was time to leave. I opened the front door and gingerly stepped outside.

Thinking back, it was extraordinary to even consider that if it hadn't been for my teenage niece Chloe, I probably wouldn't have experienced any of the incidents that led to that remarkable day.

Chloe, an incredibly lively and cheerful personality, radiated warmth and determination of character. So, it was no real surprise to witness the utter commitment she displayed with any challenge, project or hobby, and it was no different when that project was myself.

For reasons I wasn't totally convinced deserved the effort, Chloe became wholeheartedly immersed in launching my debut into the world of social media. Don't get me wrong I wasn't totally computer illiterate: back in the day I'd enjoyed the introduction of technology in the workplace, and even now with my small business it was an integral part. It was more the personal side I wasn't keen on; social media just wasn't high on my list of priorities and so that's where Chloe came in. Fully convinced it would "enhance my whole life", her words not mine, Chloe began her project in earnest: establishing social media platforms, downloading appropriate apps and the list went on…

Unfortunately, though, it wasn't too long before we encountered the first hurdle. Personally, I couldn't understand why anyone would be the slightest bit interested to know where I went to school, what I did for a living and indeed what I looked like; it was all far too intrusive for my liking. My reaction completely baffled Chloe, who decided if nothing else a profile picture couldn't possibly cause too much trouble.

However, it wasn't until we were away on a family holiday in Tuscany that Chloe finally achieved any kind of success. We were a party of seven: my sister Kim; her husband David; their son Harry; Chloe; our other sister Clare and her partner Jon; and of course me, Maria.

Our holiday home for the week was an idyllic Italian villa nestled on a hilltop, presiding over splendid views of olive groves and vineyards.

For both Harry and Chloe, initially the most important feature was the availability of WIFI, until they spotted an infinity pool and discovered a sauna along with a well-equipped gym and tennis courts. Instantly the formidable idea of being stranded in the middle of nowhere for a whole week was forgotten and their laughter filled the air.

As the lazy days of holiday life unfolded, we enjoyed cocktails by the pool, BBQs and long relaxed lunches at the local trattoria, complemented with endless hours of conversation and friendly debate.

Chloe, never one to accept defeat, quickly engaged the help of her brother and between them they went to great lengths in their quest to secure a photo I would agree to post.

Finally, realising the task in hand wasn't going to be that easy, the brother and sister duo acquired the help and support of the entire party, and so with increased pressure and desperate for some peace, I eventually had no choice and relented graciously. Absolutely elated, the pair wasted no time and with their mission complete my picture was out there for anyone who was remotely interested to peruse.

All too quickly Saturday morning dawned, the day to leave was upon us and the general mood deteriorated rapidly, all of us aware reality was just around the corner.

CHAPTER ONE

Maria – The Present

A luxury reserved for Sunday mornings, Maria snuggled even further under the duvet, the muffled sound of birdsong and the early morning sun creeping slowly through the windows, added to the peace and tranquillity of the moment.

It hadn't been too long ago that Maria had lived in a total state of disarray, with dust and rubble a constant feature while a massive programme of refurbishment was completed. On more than one occasion she'd regretted the decision to buy a property in need of so much attention, but now it was finished, and the all the inconvenience just a memory, she couldn't be happier.

Jon, an architect by trade, had been the mastermind behind the whole operation. His vision of possibilities had provided a fabulous blank canvas, from which Maria had created her perfect home. Open plan living dominated the ground floor, but it wasn't devoid of character as so many were; between them they'd managed to incorporate many of the original Edwardian features, and it had most certainly paid off, providing a subtle mix of old and new.

Admiring her own choices, it had undeniably been the right decision to ditch the chintz; she'd gone for neutrals throughout with a splash of colour to define each room. Now happy and familiar with her new surroundings, it felt good to be home.

The distinctive sound of her mobile broke through the relaxed reverie she was enjoying. Leaning over she grabbed her phone and checked the screen before answering; it was no surprise to see it was her sister Kim.

"Morning," Maria answered, trying her best to sound alert and not half asleep.

"Sorry, did I wake you?" Kim asked as she heard her sister's groggy voice. Hastily she checked the time on her watch, it was 8.30, Maria was always up and about by now, unless she was ill.

"I was awake," Maria reassured her anxious sister. "I was just enjoying my last chance to relax."

"Fine as long as you're ok." Kim quickly continued. "Anyway, two things: do you want to come over for lunch? It's going to be a late one I'm afraid, about 3.30; and a message from Chloe: have you checked your social media site yet? But I'm guessing it's a no to the latter."

"You guessed right." Maria laughed. "And thanks for the invite but I think I'll stay home today; I know I have a lot of prep to do from orders I received before I went away, and I have no idea how long it will all take."

"Ok, if you're sure, but if you change your mind later, just let me know, speak to you soon, bye." Constantly chasing her tail and living life at 100mph, Kim hung up, eager to continue with her busy day. She was the baby of the family, the youngest of the three sisters. There was an eight-year age gap between Kim and Maria, who was the eldest, and she'd always been a whirlwind, but she had the kindest, biggest heart and Maria loved her for it.

Reluctantly, Maria recognised it was time for her day to begin. Opening her business email account, her initial reaction was one of complete surprise; there must have been at least 15 new orders and a plethora of enquiries.

Born out of pure frustration and disappointment, it had been quite by chance that Maria simply stumbled into this new business venture. At no time had she ever considered herself a competent cook, so it was a shock to everyone, herself included, when having tried her hand at baking, her efforts were surprisingly very good. Originally, it had simply been the case, in her experience, cakes and pastries in coffee shops never quite lived up to her expectations. They always looked so delicious but that wasn't always reflected in their taste. Admittedly, Maria had to agree, previously she'd been completely spoilt with access to award-winning food daily. So, she became curious; how difficult could it be to create a cake that tasted as good as it looked? Sheepishly she began by baking the odd birthday cake for family members, and quickly this escalated to include friends, and before she knew it her repertoire included cakes, pastries and desserts and demand was high.

The rest of her day passed in a frenzy of baking prep and answering enquiries and at six o'clock, with just one last job on her list, she collapsed into her favourite comfy armchair in the living room. Maria picked up her phone, all she needed to do now was to check in with Louise: a young woman she'd employed to help with prep and general duties.

Surprised at the number of notifications showing on the screen of her phone, before ringing Louise Maria decided to investigate. Normally they were all complete nonsense and of no interest but as she scrolled down, two familiar names stared back at her: Lisa Golding and Karen Phillips, two names from way back, were showing as friend requests.

Maria shook her head in disbelief, this was a real blast from the past, it must be 20 years or may be even more since they'd last had any contact. This most certainly had to be a result of Chloe's work on her social media platforms, otherwise it was a huge coincidence.

Without hesitation Maria dialled Kim's number. "You'll never guess what has just shown up on my phone," she explained as Kim answered her phone. "I've had these friend requests from Lisa and Karen, two girls I used to work with years ago."

"I remember both of them," Kim admitted. "You were good friends with Lisa if I remember correctly, I hope you're going to accept."

"I don't know," Maria answered her sister honestly.

"Oh, you must," Kim urged. "Why on earth wouldn't you? Surely, you're just a little bit curious to know what they've been up to… I know I would be."

"I'm not sure," Maria said tentatively. "So much has happened, we're all different people now… Well, I am anyway." She paused for a moment before continuing. "We probably wouldn't have anything in common now anyway."

"Well, you'll never know if you don't accept," Kim said, sensing Maria didn't sound too keen.

When Maria hung up, having listened to Kim's reasoning, she still wasn't convinced. There were far too many memories relating to that period of her life, memories she'd long since filed under "Do Not Disturb". Was she ready to revisit them and everything that would entail? She wasn't at all convinced. Maria shivered, suddenly she felt cold, tired and unusually lonely; this wasn't the time to dwell on the past, she had a busy week ahead and no time for self-indulgence.

By the following Friday evening, completely exhausted, Maria had to admit she'd taken on far too much. Often to be found baking late into the night she'd struggled to complete all the orders on time, and both her sisters were very concerned.

"You need to stop and rethink this whole thing; you can't carry on like this, it's ridiculous," Clare protested during a mid-week catch up. "I thought when you sold your last business you were going to retire, not jump headfirst into something else that takes up all your time."

"I know, I know," Maria said abruptly. "But I've accepted the orders, and now I have to deliver."

"Well, I won't keep you then," Clare said. "But promise me you'll rethink this whole operation. Otherwise, you're going to make yourself ill."

"I promise," Maria agreed as she hung up, keen to get on.

By Saturday morning it was a huge relief when the last of her orders was collected and, having already accepted an invitation to dinner with Kim and her family, Maria literally had just a few hours left to check her supplies and reorder for the following week.

Later that day, with just minutes to spare, Maria turned into the quiet cul- de-sac where Kim and David lived in their beautiful family home and pulled onto their drive.

Dinner with Kim and her family was predictably a chaotic affair. Chloe, positively besotted with her new boyfriend who she'd known for all of five days, spoke of nothing and no one else, and poor Harry was suffering rejection because he'd been side lined in the school rugby team and had no idea why. Engrossed in both their conversations, Maria was surprised when suddenly Chloe changed the subject.

"Aunty M," she began curiously. "I hear you've had a couple of friend requests."

"Yes." Maria hesitated as she remembered. "To be honest I'd forgotten all about them," she confessed. "I've had such a busy week, everything else has sort of gone by the by." Maria could tell by the look on Chloe's face she was not impressed.

"Honestly, Aunty M," she began in earnest. "You don't have to instantly become best friends if that's what you're worried about. Basically, you just get to see all their posts, and you get an insight into what they're doing and likewise for your followers."

"Well, they're going to get a raw deal with me then," Maria said. "I never post anything."

They all laughed, and Maria promised her niece faithfully she would respond A.S.A.P.

Back home later that night Maria called up the friend requests, once again she examined their photos, even after all these years she would easily have recognised them both, and obviously they'd recognised her, she pressed accept and closed her laptop.

***

"She's accepted," Lisa exclaimed loudly.

Tim frowned as he looked across the living room to his wife who was curled up on the sofa. "Who's accepted what."

"Maria, I sent her a friend request weeks ago. I've been looking for her for ages and then suddenly I found her." Lisa looked up from her phone. "You remember her, don't you?" she asked her husband excitedly.

"Of course, I remember her." Tim raised his eyebrows; how could he possibly have forgotten Maria…

"It's strange," Lisa continued, "she's still got the same surname. I would have expected her to have some fancy Italian surname, so either she's divorced and gone back to her maiden name." She paused and looked at her husband. "Or maybe he died and using his surname was too painful."

"Or maybe she never married him, or anyone else, ever thought of that?" Tim stated with a sarcastic undertone that Lisa chose to ignore.

"Well, she doesn't give anything away on here, that's for sure," Lisa said while studying Maria's profile picture. "The only other information is her birthday." Lisa wasn't really talking to her husband now, merely thinking aloud, which was just as well as Tim had already turned his attention back to the film. "I know Karen sent her a request as well, so I wonder if she's had an acceptance." Lisa sent a quick message to Karen, she was interested to know, and knew Karen would message back, but probably not until the morning now, it was gone 11pm, well past Karen's normal bedtime.

***

Maria was astounded to find she'd already received a message from Lisa on Sunday morning. Apparently, it had taken quite a while for Lisa to find her. Maria smiled to herself; It was obviously the photo that Chloe put up that had helped both Lisa and Karen identify her. There was no doubt about that. Curiously Maria clicked onto Lisa's profile page and quickly scanned her information. She was still married to Tim, that didn't really surprise her, and she could see the babies she'd craved were all grown up now; how weird, she couldn't imagine Lisa with grown up kids.

Maria suddenly felt apprehensive, her own life had been a little more complicated to say the least and remembering how incredibly nosey Lisa had always been filled her with absolute dread. Lisa would want to know the ins and outs of everything, Maria just knew it, so when the next few messages arrived, she was pleasantly surprised to see how general both Lisa and Karen kept them, and soon the messages were flowing easily between all three of them. Consequently, it really shouldn't have been too much of a surprise when a few weeks later Lisa suggested that they all meet via Zoom. Realising it would be churlish to refuse, cautiously Maria agreed; she would need to engage the help of her niece for this technical dilemma.

Without any hesitation Chloe agreed to help, and in no time, she had Zoom all set up and ready for her aunt. "Would you like me to hang around a little while, until you all connect?" Chloe asked her aunt.

"If you don't mind," Maria said gratefully. "I don't want to look a complete idiot if something goes wrong and knowing my luck it will."

"I'm sure it will all be absolutely fine, but I'm happy to stay for a while." Chloe smiled warmly at her aunt, who was looking a little fraught.

Relieved her niece was going to be on hand, Maria settled herself with a mug of tea in front of her laptop and waited for her two friends to connect. Once the meeting was well under way and everything seemed to be going well, discreetly, Chloe left them to it and headed home.

It was a good hour and a half later that all three women closed their laptops. Their meeting had been a huge success, so much better than Maria could have imagined. Inevitably both Karen and Lisa had been intrigued to find out more about her; they'd both been quite shocked to hear that she'd never married, or had any kids, but sensitive enough to realise that she wasn't ready to reveal too many details at this stage, and Maria sighed with relief when Karen completely changed the subject. In the end their conversation centred around their youth and the years they'd all spent together, causing regular fits of laughter as they remembered their antics back in the day. Agreeing to do this again soon, they eventually said their goodbyes.

During the days that followed, Maria often found herself unexpectedly revisiting her past. Her thoughts and memories were centred around Andy, he'd been her boyfriend during her friendship with Lisa and Karen, and she'd been surprised that his name hadn't come up during their Zoom call. Remembering and thinking about Andy was something she'd refused to do for a very long time, and although the raw pain had long since subsided, it was still an uncomfortable memory.

***

Lisa carried two teas out onto the patio where her husband was relaxing in the chair, he'd been busy working in the garden and was now sitting admiring his efforts.

"How was it?" Tim asked as Lisa placed the tray rather noisily on the wrought iron table.

"She never married; you were right about that, never had any kids." Lisa passed a mug of tea to her husband. "We didn't really find out too much else, she looked uncomfortable talking about herself." She paused for a minute still considering why this might be. "Obviously done well for herself though," Lisa suddenly continued. "She mentioned that she'd just had her whole house refurbished, shame we hadn't met up then, she could have given the work to you." Lisa sat back in her chair and took a sip of tea.

"Where does she live then?" Tim asked his wife.

"I don't actually know her address," she admitted. "But I know it's within walking distance of her sister Kim, and I know Kim lives the other side of town somewhere. Well, she did a couple of years ago when I bumped into her in the café opposite the park."

"So, you don't have a clue then." Tim smiled; he loved his wife dearly but there was no getting away from the fact she was incredibly nosey.

"It can't be any more than six or seven miles away I wouldn't have thought." Lisa relaxed in her chair, deep in thought.

"What was really weird though," she continued, "was that she never once mentioned Andy, we talked a lot about the past, but she never mentioned him, it was like he never existed."

"Maybe she doesn't want to remember him, it was all pretty unpleasant for them both at the time." Tim looked at his wife, he recognised that inquisitive look. "Please don't get involved in any of that." He stared at his wife looking for her assurance. "Promise me, Lisa," he said sternly.

"I'm not getting involved in anything," Lisa said abruptly.

"Good, let's keep it that way." Tim closed his eyes; he knew this meeting hadn't been a good idea.

***

With intrigue getting the better of her, and keen to find out more about her old friend, about a month after their first Zoom call Lisa suggested for their next meeting that perhaps they could all meet somewhere.

"Why don't you invite them to yours, you'll be on home turf, that should help if you're feeling a little anxious?" Kim tried to reassure her sister during a quick catch up on the phone. She hadn't really made any new friends since she'd moved back, this would be good for her.

"I could do, I suppose," Maria replied, "I hadn't thought of that."

"You could do a light lunch one Saturday, make a quiche, serve it with salad, keep it easy for yourself."

"They might prefer to meet in a pub though," Maria responded thoughtfully.

"Well, you won't know until you ask."

"True," Maria agreed. "I'll send a message, that way it will be easier for them if they're not keen."

"Let me know what they say." Kim could tell her sister was troubled, Maria had never been one for discussing her past, especially the part that included Andy. After all these years, Kim was still convinced he was the main reason there'd never really been any other serious contenders. Even the infamous Italian had undoubtedly been a mere distraction.

Deciding to take Kim's advice, Maria sent a message to both Lisa and Karen inviting them to hers for lunch on a Saturday of their choice; she kept it brief, still not totally convinced it was a good idea.

***

The week ahead brought unexpected challenges for Maria. With another busy week planned, she was terribly disappointed to learn that Louise wouldn't be able to work for the next few days. Both her kids were poorly, and she had no option but to keep them home from school.

"My sister Julie is available and has offered to come up and help if that's any good." Louise felt awful, she hated to let Maria down, but she had no choice; her children would always come first.

"No, it's ok," Maria began, immediately feeling stressed. "It's kind of her to offer but I don't have the time this week to start training anyone new."

"If you change your mind, just give me a call," Louise insisted. "She's very adaptable and a really good cook, honestly she wouldn't need much training." Understandably Louise had presumed Maria would jump at the chance of help, so she'd already given her sister the address, and told her to go there straight after the school run, now she needed to get hold of her and tell her not to bother. With her two kids calling, Louise quickly rang her sister and, when she didn't pick up, left a message, she'd explain more later.

Keen not to be late, Julie hadn't bothered to check her phone since receiving instruction from her sister, and at exactly 9.30 she knocked at Maria's door. It seemed ages before a woman with hands covered in flour and looking extremely flustered opened the door.

"Hi, I'm Julie." The woman looked perplexed. "Louise's sister," she added hoping this would register. "I've come to help."

Confused but anxious to get back to the kitchen Maria invited the young woman inside. Julie was the image of her sister with long dark hair tied back in a ponytail, striking green eyes, and a sprinkle of freckles across her nose and cheeks. A lot more confident than her sister, Julie got stuck in straight away and by mid-morning she had persuaded Maria to let her bake one of her own recipes.

"It's good," Maria admitted as she took the first bite. "I love the texture: it's light, but intense in flavour." Julie watched eagerly as Maria finished the slice. "I really enjoyed that." Maria smiled as she wiped her fingers. "Do you do a lot of baking?"

"I always bake my own cakes for the children, but I try and keep it to just one a week otherwise my husband will just keep eating them." She smiled as she began to pack away the utensils she'd used.

Maria was impressed and, convinced that Julie would be a huge asset, immediately decided to offer her a part time position working alongside both herself and Louise.

With a huge grin, Julie didn't hesitate. "When would you like me to start?" she replied excitedly.

"Tomorrow," Maria said hopefully.

"Great, I'll see you in the morning then," Julie said as she collected her bag. She'd been mulling over the idea of a part time job and had already discussed it with her husband, both her kids were at school now and the extra money would come in handy. Thirty minutes later as she waited outside the school Julie remembered that she hadn't had time to check her phone all day. Listening to her messages she couldn't help laughing; so that was why Maria had looked so confused, she wasn't even expecting her. Louise was going to be so surprised.

With Julie on board the pressure of working against the clock was reduced but with three of them, there was a shortage of available workspace. It helped that the kitchen/diner was all open plan and between them they worked out designated areas for specific jobs; this was better, but it was far from ideal. Maybe it was time to look around for an outside premises from which they could work, an idea Maria was keen to explore.

On Friday evening with a glass of red and a takeaway pizza, Maria nestled down in her chair; she knew that before she started to watch the film which had been highly recommended, she must answer Lisa. Both women had accepted her invitation and a proposed date had been suggested, all Maria had to do was confirm, there was only one problem though, she still wasn't one hundred per cent convinced it was a good idea.

Unnerved by the number of times during the last few weeks she'd found herself thinking about her past, she wondered if she would still recognise Andy if she was ever to meet him. She could remember quite clearly the way he held his head slightly to one side when he spoke to her, his dark penetrating eyes and his warm smile, but what did he look like now. She tried to imagine; did he still have a full head of hair? Was it still mahogany brown or was it flecked with grey? Was he still trim or had he succumbed to middle age spread? So many unanswered questions. She finished her wine and wiped away a tear that had escaped from her eye, this wasn't any good; she needed to get a grip, she opened her laptop, quickly confirmed to Lisa, and switched on the film.

The next few weeks flew by, both Julie and Louise had been actively promoting the business to friends and family and new orders continued to arrive daily. Before Maria knew where she was, it was just a few days until her old friends were due for lunch and she'd never been less prepared.

"Any idea what you're going to serve?" Julie asked when Maria explained her predicament.

"Kim suggested quiche and salad," Maria said, glancing over to watch Julie's reaction.

"And for dessert?" Julie enquired as she poured her mixture equally into two baking dishes.

"Lemon tart," Maria answered and suddenly both women instantly burst out laughing.

"Pastry overdose comes to mind," Julie mocked.

"Maybe, do you think they'd notice?" Maria replied loudly, competing with the sound of the electric mixer.

"Do they eat salmon?" Julie asked, she was concerned, despite her flippant replies, Maria appeared troubled by this up-and-coming lunch date.

"They eat anything apparently, and no allergies." Maria switched off the mixer and was slowly adding melted chocolate to her mixture.

"What about poached salmon with a mixed salad, followed by lemon tart?" Julie suggested. "If you do something like that it can be prepared the day before, and you wouldn't need to cook on the day."

"Sounds good," Maria had to agree. "But I haven't got time to get a salmon and then poach it, I've only got tomorrow."

"When I've picked up the kids this afternoon, I can pop into the village and pick up a whole salmon. I've got a poacher at home; I'll poach it and bring it in tomorrow. I'm sure between us we can make a lemon tart tomorrow," Julie suggested confidently.

"I can't let you do that," Maria said, "I appreciate the offer though, I really do."

"Do you like salmon?" Julie continued, seemingly unperturbed by Maria's refusal.

"Yes but…"

Before she could continue, Julie interrupted, "That's settled then, I'll bring one poached salmon in tomorrow morning." She smiled at Maria and continued with her work.

By the end of the week, Maria couldn't believe how hard both Julie and Louise had worked in transforming her kitchen from a commercial workplace back to something resembling a normal kitchen.

Wanting to show her appreciation and aware they both had very young children, Maria decided to engage the help of her sister Kim. "I'd like to do something for them, I remember my old boss always gave his staff some sort of treat if they'd gone over and above and it went a long way. They've both got young families any ideas?" Maria asked.

"You could always just give them a bonus in their wages," Kim suggested as she tried to think of a better idea.

"Well, I will if I can't think of anything else, but I really wanted something more personal. If I give them money, they'll probably spend it on their kids."

"What about," Kim began, "telling them to order a takeaway of their choice and a bottle of wine, and if they bring in the receipts on Monday, you'll reimburse them as a thank you for all their help. How does that sound?"

"Sounds good, and you think that would be suitable?" Maria asked after a moment's thought.

"Well, it's something I would have appreciated when my kids were young," Kim replied reassuringly.

"Ok, well I'll go and suggest it, and see how it goes down. I'll let you know." Maria made her way back to the kitchen where both women were finishing up for the day.

"It's my husband's birthday this weekend," Louise began excitedly. "This will be a great treat, thank you very much." Completely overwhelmed, she gave Maria a hug.

"It's no one's birthday in our house." Julie laughed. "But it will be a very nice treat, nonetheless. Thank you, it's a very kind thought and very much appreciated."

***

Tim normally enjoyed Saturday mornings; they were a time to relax and recharge before he tackled the chores of the weekend. This Saturday, though, was always going to be different.

"Does this look ok, Tim?" Lisa asked her husband as she walked into the kitchen and gave him a twirl.

"It looks fine, but so did the other two outfits you've just shown me," Tim said as he poured himself another coffee.

"I didn't think you liked them; you didn't seem over keen," Lisa snapped.

Tim looked at his wife, this was one of those mornings when he really wished he was going to work. "Honestly, Lisa, you look great, don't forget though you're just having lunch at Maria's house…"

Before he could finish Lisa interrupted, "So, you think it's too much?" She sighed heavily. "I knew I should have bought something new." She turned abruptly and stomped back to her bedroom.

Tim finished his coffee and put his newspaper away, time to cut the lawn, he decided.

"Give me a call when you're ready to leave," Tim shouted up the stairs before he made a quick exit to the garden.

***

Maria was up and about early on Saturday morning, the forecast was good and with not a cloud in the sky, she decided it would be very pleasant to serve drinks in the garden; she'd let them choose if they wanted to eat in or out, she really didn't mind.

Busy chopping fruit for the punch, Maria was surprised when Chloe popped her head around the kitchen door. "Mum asked me to drop these off on my way to netball," Chloe explained as she presented her aunt with a huge bunch of fresh garden flowers.

"That's very kind of her, I'll give her a ring later." Maria smiled warmly at her niece.

"So, today's the big day then?" Chloe said as she pulled out a stool opposite her aunt. "Are you looking forward to it?"

"I think so," Maria answered honestly. "I'm not worried about the food, that's all ready, I just hope they enjoy themselves." She shrugged her shoulders. "I'm sure it will all be fine."

"Of course, it will," Chloe said as she jumped off the stool. "I'd better get going otherwise I'll be late. I don't suppose you have any spare cakes you would like me to take off your hands?" she asked sheepishly as she collected her bag.

With her hands covered in fruit juice, Maria pointed to the cupboard where she kept the cakes that didn't quite make the grade. "I'm sure you'll find something in there you fancy."

Chloe opened the cupboard. "Gosh, I don't know what to choose," she exclaimed as she peered inside several cake tins.

"Is it to take home?" Maria asked as she watched her niece trying to decide.

"No, it's for netball tea later. I don't know what to take," Chloe said as she tried to remember what all the girls preferred.

"Take a couple then," Maria said. "I imagine there'll be quite a few mouths to feed."

"Do you mind if I take the fruit cake and the chocolate cake, please?" Chloe asked rubbing her hands.

"Not at all, help yourself. Do you need to borrow the tins?"

"Yes please, if you don't mind," Chloe confirmed as she carefully packed them in her bag. Happy with her choices, she left her aunt still busy preparing her fruit punch. Once she was completely out of sight, Chloe reached for her phone.

"Mum, I've just left Aunty M and she really doesn't appear overly concerned. All the food is prepped, and she was busy making a fruit punch," Chloe explained as she hurried along the path.

"She didn't look stressed or worried?" Kim asked her daughter.

"Honestly, Mum she seemed fine; understandably she's a little apprehensive, but she wasn't stressed. I'd tell you if she was."

"Ok, thanks, Chloe. Did you get any cakes for netball tea?" Kim enquired, knowing this had been the reason Chloe had agreed to call in and deliver the flowers.

Chloe laughed. "Of course, one chocolate and one fruit… Mum, I've got to go now," she quickly explained. "I've just got to Kelly's house and she's waiting for me."

"Have a good game, see you later and thanks, Chloe." Kim put her phone down, she certainly felt better knowing Maria was ok.

***

It was exactly 12.30pm; Lisa was the first to arrive, closely followed by Karen, and any nerves Maria might have harboured were quickly dissipated as the old friends chatted freely.

"Just love what you've done with the place," Lisa said as she glanced around.

"Thanks, I'm pleased with it now, although at one time I never thought it would ever get finished," Maria confessed as she led them both out towards the garden.

"Shame we didn't reunite sooner, you know Tim started his own business, well that's what he does, refurbs, everyone wants a new bathroom or kitchen," Lisa explained while totally ignoring Karen's anxious expression.

"I do remember." Maria smiled as she offered them both a chair. "I'll give you a tour later if you want, but first and foremost." She laughed. "Let's have some drinks."

"Great idea," Karen agreed, anxious to change the subject. That was the last thing they needed to discuss, Tim's business. Goodness knows where Lisa was going with that conversation; she dreaded to think.

Relaxed in the garden, enjoying their fruit punch, Maria was more than happy to sit back and enjoy their conversation. All three of them were about the same age, mid-fifties, but Lisa, she noted, had changed the least. Her hair was a few shades lighter but still styled in a classic bob. Her clothes and shoes were good quality, although Maria thought, a little too classic for her age. She was obviously keen to impress, she'd mentioned several times how many different houses they'd lived in before they moved into their dream home, and looking at the photos she'd brought with her, it was spectacular, inside and out.

Karen on the other hand looked older than her years. Maria remembered her lovely long brown hair, which she now wore shortly cropped. Today she wore make-up, but Maria guessed she didn't normally bother.

Surprisingly, Karen had been very open discussing her daughter's problems and how it had impacted the whole family. It was a particularly sad story, she'd worked hard and secured herself a place at university. Unfortunately though, she'd become involved with a crowd that were into drugs. It had taken years with a lot of heartache to finally get their daughter clean and, even though she was fine now, she was a constant worry to them. Maria felt her obvious pain and sensed her relief once she'd told her story.

A few glasses of punch later, Maria sensed it was her turn to tell all, but she played for a little more time by suggesting they eat.

With the sun continuing to shine they'd all agreed to eat outside; quickly, Maria set the table and presented her poached salmon which she served with a crunchy mixed salad and Jersey Royals.

"Maria, this is so good." Lisa held up her glass. "Cheers, ladies." She laughed merrily.

"Yes, cheers," Karen echoed. "It's great to be here, and thanks, Maria, this is a really great lunch."

"You're both very welcome, please tuck in there's plenty to go round so don't be bashful." Maria laughed, offering the salad bowl to Karen.

"You started to tell us last time," Karen began, "all about your baking business, how's that going?"

"Yes, I did I remember," Maria said before taking a sip of wine. "We never finished that conversation, did we? Well, it was something I fell into really. I certainly didn't plan to start another business, and I can't believe how quickly it's taken off. I now employ two sisters from the village, who have proved invaluable. I must be honest though," she admitted. "I really need to find an outside premises to operate from, we need more space. It's not professional trying to run a business from my own kitchen."

Karen appeared genuinely interested. "What do you mean, a unit or a shop?"

"Originally, that was the way I was thinking," Maria began to explain. "But more recently I've been considering utilising the space I have."

Lisa who had unsuccessfully tried to steer the conversation in a different direction, suddenly became very interested. "What had you in mind?" she asked as she surveyed the garden. There was plenty of room for an extension.

"I actually thought about transforming the garage," Maria explained. "I never use it: all that's in there is a lawn mower and a few tools. I was looking at garden sheds," she continued. "They come in all shapes and sizes; all I'd need is a small one somewhere at the bottom of the garden to house the mower. That would leave the garage completely clear. It's quite a big space; I'm sure it would be enough for what we need."

"Sounds great, you should speak to my Tim, he'd give you his professional opinion," Lisa declared excitedly. "He does this sort of thing all the time."

Realising this was the first time she'd voiced this idea; Maria hastily interrupted her friend, "To be honest, Lisa, the idea is still very much in its infancy, I wouldn't want to waste his time."

"Honestly, Maria," Lisa began ardently. "He wouldn't mind, but anyway think about it."

By the time it came to serve coffee, Maria could relax, both her guests appeared to be enjoying themselves and it was a huge relief to know it was all going so well. Enjoying their coffee and petit fours, Lisa was busy regaling tales of her holidays that had taken her far and wide, and Maria was more than happy to sit and listen enjoying the late summer sun. So, it was a bit of a shock when Maria suddenly realised Lisa had moved on from that topic of conversation.

"So, Maria, you've never had any contact with Andy since you split all those years ago?"

For a second her blood ran cold, she glanced from one to the other. Karen, clearly shocked, smiled compassionately and from Lisa's expression it was obvious she meant no malice, she was just inquisitive.

"No, none at all," Maria answered honestly, stirring her coffee rapidly.

"You've never been tempted to contact him? I think I would have wanted some sort of explanation at the very least." Lisa continued, desperately digging for more information.

Maria sat back in her chair, she remembered the last time she had seen him, he'd been with someone else… He hadn't seen her. "No, not really," she replied and shrugged. "What good would it do? It wouldn't change anything."

"As long as you're happy; that's the main thing." Karen intervened and quickly changed the subject. "If that Lemon Tart is anything to go by, I totally understand why you're so very busy, it was absolutely delicious." Karen smiled warmly. "Anyway, you promised us a tour of your beautiful house before we go, and Mark will be here to collect me very soon." She finished her coffee and placed her napkin on the table.

"Oh yes, we must have a tour before we go." Silently admitting defeat, Lisa drank the rest of her coffee; she'd have words with Karen later.

Mark was the first to arrive, Maria had only met him a few times all those years ago, but she recognised him instantly. He still had the most beautiful deep blue eyes, although now they held a certain sadness about them. His face was slightly thinner, and his hair was heavily tinged with grey, you could clearly see he was a troubled man.

Tim arrived just minutes after they'd waved goodbye to Karen and Mark. He was more the rugged handsome type, still in good shape, Maria noted, more confident now than she remembered but extremely friendly.

Eventually they left and Maria closed the front door. Happy and relieved it had gone well, she made her way back out to the garden, pulling the recliner into the sunlight, the tidying could wait, she decided, as she made herself comfortable. In a desperate attempt to clear her mind she closed her eyes and fell into a deep sleep.

CHAPTER TWO

Maria – The Late 1980s

Maria filed the last of her papers and finished tidying her desk.

"I suppose you and Andy are out all weekend," Lisa enquired as she came bounding into Maria's office.

"Not all weekend." She smiled at her colleague who was fast becoming more of a friend. "Just most of it," she teased, laughing.

Only one year older than Maria, Lisa was already married. Her husband Tim was a tall, slim man with mousy brown hair that flopped over his face. Ever since Maria had known them, they always seemed to be saving, firstly for their wedding, then their house, now it seemed they were saving so they could start a family. Fair play, Maria thought, if that's what they want.

"Come on then," Lisa urged as she perched on the side of Maria's desk. "Spill the beans, what's on the agenda for this weekend?"

Having worked through lunch so she could get away earlier than normal, Maria's answer was a hurried, condensed version of events and swiftly she said goodbye and left the office.

It was Friday evening, and the traffic was heavier than normal as everyone rushed home to rediscover their freedom for the weekend. Tonight, Andy was due about 7.00 and Maria had booked a table for the two of them at a new Chinese restaurant she'd read about in the local paper. Andy loved Chinese, it was his absolute favourite, and she knew he was really looking forward to it, so she couldn't understand why she had this uneasy feeling and felt so anxious.

Annoyingly, it was later than originally planned when Maria pulled up onto her driveway. She was already feeling agitated and as she stood at the front door fumbling around in her bag for her keys, she froze for a minute as she pressed her ear to the door. It was as she thought, her phone was ringing. In desperation, she tipped the entire contents of her handbag onto the step, snatching her key from the wreckage previously considered to be essential, Maria opened the door at precisely the same time as the phone stopped ringing, and the message light began to flash.

"Drat," she shouted as she threw down her bags, collected the contents of her handbag from the front step, and slammed the front door.

Instinctively she knew who it was from, and exactly what the message would tell her. She was just about to press play when the phone began to ring again.

"Hello," she answered tentatively.

"Hello, dear," her mother replied cheerfully.

"Hi, Mum. Everything ok?" she enquired, not really giving her mother time to reply before she asked, "Did you call just a minute ago?"

"No, dear," her mother answered, "I'm just ringing to remind you Dad and I are off this weekend to visit Aunty Jean, just in case you need us that's where we'll be."

"Ok, Mum, have a great time, see you next week, love to Dad." Maria hung up and pressed play.

"Hi, it's only me." Andy always began his message this way. "I was hoping you'd be in by now." He was such a liar, she thought, he'd probably sighed with relief when the answer phone came on. "I really wanted to talk to you, I will try and call you later, but I'm sorry, Maria, I can't make it tonight, but I absolutely promise I will be at your house in plenty of time tomorrow to go to the party. I must look after Sammy tonight; I'll tell you all about it tomorrow. I'm truly sorry, Maria, I really am." His voice faded, and the message finished.

Maria sat on the stairs, staring into thin air, another lonely disappointing evening loomed before her. She'd lost count of how many times this had happened, and just recently, it was practically a regular occurrence.

She'd been introduced to Andy by a mutual friend and had instantly felt an attraction; he wasn't conventionally handsome, but he had a warm friendly smile, and his dark eyes were mesmerising. He'd been completely honest with her from the very beginning when he'd explained that, although he was single, he did have a daughter from a previous relationship. She was 18 months old and her name was Samantha, although he always called her Sammy. He'd been upfront explaining that his ex, Sharon, had a habit of using the little girl as a pawn when she wanted something, especially more maintenance, and how incredibly exasperating it could be, trying to juggle his own life with theirs.

Maria wasn't put off, she really liked him; surely they could work around his ex and a toddler.

Maria played the message again; from experience she knew she wouldn't hear from him again tonight, he hated confrontation and avoided it wherever possible. He'd wait until tomorrow and hope that Maria had calmed down.

Right from the very beginning, once they began to see one another on a regular basis, Maria readily accepted there were going to be certain times when Andy would be involved and busy with his daughter. With this uppermost in her mind, she tried her best to be considerate and sympathetic to his situation whenever she made any plans for the two of them, and at first, it all seemed to be working out well. Unfortunately, the "honeymoon" period didn't last very long and the havoc his ex was able to inflict was extremely frustrating.

Coming from a close family, Maria was baffled when it quickly became evident Andy didn't appear to have any support from his own family, when it came to looking after Sammy.

"I'm not close to my family like you," he explained one day after they'd had to rearrange their plans. "My mum and dad are divorced; Mum now lives over two hundred miles away with her new husband, and Dad has a girlfriend that I just don't get along with." He also had a younger sister who lived with her boyfriend, and she did occasionally help, but she hated Sharon, so it was sometimes more hassle than it was worth.

Not really a big toddler fan, it didn't even occur to Maria to offer any help with Sammy, and it most certainly was never a suggestion from Andy.

Maria remained uncomfortably perched on the stairs, her bags still scattered across the floor, unable to muster the energy required to move. Absent-mindedly she stared at the phone and remembered clearly the very first time this had happened, when Andy hadn't even bothered to let her know what was going on, or where he was. Andy was one of the few people she knew that had one of these new mobile phones, it was the size of a brick and just as heavy, but still he insisted on carrying it everywhere, so why he hadn't called, she couldn't imagine. As time went on, she'd become increasingly anxious; ringing his mobile she was constantly greeted with a voice explaining, "The mobile phone you are calling is switched off." She'd even resorted to calling the police, anxious to find out if there'd been any recent accidents reported. She'd checked with the local hospital to see if he'd been admitted and then, with no other choices left, she'd decided to go and see for herself if his car was outside his flat, something she would never normally do, it felt too intrusive.

It took her fifteen minutes to find his flat, she'd only ever been there once before, so she was relieved that she remembered the way. She parked up in the road and walked towards the car park; his car wasn't anywhere to be seen. Still not convinced he wasn't at home, she pressed his intercom buzzer: nothing, so he wasn't here, so where was he? In the end three days passed before he eventually rang.

Having convinced herself that she would never hear from him again, there was a certain amount of relief when Andy finally called. At first, she'd planned and rehearsed exactly what she would say, but as the days passed the anger faded and when she eventually spoke to him, she felt sorry for him, and all too quickly agreed to dinner where she made him promise that from now on, he would always let her know, even if it was just a message. He apologised profusely and readily agreed to her terms.

Eventually, with a heavy heart, Maria hauled herself up from the stairs, picked up her bags and their contents and walked into the kitchen. She opened her little freezer and selected an individual pie that her mum had made for her and pressed defrost on her new microwave. Next she opened the bottle of red wine that she'd been saving to share with Andy and poured herself a large glass. Well, he wasn't here, and her need was greater than the thought of sharing it. She sat at her small kitchen table drinking her wine and waited for her pie to defrost.

As the evening progressed, Maria continued to feel restless, even several large glasses of wine followed by a lovely herbal bath hadn't helped, so armed with a bar of chocolate she made herself comfortable on the sofa and settled down with every intention of watching the Friday film, but it didn't work, she couldn't concentrate, her mind was elsewhere.

There was no getting away from it, Maria realised as she sat in front of the T.V., She'd been in denial for a while now; her relationship with Andy was suffering under the pressure, and the constant disruption to their plans were having a profound effect on her. So much so, she was now embarrassed to admit to her own friends and family exactly how many times this was happening.

Deep down she'd known for some time something wasn't right, and at times like this, she felt as though she was just, literally, hanging on by a single thread. She deserved better, they both did, and the situation as it was, well it just couldn't continue. As far as she was concerned this whole set up had well and truly exceeded the boundaries of acceptability by anyone's standards. There was only one problem to this stark realisation and tough thinking, she didn't want to walk away, even though she knew, for her own sanity, she should. The trouble was when they were together, they had the best times; it didn't matter if they were out with friends, out on their own, or just at home, Maria enjoyed every moment they were together, and the thought of not having him in her life was far too painful to dwell on for very long.

Despite the wine it was another sleepless night for Maria, during which time she decided that tomorrow she wouldn't hang around waiting for a call, she needed to keep herself busy and deserved some retail therapy. She'd been wanting to visit the new shopping centre the other side of town and tomorrow would be the ideal opportunity. She had a plan, and a reason to get up, get herself ready and go out.

The next morning Maria arrived at the shopping centre much earlier than she would normally be up and about on a Saturday, and under normal circumstances she would have been in her absolute element. It was an impressive development with a good number of independent retailers as well as all the popular high street stores, there was an abundance of cafes and restaurants to choose from and even a small play area for the children. Nevertheless, today Maria strolled aimlessly, merely glancing at the rails of exciting new clothes and beautifully displayed shoes and bags until she decided she might feel a lot more receptive to all these wonderful shops once she'd had a coffee and treated herself to a delicious pastry.

***

Andy sat at his desk twiddling his pen, staring aimlessly out at the forecourt. It was 10.00am on Saturday morning and he'd already left two messages for Maria, this was bad news if she wasn't picking up, it meant only one thing; she was still annoyed about last night.

If it hadn't been for the fact that he had two collections arranged for today, he'd probably have called in sick, but he relied on the commission and historically Saturday was a good selling day, he couldn't miss the chance to sell a few more cars this month. Currently he was the best salesman on the team, and he needed to keep it that way, he'd pushed his luck with his boss too many times and knew he was already treading on thin ice.

Before Sammy was born, Andy was the most reliable guy you could meet, but everything changed the night she was born, and from the very first moment he held her in his arms he loved her more than life itself.

The same could not be said for her mother, Andy didn't have any feelings for her, and he'd never said anything to the contrary. In fact, as far as he was concerned, they'd never even been a couple, she was just always around wherever he happened to be. His close friends told him over and over to be careful of her, but he knew best, it was just some harmless fun…

The day she announced she was pregnant had shaken him to the core. Immediately he'd promised her financial support and was more than happy to take his turn at weekends to look after the baby, but that wasn't enough, and once she realised that was all he was prepared to offer, she made it her main ambition to destroy his life; if she couldn't have him, she decided, nor could anyone else.

Andy checked his watch, he still had time before his first client was due and he picked up his mobile phone and walked outside for some privacy. "Maria, if you're there please pick up." He paused for a few seconds hoping she would answer. "I really would like to apologise for last night, I know I ruined your evening and I'm really sorry." Still nothing, so he continued before the tape ran out. "I'm looking forward to seeing you tonight, I've already packed my bag and brought it with me so I can come straight from work. Anyway, I'll try and call you later, I've got quite a busy day with collections, but I'll see if you're home when I stop for lunch…" He didn't even have time to say goodbye as the phone went dead, the tape had run out. He switched his phone off; he hated leaving messages, he always managed to say the wrong thing or not say enough. It wasn't even any use buying flowers or chocolates, he'd long since exhausted that tactic, and he knew he was being totally selfish expecting Maria to understand his predicament, but he absolutely adored her and couldn't bear to think of life without her.

Back at his desk, he placed his mobile phone safely inside his briefcase and watched as a young couple strolled around the used car section of the forecourt. First sale of the day, he thought to himself as he adjusted his tie and made his way out to join them.

***

Maria sat in the café watching the world go by drinking coffee. By the time she'd finished her second cup she'd decided she didn't want to see Andy tonight. She was in an argumentative, stroppy mood, she wasn't even interested in going to a party; she wasn't interested in anything, apart from wallowing in her own self-pity, all in all it was probably for the best if she remained alone today. All she had to do now was leave Andy a message before he just turned up at hers.

Andy picked up Maria's message just before he left work, so made his way home before returning her call. "Ok, if that's what you want, I understand." Andy's voice was quiet, and he sounded upset. "Do you still want to go to my sisters for lunch tomorrow?" he asked tentatively.

"Honestly, I don't know yet," Maria replied, sounding as moody as she felt.

There was an uncomfortable silence before Andy continued, "Can I call you later tonight or in the morning?"

"In the morning would be better," Maria answered sullenly.

Realising there wasn't any use continuing this conversation, Andy said his goodbyes and hung up. He walked into the kitchen, he couldn't face food, but beer would do, and he grabbed four cans from the fridge and headed for the sofa.

Maria stood in the hall; she was haunted by the obvious sorrow in Andy's tone and immediately regretted her decision and the way she'd spoken to him. She fiddled with her car keys as she considered jumping in her car and heading straight over to his flat, but, thinking sensibly, she'd already had a few glasses of wine and it wasn't worth the risk.

Instead, she sat by the phone for what seemed like hours and lost count of how many times she picked up the receiver before changing her mind. How could a little girl, she thought, just two years old who she'd never even met, turn her whole life upside down?

Sunday dawned and a dark grey, wet and windy morning spanned the horizon. Maria had been awake since first light, she hoped Andy would ring early but even she hadn't considered he'd ring this early. It was 7.30am and Maria had just stepped into the shower when she thought she heard her phone ringing. Wrapped in a huge bath towel, she literally flew down the stairs desperate to reach the phone before it went to answer phone or, even worse, the caller hung up.

"Hello," she answered, almost out of breath.

"It's only me, I didn't wake you, did I?" Andy was concerned Maria sounded a bit weird.

"No." She laughed. "I was in the shower."

"Maria," Andy began humbly. "I've got freshly baked pain au chocolate and croissants can I come over for breakfast?" There was a pause. "Please, Maria."

As he was obviously on his mobile, Maria guessed he probably wasn't that far away. "Where are you?" she asked curiously.

"Outside," he whispered.

Maria hung up and opened the front door.

Andy saw her standing in the doorway and his heart missed a beat. Maria watched him as he walked towards her and her heart raced, it was that smile and those deep dark eyes, they got her every time.

***

It took just over an hour to get to Sarah and Geoff's and suddenly pulling up outside their house Maria felt a rush of anxiety, she'd been going out with Andy for well over a year now and she hadn't met any of his family, so this felt a little strange. Sensing the change of mood, Andy took her hand and squeezed it tightly.

"Thank you for coming with me today." He looked down at their entwined hands. "I know I don't deserve you, but you mean everything to me, you know that don't you?" He looked deep into her eyes; he was no longer sure she felt the same and it scared him. "We can get through all this, Maria; I know we can, and it won't always be like this, I promise."

Maria dropped her gaze. "It has to be what we both want, Andy," she answered tentatively. "On terms that suit us both."

"I think we both want the same," he replied with a definite emphasis on the "We". He smiled tenderly and jumped out of the car to open her door.

Neither Sarah nor Geoff were anything like she'd imagined. With his receding hair line Geoff looked older than his years, Sarah looked nothing like Andy, she was quite short, her face was much rounder, and she wore glasses, but they both welcomed her with open arms and immediately she felt comfortable in their company.

With Sarah busy in and out of the kitchen and Geoff busy engaging Andy with talk of last night's football match, Maria had time to relax. She noticed a few framed photos of a little girl with beautiful curly hair who she immediately recognised from the photo Andy carried in his wallet.

There were a few other photos scattered about including a couple of a new-born baby. At first Maria assumed they must be of Sammy when she was younger, but then she noted the baby wore blue bootees, so it must be another baby altogether, she decided before moving on to study a few photos of Sarah and Geoff obviously enjoying a holiday somewhere.

With the boys deep in conversation Maria made her way out to the kitchen.

"Can I be of any help?" Maria asked as she found Sarah busy basting roast potatoes.

"I'm ok I think." She laughed. "We've got roast chicken, hope that's ok I didn't check with Andy, I hope you're not vegetarian or anything?" Sarah looked hot and flustered.

"I love chicken," Maria assured her. "It's one of my favourites and honestly it all smells absolutely delicious."

"It'll be about another twenty minutes yet," Sarah said as she closed the oven door. "Would you like to have a look around while we wait? I've got before and after photos to bore you with as well." She laughed as she rummaged through a drawer to find them.

"I'd love to," Maria replied, already impressed by their pristine white and navy kitchen.

Upstairs Sarah chatted easily as they made their way from room to room.

"Andy said you have a really lovely house," she suddenly commented. "What sort of style do you prefer?"

"Well, I absolutely love what you've done here," Maria confessed. "Were these doors like this or did you bring them back to their natural wood colour?" she asked as she ran her hand over the incredibly smooth surface.

"Geoff did it," Sarah said proudly. "It wasn't our original idea, we were just going to repaint them, but once Geoff began to rub them down and discovered this beautiful wood, well, that was it, there was no way he was going to paint over that."

"There're beautiful," Maria admitted enviously. "Your house has a lot more character than mine. I really love how you've incorporated some of the classic features with the new. My house was a new build, so it is what it is really, and I've gone for semi-modern furnishings throughout," she said, wishing now she'd been a little more adventurous with her choices.

"So, you two aren't planning to live together yet?" Sarah asked, completely out of the blue, while continuing to show Maria around.

Not quite sure how to answer, Maria decided to be completely honest. "I think your brother has enough going on in his life at the moment, I don't think he has room for anything else, well not yet anyway," Maria concluded sadly.

"I understand," Sarah answered sympathetically. "It's a real shame, don't get me wrong the kids are great but Andy has changed a lot since they were born; I worry about him," she admitted as she guided Maria to the next room. "She's a real nasty piece of work his ex, and it seems to me that all she wants to do is make his life as difficult as possible. Well, I don't need to tell you that do I," Sarah said innocently as she opened the door to their newly decorated bedroom.

Maria was confused, had Sarah just mentioned "kids" plural or had she misheard? She was just about to clarify this when suddenly Geoff appeared.

"What are you two doing up here?" he asked as he met them on the landing. "I've just opened the bubbly, are you going to join us?"

"We're just coming," Sarah replied. "I've just been showing Maria all your handiwork."

"You've done an amazing job, you really have," Maria complemented him, noticing he suddenly looked awkward and a little embarrassed.

"Thank you." He smiled. "We're pleased with it aren't we?" He looked to Sarah for reassurance.

"It will do," she teased him tenderly.

Following them both back down the stairs, Maria decided this wasn't the right time for too many questions, although she would be interested to get some clarification on how many children were involved in this equation.

Andy greeted her with a glass of champagne. "You've had the guided tour then?" he joked, but his words fell on deaf ears. Maria's mind was elsewhere as she searched the room for the photos she'd previously admired. Something wasn't quite right, every single one of them had been removed, that wasn't normal behaviour unless of course you had something to hide. Now, with her imagination in overdrive, she felt uncomfortable and vulnerable among these people, as she realised there was a lot more to this story than she was aware of. Without warning her appetite completely disappeared and the aroma of a pending roast lunch made her feel nauseous. She had absolutely no idea how on earth she was going to get through this lunch, when all she wanted to do was get to the bottom of the missing photos.

"I hope everything was ok for you?" Sarah asked as she cleared away the plates. She couldn't help noticing Maria had only taken very small amounts of food and she wasn't sure whether that was normal for her or not, maybe that's how she stayed so slim, she thought, as she looked down at her own rather dumpy figure.

"It was delicious, thank you," Maria answered politely, relieved it was finally over.

Anxious to get to the bottom of the disappearing photos, Maria took the opportunity to leave the two men chatting and quickly made her way out to the kitchen where she found Sarah busy clearing the dishes. "Can I help at all?" she offered, taking hold of the nearest tea towel.

"If you don't mind that would be very kind," Sarah accepted her offer gratefully. "Geoff is great, but it wouldn't even enter his head to help in the kitchen."

Keen to steer the conversation in the right direction, Maria smiled knowingly. "Andy mentioned that you're both saving for your wedding, when do you hope to get married?"

Sarah looked up and frowned. "The thing is I really want to start a family, but Geoff is the old-fashioned sort, he thinks we should get married first." She shrugged her shoulders and smiled.

"I think that's really nice," Maria said, realising this might just be her opportune moment. "You've always got your niece, if you need to fuel your maternal instincts I suppose," Maria suggested casually.

"Yes, and now with the baby as well." Sarah laughed. "There's plenty of baby-sitting required…"

Maria didn't wait for her to finish her sentence. "Baby." She swallowed hard as she took in the enormity of Sarah's innocent comment.

Sarah kept her head down and busied herself cleaning the dishes, as she realised that she'd probably just said the wrong thing. She'd noticed earlier some of her photos had been removed, but she hadn't had the time to question Geoff, assuming it was him who had taken them down. Without making matters worse she now had no idea how to answer Maria's question. Regretfully she'd automatically assumed Maria knew about Sammy's little brother Joe, and as Andy had always denied the accusation the baby was his, she had presumed Maria knew the whole story.

Thinking that Sarah hadn't heard her, Maria continued, "Is that the baby in the photos I was looking at earlier? Is he a relation or just a friend's baby?" Maria was looking for answers, she thought the question sounded innocent enough.

Sarah blushed as she desperately searched for the correct answer: if she said relation that would no doubt cause further questions; if she said friend, well, that would be a lie.

Sensing Sarah's hesitation and obvious embarrassment, Maria regretted her question. It wasn't fair to involve Sarah, none of this was her fault, she'd shown Maria nothing but kindness. Maria would just have to wait until she was alone with Andy who she had a sneaking suspicion held all the answers to this mystery.

Sarah continued to busy herself with clearing the kitchen and was just contemplating on how to answer Maria, when quite suddenly Maria changed the subject. "You must give me your Yorkshire pudding recipe, unfortunately I have to rely on the frozen variety." Maria laughed at her own random statement a little too heartily.

Sarah had never been more grateful to pass on a recipe, anything rather than discuss Sharon and her kids. "I'm glad you enjoyed it; I know traditionally you only serve Yorkshire pudding with beef, but Geoff loves his Yorkshire pudding, so we always have it with our Sunday roast regardless of our meat choice. It's very easy to make, the secret is letting the mixture rest..." Sarah was rambling and barely knew what she was saying, and their conversation continued in a similar vein until all the dishes were clean and packed away and Sarah encouraged Maria back into the living room.

Andy could tell as soon as Maria returned to the living room something was wrong; he could sense it. He'd noticed she hadn't eaten very much and was quieter than normal during lunch and, although she continued to smile through the rest of their visit, he had a strong feeling the journey home would be difficult. "Everything ok?" he asked as he reversed the car down the driveway, and they waved goodbye to Sarah and Geoff.

Unable to hold back any longer, Maria was straight in with her first question. "Tell me more about the baby I noticed in the photos, before they mysteriously disappeared," she said with noticeable sarcasm.

Andy couldn't believe that he'd completely forgotten to ask Sarah to remove any photos she may have of either Sammy or Joe on display. As soon as he saw them, he'd guessed there would be questions, that's why as soon as he could he'd hidden them in the drawer.

"What did Sarah say then?" he asked trying to find out what she already knew.

"That's totally irrelevant," Maria replied angrily, "I'm asking you, about the baby in the photos, which I'm increasingly beginning to understand, is something to do with you."

"Well, he's definitely not mine, if that's what you're insinuating," Andy answered defensively, keeping his eyes firmly on the road ahead.

"So, is Sharon his mother?" This was the first time she had referred to his ex by name, and it felt weird, previously she'd found it easier for the woman to remain nameless, somehow without a name Maria could deny her existence for most of the time.

Andy tried to concentrate, this wasn't the time or the place to have this discussion which, with hindsight, he realised they should have had months ago.

"Andy, I asked you a question." Maria was struggling to contain her anger; she had an uneasy feeling she was just about to open Pandora's box.

"Yes, she is," he answered quietly.

"Why didn't you tell me she'd had another baby?" Maria asked impatiently. "You've never mentioned she had a new boyfriend, why all the secrecy, Andy? I don't understand." The exasperation she harboured was evident in her voice.

"She doesn't," Andy replied honestly, as he waited for the next barrage of questions.

"So, she doesn't have a new boyfriend and you're not the father, so is this baby some kind of miracle?" she snapped back at him.

"Oh, don't be ridiculous, Maria." Andy knew this conversation was never going to end well, that's why he'd never mentioned anything before.

"Don't be ridiculous," she mimicked. "I visit your sister for the first time and on display in her living room are photos of a little girl I recognised to be Sammy, and a baby boy with dark hair just like yours and dark eyes just like yours." She paused briefly before adding, "And you tell me not to be ridiculous." She shook her head in frustration.

"He's a baby, Maria, babies look like everyone, and no one."

"Well, if he's not yours, he's no relation to your sister, so why on earth does she have photos of him on display, and why did someone feel the need to remove them?" She looked directly at him, but he wouldn't turn his head.

"I removed them," Andy admitted. "To avoid a conversation just like this one."

Maria couldn't believe what she was hearing. "Ah, so you knew there would be a conversation if I spotted them, why would that be, Andy?" Maria asked sarcastically as she grabbled to understand exactly what he was saying.

"The baby is a result of a one-night stand, she doesn't even know the father's name. She tells everyone he's mine to save face, but he most certainly is not." Andy glanced briefly at Maria before continuing, "Sarah feels sorry for the baby and treats him the same as Sammy."

"And you?" Maria asked. "Do you treat the baby the same as Sammy?"

"What do you mean?"

"When you babysit for Sammy do you look after the baby as well?"

"Sometimes," he answered truthfully.

"So, you feed it, change its nappy, cradle it in your arms if he cries, and he's not yours." She stared at Andy, waiting for his reply.

"It's a baby, Maria, not another woman." He knew she would never understand, and now the whole situation had been completely blown out of proportion.

But Maria wasn't giving up, she needed more definition. "Are you named as the father on his birth certificate?" she asked indignantly.

"No," he answered quietly, exhausted by the whole conversation.

"Not convincing enough, Andy," she cried, completely enraged. "I don't believe you; I don't believe a word you've just told me. For the last three or four months, you've regularly disappeared, to supposedly look after your daughter, whereas before it was occasionally in the week and every third weekend when she came to stay with you. Now it all makes sense, of course you'd have to do more to help with two kids, to which I add: no one in their right mind would do if it wasn't theirs."

Andy pulled up onto Maria's driveway and turned off the ignition. "Maria, please you've got this all wrong." He tried to take her hand, but she pulled away.

"You spend too much time with your 'ex', Andy. Far too much time for someone who doesn't care: you stay overnight supposedly on the sofa, she's constantly calling you on your mobile and when I ask you to turn the damn thing off for a few hours so we can enjoy our evening, there's always a reason why you can't. Yet when I try to get hold of you." She stopped for breath, her voice full of emotion before continuing, "The bloody thing is always switched off."

"I do sleep on the sofa, and I've told you, I only stay when she comes in late and I'm too tired to drive, or when Sammy is unwell in the night, and I don't like to leave her."

"I don't believe you, Andy, I really don't, and now every time you disappear or cancel our plans, I'm going to have images of the four of you playing happy families. I just can't do this, Andy; I just can't do any of it, anymore." Maria opened the car door, stepped out onto her drive and made her way to the front door.

Not wanting to make matters worse and thinking perhaps it would be better to let her cool down, Andy stood by the side of his car. Maria turned to look at him. "I'm not coming in, Maria," Andy began. "I think we both need time to calm down."

Taken completely by surprise, Maria was silent for a moment; at the very least, she expected Andy would want to sort this out before he left.

"Well, that's absolutely fine," she exclaimed angrily. "But I'm telling you, Andy, if we don't sort this out today, we don't sort it ever, we're done." She could see quite clearly he was hurting too, but at that moment she didn't care; she wasn't even sure why he was upset; it obviously wasn't because of what she'd just said, more likely because he'd been caught out.

"I'm sorry Maria," he said shaking his head. "I can't stand to see you this upset, and all we're going to do today is go over and over everything that's already been said, I think it's best I go."

"Fine with me," she replied angrily. "But like I said, if you can't be bothered to sort this out today, well, that's it we're finished." She was fuming, it didn't matter how much she threatened him, nothing seemed to be getting through.

"I'm sorry, Maria," Andy said sadly as he climbed back into his car and sped away down the road.

Maria slammed her front door, kicked off her shoes and grabbed a handful of tissues as she flopped onto the sofa in floods of tears. She cried so hard it hurt, her head ached, her heart felt heavy, and she continued crying until finally, totally exhausted, she fell into an uneasy sleep.

The following days passed slowly and keeping busy was harder than she'd imagined. During the day when she was at work it was bearable; it was the evenings and weekends she found so very hard. She hungered to hear the familiar sound of Andy's husky voice and as the weeks ticked by it became clear he'd literally taken her at her word, and she missed him terribly.

CHAPTER THREE

Maria – The Present

Both Lisa, and Karen sent flowers in thanks for a very enjoyable Saturday and fabulous lunch, and another zoom call had been arranged for later in the month.

Business was booming, it was just early September but already Christmas cake and pudding orders were arriving thick and fast, all of which would require plenty of storage space of which they had very little. Julie introduced a processing system for all the Christmas orders; this way, she explained, nothing would be left to chance and would alleviate any potential disappointments later down the line. Maria was impressed, her system seemed to work well, but if the business continued to grow, and she hoped it would, there were lots of areas she still wanted to explore, vegan and vegetarian cakes and pastries for one. She would have no option but to arrange for the garage to be converted into a professional working space; for now, however, this would have to do.

In the blink of an eye autumn descended into winter. Maria had managed one Zoom call with the "girls" during which time they'd somehow managed to tie her down to meet before Christmas. This time they'd all agreed to meet at one of the restaurants in town. Maria hoped the Christmas rush would be nearly over by the time it came around.

As the weeks passed it was all hands on deck and Maria was often to be found in the kitchen up to her eyes in cake or pastry mixture late into the night and at weekends.

"Please tell me you've closed the order book for this year." Kim was concerned for her sister; it was Sunday afternoon and as far as she could tell Maria had been working all weekend. "I'll be glad when it's Christmas Eve and you're settled at ours for the festivities." She looked at her sister for some reassurance. "Honestly, Maria, you need more staff, and you definitely need more space." Kim glanced around the kitchen. "You seem to have cakes everywhere."

"I know, and I realise it doesn't look like it to you, but we have a system going on here, and so far, it's working really well." Maria placed her latest creation in the oven and set the timer. "But I have actually closed the book for this year; anyway it's too late to make a cake or pudding that would be ready in time for Christmas." Maria frowned and then smiled at her sister. "Are you staying for a cup of tea?" she asked as she filled the kettle.

"I will if it means you'll sit down for five minutes," Kim said trying to find a safe place to sit. "What about after Christmas, don't you think you'll all need a break? Surely no one will be wanting cakes directly after Christmas and New Year."

"Actually, I've already thought of that," Maria said as she made two mugs of tea. "Do you fancy a piece of cake?" She laughed ironically.

"I'll pass, but I know David will be disappointed if I go home empty-handed."

Maria laughed. "No problem, I'll pack you a cake to take home. Anyway, going back to your original question, I've already pencilled out the two weeks after Christmas, so when Louise and Julie leave on Christmas Eve, they don't come back until mid-January." She handed her sister a carefully wrapped fruit cake.

"Thank goodness for that, you're all going to need the break." Kim finished her tea and balanced the cake carefully on top of her large handbag. "Promise me that will be the last cake of the day." She pointed to the oven and gave her sister a big hug before she left.

"I promise." Maria smiled as her sister gave her the thumbs up.

As the temperatures continued to drop, the news of a potential flu epidemic began to circulate. At first it was just a news item mentioned towards the later end of the broadcast, but it soon gathered momentum, especially when it was discovered to be a completely different strain of flu, far more contagious than in previous years, and hit the headlines in all the major newspapers when it was reported that this year's flu vaccine didn't provide the necessary protection. Maria had already booked her flu jab, so decided to go ahead with it anyway hoping some protection was better than none. The last thing she needed was to catch the flu.

Before Maria knew where she was, it was the week before she'd planned to meet with her newfound friends. They were still incredibly busy and several times during the next few days she seriously considered cancelling; she didn't see how she could justify the time, but neither Louise nor Julie would hear of it.

"I can work Saturday morning if that helps," Julie explained. "You must go, Maria, you need a break; honestly, you'll feel so much better for taking a few hours to relax." She was genuinely worried about her boss; she hadn't had a day off in ages.

Reluctantly Maria took Julie's advice and, she had to admit, it did feel refreshingly good to dress up and go out. Although with hindsight she wished she'd had time to order something new to wear; she'd lost a bit of weight over the last few weeks and struggled to find something in her wardrobe that fitted. Eventually she settled on a smart pair of trousers with a long-line cardigan which covered the baggy bits ideally.

The restaurant was heaving when Maria arrived; she'd had trouble parking so was the last of the three of them to arrive, and she could see the sheer relief on their faces as she walked over to join them.

"Sorry I'm late," she said as she took off her coat and draped it over the back of the chair. "I couldn't find anywhere to park, everywhere was full, I was just lucky in the end someone was leaving just as I drove by their space, so I nipped in quick."

"I thought you would have come by cab," Lisa said, noticing how tired Maria looked.

"I would have," she began to explain, "but I left it too late and couldn't get a cab for the time I needed, anyway all good,

I'm here now." She smiled at her two friends. "Cheers, girls." Maria raised her glass of bubbles the waiter had poured on her arrival.

"Cheers," they both replied, happy to see her.

It was a bonus for Maria the food was actually very good; initially looking at the menu she'd been sceptical, there was quite a lot of choice for it all to be cooked from fresh. Sensing her hesitation, Lisa was quick to step in with a guaranteed reassurance and she hadn't been wrong.

As the waiter cleared their empty plates, he carefully placed a dessert menu in front of each of them.

"I highly recommend the homemade Christmas pudding and mince pie." He smiled. "I'll give you a few minutes and I'll come back for your orders."

Just about managing to hold it together until he was out of ear shot all three women burst out laughing.

"I think I'll pass on that one," Maria declared as she finally managed to control her laughter. "But it does remind me." She leant under her chair and pulled out her holdall. "I thought you might like these for Christmas," she said as she handed a Christmas cake and pudding to each of her friends.

"Oh, how absolutely wonderful," Lisa exclaimed. "Thank you so much; that's very thoughtful." She pulled out two gifts from her bag. "It's just a little something for Christmas." She handed each of her friends their gifts.

"Thank you," Maria said completely surprised to receive a gift.

"Thank you both." Karen had already delved into her bag and retrieved her gifts. "One for you," she said as she passed one to Lisa, "and one for you." She passed the remaining present to Maria.

"That's so kind of you both," Maria began, "but you shouldn't have. I feel embarrassed I only brought you a cake and pudding."

"Are you kidding?" Karen laughed. "I'm over the moon with these, and my family will be forever grateful."

"Here, here," Lisa added. "Tim will be in seventh heaven when he sees what I have here; honestly, Maria you couldn't have brought anything better."

"Well, I hope they're alright, you'll have to give me your feedback next time we meet."

"Have you nearly finished all your Christmas orders now?" Karen enquired.

"Oh, that reminds me, talking of your business," Lisa suddenly interrupted. "I hope you don't mind but this is Tim's mobile number, he asked me to give it to you. I was telling him about your idea to convert the garage, and he said he'd be more than happy to give you some advice and some idea of price etc." She handed a business card to Maria. "Obviously there's no obligation whatsoever, but the offer is there if you'd like him to pop round."

Maria took the business card from Lisa and couldn't help noticing Karen's concerned look as she did so.

"Thank you, I really need more space that's for sure and it would be good to get some idea of cost." She placed the card in her purse and smiled at Karen who was still looking most concerned.

***

The last Christmas order was finally collected at 1.30pm on Christmas Eve. Julie's system had been a winner and, as Julie closed the door on the last order, Maria already had the champagne opened and poured.

"To us." She held up her glass to toast her girls. "And a huge thank you from me, for your total commitment, hard work and pure genius in getting all our orders finished and ready for collection without a hitch." Maria handed them both an envelope, which they both opened immediately.

"Gosh, thanks, Maria," Louise exclaimed as she studied her voucher. "A whole day at that new posh spa the other side of town."

"Maria." Julie was shocked, she'd already looked at the prices of the spa when it first opened in the summer, and it was well out of her league. "That's very kind." She held up her voucher to her sister.

"We can go together." Louise laughed.

"That was the idea," Maria added, "I thought you'd need it after Christmas, a day of relaxation to recharge. I just hope it's as good as it looks and sounds."

Both girls gave her a big hug, finished their glass of champagne and headed home to begin their Christmas celebrations.

Packing her final bits and pieces before leaving for Kim's, Maria was beginning to wish she hadn't drunk her glass of champagne so quickly; she was feeling very hot, and she could feel a tightness in the back of her neck. Worried this would lead to a headache, Maria downed a couple of Ibuprofen. Minutes later her taxi arrived, she was finally on her way, and she couldn't wait to begin the celebrations with her dear sister and her family.

Kim's house was a delight to behold, the decorations around the outside of her house were amazing, quite clearly the best in the close. A huge fir tree stood resplendent in the centre of the lawn, covered from head to foot in baubles and flashing lights, while Father Christmas perched precariously on the rooftop.

Hearing the taxi pull up, Harry was the first out of the house.

"Let me help you," he said as he grabbed Maria's cases. "Gosh what have you got in here?" He laughed as he struggled trying to carry everything in one go.

Inside, the house was alive with the spirit of Christmas, the decorations were carefully colour coordinated to match each room and looked amazing. The kitchen was a hive of activity and the delicious aromas of mulled wine and Kim's Christmas Eve speciality of rabbit pie, all part of their family tradition, was a sure sign, if it was needed, that Christmas was about to begin.

Unfortunately, despite her best efforts, Maria struggled through dinner, her head was pounding; the ibuprofen hadn't had the desired effect. In the end she had no other choice but to make her excuses. "I'm so sorry," she suddenly declared amid the excited chatter, "I think I'm going to call it a day; I have one nightmare of a headache."

Before she could continue, Kim was already out of her chair, she'd already noticed how her sister was suffering. "I'll get you a jug of water and bring it up."

"Thanks." Noticing their concerned faces, Maria smiled. "Don't worry I just need an early night, I'll be fine in the morning, I promise."

None of them looked reassured, they'd all noticed how tired and distracted she'd been since she arrived, it was completely out of character for Maria to be the first to leave the table, especially at Christmas.

Kim placed the jug of water and a glass on the bedside table. "Make sure you drink plenty through the night, you might be a little dehydrated as well as absolutely exhausted."

"I will, don't worry, I just need to sleep this headache off." Maria gave her sister a quick hug and closed the bedroom door behind her as she left.

Desperate to rest her head she literally fell into bed and immediately closed her eyes.

Later that evening, before she went to bed herself, Kim decided to check on her sister. Maria was in a deep sleep, but she looked very hot, so as quietly as possible Kim crept over to the radiator and turned it off.

As Maria opened her eyes the following morning, the relief that her head was so much better was short-lived as she realised her nightie was drenched and her whole body ached. It took everything she had to climb out of bed and into the shower, by the time she made it downstairs she was shivering uncontrollably.

"Maria, you look terrible." Kim was shocked to see her sister looking even worse than she had the previous evening. "Are you ok?" she pulled out a stool for her sister to sit down before she collapsed.

"To be honest I feel terrible," Maria admitted as she slumped miserably over the nearest worktop. "But I don't want to ruin Christmas so please just ignore me, it will pass, and I'll be fine."

Not convinced, Kim took her sister by the arm and led her back upstairs. "You're not spoiling Christmas, if you're not well, you're not well." She pulled the duvet back for her sister. "Now get back into bed and I'll bring you a nice hot cup of sweet tea."

With total relief Maria climbed back into bed; she felt so very weak and lifeless. Hoping that a short nap might help, she closed her eyes.

***

Completely unaware that it was well over a week later, Maria opened her eyes. Struggling to focus, she looked around; this wasn't one of Kim's cosy bedrooms, nothing was familiar at all, but she didn't care, she didn't have the strength to care, she just wanted to return to her dreams.

Suddenly she felt a hand gently take hold of hers.

"Maria, my name is Ella, I'm a nurse and you're in the hospital, do you think you could tell me the last thing you remember?"

Maria squinted, still trying to focus, she couldn't answer; her lips felt tight and her tongue felt heavy, it was all far too much effort. Somewhere in the background she could hear voices, they were muffled, and it was impossible for her to understand what they were saying, but she thought she recognised them. Gradually her eyesight became clearer, and she tried her best to smile as she focused on her two sisters who, with tears in their eyes, sat side by side at the bottom of her bed.

Maria looked questionably at her sisters as she tried to gather enough strength to speak.

"Don't try and talk yet," Kim said as she walked around to the side of the bed. "Would you like some water?"

Maria nodded.

"I'll let you girls look after your sister for a bit and I'll come back later to complete my checks."

"Thanks, Ella," Clare answered with a smile as the nurse left them to it.

"Would you feel more comfortable if you sat up?" Kim asked her sister. "We'll help you and then you can have your water."

Maria nodded, and carefully they both helped her as she gradually pulled herself up.

Slowly, Maria sipped the water and gradually her lips and tongue began to feel so much better. "What's happened?" she managed to say in a husky voice she hardly recognised as her own.

"You've had that dreaded flu bug," Kim began to explain. "We had to get you into hospital on boxing day, we just couldn't reduce your temperature, you were very poorly." Kim took her sister by the hand.

"How long?" Maria managed to ask.

"You've been in here just over a week, nine days to be exact," Kim said as she pulled her chair nearer to Maria's bedside.

Clare noticed the sudden panic in her sister's eyes. "It's ok, Maria," she tried to reassure her. "It's all ok, there's no need to worry about anything at all, just relax, you're going to need all your strength to get better, don't waste the energy worrying." Clare gave her sister a gentle hug.

"Welcome back to the land of the living, Maria," the doctor said as he entered the room and approached the bed accompanied by a different nurse. "You've had these two sisters of yours a little worried I have to say." He smiled warmly at Maria, then addressed her sisters directly. "Now if I can just ask you both to step outside for a minute, I need to examine Maria."

With the examination complete, the doctor sat in the chair by the side of the bed. He was so young, Maria thought to herself, he didn't look any older than Harry.

"Now Maria," he began, "you've been very poorly, this flu virus is like nothing I have ever seen in my working life before, consequently we've had to administer various forms of strong medication. I'll be totally honest with you; it's going to be a while before you'll feel strong enough to resume everyday activities, let alone return to work."

Maria frowned

The doctor continued, "Honestly, Maria if you don't give yourself time to fully recover, you will be back in here before you know it." He looked directly at her, and she could see he meant business. "You're going to be in here for a few more days yet, then I understand your sister Kim has made provision for you to stay with her to complete your recovery."

Maria managed a half-hearted smile; it was all too much, and she had no energy to protest.

"We'll leave you to rest now and I'll inform your sisters they can return." He passed the clipboard to the nurse who hung it at the end of the bed. "I'll be back tomorrow to see how you're progressing." He smiled kindly and left the room.

Exactly one week later Maria was released from the hospital into the care of her very protective sister.

As the days passed, gradually, Maria began to feel better; she was still very weak, but her mind wasn't, and she began to stress about her business.

"Don't worry about it," Kim tried desperately to reassure her. "I've cancelled the orders that you'd received, honestly there weren't that many. Anyway, who wants to eat cake in January? Everyone's on a diet or they're still finishing their Christmas fayre."

"What about Julie and Louise?" Maria asked thoughtfully, she didn't want to lose either of them and if they weren't earning, well, they might have to look for work elsewhere. "You have reassured them haven't you? I'll be back to work soon."

"They are both fine, they wanted to come and see you, but I didn't think you'd want them to see you until you were a lot better. They both enjoyed their spa day." Kim suddenly remembered. "They were anxious for you to know that."

"Oh, that's good to hear, maybe next week I will be able to go back home and then they can come and see me."

Kim knew better than to argue with her sister, so it was better to just ignore her last comment. In truth they'd all been very busy. Julie had been instrumental in restarting the business and Kim had been particularly impressed by her aptitude and talent, and after a couple of trials, Kim felt confident to let her continue.

"What do you think?" Julie asked Kim as she proudly presented a finished birthday cake for a one-year-old in the shape of a teddy bear.

"That looks amazing, it really does; before it's packed, I just want to take a photo," Kim said as she grabbed her phone. "I'm placing a photo by the side of each order, for reference purposes."

"That's a really good idea," Julie said as she placed the cake carefully in the centre of the table. "It's something we can show Maria when she's better, hopefully that way she won't be concerned we've ruined her reputation."

Kim looked up and saw Julie's concerned expression. "Your baking is first class; you're not ruining anyone's reputation so you can dismiss that notion immediately," Kim reassured her.

It hadn't been too difficult for Kim to explain her regular disappearances. She'd decided to tell Maria that, before Christmas, she'd signed up for some voluntary work and didn't like to let them down. Knowing how kind and caring her sister had always been, Maria didn't doubt this for one moment; she was actually very proud of her.

To be perfectly honest, Kim was thoroughly enjoying herself. She met with the two girls every morning, where they discussed the plans for the day, and any other issues of concern. Admittedly it wasn't too busy, but they had enough to be getting along with and, if the enquiries were anything to go by, it wasn't going to be too long until business picked up.

Kim had easily discovered Maria's password for her computer, all three sisters used the same: it had been their Dad's R.A.F. number when he completed his national service. Once she'd found the correct files it was easy to keep all the accounts up to date, something she noticed Maria obviously hadn't had time to do for quite a while.

It was mid-February before Maria began to look and feel more like her old self. She was getting itchy feet and wanted to check on her house and, although Kim had promised her it was all fine, she wanted to check for herself. "I'd like to go home tomorrow," she announced without warning one afternoon while helping her sister prepare their evening meal. "Not to stay, just to have a look around and I can pick up my laptop at the same time."

"Well, shall we see how you feel in the morning?" Kim was playing for time. "I do have to go out first thing so I could pick up your laptop if you would prefer."

"That's kind, but I really would like to check the house."

"Ok, as soon as I get back then, I'll take you over," Kim said, realising her sister was quite adamant. "It'll be about 11.30; is that alright?"

"That's great, thank you." Maria smiled at her sister; she'd always be forever grateful for the way she had nursed her back to health, but it was time she made inroads into returning home.

The next morning, Kim arrived much earlier than normal but already the girls were in full flow. "Morning, girls," Kim shouted above the sound of the electric mixer. "We need to talk."

"Just one moment," Julie acknowledged as she let the mixer finish.

Louise made a cup of coffee for each of them as they sat for their meeting.

"Maria wants to visit her house this morning," she told the girls who, initially, looked worried. "I think she's ready and if I put her off anymore, she's going to worry. Anyway, I've given it a lot of thought and I'm not going to say anything to her until we pull into her road, and then I'll explain that you're here to see her, because obviously she'll see your cars."

"Do you want us to pack all signs of baking away?" Louise asked anxiously.

"That's all very well," Julie quickly added. "But it will still smell of baking, so she'll know we've been up to something."

"It doesn't matter," Kim explained. "I want you to carry on, we can tell her what we've been doing and show her the photos of all the orders you've completed. I think she will be very pleased, well let's hope so anyway." She smiled at both girls wishing she felt as confident as she sounded, in truth she had no idea how Maria was going to react.

"It will be so nice to see them both," Maria said as Kim explained how both the girls had been keen to see her. "We can discuss when to restart the business; that's if they still want to work for me," she added more to herself than her sister.

Maria opened her front door, it felt strange to be home, and weird that the girls were already inside. She stepped inside and stood completely still for a minute, that was definitely the sound of the electric mixer, and there was no mistaking the aroma of freshly baked cakes. Maria turned to look at her sister.

"Surprise," Kim said sheepishly. "We have quite a lot to tell you."

"What's going on?" Completely baffled, Maria looked bewildered and was eager for some sort of explanation. "I don't understand," she said as her sister ushered her towards the kitchen.

"The girls wanted to get the business up and running for you. Well, it was all down to Julie really, she asked me if any orders had come through. It wasn't too difficult to work out your password, it's the same as mine, and Clare's for that matter, anyway there were a few orders, all well within Julie's capability, so we all decided to continue."

Suddenly everything made sense, Maria thought Kim's voluntary work was taking up a lot of her time and she never seemed very keen to talk about it, now she knew why.

"There's no voluntary work, then?" Maria confirmed.

Kim shook her head. "No, sorry for that little white lie, I didn't want you to worry about what we were doing."

Maria gave her sister a big hug.

"Come on," Kim said, "let's go and see what they're up to, who knows they might even have a cake or two to spare."

Standing in the doorway, Maria felt quite emotional as she watched the activities continue; it was a few seconds before they both realised they were being watched.

"Maria how are you?" Louise was the first to notice her.

Looking up, Julie switched off the mixer, she felt a little apprehensive now Maria was here.

"I'm much better now thank you, thanks to Kim and her family." She smiled warmly at her sister. "I can't believe what you've all done here, I'm so grateful to you all for keeping the business going, I really am."

Instantly relieved, Julie made some coffee, and it wasn't long before they were all enjoying some freshly baked muffins, while excitedly updating Maria on the events of the past few weeks.

"We've taken pictures of everything that's left the premises," Julie explained.

"That's a good idea, I can't wait to have a look later," Maria said as she picked up a white chocolate and raspberry muffin and took a bite.

Immediately there was silence as they waited for her response. "What..." she said looking from one to the other.

"Is it ok?" Julie asked warily.

"It's delicious." They all looked relieved. "I've always been very impressed by your baking," Maria said to Julie encouragingly. "I certainly don't have an issue with the quality or standard you've been delivering in my absence; I'm just really grateful that you're all still here, and the business is already up and running." She finished her muffin and licked her fingers, they all laughed.

It wasn't too long before Maria sensed the girls were anxious to get on and decided to leave them to it. She'd enjoyed their meeting and even Kim had to acknowledge Maria seemed more alive than she had in a long while, so it wasn't a huge surprise when she declared that she would like to attend the meetings each morning and gradually ease herself back into work.

It was obvious to Maria from the first day as she begun to attend the morning meetings, that Kim was totally engrossed in this new role she had carved out for herself. The accounts were up to date, she'd updated the website and created social media sites for the business that already had an extraordinary number of followers.

"How do you feel about continuing with the accounts, and managing the emails, basically everything you've been doing?" Maria asked her sister as they arrived for their morning meeting a few days later.

"Are you serious?" Kim looked startled. "I'd love to I really would, I've enjoyed every minute of it."

"Great, that's settled then." Maria looked at her sister before she continued. "Because I feel ready to move back home now." She held up her hand to prevent Kim's imminent objection. "I'm more than ready and as you're going to be coming over every day, you'll be able to check that I'm ok. It will also give me more time; I must start looking into getting the garage converted, I think that's the best way to go. I couldn't go through another Christmas like the last one."

"Would you consider contacting Lisa's husband, it might be an idea to start with someone you know?" Kim asked tentatively.

"I don't really know him," Maria admitted. "But I know what you mean, that might actually be a really good idea."

The day Maria moved back home was very emotional. There was no doubt she would miss living amongst a very active, busy family, but she was more than capable now of looking after herself; she felt better than she had in ages.

***

Relieved to have finally finished this particular job, Tim sat in his truck. It had been one of those days; he'd heard his phone ringing a few times but there'd been no time today for phone calls. Four missed calls and a couple of messages: he'd deal with those as soon as he got back to the office. Thirty minutes later and stuck in heavy traffic, Tim decided, as soon as it was possible, he'd take a detour and go straight home; it was already late, and he was tired and hungry.

Finally, after what seemed a never-ending journey, Tim stepped inside the front door. He hadn't even had a chance to close the door behind him when Lisa appeared from the kitchen and promptly bombarded him with questions. "What did she have to say? You have spoken to her haven't you, please tell me you've called her back?"

"Who are you talking about?" he asked abruptly, kicking off his boots.

"Maria, she messaged out of courtesy, as she put it, to let me know that she was going to ask you for your advice on a few ideas she had in mind. She's left a message on your mobile." Lisa stopped for breath. "Please don't tell me you haven't got back to her?" She turned to stare at her husband. "You haven't got back to her, have you?" She shook her head in disbelief.

"Lisa, I've had one of those days." He took his mobile out of his pocket. "I have four missed calls to deal with plus a couple of messages and I'll deal with them all, once I've had a beer." He grabbed a can from the fridge and made his way into the study.

Maria was surprised that Tim worked so late; it was gone 8pm when he finally rang her back and they arranged a meeting at her house the following Monday morning.

"Would you like David to be here as well, just for support?" Kim asked Maria as they discussed her ideas.

"No, I don't think so, that's a kind offer but it's only an initial meeting, I'll be fine."

"Well, I'll be here anyway," Kim confirmed. "If you want me to join you, just say, it's not a problem."

"That might be a good idea actually," Maria agreed. "I'm bound to forget something."

Monday morning, Tim arrived exactly on time, and immediately Maria felt at ease and comfortable discussing her plans. He was receptive to her ideas and concise with his answers, while all the time making copious amounts of notes; it was obvious he knew his trade very well.

"I think I have a good idea of what you're looking for," Tim explained as he packed his notes away. "I can draw up a few variations for you to look at, obviously you would be responsible for ordering the equipment you need, but we can plan the layout together and I can install everything you order. For specific installations we subcontract and always supply the correct certification." He paused, watching Maria's reaction.

"Can you include costings for each of your suggestions?" Maria asked as they made their way back to the house.

"Certainly," Tim replied. "I'll have something for you by the end of the week."

"That's great, thank you." Maria smiled; she was already excited to see his ideas on paper.

"Do you email or send them by post?" Kim checked before he left.

"I can do either, it's up to you."

Kim looked at Maria. "Email," they both said together.

***

It didn't take too long for Maria to settle back to work, it was so much easier now she no longer needed to spend time bogged down with accounts and general paperwork. Kim had settled herself upstairs in one of the spare bedrooms Maria had previously used as her office and seemed extremely happy.

They all actively agreed to continue with their morning meetings; it was especially useful when prioritising orders and took a lot of pressure away from Maria. Julie continued to impress; she was keen to expand their repertoire and had already introduced several new gluten free options, which were proving to be extremely popular.

"That tastes very good," Maria said as she took another bite from one of Julie's new creations. "I like that very much; you wouldn't even know it's gluten free."

"I'll get that one onto the website today," Kim confirmed as she showed Maria the photo she'd taken earlier.

"I need to take up running or something," Louise suddenly declared, as Julie offered her a piece of cake. "Tasting all these delicious cakes is having an adverse effect on my hips."

"I know exactly where you're coming from," Kim agreed. "I don't like to weigh myself at the moment; I'm too frightened."

"Oh, before I forget," Maria interrupted, eager for their attention. "Tim has sent back several ideas of what can be accomplished by converting the garage. Kim and I are going to have a look at them later today and see if any of them would work for us. Obviously, I'll keep you both in the loop. I know we're all desperate to move into somewhere with more room, so fingers crossed."

In the end it didn't take too long for both sisters to agree on the design they preferred.

"Do you want me to send an email back, or do you think it would be better to give Tim a ring?" Kim asked her sister.

"I think I'll give him a ring just to say we would like to proceed." Maria looked pensive.

"Don't forget though," Kim reminded her sister. "We must get all correspondence in writing so David can check it over." She paused briefly. "So, with that in mind we'll need to follow up your conversation with a confirmation email."

Maria picked up her phone. "So we're agreed it's plan number three?"

"Yes, definitely, go for it." Kim sat back in her chair while Maria made a call to Tim.

Tim didn't pick up, so Maria left a message.

***

Much later that evening, Tim made himself comfortable in his study; another long day meant he still needed to catch up with his missed calls, messages and read any emails that might have come through. His last message was from Maria, checking his watch, he decided it wasn't too late to call back. He had to admit he was surprised Maria had decided to use them for the work, all things considered, but then he never could understand a woman's logic.

"Maria, hi, it's Tim."

"Tim, thanks for coming back to me. Like I mentioned in my message, I've sent you an email confirming that I would very much like to proceed, and I've settled on the third design you submitted."

"I must confess I haven't read my emails yet," Tim quickly explained. "I know that's bad, but it's been manic all week. I'm glad you liked the designs though." He hesitated, choosing his words carefully, he continued, "For the next stage, I send you a contract. I'm sorry if that sounds too official but I find it's best to have any potential issues sorted before any work begins."

"No, please don't worry," Maria assured him. "My sister's husband is a lawyer and he's already told me I must have a contract for him to check, before we go any further."

"Great." Tim sounded relieved. "I'll get that out to you, then, once that's all sorted, we need to sit down and plan the equipment you need, and where it's going to be situated. That will make it easier to get all the power points you need in the correct place."

"Thank you, it all sounds very exciting," Maria said. "In the meantime, I'll work out exactly what equipment I'll need."

"Speak to you soon then." Tim was just about to hang up when Lisa placed a handwritten note in front of him. "Oh, hang on a minute, Maria," he said quickly before she hung up. "Lisa has just handed me a note, she's apologised for not getting back to you, but she's having trouble with her phone. That's also a dig at me." He laughed. "She's been telling me she needs a new phone, guess that's a job for the weekend now."

"Tell her not to worry, I know Kim kept in touch while I wasn't well, and I just wanted to thank her for the lovely flowers."

"Ok, I'll tell her. Speak soon, enjoy the rest of your evening." Leaning back in his chair with his hands behind his head, he stretched out. He knew he'd offered a very competitive rate, but he didn't think for one minute anything would come of it, he just hoped there wouldn't be any repercussions, they were all adults after all, but probably best if he took the lead on this job, he decided.

***

There was great excitement when Kim confirmed they'd received their first wedding cake enquiry. It had been less than a week ago, after several trial runs, that they'd agreed to test the water, so to speak, and Kim had added it to their repertoire online.

"It sounds like she's got very definite ideas of what she wants, do you think she's actually looked at what we're offering?" Julie enquired after listening to the contents of the email.

"I still think it would be worth inviting her in, it can't hurt," Kim explained. "She's mentioned she's interested in having the four-tiered wedding cake in different flavours, but she's just ignored the flavours we've offered and chosen her own." They all laughed.

"Are we all in favour of meeting her?" Maria asked, concerned; they were all in agreement, it would be a huge undertaking and they all needed to be on board.

"Oh yes, definitely, she can have whatever flavours she likes, that's not a problem," Julie replied, anxious not to sound negative.

"I'll email her back and get a time booked in, what's the betting she wants to come one evening?" Kim laughed. "Don't forget, Maria," she added hastily, "when you've got a minute, David has sent the contract back, so we just need to read through his email."

"I'll be with you in a minute," Maria replied as she quickly finished checking off today's delivery.

Satisfied with David's conclusion, Maria signed the contract and sent it back.

Tim hadn't expected any issues with the contract, the company had a good reputation, they were always highly commended for their work and provided excellent after sales care and guarantees. But he still couldn't believe they were going to be working for Maria.

Initially he'd been wary of her, he'd never really got to know her very well when they were younger. He'd witnessed first-hand the pain and heart break she'd caused his friend, and that had been more than enough for him to draw his own conclusions. Lisa, however, had always insisted he'd got her all wrong and now after meeting her he thought maybe he'd been a little harsh.

She hadn't altered that much over the years; she'd always been immaculate in her appearance, she still wore her hair short, but it seemed softer in its style and colour, and she looked thinner than he remembered, unlike his poor Lisa who was constantly fighting the battle of the bulge.

Before he filed this contract and took this job to the next stage, he needed to have a conversation with his partner, but that could wait until Monday morning, no need to call him into the office tonight, but it was most certainly something he needed to do face to face.

***

It was this Saturday that Lisa had organised one of her "date nights". Relieved to hear it only involved a meal in a restaurant, Tim had willingly agreed. On a previous occasion Lisa had booked tickets for the movies, that hadn't worked out at all well as he'd slept right through the entire film. Tonight, he'd been told he needed to make more of an effort.

"Can I interest you in an aperitif?" the young waiter asked as he sat them at their table.

"I'll have a champagne cocktail please," Lisa answered without hesitation.

The waiter turned his attention to Tim. "For you, sir?"

"What beers do you have?" Immediately Tim noticed Lisa's wide eyed expression. "Don't worry, I'll have a G&T." He smiled knowingly at the waiter.

"Any preference for your gin, sir?"

"Monkey 47 with Mediterranean tonic."

"Thank you, sir." The waiter smiled, handed them their menus and walked away.

Minutes later Tim closed his menu and placed it on the table. "I've decided," he declared happily. "How are you getting along?"

Lisa looked up. "There's just so much I like; I don't know what to choose. What are you having?"

"I'm having the cauliflower velouté with crispy hen's egg, followed by the hake with gnocchi, leeks and black truffle." Tim rubbed his hands together, pleased he wasn't the one still deciding.

"Sounds delicious." Lisa closed the menu. "I've decided," she said as she took a sip of her champagne, already excited to taste the delights she had chosen for her meal.

"That was divine, thank you," Lisa said as the waiter cleared their plates. "I think I'm going to need a break before dessert though."

"I agree," Tim said as he sat back in his chair. "It will give me time to update you on Maria and her commission."

"There's an update already?" Lisa was surprised, it had only been a few weeks since Tim first quoted.

"I know." Tim began. "Well, it's all moved pretty fast, but it's understandable, having seen the set-up they have. They desperately need more space."

"What stage are you at now then?" Lisa asked, suddenly feeling extremely anxious and fiddling with her napkin nervously.

"To put it in a nutshell, I received her signed contract yesterday."

"Why didn't you tell me you were getting to that stage?" Lisa asked, obviously quite shaken. "Honestly, Tim, I can't believe you never mentioned this before, this is just crazy."

"Lisa," Tim exclaimed, completely stunned by her sudden change of mood. "I know she's your friend, but I know what I'm doing, she won't be disappointed."

"I know that," she snapped back.

Tim noticed Lisa's rosy cheeks had been replaced with a pale pallor and the penny suddenly dropped. "Lisa, I asked you before you gave her my card to explain the situation, you promised me that you would." He stared at her in disbelief. "I didn't think for one minute I would need it confirmed, you're my wife, I believed you."

"It wasn't the right time," she confessed. "I'd planned to ring her, but you know my phone's been playing up for weeks, anyway, I thought I had plenty of time; it normally takes ages to get to this stage."

"She doesn't know then."

"No, she has no idea," Lisa practically whispered.

Tim held his head in his hands, this was unbelievable. There was only one way out as far as he could see.

"Tim," Lisa said reassuringly. "Please don't worry, I'll give her a ring and explain everything. Honestly, Tim, I promise it will all be fine, it was all such a long time ago; I'm sure Maria will understand, I'll explain it's all my fault."

Tim stared at his wife; he was so angry it was a while before he could speak. "This is just so unprofessional, Lisa, and not how we work. I suggest you arrange to meet her; this is something you should explain face to face not over the phone." Tim pushed the dessert menu to one side. "I've lost my appetite; if it's all the same with you, I'd like to leave."

Lisa knew better than to argue. Tim paid the bill and they left.

***

Sunday mornings were Maria's favourite, with a fresh pot of coffee, a plate of bacon sandwiches and several newspapers, she made herself comfortable for the next few hours, while she caught up with all the news and gossip.

"Hi, Lisa." Maria tried to sound upbeat as she answered the call, she hoped this wasn't going to be a long conversation, she hadn't quite finished her breakfast…

"Maria, would it be possible to pop over today at some stage? I need to have a chat with you about something." Lisa swallowed hard, she had everything crossed Maria would agree, she hadn't slept a wink all night, and Tim was still so angry he could barely look at her. She had to sort this out as soon as she possibly could.

"Today…" Maria had hardly begun her sentence when Lisa interrupted.

"Please, Maria, I wouldn't ask but it's very important to me."

"Has something happened, Lisa, are you ill, what on earth is the matter?" Maria felt uneasy, her friend sounded incredibly upset.

Ignoring Maria's questions, Lisa continued, "I can be with you in 45 minutes if that's ok. Please, Maria, I wouldn't bother you if it wasn't absolutely necessary, and this is something I need to explain face to face; I can't do it over the phone."

There was no mistaking the urgency in Lisa's voice and so Maria agreed, and a few minutes later Lisa was in the car on her way.

In record time Lisa pulled up outside Maria's house; she was really nervous and had absolutely no idea where to start this confession, even Karen had deserted her on this one.

"I'm sorry, Lisa, I'm with Tim on this," Karen explained, not at all surprised; she'd had an uneasy feeling about all this from the beginning. "You should have explained when you first gave her Tim's card, especially as you'd promised him you would, what were you thinking?" This was probably the first time she hadn't had Karen's support; she was all alone on this one and she felt incredibly vulnerable. Nervously she pressed the doorbell.

The tense nervous expression etched across Lisa's face and the way she sat on the edge of the seat had Maria worried. "Would you like some tea, coffee or something stronger?" Suddenly Maria wasn't sure she wanted to know why on a Sunday morning Lisa was sitting in her living room.

"Tea would be good, thank you." Lisa attempted to smile but her lips were already quivering, and the smile didn't really happen.

Minutes later, Maria placed a tray of tea and a plate of homemade biscuits on the table. "Shall I be Mum?" she asked, desperately trying to ease what was feeling like a very tense situation.

Lisa nodded, and Maria noticed the tremor in her hold as she took her cup of tea. Sitting bolt upright, Lisa drank her tea straight down and replaced her teacup on the tray. She took a deep breath and with a croaky voice she began, "Firstly, Maria I would like to apologise for interrupting your Sunday." She tried again to smile, but she was so nervous this time it looked more a snarl. "I've made a huge error of judgement, in doing so I've let my husband and his company down." She stopped for a moment and lowered her gaze.

Relieved to hear that it wasn't a health issue, Maria, still not exactly sure what this had to do with her, relaxed back into her chair. "I'm sure it's not that bad." Maria smiled. "Whatever it is, Tim loves you, he always has, I'm sure it can be sorted." Maria smiled at her reassuringly.

"It's not just Tim that needs to forgive me though." Lisa looked directly at her newfound friend and took a deep breath. "I realise I should have told you this when I first gave you Tim's business card and don't ask me why I didn't, because I just can't answer that." Lisa stopped for what seemed like an eternity.

"Tell me what exactly?" Maria asked nervously.

"I just had no idea how quickly everything was proceeding, normally, well sometimes, most times actually—" Lisa was mumbling, and Maria was finding it hard to keep up. "It takes months before the client gets to the contract stage, so you can imagine how surprised I was when Tim said the contract had been agreed and signed."

Maria shrugged. "Sorry, I don't understand. I had no idea you were even part of Tim's business." Maria was puzzled, this was a weird conversation.

"Oh, I'm not," Lisa was quick to reassure her.

"Then I really don't understand, why is the contract any concern of yours?"

"Because there is something I promised Tim that I would tell you, and he thought I had, but in my defence, I thought I had plenty of time." Lisa was stumbling over her words and hardly making any sense, and Maria was losing her patience.

"Lisa," Maria almost shouted. "Please just tell me, what it is you're trying to say?"

Lisa sighed and looked down at her feet, unable to look Maria in the eye. "Do you remember years ago you told me that your car was due for a service and how you were dreading taking it back to the garage in case you saw Andy?"

"Yes," Maria confirmed, surprising herself that she remembered it so well. "You told me not to worry as he didn't work there anymore; when I asked you how you knew you just said Tim told you." Second guessing what was coming next, Maria felt goose bumps cover her arms and she shivered.

"Well." Lisa looked up to face Maria directly. "Tim knew because Andy went to work for him, and now they're business partners." Lisa watched as all the colour drained from Maria's face.

There was a deafening silence while Maria digested Lisa's last sentence. "So, I've just signed a contract employing my ex, who absolutely broke my heart and who I haven't seen for over thirty years, to convert my garage, is that what you're telling me?" Maria practically whispered unable to belief what she'd just heard.

"No," Lisa said confidently. "Tim was adamant that you know, the contract can be void with immediate effect, that is no problem at all." Looking directly at Maria she continued, "Maria I'm really sorry that I've put you in this predicament, why I didn't mention it at the very beginning I have no idea, and if I could turn back time I most certainly would."

Hardly able to look at Lisa, Maria was struggling to retain her composure. "Does he know?" she asked in a voice full of emotion and disappointment.

"No, Tim had planned to tell him on Monday morning," Lisa answered honestly.

"Isn't it a bit strange that Tim didn't see the need to check with his business partner, before accepting this work?"

"Not really," Lisa said in Tim's defence. "Andy wouldn't object; he's not that sort of guy, anyway they normally work on different jobs. It's very rare they work on the same project. Tim would have undertaken all your work."

Maria was stunned, there was no other word for it, this had taken the wind out of her sails. Although it did explain Karen's concerned expression that Maria had witnessed whenever Tim's business was discussed. Now she felt betrayed by all of them.

Taking the continued silence as her cue to leave, Lisa picked up her handbag and stood ready to leave. "I am truly sorry, Maria…" Before she could continue Maria interrupted.

"Can you tell Tim I'll give him a call in the week? Do you mind seeing yourself out?" Maria could hardly bear to look at

Lisa, this had stirred so many emotions it was taking all her strength just to remain civil.

"Of course," Lisa said as she made her way out of the house and back to her car.

Maria didn't have the energy to move from her chair in the living room, she'd heard Lisa's car drive away ages ago, but this unexpected visit had left her feeling numb and lifeless. No one knew the whole story of her breakup with Andy, not even Lisa. No one knew the pain she'd suffered, the feelings of betrayal, emptiness, worthlessness, and total heartbreak, that had taken forever to fade. For such a long time now, she'd refused to allow any of those feelings to resurface up until today, and now she could remember every detail as though it was yesterday, and it was an uncomfortable painful memory.

CHAPTER FOUR

Maria – The Late 1980s

The pain of heartbreak wasn't something Maria acknowledged as a real emotion, until now. Sobbing into her pillow late at night, the misery and sorrow each morning when she opened her eyes to the realisation there was no happy ending to this story, and the perpetual feeling of loneliness as she cancelled all the up-and-coming events they would have experienced together, were all taking its toll.

She had no appetite for clubs or parties but went along dutifully, knowing her friends were trying their very best to keep her occupied, and Maria was appreciative of their continued support and loyalty, more perhaps than they realised.

With a fine-toothed comb she searched out every piece of evidence that may have any link to their life together; she ripped photos from their frames, nothing escaped, everything was destroyed.

"Extreme" was the comment from some, "understandable" was the comment from others, but for Maria it was a necessity, there was no way back from this, so it was a case of moving on, or stay broken forever.

For Andy it was the complete opposite; he treasured every photo he possessed and savoured all the memories they had shared together. For him though, it wasn't over, he wasn't one to give up lightly; he knew Maria felt betrayed, he knew he'd stretched the truth to its limits, but the way he felt about her, he couldn't envisage life without her for too long.

He had a plan; he would give Maria some time and space, not sure how long, he hadn't quite got down to specifics, and in the meantime, he was going to sort all the reoccurring issues with Sharon. In his mind it was all settled, all he had to do was put it all into action...

***

Family lunches hosted by Maria's parents were historically chatty, jubilant affairs that lasted most of the afternoon. Her father always carved the joint at the table, there were dishes of scrumptious crispy roast potatoes and parsnips, alongside several varieties of fresh veg, followed by mouth-watering homemade desserts.

It was always very serious business helping oneself and passing the dishes of delicious food, so the family were all quite genuinely surprised when Maria chose this particular moment to make her sudden announcement. "I've been for an interview this week." There was a short silence as everyone stopped for a moment to digest Maria's statement.

"Doing what exactly?" Kim asked looking puzzled. "I thought you loved your job."

"I do, I did, but I just need a change," Maria began to explain. "I need a whole new challenge." She glanced around the table; it wasn't very often she held everyone's attention. "The interview went well, I think, and if I get offered the job, I may even look to move house."

"Where is this new job then?" her father enquired as he helped himself to a few more potatoes.

"It's the other side of town, it's not really the distance," she pointed out. "It's trying to cross town during the rush hour, it could add 20 to 30 minutes to the journey each way."

"Have you started to look already?" her father enquired.

"No, I don't want to jinx anything." She laughed. "I was really hoping you and Mum would come with me to look around, if I get the job that is."

"Of course, darling, we'd love to," her mum confirmed.

By the end of the following week, Maria received the written confirmation she'd been hoping for. She was the successful applicant, and the job was hers. Immediately she accepted and set about compiling her letter of resignation.

"I understand, I really do," Lisa said miserably as Maria tried to explain her decision to leave. "Does it really have to be so drastic though?"

"You know as well as I, Lisa, now Andy has resurfaced, he'll keep on until I agree to see him. A few months back I would probably have given in, but now…" She shrugged her shoulders and looked bleakly at her friend. "I just don't want to see him or talk to him, and every day I dread the fact he could just turn up here and waltz into the office, all smiles."

"Can't you just talk to him and tell him straight? You don't need to change your job surely." Lisa hadn't seen this coming at all, she'd presumed it was just a matter of time and they'd be back together, that's what normally happened.

"I'm sorry, Lisa, it's for the best; I really need a change and I certainly need a new challenge and I'll have all of that with this job." She gave her friend a big hug. "We'll still be friends, that won't change," she reassured her.

Lisa managed a smile as they headed into work.

By Saturday morning, Maria had three properties lined up to view; by Saturday lunch time, with just one left to view, disappointment reigned heavy.

"How on earth did they get this photo?" Maria showed her father the exterior photo of the house they were just about to view.

"Don't write it off just yet, it might surprise you inside," her mother said encouragingly.

"I'm not holding my breath," Maria replied, looking as disheartened as she felt.

Fifteen minutes later they were already heading back to the car.

"That was worse than terrible." Maria shuddered. "There's no way I could ever walk barefoot on that carpet, it was filthy, and that kitchen, half the wall tiles were missing and when was orange a fashionable colour for kitchen cupboards?"

Her mother laughed. "I don't think that was their original colour, it looked to me as though they'd had several coats of paint over the years."

"It does say on the description the property needs updating," her father explained as he handed all the paperwork back to Maria.

"That's an understatement," Maria replied, irritably despondent; all three properties had been a complete waste of time.

"Shall we find a pub and get something to eat?" her father suggested as he unlocked the car.

"That's a great idea," both women answered in unison as they jumped back into the car.

***

Early Sunday morning, Maria was up and out in search of the local paper and any other information she could find relating to properties on the market; there had to be something out there somewhere, surely? Armed with enough reading material to keep her busy for the next few hours, Maria returned home, made herself a pot of coffee and settled down with her papers. Literally a few minutes later, Maria was distracted by the sound of her telephone, tempted to let it ring and go onto answer phone, reluctantly she left her papers and answered her phone.

"Morning, Maria," her mother said cheerfully.

"Hi, Mum, everything ok?" Maria asked, surprised to hear from her mother so soon.

"Oh yes, everything's fine, no the reason I'm calling is because your dad and I would like you to join us next weekend, we're going to this lovely hotel we found a few months back." She stopped for a second expecting Maria to object, when she didn't, she continued. "Anyway, your dad has already booked you a room; I'm sure you'll love it, there's a fabulous spa, swimming pool, gym and lots of incredible walks, not that we've managed any of them yet." She laughed. They'd both been concerned for their daughter; she hadn't been the same since the split with Andy and then after yesterday's disappointment, they were hoping a change of scenery might help.

"That will be great, Mum," Maria answered without really giving it much thought. "That's really kind of you both, I'll look forward to it." Realising they were only trying to help, she hadn't the heart to object, it might even be fun, she considered as she said goodbye to her mum and hung up.

By the time Saturday arrived it was well over three months since she'd seen Andy, and still silly little things would suddenly remind her, and along with a memory came the raw pain that spread like fire in the pit of her stomach. This weekend, she hoped, would be a turning point: somewhere with no memories, somewhere she could relax knowing he wasn't going to suddenly appear, somewhere to recharge and hopefully enjoy.

After a three-hour journey, they turned into a stunning tree-lined driveway where the trees were so old, they formed a canopy, and right at the end of the impressive drive sat a magnificent Victorian residence, now a five- star hotel. Typical of the era, a decorative porch wrapped itself around the front and one side of the building, where in warm weather residents could relax and enjoy great views while enjoying drinks served from the bar.

Inside was a hundred per cent luxury, a grand sweeping staircase adorned with original works of art was a showcase for Victorian lifestyle at its best.

"Wow, Dad," Maria exclaimed. "This place is incredible."

"Wait until you see your room," he replied, smiling.

Check-in was quick and precise and when the porter opened the door to her room, opulence positively oozed from every corner. Kicking off her shoes, her feet sunk deep into the soft velvety pile of the carpet; there was a comfy sofa and armchair by the window, a bowl of fresh fruit and a plate of homemade cookies placed on the table along with freshly laundered napkins.

"Oh, Mum, this room is an absolute dream." Maria hugged her mother who had literally just popped her head around the door.

"It's our pleasure, dear." It was a refreshing change to see her daughter genuinely happy. "We're just going down for afternoon tea if you would like to join us. We have dinner booked in the restaurant later tonight, so we thought afternoon tea would suffice until then."

"Thanks, Mum," Maria beamed. "I'll see you down there, I just want to finish unpacking and I'd really like a swim before dinner, so I won't want too much to eat."

Afternoon tea served in the grand lounge was a very civilised affair, and Maria couldn't resist the delicate finger sandwiches and the warm scones with clotted cream and delicious homemade strawberry jam.

"So much for not eating too much." Maria laughed as she heaped cream and jam onto her scone.

A couple of hours and far too many cakes later, Maria dived into the pool; it was practically empty with just one other couple in the shallow end with their children. She swam vigorously, determined to burn off the calories she'd happily consumed earlier.

***

While Maria swam, Andy sat at his desk; this weekend it was his turn to work and today had been particularly quiet for a Saturday, which meant there had been far too much time to think. Maria filled his head; he couldn't believe that despite his best efforts she'd remained adamant, she wanted nothing more to do with him, it was so frustrating.

Quite by chance later that evening, Andy bumped into Lisa and her husband Tim, he'd decided to have a quick drink on his way home and had been standing at the bar when they walked by.

"Hi Andy," Lisa said, as she recognised him. "How are you?"

"Not so bad," he said trying to sound upbeat.

"If you're on your own, why don't you join us?" Lisa said, feeling sorry for him; he looked so lonely as he stood leaning against the bar.

Andy looked at Tim; he didn't know him as well as he did Lisa, and the last thing he wanted was to disrupt their evening.

"Yes, mate, join us; we're just making our way to the table in the corner," Tim said, sensing Andy's hesitation.

Chrissy Ward

"Thanks, I'd love to," Andy said, grabbing his glass as he followed them over to their table. At first, his objective was to use this unforeseen opportunity to gain some inside information. Lisa always made it her business to know exactly what everyone around her was doing and would most certainly know all the latest news on Maria, but unfortunately that wasn't to be, as Tim had more pressing issues he was keen to discuss.

"I'm glad we bumped into you." Tim took a sip of his pint before continuing, "Don't know if you've heard, but I'm starting out on my own."

"No, I hadn't heard," Andy answered honestly.

"Well, it's something I've been considering for a while now, so I thought I'd bite the bullet and give it a go," Tim explained as he opened a packet of crisps. "The thing is, originally, I'd agreed with my boss to buy the truck that I currently use, but he's turned a bit funny on me and changed his mind, so I need a truck urgently."

"What do you call urgent?" Always the salesman Andy was all ears.

"Realistically I need it on the road ready to go in less than a month."

"In that case," Andy explained, "you're probably looking at a used truck rather than brand new."

"As long as it comes with a couple of years' warranty, four wheels and a steering wheel I really don't mind." Tim laughed.

Andy already had a few in mind so they both agreed to meet at the garage in the early part of the next week. For the next couple of hours, they discussed Tim's ideas for his new business and the two men chatted easily, occasionally stopping to include Lisa in the conversation, although she seemed perfectly happy to just sit back and listen.

***

At 8pm precisely, Maria made her way down the grand staircase to join her parents in the library for pre-dinner drinks. For the first time in ages, she felt confident; she'd bought a new dress, a little

83

different from her usual type, this was a looser asymmetrical style, extremely flattering and definitely very comfortable.

The library was a beautiful unique room, with a faint aroma of antique books that probably remained untouched for most of the time. Another huge fireplace was the centrepiece set against oak-panelled walls and the overall ambience was cosier than the more formal lounge areas.

Quickly scanning the room, Maria spotted her parents, they'd positioned themselves by a huge window, and were busy admiring the stunning views where beautifully manicured lawns were bordered with an abundance of Hydrangea, Aster and Salvias to name but a few.

"Darling, we've ordered you a glass of champagne," her mother said indicating the glass on the table.

"Thanks, Mum," Maria said as she savoured her first sip. "Gosh, that's really good." She placed her glass back on the table and picked up the large leather-bound menu. "I don't think I've ever seen such an impressive menu," Maria had to admit, as she scanned each page.

Her father, inquisitive to see what delicacies were on offer this evening, was now fully engrossed in his copy of the menu and absent-mindedly tapped the side of his chair while deliberating. "I'm not sure if I fancy the scallops or the carpaccio for my entrée," he mused more to himself than anyone in particular.

"I have no idea what to order," Maria added, shaking her head, "I like everything."

Suddenly, from nowhere, dressed in a smart black evening suit, a young man appeared. "May I be of any help?" he enquired politely in a very strong Italian accent.

"Thank you," her father replied looking up from his menu, "but I think we just need a little more time if that's ok."

"That's absolutely fine, sir, I'll come back for your order in a short while." He smiled at Maria and swiftly made his exit.

Inside the room designated as the main restaurant, crystal chandeliers hung from the ceiling and thick heavy drapes framed each window. The tables were adorned with crisp white linen, highly polished silver cutlery and fine cut wine glasses. The luxurious surroundings, excellent food and incredible attention to detail, set a whole new precedence to "dining out".

"I'm not sure any of the other tables are receiving quite as much attention as we are," her father unexpectedly announced towards the end of their meal.

"What makes you say that?" Maria asked, completely unaware that her father had been paying that much attention to the other tables.

"I've been watching, and as far as I can tell we were the only table to receive the extra fish course, and, so far, only one other table has been offered the sorbet before dessert."

"Well, I'm not complaining." Maria shrugged her shoulders, not too bothered about the other tables; she was enjoying herself for the first time in ages.

"The restaurant manager has been particularly attentive don't you think?" Her mother smiled knowingly. "Although I do believe, that's more to do with you, Maria, than us."

"I don't think so, Mum," Maria said, slightly irritated by her mother's assumption and was grateful when her father promptly changed the subject. In all fairness Maria had already noticed the waiter was "a little over the top" but he was Italian, and she'd just attributed it to his culture.

The weekend was over all too quickly, and first thing Monday morning, Maria sent her parents a huge bouquet of flowers. They had showered her with kindness and generosity all weekend, and she returned home on Sunday feeling refreshed and relaxed.

***

Having completed two interviews, both held on site, Maria couldn't believe she hadn't noticed the drabness of her new surroundings. The building, housing both the warehouse and the offices, was situated in the middle of a busy trading estate; the car park was limited, it was first come first served, other than that, parking was in the next road. The offices were clean but far from luxurious, the flooring was a heavy-duty carpet tile, the walls were stark with a thin coat of emulsion and the windows were completely devoid of any sort of covering. The desks and chairs, however, looked reasonably new and were quite comfortable.

She'd been employed as "office manager". Her priority being to introduce and implement a new system of computerised accounting and ordering, using the new software systems already in place. The challenge and competitive salary had sealed the deal for Maria and now she was keen to get started.

As expected, the journey to and from work was a nightmare, hitting heavy traffic for miles reignited her search for the right property, but for now, nothing seemed to fit the bill.

***

"Don't forget Tim, if Andy mentions Maria, you know nothing," Lisa reminded her husband before he left.

Tim looked at his wife and frowned. "You've already told me that, several times."

"I just need to be sure you remember, the last thing I need is for Andy to find out through us, or you, to be exact, that Maria has changed her job."

"I'm going to look at trucks," Tim reminded his wife. "This is a business meeting, not a coffee morning." He collected his sandwiches from the fridge. "I'll see you tonight, have a good day." He kissed her goodbye and left.

Tim walked into the showroom at exactly 9.30am, shaking hands; Andy led the way. "How many miles on the clock?" Tim enquired as they approached the truck he had come to view.

"16,000, which is very low, it's two years old and, as you can see for yourself, it's in very good condition." Andy had pulled out all the stops to get his hands on this truck and called in a few favours to get the best possible price.

Tim was no stranger to buying used vehicles and knew his way around a truck blindfold, so he was certainly no pushover, but even he had to admit this was an excellent purchase. Within one hour the two men shook hands for the second time that morning; the deal was complete, and Tim was looking forward to collecting his new truck the following weekend.

Back at his desk, Andy watched Tim as he pulled out onto the main road and drove away. He'd really hoped that Tim might have mentioned Maria, but then thinking about it, why would he? This was business and Andy, as always, had been the ultimate professional. He sat for a while studying all the paperwork on his desk; it all needed his urgent attention, but his mind was elsewhere and wandering, he was desperate for some sort of contact with Maria, then completely out of the blue he had an idea.

Not brave enough to go directly to her house, Andy thought it might be easier all round if he met her one evening as she left her place of work. Starting from Monday, for the next three evenings he pulled up opposite her office at the exact time she should be leaving. Believing at first he must have just missed her, by the third evening he was convinced she must be ill; there was no other reason that he could think of to explain her absence. Realising this might be the excuse he'd been searching for, he switched on the engine and headed straight for her house. No sooner had he turned into her road than he could see that her car wasn't on the drive and, as he approached nearer, he noticed all the windows were closed, a sure sign she wasn't in. Parking up, he waited for over an hour, but still there was no sign, so his next conclusion was that she must be away somewhere, maybe even on holiday.

The idea of Maria on holiday, and possibly with someone else, haunted him for the remainder of the evening and after a restless night, the following morning he'd decided, he would make one more journey to see if she had returned home later last night. It would only mean a slight detour on his way to work, and if her car still wasn't there, it would confirm she was away. He pulled into her road at the same time as she reversed down her drive; desperate not to be seen, he dived in between two parked cars. This was much earlier than she normally left for work.

Intrigued and convinced he hadn't been seen, Andy decided to follow her, carefully staying just far enough back not to be recognised and only just managing to pull over before she unexpectedly parked up outside a rather large industrial unit. What on earth was she doing here? he thought as he watched her take her briefcase and enter the building.

Confused, he drove back to his own place of work arriving late for the second time that week.

Maria walked into her office with a face like thunder, her hands were shaking, and her knees felt like jelly. She'd spotted Andy from the moment he dived into a space between two parked cars in her road and watched as he followed her all the way to work, unsuccessfully trying to maintain a safe distance so he wouldn't be recognised.

Returning home after an excruciatingly long day, Maria, still fuming from earlier, picked up the phone and with trembling fingers dialled his number. All day, over and over she'd rehearsed her speech; she would explain to Andy, once and for all, that it made no difference how many times he followed her, it was over. One hour later, emotionally drained, Maria hung up, his words echoing inside her head.

"Please, Maria," he pleaded, "just one drink, let me at least have the opportunity to explain."

"You'd be wasting your time, it's not going to make any difference whatsoever, it's over," she explained firmly.

"I understand that Maria, I really do," he answered quietly, "but I would still very much appreciate just one hour of your time, it would give me closure if nothing else," he added hopefully.

Exhausted with the whole scenario, finally, Maria agreed to one last meeting straight from work on Friday evening for one hour only.

"I can't believe you've agreed to this," Lisa said as she spoke to her friend later the same evening. "You've changed your job in order to make it harder for him to reach you, now you're telling me you're going to meet him for a drink." She was miffed to say the least; Maria's replacement had only lasted a few days and now, while they searched for another suitable applicant, they'd all had to share the extra workload. It wasn't just that though, she really missed working with her friend.

"To be honest I can't believe it either," Maria admitted. "Hopefully though it will give him the closure he obviously needs."

"If you believe that..." Lisa began. "The last thing he's looking for is closure; of that I'm absolutely sure, anyway, promise me you'll let me know how it goes."

"I promise," Maria agreed as they said their goodbyes.

By Friday evening, Maria was ready for the weekend. They were nearly ready to go live regarding the invoicing, but the week hadn't been without its setbacks and anxious to prevent any further delays Maria had worked late most evenings.

"Maria." Taken by surprise she looked up. "I'm glad I've caught you," her boss, Charles Maitland, continued as he walked over to her desk. "I won't keep you long, just a quick word."

"That's fine, is everything ok?" she asked him anxiously.

"Very much so." He smiled warmly. He had to be in his early sixties, a very astute businessman who certainly wasn't afraid of hard work. He could often be found helping in the warehouse, even did the occasional delivery if needed, and he had this uncanny knack of seeing absolutely everything that happened during the course of the working day.

"I understand we're nearly ready to go live for the sales invoicing?"

"I'm really hoping to get started on Monday," Maria confirmed. "If everything goes to plan that is."

"Well, I'm sure it will; I have every confidence in your ability." He paused briefly. "It hasn't gone unnoticed how much time and effort you've dedicated to this project, that is why I would like you to accept this." He handed her a plain white envelope. "It's just a little incentive and may help you relax after an exceptionally busy week."

"Thank you," she said, accepting the envelope he offered. "It's not necessary, I've enjoyed the challenge."

"I'm sure there'll be a lot more challenges before too long." He laughed. "Thanks again, Maria, enjoy your weekend, and don't be too much longer here. Goodnight."

"Good night," she replied as she watched him leave. Sitting back down in her chair she opened the envelope. "Wow," she said out loud as she examined the gift voucher that entitled her to a very generous spending spree at the new beauty shop in town.

***

Andy finished work early on Friday; he'd called in a favour from a colleague which left him plenty of time to get home, shower and change. The last thing he wanted was to meet Maria in his work clothes, although she always said he looked good in a suit, anyway, he'd bought a new pair of casual trousers and shirt and felt relatively confident as he left his flat. He sat in the car for a while before he drove off; he had no idea what to expect from this evening, he hoped for a reconciliation, but at the end of the day, just a chance to speak face to face would be better than not. Feeling like a teenager on a first date, he started the car and drove off. He hadn't told anyone about his plans for this evening; he'd realised that if Sharon thought he was at home alone with nothing much planned, miraculously, there would be no dramas. If she knew he had plans, well, there'd be a catastrophe of some sort.

Andy had never been to this pub before; it had been Maria's choice, and as he pulled into the car park, he was relieved to see there was no sign of Maria's car. He'd wanted to be the first to arrive, and he quickly parked up and made his way inside desperate for something to calm his nerves. Looking around as he waited at the bar, he could see why she'd chosen this place. It was cosy and comfortable inside with low ceiling beams and a huge inglenook fireplace. Choosing a table with a good view of the door, Andy sat in one of the comfortable armchairs and sipped his pint. The last few months had been insufferable, he'd never experienced such feelings of despair and now he had a chance, a chance to explain, he sat on one hand fingers crossed.

With her heart pounding against her rib cage, Maria walked into the pub, instantly she spotted him and, smiling, made her way over to join him.

Without thinking, Andy stood and kissed her on the cheek; it felt the most natural reaction, but he sensed she didn't feel the same.

"What can I get you?" He smiled nervously.

"G&T please, ice and lemon."

"I know," he said, smiling, as he made his way to the bar.

Maria made herself comfortable and discreetly checked her watch; she wasn't staying any longer than one hour, after all, that was the agreement.

As Andy stood at the bar the speech he'd rehearsed over and over completely disappeared from memory; yesterday he'd been pitch perfect, now he couldn't remember a single word. Turning from the bar with a G&T, Andy was surprised to see Maria deep in conversation with a couple of young men that had already made themselves comfortable; as he approached the table, they both stood.

"See you Monday, Maria, enjoy your evening," one of them said as they both acknowledged him before leaving.

"A couple of guys from work," Maria explained. She couldn't help noticing the relief spread across Andy's face. "Thanks for this." She raised her glass to his.

The next time Maria checked her watch it was two and a half hours later. Once the ice had been broken, the conversation and laughter flowed freely and Maria was struggling to remind herself how much pain and suffering this man sitting opposite had inflicted upon her life.

"Andy, it's nearly nine o'clock," she suddenly exclaimed, hardly able to believe it herself.

"Should you be somewhere else?" he asked with a concerned expression.

"It's not that." She looked at him trying to remain strong, it would have been so easy to stay chatting, but she mustn't give in. "I have things to do," she finally explained.

Andy wasn't ready for the evening to end. "Are you hungry?"

he asked with a little trepidation, sensing immediately the change of atmosphere between the two of them.

"Sorry." She faltered a little before continuing, "I really should be leaving." Fumbling in her bag for her car keys was purely an excuse; if she looked directly at him, she'd crumble and give in.

Realising this wasn't up for negotiation he accepted her decision. Walking her to the car, the silence between them was palpable, and before he knew it Maria was in her car with the engine revving.

Initially, her plan had been to jump in the car, say a quick goodbye and drive off, but it wasn't that easy; he looked forlorn and desperately sad. Maria opened her window.

"Thanks, Andy." She smiled up at him; she'd enjoyed the evening, but they hadn't discussed any of the issues responsible for their breakup, let alone resolve them. At least, she hoped, the evening had given Andy closure although, she had her doubts.

Andy just about managed to return her smile, his lips were dry, and he couldn't speak, so instead he raised his hand and waved her goodbye.

"Idiot," he shouted as watched the rear of her car disappear from the car park. He couldn't believe he'd stood there and let her drive away, and out of his life. He felt physically sick and bent over holding both knees with each hand while taking deep breaths as he tried to regain some composure before driving home.

After a sleepless night, replaying the events of the previous evening over and over until she nearly sent herself insane, Maria poured all her frustrations and anxieties into the overdue chore of housework. She cleaned and polished everything in sight, choosing to ignore the phone each time it rang, today wasn't the day for explanations or even general chit chat, she wasn't in the mood.

***

Having tried unsuccessfully throughout the day to contact her daughter, Delia decided to ring her youngest daughter, if anyone had heard how last evening went it would be Kim. "Hi, darling, it's Mum."

"Hi, Mum, you ok, bit late for you isn't it?" Kim replied checking her watch.

"I'm fine, I was just wondering if you've spoken to Maria today, I've been trying to get hold of her for the best part of the day; I can't even leave a message as her answer phone doesn't appear to be switched on."

"No, Mum I haven't, I did mean to, but time run away with me today. Don't worry, she met Andy last night, she's probably still with him." Kim had instantly picked up on her mother's anxiety.

"I knew she was seeing him, that's why I wanted to check she was ok."

"Please don't worry, Mum, I'm sure she's fine and I'll pop over first thing in the morning if she's still not picking up and I'll let you know."

"Thanks, darling," her mother replied sounding a little less anxious, "that's very kind and like you say I'm sure she's probably still with him." They both laughed and said goodnight.

***

Saturday morning dawned with a beautiful clear blue sky, but the weather didn't reflect Andy's mood; he was restless and agitated, he needed a change of scenery. Jumping into his car with no definite destination in mind, he drove and drove until he realised the coastline was in sight. The invigorating sea breeze was a refreshing change, breathing in the sea air, he strolled along the pier until the aroma of freshly cooked bacon wafted his way; like a magnet he was drawn towards a typical seaside café. Inside were a few small tables dressed in gingham tablecloths and several bar stools against the counter, Andy managed to take the last available stool.

"What can I get you, love?" the rosy-cheeked woman behind the counter asked with a friendly smile.

"Bacon sandwich and coffee please," Andy answered, suddenly feeling extremely hungry.

"Coming right up, sweetheart," she answered, placing a paper napkin and cutlery in front of him.

It was a busy little place with a great atmosphere and behind him Andy could hear the excited chatter of a young group of students, that had obviously just visited the fortune teller at the Fair.

"If you think about it, everything she said was pretty general," one of them said quite cynically. They all agreed until one spoke out.

"Actually, I don't agree." The young girl was softly spoken and Andy, suddenly very interested, had to concentrate to hear what she had to say next. "There's no way she could have known that my grandpa died of a massive heart attack."

"Clever educated guess I say," the same cynical young man replied.

"You say that" the young girl sounded more confident as she continued. "My grandpa had locked the bathroom door, by the time the emergency services arrived and knocked the door down, my grandpa had died. My grandma never forgave herself; she always thought that if she had somehow managed to break the door down herself, she might have been able to administer C.P.R. and my grandpa may have survived." She stopped to take a sip of her tea. "After recalling this story to me, the fortune teller told me to tell my grandma not to blame herself, my grandpa died instantly, there was nothing she could have done." Andy couldn't help himself, he turned around to see the reaction of the rest of the group; they were silent as they digested this information until one of the other young girls asked.

"She actually regaled the whole story, in that much detail."

"Pretty much," the young girl confirmed.

"Pretty much, that doesn't cut it for me," the young cynic added. "That's what they do, they say a few things and before you know it, you've told them the whole story."

Still debating the facts, they collected their coats and bags and left the café.

"Can I get you anything else, love?" the same rosy-cheeked woman asked as she cleared Andy's empty plate.

"No thank you, that was great, I really needed that." Andy paid his bill and left.

Lost in thought, Andy meandered towards the fair ground; the loud squealing, laughter and the sight of bright pink candy floss made him smile. He passed the dodgem cars, the carousel, popcorn stalls, and there tucked away in the corner was the brightly lit tent of the fortune teller.

***

Having totally exhausted herself yesterday, Maria slept heavily and on Sunday morning was woken by the sound of loud banging. Sitting up in her bed, desperately trying to clear her head, she realised it was someone banging on her front door. She climbed out of bed and peering out from the bedroom window she could see Kim's car parked on the drive; panicked by her sister's reasoning, she flew down the stairs and opened the door.

"For goodness' sake, Maria, why haven't you answered your phone, we've all been so worried?" Kim said, relieved when Maria finally opened the door.

Sensing her sisters anguish, Maria couldn't stem the flow of tears; guessing the situation was completely Andy related, Kim put her arms around her sister and led her towards the kitchen. "Sit down and I'll make us some tea and you can tell me all about it."

Feeling desperately sorry as it was clear her sister was in complete turmoil, Kim listened for over an hour as Maria confided her innermost thoughts and fears.

Later that morning strolling back towards his car, Andy couldn't stop smiling; that was an experience he would never divulge, no one would believe him anyway.

CHAPTER FIVE

Maria – The Present

Over the last couple of days, having discussed the whole situation with both Kim and David, Maria finally decided she would go ahead with the planned conversion. It would provide the space they desperately needed and apart from that, despite the last little hiccup, she liked Tim and trusted him to be good to his word and provide a professional service.

In all honesty, Maria felt slightly embarrassed when she made the call to Tim, with hindsight she suspected her reaction had been completely over the top. Admittedly, Andy had been a huge part of her life, it was true, but it was all many moons ago now in a different lifetime. Tim, however, was his usual calm, professional self when he answered her call and suggested it might be more civilised to meet, have a cup of tea and discuss where they go from here.

A few days later, sitting in Maria's living room, Tim looked more relaxed than he felt. "Firstly," he began, "I apologise, Maria, I should have told you myself when I first came to see you that Andy was my partner; I can't tell you how much I regret that." He paused and fidgeted in the chair before continuing. "It's important to me that you understand, I certainly wouldn't dream of holding you to the contract; I truly don't want you to feel that you have no other option." He paused again and took a deep breath. "If, however, you do decide to continue, I can assure you I will be the one working on this project with a couple of our team; Andy wouldn't be involved, in actual fact it's very rare we work together anyway, so it wouldn't be unusual." He shrugged his shoulders and looked genuinely sorry.

Right on cue, Kim entered the living room with a tray of tea and some delicious jam tarts. "Shall I be Mum?" she asked as she placed the tray carefully on the table.

"Milk and two sugars for me please," Tim answered, grateful for the distraction.

"Help yourself to a jam tart." Kim said as she passed him his tea.

With the pleasantries over, Maria was keen to get back to business. "As I mentioned on the phone," she began to explain, "I have decided, Tim, that I do want to proceed with our original plans and get started as soon as possible."

"Do you mind if I ask something first?" Kim said, interrupting.

"Of course," Tim said, guessing the question was directed at him.

"Does Andy know this project is for Maria and, if so, how does he feel about it?"

There was a short silence before Tim replied. He'd rehearsed his opening speech over and over, but now he'd need to think carefully before answering any questions. "Well, he does now." He paused for a minute before continuing. "To be honest, he was more concerned how Maria felt." He leant over and helped himself to a cake. "Obviously, I've told him the whole story, and he was in total agreement with me, under no circumstance would we hold you to the contract if it was your wish to find someone else to complete the work." He took a bite of his cake and waited for Maria's reply.

Over the years, Tim and Andy had become close friends, as well as business partners, and Tim recognised Andy hadn't had it easy, experiencing more than his fair share of heartbreak. However, he'd always remained a good father to his daughter Sammy, and she'd repaid him by growing into a lovely, successful young woman, who Tim believed had just announced her engagement. Tim had no idea how much Maria knew of Andy's life, it wasn't his place to say, it was a shame though that Maria still felt so bitter, but at the end of the day it wasn't any of his business.

"I appreciate the gesture, I really do," Maria said. "But, like I said earlier, I have decided to go ahead with our original plans." At first Maria thought Tim wasn't listening, but witnessing his heavy sigh, she took that as a sign of pure relief.

"Thank you, Maria," he said finally. "I can assure you we are a professional company, and you won't be disappointed with the finished conversion."

Finally, with everything now settled, the two sisters watched Tim drive away and Kim put her arm affectionately around her sister. "That wasn't too bad, was it?" she asked thoughtfully.

Maria turned to look at her sister. "Tell me honestly, do you think I made too much of all this? For all I know Andy is happily married and hardly remembers anything about me."

"He may be happily married, he may even have a load of kids, but I bet he remembers everything about you," Kim answered cheerfully. "Why didn't you ask Tim about him, it wouldn't have looked odd, after all you went out with one another for years?"

"Never," Maria exclaimed in absolute horror. "He'd tell Andy I was asking, how embarrassing would that be?"

Kim couldn't help smiling at her sister's indignant response. "Why would that be embarrassing?" Kim felt compelled to ask. She'd already tried searching for any details she could find on social media, although as of yet, her efforts had been in vain. "Anyway, how do you know he's not given Tim the third degree? I bet he's asked all sorts of questions about you," Kim persisted. "In my experience men are far nosier than women."

"I bet he's not in the slightest bit interested," Maria said, completely unconvinced. "Anyway." Maria continued as she suddenly remembered Kim had mentioned to her earlier that they'd heard from the bride to be. "Don't forget you were going to tell me what the bride had to say."

"Oh yes, I nearly forgot." Kim smiled. "She's emailed to say she can make next Wednesday at 4.30pm. As we were expecting her to want a weekend appointment, I thought you'd be pleased so I confirmed."

"Next Wednesday I've got my last appointment at the hospital at 3.30pm," Maria explained reluctantly. "They always overrun, I'll never get back in time, and I can't change it; I've already changed it once."

"As it's just a preliminary meeting I'm sure I can cope." Kim tried to reassure her sister. "How about if I ask Julie to come back if she can get someone to look after her kids?"

"Don't you think it will look bad that I'm not here?"

"I'll explain, I'm sure this won't be the only meeting we have with her."

"Well let's see if Julie can help out, if not I'll cancel the hospital, I'll have to," Maria concluded.

Sensing this was Maria's final word on the matter, Kim decided to leave it as it was for now.

***

Having agreed work could begin on Monday, Maria was up and about earlier than normal. Tim had mentioned he'd be there by 7.30 and, although Maria had given him a key to the garage, she still wanted to be presentable by the time they arrived. In her past experiences there was always some sort of question to be answered and she didn't doubt this would be any different. She wasn't wrong: 7.45 and already the first question of the day...

"I'm sorry to disturb you, Maria," Tim said as she opened the front door. "Just to let you know, we're going to start this morning by taking out most of the back wall, as we agreed that will become the main entrance, so it's going to be a bit noisy for a while, if it gets too much just let me know."

"Thanks, Tim." She smiled back at him. "I guessed as much, it was the same when I had the house refurbed, and I've already warned the girls, so hopefully we'll be fine."

Tim hadn't been kidding, the next few days were particularly noisy, and Maria was relieved when Wednesday seemed a lot quieter. Tim on the other hand was tearing his hair out; one of his guys had gone sick and he knew this was going to put him behind if he didn't return this week. He couldn't afford to fall behind; he'd got a cement delivery booked for Monday and at this rate he'd have to cancel it. By Friday afternoon Tim could see they were just one day behind schedule.

"Sorry to disturb you again," Tim began as Maria answered the door, fully aware he'd had to check on several issues already today. "I know I said we wouldn't be working weekends, so you would get some peace, but due to Phil going sick mid-week, I was wondering if you wouldn't mind if I did actually work tomorrow?"

"I don't mind at all," Maria replied, grateful that she had already made plans for the weekend. "I won't be here, so it makes no odds to me."

"That's great, as long as I won't be disturbing you." Relieved, all Tim had to do now was explain to Lisa, but that would have to wait until later.

Back at the unit after a busy day, Andy pulled up next to Tim's truck. "Why are you loading your truck tonight?" he asked as he dropped the side panel, ready to unload some equipment.

"I've got to work tomorrow otherwise it means cancelling the cement delivery for Monday."

"Who's working with you?" Andy asked as he begun to unload some of his own tools.

"I'm just doing it on my own," Tim explained. "I should catch up, I can work all day, Maria is out so she doesn't mind."

"In that case, there's no reason why I can't help you," Andy quickly offered.

"Are you sure, mate," Tim asked, he would certainly welcome the help. "If you don't mind, that would be great."

"What time are you starting in the morning?" Andy asked as he reloaded his tools.

"Maria is leaving home early, she said she'd be gone by 8.00am, so I thought 8.30am."

"I'll see you there at 8.30am then," Andy called out to his partner as he drove off.

Andy couldn't help smiling, he'd been wondering how he could feasibly wheedle his way around to Maria's house; even if she wouldn't be there, it might give him a little more of an insight into her life. He hadn't managed to find out very much from Tim, other than the fact that she'd never married and never had any kids. It hadn't really surprised him to learn she'd never had any children; she'd never shown any real interest in Sammy, but he'd been shocked to hear she'd never married. He couldn't understand that and wondered why.

Many a time over the years he'd wondered how she was and what she was doing. He'd tried searching her out on social media a few times without any luck, but the other day when Tim told him about this job, he'd looked her up again and found her by recognising her profile picture. She really hadn't changed that much; she still wore her hair short, but the highlights had been swopped for lowlights and somehow the style was softer, other than that he thought she looked just the same. Apart from the picture and her birthday there was no other information available; funny really, he'd always remembered her birthday. When they first met it had taken him a while to get used to the way her family went to town over birthdays: loads of presents, celebrations, parties, they went wild in comparison to his own family who just about managed a card. It was purely because of this that he'd always made birthdays so extra special for Sammy, and now the tables had turned, and Sammy made birthdays extra special for him.

"What are you doing?" Tim spoke in a whisper as he found Andy peering through Maria's patio doors.

"Why are you whispering?" Panicking, Andy stepped away from the patio doors. "You told me she'd be out."

"She is, mate." Tim couldn't stop laughing. "That got you going though didn't it?"

"I'll get you back for that," Andy said, regaining his composure. "It looks lovely inside, very stylish and all quite new."

"It is, she had the whole place refurbed just a few years back, don't think she's lived here much longer than two or three years."

"Where did she live before that then?" Andy asked as he made his way around the house peering through each window.

"No idea," Tim said as he started to unlock the garage. "She doesn't give much away, bit of a closed book, but very nice and very house proud and she'll spot your greasy imprints on her windows, so you better polish them off." He laughed as he watched Andy desperately polishing away any evidence Maria might discover. "Come on, mate," Tim called. "Otherwise, we're never going to get finished."

Andy, who had always preferred a cotton handkerchief as opposed to tissues, quickly stuffed his hanky back in his pocket but, in his haste, it became caught on his cuff and fell to the ground.

***

Despite her best efforts, Maria arrived home from her hospital appointment just as the bride-to-be drove away.

"How did it go?" she asked as she dropped her bag on the chair.

"Very well." Julie was excited to relay the details to Maria. "She's very nice, very friendly and was quite receptive to our ideas. The only specific, really, is that one of the tiers, probably the smaller one on the top is carrot cake, which is her dad's favourite apparently."

"That's nice, what flavour is for her mum then?" Maria asked, expecting that to be the next request.

"She's having pale pink peonies for her bouquet, in memory of her stepmum," Julie answered quietly.

"Ah that's sad, but a really nice gesture." Maria was already warming to this woman, even though they'd never met.

"I've actually got most of the meeting in note form for you to go over, and then I'll draft a confirmation reply." Kim passed the notes to her sister.

"She's also interested in a cheesecake." Julie suddenly remembered. "Well, it's a cake of cheese actually, but she wondered if we would be able to do that as well." Julie passed the picture she'd been given to Maria.

"I've seen quite a lot of these in magazines," Maria replied as she looked at the picture. "I can't see it being too much of a problem."

"Great," Kim quickly added, "I could do with a new addition to our wedding page, on the website." They all laughed as Maria raised her eyebrows to Julie in mock amusement at her sister.

"How have we left it?" Maria asked, anxious to meet their very first bride.

"She's going to give us a few dates when she can come in again, in about a month's time to taste test some samples of other flavours for the actual cake," Julie explained.

"She's a teacher apparently," Kim added. "So, it's not easy in the week unless it's after school, but I've told her that's not a problem for us at all."

Satisfied it had all gone well and concerned that Julie had young children at home probably waiting to see their mummy, Maria wrapped up the meeting and work for the day.

"See you both in the morning," Julie called out as she collected her coat and bag.

"Take care and thanks for today." Maria waved as Julie left for the day, followed closely by Kim.

***

As the weeks passed and the garage gradually became less garage and more kitchen, the girls were becoming just as excited as Maria. Both Julie and Louise supplied regular hot drinks to Tim and his team just to see how it was all coming along. Kim had deliberately kept her distance from the conversion; she preferred to wait and see more of the finished product, but the excitement was contagious, and it wasn't long before curiosity got the better of her.

"I thought you weren't that interested," Maria teased her sister, "you said you'd rather wait, what made you change your mind?"

"Listening to you lot, it's all you talk about."

"Would you like to take the teas round this morning?" Louise asked, thinking it might be the perfect excuse to have a quick look.

"Oh, ok, why not?" Kim laughed.

Maria looked up briefly from icing her cake. "That didn't take very much persuading."

Kim grinned at her sister. "Do you give them anything to eat with their tea?" she asked as she picked up the tray.

"Not normally, but there's those mini carrot cakes we made as a trial, you can take those if you want to look good." Maria pointed to the tin on the other side of the kitchen.

"I might as well," Kim said as she balanced the tin of cakes carefully on the side of the tray before making her way out to the garage.

Thirty minutes later Kim returned to the kitchen with two empty mugs and one empty cake tin.

"Don't tell me you've been in there all this time?" Maria said as Kim packed the mugs straight into the dishwasher.

"I know, I couldn't get away." She laughed. "I can't believe how much they've already managed to complete, now I understand why you're all so excited."

"I actually forgot you were out there," Maria confessed as she finished the 60th birthday cake she'd spent most of the morning working on. "What do you think of it so far?" she asked.

"I'm no expert," Kim admitted. "But it certainly looks promising."

"I'm actually extremely pleased with it all," Maria admitted to her sister. "I think when it's finished it's going to be better than I'd imagined."

"You might be right," Kim agreed as she turned and showed the empty cake tin to Julie.

"They ate the lot," Julie exclaimed as she took the empty tin.

"Mainly." Kim nodded. "I noticed Tim wrap a couple in tissue, probably taking them home or saving them for later."

Later that day back at their office Tim and Andy sat down to catch up on some paperwork and discuss the next project Andy was keen to begin the following week.

"Oh, by the way I saved these for you today," Tim said as he took out a couple of mini carrot cakes from his lunch box and passed them to Andy, who sat at his desk directly opposite Tim's.

"Carrot cakes." Andy grinned as he took his first bite. "Thank you, these are very good, Maria's, I take it." He looked at his partner for confirmation.

"From her kitchen, don't know if she actually made those very cakes," Tim replied as he switched on his laptop.

"Did Maria actually remember carrot cake was my favourite?"

"I've no idea," Tim admitted. "Kim gave them to us when she brought out our morning tea. Maria might not even know she did that, and anyway I didn't say I was taking two for you. Kim just said finish them up, so I saved those for you."

"Well thank you, they were delicious," Andy said as he tried to hide his disappointment.

***

"I take it you're impressed with the work they've done so far then," David acknowledged after listening to his wife talk of nothing else all evening.

"Honestly, you should see the attention to detail," Kim explained as she waited for the pie to finish cooking for their supper. "Tim has thought of absolutely everything, I know Maria was only saying the other day she really wishes she'd employed Tim for her house refurbishments, she's that impressed."

"If I can get away a little earlier tomorrow afternoon I might pop over and have a look," David said as he poured a couple of glasses of wine.

"Well let me know if you're coming and I'll wait for you, otherwise I'm leaving at lunch time tomorrow," Kim explained as she carried their supper through to the dining room.

The next morning began in chaos, when the food delivery Maria was eagerly awaiting had been delayed and wouldn't now arrive until the afternoon. With all the rescheduling of their plans for the day, and Kim keen to get away at lunch time, she had completely forgotten to mention to Maria that David might pop round.

"Kim," Maria called from the bottom of the stairs, "David has just pulled up outside."

"Ok thanks," Kim called out in response. "I forgot he said he might come over," she admitted as she leant over the banister. "He's early, he said in the afternoon."

"It's 12.15 so in theory he could be on time…" Maria replied as she opened the door to her brother-in-law.

"How come you're so early?" Kim greeted her husband as she quickly ran down the stairs.

"I thought I'd surprise you and take you for lunch, you said you'd be finishing at lunch time, so I thought why not?" Affectionately, he put his arm around his wife. "Are you still on for finishing at lunch time?"

"I certainly am." She smiled. "But first let me show you how the conversion is coming along."

"I'll join you in a minute; I've just got to wait for my cake to cool a bit," Maria explained as she made her way back to the kitchen, leaving her sister and brother-in-law to make their own way to the garage.

"It's all looking pretty good to me," David said as he shook hands with Tim. "You've done an amazing job, how long now until it's all finished?"

"Another couple of weeks until we're ready to fit the equipment, so probably another three weeks and we're out of your hair," Tim said looking at Maria who'd just joined them.

"That's great, Tim," she said excitedly. "We're desperate for the extra space."

"Well, we better leave you to get on if you're on a deadline." David laughed before they all said goodbye.

Making their way back to the house, David noticed what he originally thought to be an old rag caught on a rose bush.

"Looks like something is caught on one of your roses." David stopped and pointed to a white piece of fabric flapping in the breeze.

"It's a hanky," Kim explained as she carefully released it from a thorn.

"Well, it's definitely not mine, I only use tissues," Maria said as she watched her sister successfully release the hanky.

"It could belong to anyone; it's obviously just blown in and got caught up."

"Don't touch it then," David called to his wife.

"It looks clean enough," Kim said holding it up. "It's soaking wet from the rain earlier."

"Just put it straight in the bin," Maria said, laughing at the two of them.

"Look it's embroidered with initials," Kim said, instantly regretting mentioning that out loud.

"What are they?" Maria asked casually as she made her way back in doors.

"I didn't really look," Kim answered quickly. "I've put it in the bin now anyway."

"Are you joining us for lunch today?" David asked Maria as they made their way through the house.

"That's really kind," Maria replied. "But I want to wait and make sure my delivery arrives, otherwise I'm going to need to make a few phone calls."

"Ok, well you're always welcome." David smiled as he headed towards his car.

"You sure you don't mind me leaving early?" Kim checked with her sister.

"Don't be silly, go and enjoy your lunch, I'll see you in the morning." Maria kissed her sister on the cheek and gently guided her out the door.

It was gone five o'clock when the delivery Maria had been waiting for finally arrived; by the time she'd checked everything and packed it away it was pouring with rain and she decided emptying the rubbish would have to wait, until the morning.

***

Having enjoyed a rather large lunch, Kim was enjoying a relaxing evening watching T.V.

"I knew there was something I was going to ask you," David asked looking up from his paper. "What were the initials on that hanky you were suddenly so keen to throw away."

"Why?" Kim looked over to her husband.

"Just wondered," he answered still looking at her.

"A.P.," she replied.

"I thought so." He smiled. "So he must have been there at some stage then."

"I don't know when," Kim muttered. "I see all the guys coming and going, I've got a bird's eye view from my window, and I've never seen him."

"Would you recognise him if you saw him?" David asked his wife. "I don't think I would. I can honestly say I wouldn't have recognised Tim in a crowd that's for sure."

"I think I would," she said, making a mental note to have another search on social media.

***

At last, it was the day all the equipment Maria had ordered for her new kitchen was due to arrive. Maria checked her watch; it was just 8.30am, the delivery was due any time between 7.00am and noon and neither Tim nor her sister Kim who had both promised to be in early had arrived, not that it really mattered; nothing had turned up yet.

Kim had set her alarm for thirty minutes earlier this morning and had been aiming to leave as early as possible, in order to get their morning meeting finished before the new equipment arrived. Despite that, after a call from Chloe who suddenly needed some reassurance about one of her papers, Kim ended up leaving even later than normal and consequently got caught in all the school traffic.

Returning to the kitchen, Maria decided to begin the prep for the day, both Louse and Julie would be here soon, so she was keen to get them started as once the equipment arrived she would be busy.

For the third time that morning Tim tried to speak to Maria on her phone. "Maria, it's Tim. I'm sorry I'm going to be late; I've been involved in a car accident; I'm just waiting for the police as there's quite a few cars involved." He paused waiting to see if she would pick up. "I'm fine, just a bit of whiplash I think, anyway when you get this message can you ring me, please?" Tim put his phone on the dashboard, this could take a while; there was no sign of the police yet, although he could see an ambulance had just arrived.

It was a four-car pile-up. With no easy escape route, Tim had been caught right in the middle, he'd never been involved in anything like this before and, checking the front of his truck, he even began to wonder if it was still roadworthy; it didn't look that safe. This was typical, the one day he needed to get to Maria's early and this happened. It was all so frustrating, and he could kick himself, he'd seriously considered leaving the plans on site, but then he'd decided against it and packed them in the truck. Now, when the equipment arrived, Phil wouldn't have a clue where any of it was going. Getting impatient, he picked up his phone and dialled Andy.

"Andy, it's me." Tim sighed with relief, at last someone was picking up.

"What's up, mate?" Andy replied, trying to hold his phone as well as a plank of wood.

"I've been involved in an accident."

"Are you ok?" Andy immediately put the wood down and listened anxiously to his friend.

"I think so, my head has begun to throb, but I think that's just me panicking." Tim sat back and rested his head on the head rest before continuing. "I don't think I'm going to get away any time soon, and to be honest it looks like the truck is heading straight for the repair shop."

"That bad," Andy replied before adding. "If the truck is that bad you most certainly need to get checked out."

"Don't worry I'm fine," Tim assured him. "Anyway, there's an ambulance crew making their way through all of us. But that's not what I'm worried about, I've got the plans for the equipment that's due for delivery at Maria's today, if it's not already there that is, and so Phil won't have a clue where it's all supposed to go. I've tried ringing him, but it just goes straight to answer phone."

"Is there anything I can do to help, apart from trying to get hold of Phil?" Andy asked.

"Well, I don't want to leave here until the police arrive, this was all the fault of the second car as far as I can tell, so I need that confirmed so I can communicate that to the insurance company. Is there any way you can collect these plans and get them over to Phil?"

"I can, but where are you?"

"I'm just off the new Bellway interchange," Tim explained.

"Ok, so that's about 20, 25 minutes away," Andy guessed.

"Can you leave straight away?" Tim asked uneasily.

"I'm on my way, but will Maria mind, if I suddenly turn up with the plans?"

"I've no idea, I can't get hold of her, but the electrician is due this afternoon and if Phil doesn't know where everything is supposed to go, well, it's just going to be a disaster." Tim was beginning to sound extremely anxious, an unusual trait for him and it didn't go unnoticed.

With Tim's exact location in mind, Andy jumped straight in his truck, he was on his way within minutes.

Finally, over an hour later than planned and seriously harassed, Kim arrived at Maria's. Anxious to explain and reassure her sister she was ok she made her way straight into the kitchen.

"Hi, Kim, are you ok?" Maria asked casually as she finished explaining today's workload to Julie.

"Where's your damn phone?" Kim sounded exasperated and Maria looked shocked at her sister's unusual outburst. "I've been ringing and ringing, I wanted to let you know I was ok, and that I had unfortunately got caught up in the school run."

Maria checked her back pocket. "I must have left it in the living room," she admitted. "I can normally hear it from there, but I'll go and get it. Tim's not here yet, he might have been trying to ring as well." Maria jumped off the stool and went in search of her phone.

"I need a strong coffee." Kim explained to Julie as she grabbed the kettle.

Maria walked back into the kitchen already speaking with Tim, and it was obvious to both Julie and Kim something was wrong. "Tim, I'm really sorry to hear that, are you injured?"

"Don't worry, I'm fine, might have a bit of whiplash and I've got a headache but that's all, anyway I'm next in line to be checked over by the medics," he reassured Maria before continuing. "Maria, the problem is I have the plans here with me, so Phil won't know where to place the equipment ready for the electrician, who's due this afternoon." He stopped for breath, dreading her reaction to his next statement. "Maria, I had no option other than to ask Andy to collect the plans, he will drop them off for Phil and if the equipment has already arrived, he'll just help him get it in the correct place. If it hasn't arrived, using the plans, Phil can get the delivery guys to help place it correctly."

There was complete silence at the other end of the phone as Maria registered exactly what Tim was explaining. Sensing an issue on the horizon, Kim urged her sister to continue the conversation in the privacy of the living room.

"Don't worry, Tim," Maria eventually replied, realising this wasn't the time for a meltdown. "That's fine, no problem at all."

"I assure you, Maria, Andy has no reason to disturb you, you won't even know he's there." Tim was grateful for her understanding, the last thing he needed now was any more stress; his headache had progressed to a migraine, and he felt nauseous. Relieved that was all in hand, he picked up the phone and rang Lisa.

Finishing her call, Maria made her way upstairs to find her sister who had already made herself comfortable ready to begin work in the room now referred to as Kim's office.

"What's going on?" Kim asked as Maria flopped into the chair in the corner.

"It's Tim, he's been involved in a car accident; he's fine apart from whiplash," she quickly added. "Apparently, he's got the plans that Phil needs in order to place the equipment correctly ready for the electrician, who's due later today."

"Ok, so what's going to happen?" Kim could tell by the look on her sister's face, there was still more to be told.

"Andy is going to collect the plans and bring them over to Phil, if the equipment has already arrived, he will help Phil get it in place, if it hasn't, Phil can get the delivery drivers to help."

"When is he due then?" Kim asked as she looked out of the window. "I think all your equipment has just arrived." Kim pointed to the large lorry parked outside.

Maria walked over to the window. "Oh well," she exclaimed. "Looks like Andy will have to help Phil get it all in place." She shrugged her shoulders and silently made her way back down to the kitchen.

Twenty minutes later, Andy pulled up just behind the accident site, it was a lot worse than he'd imagined with broken glass and car parts strewn all over the road. The police had obviously just arrived as they were still assessing the situation and didn't really take too kindly to his request to speak with Tim, eventually they agreed and, carefully, Andy made his way on foot towards Tim's truck.

"You don't look too good, you sure you're ok?" Andy said, concerned for his friend.

"To be honest I've got a bad headache, the medic wants me to go to the hospital for a scan."

"Good, make sure you do, and don't worry about anything, we'll get by for one day I'm sure." He touched Tim affectionately on the shoulder. "Sit back and relax while you wait."

"By the way, Maria was fine when I explained the situation, but I did emphasise she wouldn't even know you were there."

"Don't worry, I'll be very discreet." Andy smiled reassuringly. "Unless of course she comes out offering cake and refreshments, then it would be rude to ignore her."

"No chance of that, she doesn't do the tea run." Tim tried to laugh, but it hurt to even attempt a smile.

Andy jumped back in his truck; why on earth did he feel like a teenager on the way to his first job instead of a middle-aged man on his way to complete the simplest of tasks?

Finally, the delivery lorry pulled away considerably lighter.

"Gosh, Maria, that's a lot of equipment they've just unloaded," Kim said as she made her way back down to the kitchen. "Are you sure there's enough room for that lot?"

"I hope so." Maria noticed the concerned expression on her sister's face. "Well, both Tim and I measured it all out, so it should be ok, but I do agree it did look like an awful lot of equipment."

"Do you think one of us should check Phil is ok?" Kim asked.

Maria shook her head, the last thing she needed was to be caught outside when Andy arrived. "I'm sure Andy has kept him informed of what's going on, but if you want to check, go ahead."

"No, you're right," Kim acknowledged. "I'll ask Louise to take him a drink, that way if he's got a problem, I'm sure he'll mention it."

Approximately 45 minutes later, back in her office, Kim watched Andy as he pulled up outside the house. He parked in the road as opposed to pulling onto the driveway which gave Kim a better view. She could see him quite clearly sitting in his truck, he was checking through some papers, probably going over the plans before he began to place the equipment; it seemed ages before he finally opened the truck door and stepped out onto the pavement. Kim smiled to herself, he was still a very handsome man, he'd always been fussy with his hair and today was no different; it was well groomed and much lighter now it was sprinkled with a little grey, he'd kept himself trim, she noted, unlike her David who'd clearly grown at least two sizes since they'd first met. Kim stepped back from the window careful not to be seen as he walked towards the side entrance, clearly, he knew exactly where he was going; he'd obviously been here before, she smiled as she watched him disappear through the side gate.

Maria was preoccupied in the kitchen, assembling a true masterpiece that had been especially commissioned for a little girl's sixth birthday and would eventually resemble a fairy castle. It had taken huge amounts of sponge cake, butter cream and icing and was already looking quite magical. As the last turret stood firmly in place, Maria looked up and stretched; looking out of the window, she glanced the rear view of a man she would have recognised anywhere as he entered the new entrance of the conversion. At practically the same time, Kim entered the kitchen and stood beside her sister.

"I see you've already spotted him, are you ok?" she asked quietly, trying to be out of earshot of both Julie and Louise.

"I'm fine." Maria turned and smiled at her sister, always grateful for her concern. "Honestly, I'm absolutely fine, and I need to get on, we've got to have this finished by tonight." She looked back down at the castle but all she could visualise was the memory of a man she had once absolutely adored.

"Looks like the guy Phil was waiting for has just arrived," Louise said as she glanced out of the back door window. "I'll just go and offer him a cup of tea."

"He doesn't drink tea only coffee," Maria replied automatically, without even giving it much thought.

Wide eyed, Louise nodded in acknowledgement. "I'll make a couple of coffees then," she said, filling the kettle at the same time, trying to catch her sister's attention. There'd been a few weird vibes since this building project first began and Louise was intrigued.

"Well," Louise said as she returned to the kitchen. "The new guy is very nice, and reasonably handsome for an older man." As she placed the empty tray back on the shelf, she continued, "He seemed surprised that we knew he only drank coffee, has he been here before?" She looked at Maria waiting for a response, but Maria was still a million miles away and hadn't even heard the question.

With all the equipment in place and ready for the electrician, Andy climbed back into his truck. An overwhelming feeling of disappointment hovered; he hadn't even caught a glimpse of Maria, one of her staff had kindly brought out a coffee. That had surprised him though, when she told him Maria said he doesn't drink tea, fancy her remembering that, he thought as he drove slowly away.

At the end of the day relaxing on the sofa, Maria checked her phone again, she really thought she would have heard from Tim by now; he'd promised to keep in touch. She checked the time; 21.05, it wasn't too late, she thought as she dialled his number.

"Hi, Tim, it's Maria," she began as it went straight to answer phone. "I was just wondering how you're feeling, anyway hope everything's ok and hopefully catch up in the morning." She hung up and switched on the T.V. It was a few hours later when having dozed off watching a film Maria was woken by the sound of her phone. Checking the number calling, Maria was somewhat surprised to be hearing from Karen so late. "Hi, Karen, I've been meaning to ring, but it's all been very busy …" Maria didn't get the chance to finish her sentence before Karen interrupted.

"Maria, this isn't a social call," Karen sounded distressed as she continued. "I'm sorry to have to tell you this but Tim has been admitted to hospital."

"What's wrong with him?" Maria asked anxiously.

"As far as I understand, he was checked over at the scene by an ambulance crew who became concerned when he was unable to walk in a straight line and suffered several bouts of vomiting."

"Gosh, that sounds awful, what's the diagnosis?" Maria asked, genuinely concerned for Tim.

"I'm sorry, Maria, I don't know any more details at this moment in time. Lisa rang me with a list of people to notify, obviously she's at the hospital with Tim, but if I hear any more, I'll let you know."

"Thanks, Karen. I appreciate that."

Maria hung up, still in shock, she sat for a while digesting this information. It was too late to ring Kim; she'd wait now and speak with her in the morning.

The next morning, determined to keep everything in order, Andy was in the office before 07.00. Tim had always been particular in logging all their jobs, quotes, orders in fact, everything business related could be found somewhere on his laptop, so logging on, Andy begun to plough his way through Tim's files.

The electrician arrived back at Maria's before 07.30 the next morning keen to continue, he'd tried to speak with Tim, but he still hadn't returned his call, and now he was here and there was no one to let him in.

Maria heard the electrician pull up onto the drive and instantly made her way down to meet him as he collected his bag of tools from the back of his van.

"Morning. It's Ian, isn't it?" she asked as she made her way outside.

"Yes, that's me," he answered, pleased to see that someone was around. "I was hoping to get this finished today, but I can't get hold of Tim, I don't suppose you have a key to let me in?"

It was clear he had no idea that Tim was in hospital; not quite sure how much information to divulge, Maria decided to keep it brief.

"That's no problem I can let you in. Tim was actually involved in an accident yesterday so he might not be feeling too well this morning, but I'm sure someone will be in touch with you soon."

"Oh, that's a shame, thanks for telling me. I'll give his partner a call then, just to let him know I'm here."

***

After what had seemed like days instead of hours, Lisa sat bolt upright as the doctor she'd seen previously, and a nurse, entered the relatives' room where she'd been patiently waiting. Initially she'd been allowed to sit with Tim but as his condition seemed to deteriorate, they'd ushered her away and eventually she'd been informed that Tim was going down for an emergency procedure… whatever that meant.

"Mrs Golding," the doctor began as he took a seat next to hers. "We have successfully drained the excess fluid from within the brain and this in turn has reduced the pressure on the brain…"

The rest of his words were lost on Lisa as she struggled to appreciate the enormity of the situation. Sensing her vulnerability and obvious total lack of comprehension, the nurse gently took her hand.

"I can take you to see him now," she offered. "He will sleep for a while yet but you're very welcome to sit by his bedside. I'll bring you a nice hot cup of sweet tea." She took Lisa to Tim's room and pulled up a chair for her, right next to his bedside.

***

Kim pulled up behind the electrician and made her way around to the back door; she was keen to speak with Maria, overnight they'd received some promising enquiries, it was going to get very busy if they all came off, in fact she was going to suggest that Chloe might be able to help when she finished university for the summer break. Nevertheless, as soon as Kim walked into the kitchen, she could tell immediately there was something wrong, Maria looked upset.

"What's wrong?" she said as she dropped her coat and bag in the corner out of the way.

"I got a call from Karen late last night," Maria began to explain. "Apparently Lisa asked her to let me know that poor Tim has been admitted to hospital. From what she told me it sounds very much like a head injury, but Karen was vague and non-committal, although she did say when she had any further news, she would let me know, but I haven't heard anything more this morning."

"That's absolutely awful," Kim replied, shocked to hear this news. "I can't imagine how Lisa must be feeling right now."

"Nor can I," Maria answered. She'd grown fond of Tim and was genuinely worried for him.

It was gone six o'clock that evening when the electrician knocked lightly on the back door. "It's all finished as far as I'm concerned," Ian explained as he handed the key back to Maria. "My boss will be here tomorrow to sign it all off; is it ok if I tell him to knock for the key?"

"That's absolutely fine, do you know what sort of time he'll be here?" Maria enquired.

"Not really, but I can give him a ring and check."

"No, please don't worry, I'm here all day," Maria assured him. "I'm anxious to see how it looks, so I might go take a sneak peek later."

"I should explain then." Ian suddenly looked concerned. "I've had to remove some of the wall tiles to fit the power points completely flush and some of the floor tiles will need replacing, but don't worry about any of that, I've already mentioned all that to Andy, who by the way was extremely grateful to you for letting me in. I think with everything he forgot I was due here today."

"Did he tell you how Tim was doing?" Maria asked, hoping he might have an update on the situation.

"When I spoke with him, he'd been informed Tim was in hospital, but he was still waiting for more news," Ian replied honestly, realising her genuine concern.

"Hopefully, he's back home by now. Well, thanks for today and I'll see your boss in the morning." Maria closed the back door and hung the key on the hook, she would go have a little look around later but first she needed to eat.

***

Andy's day was manic, but thanks to Tim's fastidious way with paperwork, it was relatively easy for Andy to pick up where they were and where they were going next. It was typical though, he thought, as he sorted through endless job lists, there wasn't very much that he could find re Maria's conversion; he knew it was pretty much near completion, although he'd forgotten the electrician was having to go back today to finish off, so was grateful when Ian rang to let him know Maria had let him in. Under normal circumstances he would have called her out of courtesy, but as things were he didn't think that would have gone down too well. Satisfied everything was in place for tomorrow, Andy locked their unit and decided a quick pint was needed before he headed home; it was his turn to ring Sammy tonight, so he couldn't be too long.

Maria switched on the lights, she had deliberately kept away since the equipment arrived and now, she couldn't believe it, the electrician had done an amazing job with the lighting.

She walked around in wonderment; she switched on several ovens, yes, she acknowledged, they all worked. The surfaces were still protected by their packaging and there was a lot of washing down and polishing required; it was quite dusty in places, especially the floor and windows, but it was perfect, the three of them would be able to work in here with plenty of room to spare, and it would be far more professional than trying to work from her kitchen. She switched off the lights and locked the door. What a shame Tim hadn't been here to share this moment; he'd been the ultimate professional and his attention to detail had ensured this kitchen layout was perfect in every respect. Maybe she'd ring Karen and see if there was any news.

Andy took the first sip of his pint just as his phone begun to ring.

"Hi, Karen," he answered straight away, anxious for any news of his partner.

"I've just had an update from Lisa, and she asked me to let you know straight away," Karen began to explain. "Tim's had a successful procedure today to relieve the pressure on his brain, he will have to remain in hospital for at least the next week, but she did ask me to warn you he wouldn't be able to return to work for quite some time."

"Gosh, I'm sorry to hear that," Andy said, completely shocked the situation had been that serious. "As I hadn't heard anything I just presumed he was at home resting. Can he have visitors do you know?" Andy enquired.

"I have no idea," Karen admitted, keen to ring off and get on with the next call.

"Ok, well thanks for letting me know," Andy said, realising he wasn't going to learn any more from Karen, he'd give it a day or two and he'd ring Lisa direct, after all he was Tim's business partner and he knew the business would be one of Tim's main concerns, even if it wasn't Lisa's. He finished his pint and made his way home, eager to speak to his daughter.

Karen put the phone down from speaking with Andy and immediately dialled Maria, she kept the call short and sweet, passed on the relevant information and said her goodbyes. She had no intention of becoming involved in this potential can of worms, she had more than enough of her own problems to deal with.

Maria couldn't help feeling disappointed to learn Tim wouldn't be returning to work anytime soon, she'd been shocked to hear the severity of his condition, she assumed, as she hadn't heard otherwise, Tim was already at home. No doubt she would hear from Andy now, as Tim's partner he would have no choice, and nor would she if she wanted the work finished. Anyway, she decided, if Tim was still in the hospital at the weekend she would like to visit; the hospital was about thirty minutes away, maybe Kim would like to go with her, she'd ask her in the morning.

By 11.30am the following day, Andy received confirmation all the electrics had been signed off, he knew now he had no option; he would have to make contact. Deciding email was probably his best way forward, he carefully drafted a letter requesting permission to visit the premises in order to assess the work that still needed completing.

He needn't have worried too much, Kim answered all the business related emails and she laughed to herself when she read it; she guessed he'd written this several times over before he sent it, it was direct and grammar perfect. There was only one problem, Kim realised, he'd obviously forgotten how impatient Maria could be, she'd spent all morning cleaning with Louise and now the two of them had already started to move other bits and pieces over to their new home.

"Maria," Kim called to her sister as she heard her back in the house, "I need a word."

"What is it?" Maria asked as she made her way up the stairs to Kim's office.

"I've just had an email from Andy, he needs to visit the property so he can sort out what needs to be finished."

"Just tell him we're quite happy to wait until Tim returns to work," Maria replied flippantly.

"You're not serious." Kim frowned at her sister. "Who knows when that's going to be? Anyway, they probably need to get it finished, they might need the money, they've been very good; they haven't asked for any monies up front." Kim could tell by her sister's expression she was fighting a losing battle. "I can show him around if you want," she conceded. "It's no problem."

"Well explain to him it's not really convenient until Monday morning."

"Why Monday morning?" Kim asked looking puzzled.

"'Cos I've got the dentist, so I won't be here." Maria laughed. "Oh, I nearly forgot, do you fancy coming with me on Saturday morning? I'm thinking of visiting Tim in the hospital."

"I'm sorry, I can't on Saturday, David and I have promised his parents we'll sort their garden out this weekend, but Chloe is home this weekend; she'll come with you if you'd like some company. She can always wait in the relatives' room if she doesn't feel comfortable visiting Tim in his room."

"Check with her first then, if she doesn't mind, we can have some lunch together somewhere on the way back." Maria made her way back to the kitchen; there was still so much to do.

Returning her attention back to her laptop, Kim sent a friendly reply to Andy asking if it would be possible if he could pop round on Monday afternoon, with her fingers crossed, she pressed send. Later that afternoon Kim confirmed to Maria that Andy had agreed to Monday, and Chloe would love to accompany her aunt on Saturday.

Lisa was relieved to see, day by day, how well Tim was recovering and was now anxious for him to return home. It was Friday morning and Tim was sitting in the chair next to his bed when Lisa arrived; he looked well but a little sad.

"What's wrong?" Lisa asked anxiously as she bent to kiss him.

"The doctor has just completed his rounds and I can't come home until Monday at the very earliest, which means I'll be here all weekend."

Always fearing the worst, Lisa was relieved that's all it was. "Never mind, it's just one of those things, good job I brought these then," she said as she pulled out a clean pair of pyjamas and a brand new pair of slippers.

Tim laughed, and then frowned. "I don't wear slippers."

"You do now," Lisa said as she placed the slippers by his feet.

"Did you remember my mobile?" Tim asked casually as he wiggled his feet into his new slippers.

"No, because as soon as I leave, I know, you'll be straight on the phone to Andy and the doctor said to avoid all stressful situations."

"It's more stressful not knowing how he's coping and what's going on if you must know," he replied, a little angered at her response.

***

Sammy was shocked to hear from her father that Tim had been involved in an accident and had been admitted to hospital.

"Dad, will he be, ok?"

"Oh yes," Andy assured his daughter. "It's just going to be a while before he's up and running and ready for work."

"Are you going to be alright? Would you like me to help with the paperwork or anything?" Sammy loved her dad, and they had a great relationship, but she couldn't help worrying about him. She would have loved to see him in a happy relationship; she was sure he was lonely even though he insisted he was fine as he was.

"Thank you, Sammy, that's very kind but I think have everything under control, I hope so anyway," he added tentatively. "If you're free on Saturday though, do you fancy coming with me to visit Tim? I might need a bit of back up if Lisa is around."

"Of course, I'll go with you, we can have lunch somewhere before or after depending on what time you want to go."

"Thanks, Sammy, I look forward to it." Andy smiled to himself knowing his daughter wouldn't stop talking the whole way, at least she'd keep him awake.

***

David was already sitting in the car waiting for Kim who was still busy desperately trying to leave the house in some sort of order. Every morning was complete chaos, usually the weekends were a lot calmer, but not this Saturday.

"Chloe if you want a lift to Aunty M's we're going now," Kim shouted up the stairs as she collected her bag and keys.

"Five minutes, Mum."

"No Chloe, your dad's already in the car; it's now or you'll have to walk," Kim answered in an agitated tone that Chloe immediately recognised.

"What's the rush?" Chloe mumbled as she scrambled into the back of the car.

"You know what Granny and Grandpa are like, if you say you'll be there first thing, they expect you first thing, not halfway through the morning." David caught the raised eyebrow expression in his rear-view mirror. He couldn't help but smile, she drove them mad when she was home, but they missed her terribly when she was away.

***

Andy had to admit he was surprised he hadn't spoken with Tim directly since the accident; he'd considered ringing his mobile on more than one occasion, but something always held him back and, in the end, he'd decided to just turn up at the hospital on the Saturday. If Lisa was there, no doubt she'd soon make it known if he wasn't welcome.

As predicted, Sammy didn't stop talking for the whole journey. She was excited about her new promotion as head of department at her new school and even more excited about her recent engagement and forthcoming wedding. Andy had been so engrossed in listening to her he'd missed the last instruction from his satnav.

"Dad, why don't you keep an eye on the map? Then you would have noticed that you missed the last turning." Sammy laughed as she witnessed her dad try and turn the car around in a tiny narrow lane.

"Not my strong point, taking instruction," Andy admitted as he joined the main road heading, at last, in the right direction. Thirty minutes later they both walked into the hospital.

"You alright, Dad?" Noticing her dad had gone quite pale, Sammy took his arm.

"I'm fine," Andy replied. "Hospitals aren't really one of my favourite places," he admitted to his daughter as they made their way to the relevant ward.

Maria managed to get one of the last spaces in the hospital car park and, as she switched off the engine, she suddenly thought that maybe she should have checked with Lisa or even Karen that it would be ok to visit Tim. Well, she was here now, if it wasn't convenient, she'd leave the muffins and cookies and head off for an extra-long lunch with Chloe.

Quite by chance they passed the visitors' room before they entered the main ward and Chloe decided she would prefer to wait here, where she could happily spend the time messaging her friends.

"You sure you want to wait in here?" Maria checked with her niece as she peeped through the window, there was only one other young woman sat in the corner so she should be ok.

"I'll be fine, don't worry," Chloe said as she opened the door and walked in.

The young woman looked up from her magazine and smiled as Chloe sat down.

"Hello, Miss Porter." Chloe recognised her immediately.

"Hello," Sammy replied not wanting to appear rude but clearly not recognising the young woman.

"I used to go to Lakeview secondary, I was in the sixth form when you arrived, you never actually taught my class though," Chloe was quick to explain.

Pleased Chloe would have someone to talk with, Maria closed the door behind her and left them chatting. What a small world, what were the chances of Chloe meeting one of her old teachers here at the hospital?

Behind closed double doors the main ward was divided into smaller rooms, all leading back to the main corridor and held six beds in each. Maria had been instructed by one of the nurses to head to the last room on the left. She peered through the door before entering and spotted Tim right at the end. There was no sign of Lisa, although she could see he already had one other visitor, who from this distance looked more like a man.

Not wanting to intrude, and wishing now that she'd rang before just turning up, Maria decided she definitely wouldn't stay, she'd politely enquire how Tim was, leave the goodies she'd brought with her and make her excuses.

Tim spotted Maria as soon as she walked through the door, the look on his face caused Andy to turn and look straight into the eyes of the woman he'd never forgotten and had been desperate to see for a very long time.

Maria was smiling broadly, happy to see Tim sitting up in his bed and looking much better than she'd anticipated until the look on his face caused her to glance directly at the man sitting next to him. Immediately, Maria recognised the face staring back at her. As she quickly looked away, suddenly everything appeared to be happening in slow motion and the relatively short walk towards Tim's bed seemed endless. For a split second she considered turning and leaving, but her legs wouldn't change direction and they kept walking towards Tim's bed. Eventually, with her heart pounding so loudly she imagined everyone could hear it, she reached the end of the bed and gripped the iron bedstead tightly.

"Maria, how lovely to see you," Tim said genuinely touched that she would spare the time to visit. Sensing her embarrassment, Tim quickly continued, "Obviously there's no need for any introductions."

"Hello, Maria." Andy was the first to speak. "Please have a seat." He indicated the chair next to himself. "I was just leaving anyway." A statement that wasn't strictly true, Maria looked amazing and the last thing he wanted was to leave.

"Please don't leave on my account," she said, having quickly regained her composure. "I can't stay too long, I brought my niece along for the ride and she's waiting in the visitors' room, I promised her lunch." She glanced briefly in the direction of Andy then, concentrating her attention on Tim, she continued, "Well, Tim, how are you?"

"Better than I was." He smiled broadly before he began a brief synopsis of the last week, all the time fully aware how awkward this situation must be for her. Andy on the other hand, he suspected, was thoroughly enjoying the experience; he hadn't taken his eyes away from her the whole time.

Maria listened a little too intently, desperately trying to drown out the sound of her rapidly beating heart, was she really doing this after all these years? Standing just a few feet away from Andy was intoxicating, it took all her strength to appear calm and in total control; suddenly she realised Tim was still talking to her.

"I'm so sorry, Maria, that I haven't been able to…"

Before he could finish, Andy interrupted, "No work talk, you agreed."

"Please don't worry, Tim, just concentrate on getting yourself better." Maria smiled warmly at the man she now considered to be her friend. "I've brought you a little something to help you on your road to recovery." Maria produced a box containing the cookies and muffins she'd baked for him.

Tim lifted the lid and raised his eyebrows in astonishment. "Wow, look at these," Tim said as he showed the contents to Andy.

"Are you offering me one, or just showing me." Andy laughed as Tim quickly closed the lid.

Deciding it was probably time to leave, Maria lent over and squeezed Tim's hand. "Now you take care and when you're feeling better you must come over for a cup of tea." Not quite sure how to say goodbye to Andy, she hesitated, which gave Andy the opportunity to speak.

"I have a meeting at your place on Monday afternoon, I understand it's with your sister Kim."

"I think you'll find the meeting is for Monday morning," Maria replied in a very businesslike manner, that certainly didn't betray her true feelings. "I won't be there; I have a meeting elsewhere, but Kim will look after you." She smiled at them both before saying goodbye, and with her legs quivering like jelly, somehow, she managed to walk away.

"I know I said no talk about work, but that meeting is definitely for Monday afternoon," Andy said as he watched Maria leave. "I'll show you the email I received from her sister."

"That's very strange, she doesn't normally make a mistake, well, not in my experience anyway," Tim said as he watched Andy search his phone for the email.

"Look, read this," Andy said handing his phone to Tim.

"You're right, it definitely says afternoon, that's weird, why would she be so adamant it was the morning?" Tim handed the phone back to his partner.

Returning to the visitors' room, Maria found Chloe still in conversation with the teacher, she looked up as Maria opened the door.

"You weren't very long, Aunty M."

"Tim already had a visitor; I didn't like to gate crash for too long," Maria said, smiling.

"Would that be Tim Golding?" the teacher asked Maria inquisitively.

Looking directly at her for the first time, Maria's stomach lurched. "Yes," Maria managed to say knowing exactly what was coming next.

"That would have been my dad then, he's here visiting Tim, they're business partners."

Chloe was intrigued. "Tim built Aunty M's new kitchen for her new baking business," Chloe stated proudly.

"No way," was all Sammy managed to say while unable to take her eyes away from Maria, the penny dropped, and she realised that Aunty M was in fact Maria. Suddenly she remembered the building work at the house she went to for her wedding cake meeting. Surely not, it couldn't be could it? Surely it had to be just pure coincidence.

"Well, it's really nice to meet you." Maria needed some air and was anxious to get out of the hospital. "We should go, Chloe, if we're going to find somewhere nice for lunch."

"Lovely to catch up, Miss Porter," Chloe said as she gathered her bag and phone.

"You can call me Sammy, now you're a university student," she quickly added, watching intently for Maria's reaction, but it was too late Maria had already turned her back to leave.

A few minutes later having said goodbye to Tim, Andy returned to the visitor's room. "Sammy, you, ok?" He asked as he stood directly in front of his daughter.

Sammy looked up, she had absolutely no idea how long he'd been standing there. She smiled. "I'm ok, but I think I've just met Maria." She looked at her dad for the answer.

"Probably," Andy answered his daughter, "she's been to visit Tim and brought her niece along for the ride." He sat down next to Sammy and took her hand. "I've just met her too." He smiled reassuringly at his daughter and answered her next question before she had the chance to ask. "There's no story to tell, she could hardly bring herself to look at me."

"I'm sorry, Dad." Sammy said, moving closer to her dad.

"Don't be silly, it's not your fault." He gave her a quick hug. "Come on let's go get some lunch." He stood and pulled her up, and together they left.

***

For a Monday morning the dentist was particularly busy, they'd had an emergency first thing and now they were running considerably late. As Maria checked in, she was immediately offered an alternative appointment if it wasn't convenient to wait. Normally she would have opted for another appointment but today she was in absolutely no rush to return to work. She wanted to be as late as possible, but just so Kim wouldn't worry she gave her a quick ring, purposely not mentioning the offer to reschedule.

Andy pulled up outside Maria's house just after 2pm, having double checked with Kim by email earlier the exact time he was expected.

Having spent well over two hours in the dentist waiting room, Maria was convinced that by the time she arrived home Kim's meeting with Andy would be over. So, when she learnt he'd requested a later time and the meeting hadn't even begun, she felt cheated, all that time sat in the dentist for absolutely no reason, what a complete waste of time.

From her office, Kim watched as Andy collected a few papers from the back of his truck. It had been a shock to learn from Chloe all about the teacher who she'd recognised in the waiting room, and then to realise she was Andy's daughter. A day full of surprises, Kim thought to herself as she continued to watch Andy walk up the driveway.

Feeling guilty now about deceiving her sister, Kim changed her original plans and ran down the stairs, anxious to take control of the situation.

"Andy," she called just before he reached the door of the new kitchen. "Wait for me a second."

"Oh, hi, Kim," Andy said as he watched her stumble out of the back door.

"Andy, I need to explain," Kim began as she caught up with him. "Maria has already moved into the new kitchen, she couldn't wait, so it might not be as easy as you imagined assessing the outstanding issues."

"That shouldn't be too much of a problem." He laughed. "I've already got a rough idea from what Ian the electrician reported." He smiled reassuringly. "I can always arrange for the outstanding works to be completed either at night or at the weekend, if that would help."

"Thank you, that might be most helpful," Kim said as she led the way inside.

The delicious aroma of freshly baked cakes and pastries instantly reminded Andy that he hadn't even had time to stop for lunch. "Gosh, it smells wonderful in here." He laughed as Kim closed the door behind him.

Kim watched as Andy worked his way swiftly around the kitchen, making notes as he went. She also kept a watchful eye on

Maria and noted how many times she accidently glanced in his direction, maybe there was some unfinished business here after all.

"Well Kim." Andy broke into her thoughts. "I'm pretty sure I've noted all the outstanding work. I'll put it all in an email, let me know if I've missed anything, and as I said I'm happy to have the work completed out of hours so to speak."

"Thank you so much, Andy, can I tempt you to a cup of something and a warm muffin before you go?" Kim said, hoping this might give her the opportunity to find out a little more about this man.

"You can most certainly tempt me to a muffin, unfortunately though, I don't have time to stop for a drink," he replied.

"Maybe another time." Kim was disappointed. "Anyway, not to worry, I'll pack you a couple of muffins. Would you prefer chocolate or fruit?"

"It has to be chocolate." He laughed. "There's no contest I'm afraid."

Maria, who had been listening intently to their conversation, couldn't help smiling; even after all these years he was still a chocoholic and without giving it much thought she packed a white chocolate and double choc chip muffin in a small package and handed them to Andy.

"Thank you very much," he said as he peeped inside the box. "I'll enjoy these." He smiled at Maria, but she missed it; she'd already returned her attention back to her cake mixture.

"I'll see you out then," Kim said as Andy packed away his papers and carefully carried his muffins. "I hope you save one of those for your wife and don't eat them both," she said, smiling widely, as she walked him to his truck.

"There's no way I'm sharing these with anyone," Andy replied climbing into his truck. "I'll send you that email by the end of the day," he called as he drove away.

Kim, disheartened with that answer, made her way back to her office; somehow, she needed to find out a little more about Andy Porter. She'd try again with social media, maybe he'd added some information, or she could check out his daughter; that might be a better option. She was bound to have a comprehensive social media account. She switched on her phone and searched Samantha Porter.

Maria finished mixing the ingredients of a fruit cake that would eventually be a 25th wedding anniversary cake, and carefully placed the mixture in the oven. While that was baking, she could take a quick break. She needed some fresh air; it would be good to clear her head.

"That was weird," Louise whispered to her sister as soon as Maria left. "Did you sense an atmosphere just then?"

"Can't say I did," Julie replied as she put the finishing touches to her latest creation.

"Well, I did," Louise continued, with a knowing look. "I'd say something's definitely going on with Maria and that guy."

"Honestly." Julie looked at her sister and shook her head in amazement, "You read far too many romantic novels."

"Maybe I do," Louise admitted. "But I bet you any money you like, there's something going on with those two, take my word for it."

Unable to resist the aroma of freshly baked cakes, Andy drove into the next road, parked up and pulled out the package containing the two muffins. He was absolutely starving, and these were just what he needed. They were still slightly warm and truly delicious; he could understand why they were so busy but what amazed him more than anything was why Maria had chosen this business. She'd never shown the slightest interest in any sort of cooking, and he'd never known her to bake a cake. Strange how people change. He screwed up the packaging as he took the last mouthful, wiped his hands on his hanky and drove off keen to get back to the unit where he could confirm these details by email to Kim.

Over the days that followed Andy found it increasingly difficult to think of anything other than Maria. He imagined what it would be like to sit and have a proper conversation. He was interested to find out more about her life, but he had to acknowledge, she hadn't shown the slightest interest on either of the occasions their paths had crossed and that made him sad.

For the rest of the day, Maria couldn't settle; she was restless and irritable. Even Kim, sensing she was in no mood for talking, kept her distance. Later that evening as she cleared away her supper dishes, Maria looked out of her side window where she could see her new business premises dimly lit for security purposes. For her business it had been the right decision; on a personal level with the return of Andy into her life she found it extremely disturbing.

The following morning with the sun shining brightly, everything in her life seemed so much better and suddenly Maria was hungry. It would be a good idea to get out of the house for a while and an ideal opportunity to try breakfast in the new café which she'd heard rave reviews about.

"Kim, it's only me," Maria said as her sister answered her phone.

"Everything ok?" Kim asked, sounding worried. Maria never rang this early unless there was a problem.

"Yes, fine, I was just wondering if we could have that meeting you keep asking for this morning? Over breakfast at Amy's, we could call it a breakfast meeting." Realising how miserable she'd been yesterday, Maria laughed trying to sound much happier.

"Sounds great, what time?" Kim asked as she checked her watch.

"About 9.30am, is that ok?"

"That's fine, I'll see you there," Kim agreed, realising she would have to get a move on if she was going to be on time.

Amy's was extremely busy; it hadn't been open that long and was already a firm favourite with the locals. The interior was all shabby chic with odd tables and odd chairs; not necessarily Maria's taste, but it was comfortable enough, and as Maria was shown to her table, she was pleased she'd had the foresight to phone ahead and make a reservation. This was such a good idea; the change of scenery was a refreshing break from the four walls of the bakery. She sipped her freshly made smoothie and waited for her sister to arrive.

"We should do this more often," Kim said as she dabbed each side of her mouth. "That bacon sandwich was to die for."

"I'm glad you enjoyed it, and we've covered a lot of outstanding issues." Maria was pleased, it had been a successful morning.

"Now you're sure it's fine for Andy, and one other chap, to come around on Saturday and finish all the odds and ends?" Having witnessed Maria's reaction to his visit on Monday, Kim was looking for definite clarity.

"Yes, let's just get it all done and dusted," Maria answered, confident that she would be ok. All she wanted was to get it finished, so she could enjoy her new premises and move on; the constant flash backs and dreams were driving her insane.

CHAPTER SIX

Maria – The Late 1980s – Early 1990s

Delia and Richard were incredibly excited; they'd just booked their 35th wedding anniversary party at Mulberry Court Hotel. With only limited funds available their wedding day had been for immediate family only, but now they were able to realise and share their dream with their three wonderful daughters: Maria, Clare and Kimberley; the rest of the family; and lots of friends. With the invitations in the post the countdown was on.

Filled with confidence and real belief from his visit to the fair ground and its occupants, Andy drove home excited, he had a definite plan. He was under no illusion. It wasn't going to be easy; he had a lot of work to do to win back the trust of the woman he adored, but he could do it, slowly; he wasn't going to rush anything. He would prove to Maria just how much she meant to him. He drove home in high spirits, enjoying his music and the scenery all around him.

Maria always knew Monday was going to be challenging and by noon, with the constant sound of the printer beginning to rattle her brain, and up to her eyes in reams of paper, Maria chose to take an early lunch and enjoy the solitude of her car for an hour. Having enjoyed her sandwiches, she reclined her chair and closed her eyes; listening to the music she could feel the tension of the morning slowly begin to fade.

Exactly one hour later Maria returned to her office immediately noticing a rather large bouquet of flowers on her desk.

"Who are those flowers for?" she asked her colleague, who was now desperate for her own lunch break.

"You," her colleague answered as she made a quick exit.

Maria opened the small envelope attached to the cellophane at the top of the bouquet. "Thanks for a great evening. Andy." She read the card several times before popping it back into the envelope. To be honest she'd expected a phone call after their meeting in the pub, but she'd heard nothing, so the last thing she expected was flowers; this wasn't his normal style that was for sure. Unnerved by this unusual turn of events Maria's mind went into overdrive. The rest of the day passed in a similar vein to the beginning, chaotic, and by 5.30pm they'd only managed to accomplish half the day's invoices, not a good start to the week but Maria felt exhausted and couldn't face the prospect of working late to catch up. Hoping for a better day tomorrow, Maria packed away her work and, collecting her flowers, made her way home.

By Wednesday evening as Lisa still hadn't heard how Maria's meeting with Andy had gone the previous Friday, she presumed it hadn't gone that well and there wasn't too much to tell. So, when she saw Andy in the pub later that night with a few other guys, she was absolutely convinced it hadn't gone that well with Maria, otherwise, she was sure, they would have been out together. Andy had never really been one for going out with the guys and, noticing they were all dressed in suits, Lisa assumed they were work colleagues, out for a drink after work.

Andy had spotted Lisa as she entered the pub alongside her husband Tim but, for no particular reason, didn't acknowledge them until they were leaving.

"That was weird," Lisa commented to her husband as they approached their car.

"What was?" Tim replied, completely unaware of where Lisa was going with this comment.

"Andy," she said. "I'm sure he saw us when we arrived, yet he didn't acknowledge us until we left. How was he when you collected the truck?"

"He was fine, just normal really," Tim said realising he probably wouldn't have noticed if he wasn't; he didn't really know him that well. "He asked how the business was going, joked about if I was ever looking for a partner to let him know, and that was about it, why?"

"No reason," Lisa replied, already deep in thought and keen to return home so she could ring Maria and find out exactly what had happened.

By the time Maria returned home from work on Wednesday evening, Lisa had already left a couple of messages. Tired and still not really in the mood for a heart-to-heart, Maria made her call to Lisa brief but did agree to meet for a quick drink on Friday straight from work.

As the clock struck 6pm on Friday evening Maria filed the last invoice of the week. She'd worked late Tuesday, Wednesday and Thursday evening and now finally they were completely up to date. Now all she wanted to do was head home, but she'd promised Lisa and checking the time she realised it was too late to cancel, Lisa would be on her way by now.

Reluctantly Maria made her way to meet Lisa, she knew her friend was desperate for all the news and gossip re her meeting last Friday with Andy, but there really wasn't that much to tell and in truth Maria was dreading spending the next couple of hours talking about Andy. Still, she consoled herself, she didn't want to be late getting home; she had a very busy day on Saturday as all three sisters had decided to spend the day together shopping for their new outfits for the big anniversary party.

***

Unfortunately, Andy's original plan was proving a far greater challenge than he could have imagined. On Monday he'd sent a large bouquet of flowers to Maria at her place of work. He'd deliberately kept the message short and to the point and had been determined not to ring. It wasn't part of the plan to bombard her; he was playing the long game but by the end of the week, disappointed that she hadn't even left a message of thanks, his strength of character was waning fast.

Andy checked his watch, it was time he finished up for the week. It was his weekend to look after his daughter Sammy. At least he acknowledged she would keep him busy; her energy levels were off the chart so he'd be kept fully occupied for the next couple of days. He thought of her gorgeous little face; one smile from her could melt his heart. He closed his briefcase firmly shut and headed off to pick up his daughter.

***

Having managed to secure a couple of cosy chairs in the corner of the pub, Lisa and Maria chatted easily while enjoying their drinks. They covered all the general gossip and, as predicted, as soon as she could Lisa turned the conversation to the subject of Andy.

"So, you haven't heard any more since the flowers?" Lisa asked, keen to learn all the details.

"No, nothing at all." Maria took a quick sip of her gin and tonic before continuing, "It's not his style at all," she admitted. "Flowers and just a brief, well very brief, note, and then nothing, but…"

"I wasn't going to mention anything," Lisa interrupted her friend. "But he was in The Greyhound the other night." She paused again before adding, "Not with another woman or anything; it looked like they were work colleagues, all suited and booted."

"That's good to hear." Maria tried her best to sound convincing. "Why shouldn't he go out? After all, I'm here with you."

"Do you think he's finally got the message?" Lisa asked delicately.

"It looks that way doesn't it?" Maria concluded as she finished her drink.

By the end of the evening Maria was convinced that she'd probably heard the last of Andy. Why then, she thought to herself, did she feel so incredibly sad?

***

The three sisters had agreed to meet on Saturday morning at 9.30 for a quick coffee before hitting the shops. The café was already busy but Clare being the first to arrive had managed to secure the last table. She waved frantically trying to attract the attention of Maria who was desperately searching for a familiar face.

"No sign of Kim yet then?" Maria noted as she gave Clare a quick hug.

"No, but I think we'll order otherwise we might be asked to vacate the table," Clare said as she indicated to the waiter that they were ready to order.

Kim arrived just minutes before three steaming coffees and a plate of freshly baked pastries were carefully placed on their table.

"Sorry," she explained as she made herself comfortable. "I wasn't sure where would be the best place to park; anyway I've ended up on the top floor of the multi-storey. Gosh these look good," she said as she helped herself to one of the pastries.

Less than one hour later in the first department store on their list, Clare was lucky enough to find exactly what she was looking for. It was a relatively plain shift dress in French navy, but the sleeves were pleated chiffon, with deep cuffs secured by four covered buttons and transformed the outfit into sophisticated elegance.

"You sure it's not too much?" Clare asked as she cautiously pulled back the curtain of the changing room.

"No way," Maria assured her, "you look amazing, it fits like a glove. It's perfect for the occasion, trust me, absolutely perfect."

"I agree, totally," Kim added admiring her sister's choice.

"That's me sorted then." Clare smiled as she returned to her fitting room. "One down two to go," she called out as she changed back into her own clothes.

Kim had been instructed by David to wear red, his favourite colour, but that was proving easier said than done. Red didn't appear to be a high fashion colour this season and anyway Kim had fallen in love with a floaty tiered dress in a beautiful sea green; it really suited her, and she felt comfortable and confident.

"I'd go with that, I really would," Clare encouraged her sister. "David will love it, and he'll understand. I mean if there's nothing in red available to buy, well there's nothing in red, it's as simple as that." She shrugged her shoulders and smiled reassuringly at her sister.

"Kim, you look truly gorgeous; it's by far the best one you've tried today, honestly it really is," Maria said watching her sister as she gave them a little twirl.

"Well, I do love it," Kim confirmed. "I think this is the one." She paused briefly. "Yes, I'm going to take it." She did another little twirl for her sisters and happily headed back to her fitting room.

Several shops later and with nothing really catching her eye, Maria had more or less given up hope of finding her outfit, when purely by chance Clare spotted a few sparkly outfits hanging in the corner of the shop.

Always attracted to a little sparkle, Maria flicked through the dresses. The last one on the rail immediately caught her attention; it was black with thin diagonal silver stripes. Encouraged by her sisters Maria made her way to the changing room. Staring at her reflection, she couldn't help smiling; she felt a million dollars. The dress fitted perfectly, and the diagonal stripes had the most alluring effect. Suddenly she felt sad. Andy would never get to see her wear this dress, and she knew he would have been extremely impressed and equally as proud.

***

By Sunday evening Andy returned one very tired little girl. They'd had a really great time: lots of fun and laughter, enjoying afternoons in the park playing on the swings, riding the roundabout, making chocolate rice Krispy cakes for their tea and snuggling up after bath time reading a story of her choice. With a big hug she waved goodbye to her Daddy, happy to know that in just a couple of weeks he'd be back to collect her once again. It was all normal for Sammy; she'd never known a different way of life. Andy continued to wave with his arm leaning out the car window until he knew Sammy could no longer see him. He turned left at the bottom of the road and headed home. The car was quiet; he missed the sound of her chatter, and he missed her big smile. He missed everything about her, he decided, as he turned up the volume to drown out the silence that surrounded him.

By Monday morning having spent Sunday evening deciding the next best course of action, Andy walked into work with an unusual spring in his step. Normally he gave the impression he was struggling with the whole world resting upon his shoulders, but today he was alive and buzzing with anticipation.

***

Maria was struggling. Although never actually alone for very long, she was lonely; she missed Andy more than she ever thought possible. Why had it always been so complicated? Why hadn't he felt he could be completely honest with her? Why had he always put his ex and her demands first? There were so many "whys" and so many unanswered questions but above all else she was sad; she'd really thought that despite their troubles, he was her soul mate, and it hurt to realise that she'd got it so wrong. Funnily enough, previously knowing he was desperate to see her made it bearable; even when she'd spotted him following her, she'd been angry, but also reassured that at least he was suffering just as much as her. Now with complete silence and no attempt at any contact she was in no doubt it was over, and the realisation was breaking her heart.

On Wednesday morning for the very first time Maria was late for work. Unexpected major roadworks had appeared overnight and were causing mayhem and huge delays. It was at moments like this she really wished she'd paid more attention when Andy had installed her car phone. She picked up the handset; there was no dialling tone. She opened the glove compartment, desperately searching for the instruction leaflet when she suddenly remembered she'd taken it indoors to read, then never actually got round to it. Eventually she arrived at work. Flustered, she grabbed her bag and rushed into the building; she absolutely hated being late.

"Morning, Maria, everything ok?" her boss enquired as he watched her rushing to the office.

"Sorry I'm late," she called out in response.

"Don't worry, we've all been caught out today." He laughed trying to make her feel better. "Oh Maria, I nearly forgot; a package arrived earlier for you. I've put it on your desk."

"Really?" Maria looked puzzled. "Thank you, I'm not expecting anything." She shrugged her shoulders and made her way to the office.

Susan was the only other office staff in today. She was Maria's favourite; she was hard working and never pried.

"Morning, Maria," Susan said as Maria hurried into the office.

"Morning, Susan, everything ok? What have you started on this morning?" Maria asked as she hung up her coat.

"As you weren't here, I wasn't quite sure, so I thought I'd start with the invoices that have been sent up from downstairs."

"Just give me a minute and we'll plan the rest of the day," Maria said as she sat at her desk.

Picking up the very slim package, Maria noted it was a local postmark. She studied the handwriting; she didn't recognise it at all. Curiosity getting the better of her she ripped open the package. An envelope fell from the packaging. Maria opened it carefully and placed the contents on her desk: a letter and two tickets for the variety show at the London Palladium. How very strange, she thought to herself as she opened the letter.

"Dear Maria," she began to read, "I won these tickets in a raffle. As you can see, they're for this Saturday evening. I don't have anyone to take so knowing the variety is one of your favourites I thought you might be able to make use of them and enjoy the evening. Andy x."

Stunned, Maria placed the envelope and its contents in her handbag. Her mind was a whirlwind, why had he posted them to her place of work when he could have just popped them through her door at home? Why hadn't he just rung her and asked if she'd wanted them, or even just asked if she wanted to go with him? None of this made any sense to her. Quickly she made up her mind exactly what she would do next. With that decided she re-engaged her brain into work mode and carried on with her day.

Throughout Wednesday morning, as busy as he was, Andy couldn't truly concentrate. He was like a cat on a hot tin roof, constantly making trips back to his desk to check if he had any messages. He knew for sure the package was due for delivery today and by lunch time he was under no illusion, this idea wasn't going to pan out quite as he'd expected. He was disappointed; if this didn't spark a reaction, he had no idea where to go from here. He had no plan B; basically it was back to the drawing board.

Maria kicked off her shoes as she walked through the front door. She'd begun to think the day would never end. Home at last, she poured herself a large glass of wine. Recognising it was probably now or never she took the envelope from her handbag and opened the letter. She reread it over and over before she picked up the phone; her heart was beating fast and loud, and she dialled the number twice before allowing it to go on, to actually ring.

"Hello," Andy answered, sounding as weary and disillusioned as he felt.

"It's Maria." She paused. "Is it convenient to talk or shall I call you back?" she asked politely.

"No," Andy answered, suddenly wide awake and very upbeat, "it's fine. I can talk now, of course." He stopped before he made a complete fool of himself.

"Andy, I received the tickets this morning," Maria began, her voice a little shaky. "It's very kind of you but wouldn't you rather give them to one of your family, or maybe take one of them yourself?"

"They can't make it," Andy said, surprising himself at his quick response. "I thought you would know more people to ask than I." His voice trailed off leaving an uncomfortable silence.

"Maybe..." Maria finally spoke.

"Maria, if you're too busy, don't worry," he interrupted. "I realise it's very short notice, that's probably why they were in the raffle." He tried to make light of the whole situation. "It's just I remembered how much you always enjoyed the variety show when it was on T.V. so I thought, well, I'd send them to you."

"Actually, it was you that always enjoyed the variety show." She laughed, remembering.

"Well, why don't we just go together then?" he said timidly. "Just as mates of course," he quickly added. "It would be a shame to waste a couple of really good tickets."

"Why not," Maria replied, perhaps a little too quickly, and now she could feel her face blush and she was glad he couldn't witness her embarrassment.

"If you're sure, that would be truly amazing." Andy's heart was soaring; he'd planned this over and over and earlier today he'd thought all was lost and now, well he couldn't believe it, he was going to see Maria on Saturday night. This was an incredible outcome and once again he gave thanks for his unexpected trip to the fairground.

Finishing the conversation Maria hung up; what on earth had she just agreed to? She sat with her head in her hands, a mix of emotions flooded her whole being, half of her was disappointed at her total lack of self-preservation and utter weakness, the other half excited; just the sound of his voice had given her goosebumps and she'd missed that feeling so very much.

***

The variety show had been spectacular; they'd had excellent seats, just three rows from the front, and the whole theatrical performance, from the costumes to the singing and dancing had been magical. Andy was on top form, and it was so easy for Maria to forget all the complications and baggage he carried with him that had, ultimately, finished their relationship.

"Fancy a drink before we head back?" Andy whispered as they were swept along with the crowd towards the exit.

Not wanting to sound too keen Maria hesitated just long enough to let him believe she was going to refuse. "Ok, just a quick one," she said, smiling as he realised she'd been teasing him. "But I definitely don't want to miss the last train back."

"We've got over an hour until the last train leaves." He laughed, guiding her across the road heading to a bar he knew not too far away.

To Maria it seemed they'd only just arrived at the bar when it was already time to leave. They arrived at the station with seconds to spare, and realising they were really going to have to run if they were to catch this train, Andy grabbed her hand and they both ran as fast as they could. This was the first physical contact they'd had all evening and Maria wasn't sure whether her heart was beating fast and loud because she was so unfit or because she could feel the gentle touch of his hand in hers. They climbed into the first carriage just as the final whistle blew. Holding on tight to her hand, Andy led the way through several carriages before he was convinced they would be near the exit of their station when they finally arrived.

"We should be alright here," he explained as he chose a seat where Maria could sit next to him. "That was close," he said as he sat down still slightly out of breath.

"Very," Maria just about managed to answer, still struggling to regain her composure.

Andy turned to look at Maria, her face was flush from running, but still she managed to look so incredibly gorgeous and there was no way he wanted this evening to end.

"I think we're going to have to leave our cars in the station car park after all the cocktails we've managed to drink," Andy suddenly announced. "What do you say we get a cab?"

"There's only ever one cab this time of night." Unexpectedly Maria felt strangely uncomfortable, she wasn't sure if he meant get separate cabs or just one.

"We can ask him to drop you off first." He shrugged his shoulders. "If he's not keen to take me on from yours I can walk, it's a lovely evening."

"It's five miles," Maria stated, looking at him in amazement.

"It's four and a half actually," he corrected her, smiling. "Don't worry, Maria, I'll be fine, and if I'm not, I can crash with a mate of mine that doesn't live that far from you."

"What mate is that?" Maria questioned him. "It's a bit late to just turn up at someone's house, even if they are a mate," she added, anxious that he would end up walking the whole way home.

"One of the guys from work, doesn't live that far from you; I'm sure he wouldn't mind if I crashed on his sofa if need be."

Maria grinned, she still wasn't convinced Andy knew anyone who lived anywhere near her.

As they'd expected, the cab driver was only able to do the one drop off due to a pre-booked pick up. As he pulled up outside Maria's house the heavens opened, with no umbrella and only wearing a short jacket, Maria ran for shelter in her porchway while Andy paid the driver.

"At least come in and have a coffee, by which time it might have stopped raining, otherwise you're going to get very wet." She laughed as he desperately tried to shake off the rain drops from his hair.

"Are you sure?" Andy replied, already following her inside.

"No, I'm not sure," she said in a whisper as she turned to face him. "I'm not sure at all."

"Well, I am," Andy said as he closed the front door behind him. "I'm one hundred per cent sure." He placed both arms around her waist and pulled her close, he kissed her gently, teasing her lips and Maria took him by the hand and led him towards the stairs.

The next few weeks were amazing; apart from his allocated time with Sammy, Andy devoted every second to regaining Maria's trust and she was enjoying every minute.

No one, friend or family, were particularly surprised to learn that Maria and Andy were back together. Maria, though, had been reluctant to reintroduce Andy back into her family circle. Conscious of their continued support and concern over the last few months, she recognised that her family, having witnessed first-hand how she had suffered, would probably be less forgiving. It was an unfortunate situation especially with her parents' anniversary party looming; so, she was shocked when, during one of her regular phone calls, her mother casually broached the subject of their up-and-coming party.

"Maria, I have to confirm final numbers this week so if you would like to bring a guest, I really need to know."

There was a short silence while Maria hurriedly decided whether to ask or not. Finally, she answered, "Would you and Dad mind if I brought Andy along?" She held her breath as she waited for her mother to reply, not at all convinced the answer would be favourable.

"No, darling, we don't mind at all." Her mother wasn't surprised, she'd already warned her husband this question was on the horizon. "If that's what you want and you're happy, it's fine by us." She'd always liked Andy, but she couldn't help feeling concerned; she had a feeling his daughter would always be a cause for concern for them both one way or another, for a very long time.

"I haven't actually asked him yet, Mum." Maria was keen to point out. "I wanted to check with you first."

"Well, you have a chat with Andy, but I do need to know by the weekend; that's my deadline," her mother explained.

"Will do, Mum," Maria confirmed. "I'll let you know but I'm sure he'll jump at the chance."

"Ok, darling, take care and I'll speak to you soon."

"Bye, Mum." Maria hung up and immediately decided she would wait until Friday before she asked Andy. She preferred it to be face to face rather than over the phone, that way she would be able to judge for herself his initial reaction. It frightened her a little the prospect of inviting him; he'd let her down so many times in the past. She would be wary and place herself in a very vulnerable position but come the night of the party, if she hadn't invited him, she would always regret her decision. It would be different this time, it had to be, and in all fairness since they'd been back together, Andy hadn't let her down once and was going out of his way to prove his commitment to their relationship.

Andy had already guessed Maria was stalling before inviting him back into the fold of her family. There'd been ample opportunities over the last few weeks, but he couldn't blame her, and over the weeks he'd come to terms with the idea she wasn't going to invite him to her parents' anniversary party. So, when casually over fish and chips on Friday evening Maria began to test the water, Andy wasn't going to pass up on a possible invitation.

"Maria, if you're trying to invite me to your parents' anniversary party, I would be honoured to accept," he said graciously, hoping he hadn't got this all wrong.

"It's going to be quite formal." She looked concerned as she spoke.

"I can do formal," he said quite indignantly.

"I know you can." She laughed still not really convinced this was a good idea.

"To formal for our relationship at the moment, is that it?" he asked, disheartened this might still be the case.

"I don't want it to be," she answered honestly while swirling the last of her wine around the bottom of the glass.

"Well as I see it," he began, "this is my chance to prove to you that it isn't. Please, Maria, trust me, one more time."

She looked deep into his eyes, searching his soul. "One more time," she finally agreed, pinching his last chip.

The following days were busy, and Maria couldn't hide her excitement; it was going to be a great anniversary party and a bonus to have Andy by her side.

***

It wasn't unusual for Andy to hear from his ex a couple of times a day, especially if she wasn't seeing anyone. Her calls could be for a variety of reasons: a tap needed fixing, or she'd run out of money and couldn't afford to buy food. On this occasion he'd gone straight out after work, bought a couple of bags of food and taken them straight down to her, only to find she'd held a party the night before and spent all her money on booze. From experience he'd learnt that she contacted him less if she thought he was just home alone. If she knew he was going out, that's when the problems started, so there was absolutely no way he was going to mention this weekend.

This particular week he'd heard from her every day, but nothing too serious. So on Thursday, knowing he had a busy day, he decided her call would have to wait until his lunch hour when he'd call her back. As it happened, nothing that day went to plan; the delivery of new vehicles was unusually early and arrived before they'd had time to clear the forecourt, customers were late to pick up their vehicles and the whole morning was unorganised chaos. Consequently, his lunch hour was much later than normal and after a quick call to Maria, Andy picked up the phone and dialled his ex.

"What's the matter? You rang earlier," Andy said as Sharon answered the phone.

"Some sort of father you are," she scolded him. "I've been calling and calling you." It was clear she was angry; something obviously hadn't gone her way today.

"I take it there's a problem," Andy said, he was used to her outbursts so wasn't too concerned.

"Yes, there is, as you'd already know if you'd bothered to answer your phone."

"What is it?" Andy was already losing his patience.

"It's your daughter, she won't stop crying; she says she has pains in her tummy."

Ignoring her sarcasm, Andy persisted with his questions. "Have you called the doctor?"

"Of course, I have," she practically screamed down the phone. "He said it was just a tummy ache and she must have eaten something that didn't agree with her."

"Ok, well listen, I'll come straight from work, if that's ok with you?"

"Good because I'm going out tonight. I've put up with her crying all day and I need a break." She slammed the phone down and immediately went in search of something she could wear tonight.

Hearing her last comment, Andy raised his eyebrows and shook his head; so that was it, she needed a babysitter. He wouldn't be at all surprised to find Sammy wasn't ill at all; it wouldn't be the first time she'd pulled a stunt like this.

It was nearly 7.00pm when Andy finally arrived. He'd been late leaving and then hit heavy traffic, so he was tired and hungry when Sharon answered the door.

"At last," she sneered, leaving him to close the door.

He wasn't in the mood for her and was just about to give her a piece of his mind when he saw his daughter curled up on the sofa. Her face was red and blotchy, and she had her knees pulled up under her chin.

"How long has she been this bad?" he asked Sharon as she continued getting ready to go out.

"I told you earlier, all day."

"And what exactly did the doctor say?" he questioned her again.

"He said it was just a tummy ache, anyway I've got to go, I'll be back about eleven, see you." The front door slammed behind her as she swiftly made her exit.

Grateful Sharon's sister had the baby, Andy sat on the sofa next to his daughter. "It's ok, darling," he spoke gently. "Tell Daddy where it hurts." Sammy pointed to her tummy.

"It hurts, Daddy, it really hurts." She began to cry.

"Ok, darling, don't worry, Daddy's here." He went to give her a cuddle just as she vomited all over the sofa. Andy quickly cleaned up the sofa, wrapped Sammy in a blanket and carried her out to his car, he was taking her to A&E, something was wrong; this wasn't just a tummy ache.

It was extremely busy at the hospital, but they were lucky, the nurse looking after Sammy suspected this was a little more than just a tummy ache and quickly put a call out for the on-call paediatrician.

"I'm afraid, Mr Porter, Samantha will need surgery to remove her appendix," the doctor explained after he'd given Sammy a thorough examination and checked her test results. "We aim to prep her for surgery later this evening, could you please confirm Samantha hasn't eaten in the last few hours?"

"I've been at work, but she tells me she hasn't eaten since breakfast," Andy answered still in shock.

"Ok that's fine, you can stay with her until we take her to theatre." The doctor smiled reassuringly. "Try not to worry, she's in good hands."

Andy gave his daughter a cuddle.

"It's alright, baby, it's all going to be fine; the kind doctor is going to take all the pain away."

"Promise?" Sammy whimpered, snuggling into her daddy.

"I promise sweetheart," he said as he stroked her face.

It seemed ages before they finally came for Sammy and although she frequently fell asleep it was never for very long, constantly being woken by the acute pain. It broke his heart as eventually he watched the orderlies wheel her away.

He checked his watch, he had no idea where Sharon had gone for the evening, so he had no idea how to get in touch with her. He'd just have to wait until she arrived home, or maybe when she got home and realised they weren't there she'd ring his mobile. Deciding this was probably what she'd do, he quickly ran down to his car to retrieve his mobile phone.

***

Thursday had been eventful to say the least; Maria was now on the final stages of completing the whole programme and it was now just a couple of days until the whole company would be fully computerised. She'd thoroughly enjoyed the challenge and her boss had been extremely generous with a healthy bonus at the end of each stage. Finishing up on Thursday evening Maria was relieved that she'd booked half a day's holiday for tomorrow and would be leaving promptly at lunch time. It would just give her a little bit of time to herself before Andy arrived on Friday evening.

With her supper in the oven Maria had 30 minutes to spare and thought she'd use the time to find something to wear to travel to the hotel and something else for the Sunday morning. She made her way upstairs and opened her wardrobe. Her sparkly evening dress had centre place and Maria couldn't resist the urge to try it on again. She posed in front of her full-length mirror and admired her reflection. This was a fabulous dress, and she couldn't wait to see Andy's reaction when he saw it for the first time. Suddenly she missed him; they'd had a quick conversation at lunch time and, although they'd agreed not to speak now until Friday evening, a quick call couldn't hurt.

His phone rang and rang. Maria checked her watch, 7.50pm, he should be home by now. He hadn't said he was working late but that didn't mean he wasn't, or he could just be enjoying a pint before heading home. Maria hung up and decided to try his new mobile phone. She picked up her phone, and then immediately replaced it; they had already spoken once today. Andy would have no reason to expect a call from her tonight, so if he was out, he was out, and she should respect that.

She consoled herself with the idea she would give him a call later this evening, just before she went to bed; he would most certainly be in by then.

On the other side of town waiting patiently in the hospital for his daughter to return after her operation, Andy was relieved that he'd already spoken with Maria today. They hadn't made any plans to speak again today, and their arrangements were for Andy to meet Maria at her house on Friday evening. He was really looking forward to this weekend and couldn't afford any unforeseen problems or issues to affect their plans. It didn't bear thinking about: the possible repercussions if Maria knew he was in the hospital with Sammy, she'd start to panic, and he didn't need that right now. He sat in the waiting room for it seemed an absolute age; the nurse had promised to come for him the moment Sammy was back. In the meantime he'd found a nearby vending machine and drunk too many cups of bad coffee and eaten far too many chocolate bars. Finally, the kind nurse came back but instead of just telling him Sammy was back she took the seat next to him.

"Mr Porter," she began.

"She's ok," Andy interrupted, "please tell me she's ok." He stared at the nurse desperately seeking her assurance.

"She is now," she answered.

"What do you mean, now?" Andy interrupted her again.

"Mr Porter, please let me finish." She smiled. "The operation to remove her appendix was a complete success but we had a little trouble bringing her round after the anaesthetic."

"What do you mean had a little trouble?" Andy couldn't help it, he knew it was rude to interrupt but he was really panicking, if anything happened to his little girl, his life would be over.

"I just wanted to explain that for the next 24 hours she could suffer bouts of vomiting and extreme fatigue," the nurse concluded, having decided to keep any more explanations brief and to the point.

"Can I see her?" he asked tentatively.

"Of course, follow me."

Sammy looked so tiny tucked up in her bed. She tried to open her eyes when she heard her daddy's voice, but it was too much effort when all she wanted to do was sleep. Andy sat by her bedside and held her hand gently while she slept. It was 3am and he hadn't heard a word from Sharon. If this was the other way around and she was here at the hospital, she'd be ringing him every five minutes. He leant back in his chair and closed his eyes.

After supper Maria curled up on the sofa and before she knew it fell into a deep sleep. It was gone midnight when she stirred; the house was in complete darkness; the only light came from the T.V. Acknowledging it was far too late to call Andy, she made her way upstairs; she'd call him in the morning, she thought to herself as she climbed into bed.

Andy was woken by someone touching his shoulder; he opened his eyes, startled. It took only seconds for him to remember where he was.

"Mr Porter, sorry to wake you but you're in the way now," the nurse said indicating that she needed him to move his chair away from the bed.

"I'm so sorry," he said jumping out of his chair. "You ok, honey, how do you feel?" he asked as Sammy slowly opened her eyes.

"I don't feel well, Daddy," she answered tears spilling down her cheeks.

"What is it, baby?" Andy asked, moving around to the other side of the bed, keeping out of the way of the nurse.

"I feel sick, and my tummy still hurts."

"I can give you some medicine that will take the pain away," the nurse quickly said.

"There you go, honey," Andy tried to reassure her. "The nurse will make it all better."

"The doctor will be around to see her between 9.00 and 10.00am," the nurse said as she finished her checks.

"Thank you," Andy said as she left.

Sammy was already dozing by the time the nurse left so Andy sat back in his chair, it was just 7.00am. He checked his mobile phone; the battery was getting low. He'd leave a message for work then he'd wait until the doctor came round before he decided what to do next.

**

Maria was in work before any other office staff on Friday, so she took the opportunity to give Andy a quick ring at work. Unusually the receptionist kept her hanging on for quite a while; she was just deciding if she should hang up and redial when she heard her call being transferred.

"Hello." It was a man's voice that she'd never heard before.

"Oh, hello, I was just wanting a quick word with Andy if that's possible," Maria replied suddenly realising this could well be Andy's boss.

"Is this Maria, by any chance?" the unfamiliar voice enquired.

"Yes, it is," Maria confirmed suspiciously.

"Well, I'm afraid Andy hasn't turned up for work yet."

"Oh, well I'm so sorry to have disturbed you," Maria said as her stomach lurched from panic to annoyance and finally to worry.

"Obviously you haven't heard from him either," the voice asked mellowing slightly.

"No, I'm afraid not," was all she could manage to answer.

"Well, if you do hear from him perhaps you could ask him to give his boss a ring?" He sounded angry again.

"I certainly will," she replied as already deep in thought she hung up.

Maria sat in her chair. What on earth had happened? Had he been in an accident? Was he unwell? All these thoughts were running wild in her head as she begun to face the reality; this had all the hall marks of life with Andy, and she felt nauseous. By lunchtime Maria still hadn't heard from Andy. Packing away the last few bits and pieces left on her desk, she could feel the all too familiar feelings of dread welling up inside. All the excitement of the weekend had disappeared and was slowly being replaced by anger and frustration.

Having said her goodbyes to the girls and her boss, Maria made her way out to her car. Where to go first? she thought to herself as her fingers played irritably on the steering wheel. It wasn't any good going home; she wouldn't settle until she'd checked out a few things. Thirty minutes later she pulled up outside Andy's flat. There was no sign of his car in the car park, but that didn't really mean anything, and she still needed to check to see if he was actually at home. With no reply to the intercom, she stood outside for a while considering her next move when a resident she recognised returned, opened the main door and held it open for her to enter.

"You're Andy's friend, aren't you?" the kindly faced gentleman said as Maria followed him into the building.

"Yes, I am and thank you for letting me in," she quickly replied, not really wanting to get too involved in a conversation.

"You're welcome." He smiled making his way to the lift.

Maria hurried down the corridor towards Andy's flat. Not wanting to draw too much attention to herself, she knocked gently a couple of times, but there was no answer. Checking there was no one around she bent down trying to peer through the letter box; there was absolutely no sign of life at all. Convinced he wasn't here she stood up and straightened her clothes. Slowly she walked back to her car; she could no longer differentiate between feelings of worry, concern and anger. Trying to think logically, she started the engine; maybe the most sensible idea was to head home and see if Andy had left a message on her answer phone. She reversed out of the carpark and headed for home, secretly hoping his car would be parked on her driveway waiting.

Maria could see her house from the top of the road; so that was another disappointment for the day, she thought, as she stared at her empty driveway. She could hardly bear to look as she opened her front door; would she be welcomed by the flashing light on the answer machine or would she not? With everything crossed she opened the door.

"Yes, yes," she practically screamed as total relief flooded over her. She had two messages; she pressed play and sat on the stairs.

"Hello, darling, thought you might be home from work by now, anyway it's just a quick call to let you know we've arrived at the hotel safe, and sound and I'll give you a call later this evening, bye, darling." With everything else going on Maria had forgotten her mother promised to let her know as soon as they arrived. Anxiously now she pressed play for the second message.

"Hi, it's only me," her sister Kim said. "Just to say I'll pick you up at 8.30am and we can go the hairdressers together, speak later." The phone went dead; there were no further messages. Ten minutes later still sitting on the stairs, Maria picked up the receiver. She dialled Andy's home number and listened as it went straight to answer phone. She dialled his mobile and listened as it again it went straight to answer phone.

Suddenly the house felt claustrophobic. Maria could literally feel the walls closing in as she strolled aimlessly from room to room unable to concentrate on any one thing other than "Where was Andy". She was way past the stage of worrying if he'd been involved in an accident or injured in any way; he would have got a message to her somehow. No, this had all the familiar traits of his ex and his daughter. In hurricane proportions anger swept right through her whole body.

"Why, why," she screamed as she marched heavily up the stairs and flopped onto her bed, barely managing to grab the pillow before a waterfall of tears cascaded down her cheeks. Unable to stop, she cried until her tears ran dry.

***

"I think it's best if we keep Samantha in for at least one more night, just to be on the safe side." The doctor smiled at Sammy. "I'll be back later this evening to see how you're getting along; we'll also be moving you into the main ward today, so you'll have some other children for company. That will be better won't it?" he spoke tenderly with genuine concern.

"Thank you, Doctor," Andy said acknowledging him as he left.

"Daddy, where's Mummy?" Sammy asked for the first time.

"I don't know, darling, but I'm going to have to go home and collect you a clean nightie and get some clean clothes for myself, then I'll come straight back, will you be ok for a very short while?"

Sammy's face crinkled and her top lip quivered as tears began to spring from her eyes. Andy sat on the bed and cuddled his daughter.

"It's ok, it's ok," he desperately tried to reassure her. "I won't go anywhere; I'll stay here with you, don't worry."

With one arm around his daughter, he carefully manoeuvred his other arm so could reach his mobile phone. It was just as he thought, the battery was completely flat.

While the nurses were busy settling Sammy into the new ward, Andy took the opportunity to search for a pay phone. He was sure he'd seen one near the reception area, so he hurried there first. Having completely forgotten that Maria was finishing at lunchtime he decided that he wouldn't call her, they hadn't arranged any contact until Friday evening so as far as he was concerned, she need never know about all this, well not until after the party anyway. He knew they wouldn't be too happy with him at work; he'd realised early hours this morning that at the very least he would be late, so before his phone went flat, he'd left a message for his boss explaining everything, so at least they knew where he was. With all that sorted, as far as he was aware, the only one he needed to call was Sharon. Dialling her number he checked his watch. "Gosh," he thought to himself; it was much later than he realised.

"Hello," Sharon's voice sounded husky.

"Please don't tell me you're hungover?" Andy asked her angrily.

"No, I am not." She tried her utmost to sound awake and sober. "Anyway more to the point where are you?"

"Nice of you to ask, at last," Andy replied sarcastically. "I'm at the hospital with our daughter." He waited for a panicked response, but it never materialised.

"Why?" she asked calmly, struggling to remember any of the events of yesterday and last night.

"Sammy had to have an operation to remove her appendix last night, well, early hours this morning." He waited again for several seconds before she responded.

"Oh." Feeling unwell herself a one-word answer was all she could manage.

"What do you mean 'oh'? Had you even realised we weren't there when you got in last night?" Andy was furious, she sounded completely spaced out.

"Is she ok?" Sharon asked, deciding to ignore his last question.

"She is now, but they're keeping her in tonight. I've been here since last night and I need to go home, have a shower and change my clothes so you need to get yourself over here with a clean nightie for Sammy, she's asking for you." He waited for her excuses, but there was nothing but silence, so he continued. "Get a cab, I'll pay for it when you arrive." Still there was no reply. "Sharon—" he raised his voice "—are you listening to me?"

"Yes, I'll do that," she replied and hung up. Leaning against the wall, she tried to comprehend the conversation; there'd been some mention of going to the hospital and she would do that, but for now she needed her bed, she needed to sleep.

***

Always on Friday afternoons, Andy's boss, Ian Kendrick, left early, but today before he left, he decided to check one more time to see if there had been any news of Andy. He was disappointed; he really thought Andy had sorted himself out. He'd promised profusely to always contact them in future having had goodness knows how many second chances. He was without doubt a very good salesman, probably the best of the team, but these disappearing acts where no one could contact him, and he didn't bother to contact them were causing Ian Kendrick serious headaches and were going to cost Andy his job if he wasn't careful.

"Jenni." Ian Kendrick pulled up the chair opposite the receptionist. "Still no news of Andy?"

"No, Mr Kendrick, nothing I'm afraid," she replied.

"Let me know on my home number if you hear anything from now until you finish." He stood up and pushed the chair back. "Goodnight."

"Goodnight," she replied, relieved to see her boss leave.

Jenni leant back in her chair; this telephone system had been much harder to fathom than she could have imagined, she'd already made more than her fair share of errors, cutting people off, transferring them to the wrong department or person and now this… Sighing heavily she felt weighed down with guilt, but what could she do? There was no way she could afford to lose this job; she'd only been here six weeks and was only halfway through her trial period, she had no option but to remain silent.

From the moment she arrived this morning the phone had been manic; it had been one query after another. At one time she had so many people hanging on she'd been tempted to cut them all off just for some peace, so it really wasn't her fault, she decided, that she hadn't noticed there were two unread messages in the system. She had no idea if they'd been there from first thing or more recent and now, desperately trying to remember how to retrieve messages, somehow, she managed to delete them both. At first, she hadn't been too worried, whoever it was would probably call back, if they hadn't already, she convinced herself. As the day went by though, she begun to feel increasingly uncomfortable. She'd had her boss question her more than once and several of the sales team, all desperate to find out if Andy Porter had been in touch or left a message. Now she really hoped it wasn't the case, but what if one or both of those messages were from Andy? Trying to push the matter from her mind really wasn't working. She hoped this wasn't going to cause Andy any real trouble if the messages were from him, he was, she acknowledged, one of the kindest members of the team; he'd often helped her when he could have made life extremely difficult. Surely, he would have called back if they'd been from him? She checked her watch, another hour to go, she just wanted to get out of this place and go home to her family.

***

Andy made his way back to the ward where Sammy was already settled and busy checking out her new neighbours. They all seemed to be very young children, he noted, and they all had their mummies by their side apart from Sammy. The rest of the day passed in a flurry of activity; there was always so much going on and in between Sammy's naps he managed to try several times to get hold of Sharon, but there was never an answer. He was absolutely disgusted with her; he'd been here nearly 24 hours and was tired and hungry.

"Mr Porter," a nurse interrupted his thoughts. "We are going to be settling the children down for the night very soon and we don't encourage parents to stay overnight in this ward as all the children are in recovery and need a good night's sleep." She smiled warmly before she continued, "You can return in the morning anytime from 8.00am."

"That's fine," Andy replied, slightly relieved to see Sammy was already beginning to doze. "Did you hear that, honey? I must leave you now as the nurses are going to turn all the lights out so you can all get some sleep."

Sammy tried to open her eyes, but she was tired and they only quivered. Andy leant over and kissed her goodnight.

"Night, night my precious one," he whispered in her ear. "Daddy loves you very much, sleep tight." He was just about to leave when a little voice piped up.

"Daddy, you will be back in the morning won't you?"

"Of course, I will, darling," he assured his daughter, squeezing her tiny hand before he left.

Although he didn't use it very often, Andy opened Sharon's front door with his key; the house was in darkness and completely silent. At first, he thought she'd gone out again but then he saw her handbag on the floor next to her shoes.

"Sharon," he called out as he made his way from room to room, "you here?" He listened for a moment, nothing, just silence. Slowly he made his way up the stairs; he reached her bedroom, the door was wide open and there she was slumped across her bed, fully clothed in the same clothes she was wearing last night. He switched on the light and shouted her name. She stirred and slowly turned her head to face him; she looked like Alice Cooper with black eye liner and mascara smudged all around her eyes.

"For goodness' sake," Andy shouted. "You are an irresponsible, selfish…"

"Shish, Andy please." She sat up. "What's the time?"

"7.30pm Friday evening, you've slept the whole day away, what on earth were you drinking last night?"

"I think someone spiked my drink," she mumbled, holding her head.

"How did you get home?"

"I don't remember," she answered honestly. "I remember it was daylight."

"That means you didn't get home until this morning," Andy said in disbelief. "Where did you spend the night then?"

"I don't know," she shouted, "but at the end of the day it's none of your business anyway."

"It is my business when you're too drunk to care for our daughter," he shouted. "You're a disgrace, do you know that? An absolute disgrace; well I suggest you get your act together and make sure you're at the hospital to see Sammy by 8.00am tomorrow."

Sharon slumped down and buried her head in her pillow, desperately trying to drown out his words, Andy switched off her bedroom light and left.

Back in his car, he noted the time; he could still make it. He'd go straight home, quickly pack, have a shower and head straight to Maria's. He briefly considered giving her a quick ring, but then decided against it, if she knew what had been going on she'd go straight into panic mode. No he'd be as quick as he possibly could and, hopefully, she'd understand why he was a little later than they'd originally planned.

It was dark when Maria woke. She must have cried herself to sleep, she realised, as she sat up; everywhere was in darkness. As she reached for her bedside lamp she checked her watch; it was nearly nine o'clock and still there was no sign of Andy. Making her way to the bathroom she examined the image starring back at her: puffy, sore eyes, a blotchy complexion and a vibrant red nose stared back. She looked terrible and couldn't help it when more tears began to stream down her face as the realisation began to dawn all over again. Needing to numb the pain, Maria headed downstairs in search of some wine. She poured herself a large glass and sat at her kitchen table.

"Cheers, Maria," she toasted herself. "Here's to life without the evasive Andy Porter." She drank one glass straight down and instantly poured another. It was at this moment she decided; it wasn't like she'd never been here before but for her own self-worth she couldn't live like this. It wasn't fair, no, she had no choice. This had to be the end; there was no way back from this, ever.

Andy woke to the sound of his phone ringing. He rolled over on his bed. At first, he felt confused, it was daylight, and he still had the towel wrapped around his waist from his shower last night. He reached out for his phone.

"Hello," he managed to say still trying to wake.

"Why aren't you on your way to the hospital?" Sharon enquired sarcastically.

"What…"

"If you've just woken up, it's 9.30 Saturday morning and apparently you promised Sammy that you'd be back at the hospital by 8.00am."

"Where are you then?" he asked her abruptly.

"I can't go to the hospital; in case you've forgotten, I also have a baby to look after. He's far too noisy for a hospital."

"Oh, just great, so you're not going to the hospital at all today?"

"I've just told you I can't, but I have rung and that's how I know you promised Sammy; the nurse made it very clear she was expecting you to arrive imminently."

"I'm on my way," he said as he hung up. He couldn't allow himself the time to think of anything apart from the fact that once again he'd let his little girl down.

Naively Andy was convinced this weekend was still salvageable. He remembered Maria was going to the hairdressers first thing and he also remembered talk of them heading off to the hotel about noon. He could still make it; he just had to. It wasn't any good ringing, he decided, he knew Maria well enough to know she would already be furious. Once she heard his voice she'd just hang up; he had more chance of forgiveness face to face.

Andy arrived at the hospital and made his way straight up to the paediatric ward. Sammy was sitting up in bed and waved excitedly when she saw him. "Hello, sweetheart, how are you feeling today?" he asked as he bent down to kiss her cheek.

163

"The nurse made all the pain go away with her magic medicine," Sammy informed him as he pulled up a chair next to her bed.

"That's good to hear and did you manage to eat any breakfast this morning?"

She shook her head. "No, it was disgusting, so the nurse brought me a chocolate milkshake and I drank it all, and she said I was a very good girl." She looked so pleased with herself Andy couldn't help smiling.

He was just about to explain to his little girl that unfortunately he wouldn't be able to stay with her all day, when the doctor appeared ready to do his rounds. It was a different doctor today; he looked more like a student than an actual doctor. He stood reading Sammy's notes before he examined her tummy.

"Well, young lady, just a few more tests today and if they all come back good, you're free to go home." The doctor looked directly at Andy. "I would like the physio to see Sammy this morning to make sure she feels comfortable walking, and she's not disturbed or worried by the sight of her wound. Once that's all in order we can complete her release papers and of course, organise for her medication. Will you be here while we sort this?"

"Of course," Andy answered. "I'll be here."

"Jolly good." The doctor smiled and moved onto the next bed.

***

Kim hadn't even pressed the doorbell when Maria flung open the door.

"What's the matter?" Kim asked, instantly aware something was very wrong. She held out her arms and Maria clung to her sister sobbing into her shoulder. "It's ok, honey, let it all out." Kim held her sister tight until eventually the sobbing subsided. "You don't need to go into detail, but I take it Andy's not coming."

Maria wiped her eyes and nodded. "Just give me five minutes to wash my face." She turned and slowly walked back up the stairs, everything was an effort, even breathing.

Absolutely devastated for her sister, Kim watched her until she disappeared into the bathroom. As quietly as she could she picked up Maria's phone and rang David.

"It's only me," she whispered, "don't ask but there's a change of plan; after the hairdressers I'll be bringing Maria home and she'll be travelling down with us."

"No problem, I guess Andy's disappeared again?"

"I'll explain later. I've got to go now, bye." Carefully she replaced the receiver and stood waiting for her sister, grateful that with David she'd found her soulmate.

Kim had been "going out" with David for just over a year now and already the pair were pretty much inseparable, spending their time together either at her parents or his, both of which were happy to have them. They were a delightful couple, always happy and laughing, an absolute joy to be around.

"Wow you both look amazing," David said as both sisters climbed out of the car. Kim did a little twirl showing the back of her hair, Maria just about managed a smile. David felt sorry for her; she looked so sad, and in desperate need of a hug, but he wasn't that confident, so he decided to offer everyone a cup of tea, David's answer to everything.

"I'd love a cup of tea, thank you," Maria said, trying her best to smile and turning to her sister she whispered, "Kim, would you do me a huge favour?"

"Absolutely," Kim replied without hesitation.

"Would you try and get hold of Mum and Dad and just explain Andy isn't going to be coming. Please stress I'm fine, I don't want them worrying and just say we'll talk about it after the weekend, but not while we're away."

"Of course, I'll do that now." Kim gave her sister a quick hug. "Consider it already done."

"Maybe they could rearrange the table plan, so I'm not sat next to an empty place," Maria quickly added.

"No problem, I'll give them a call now."

***

As the morning passed, and now under no illusion that he was in serious trouble, Andy began to realise with hindsight that he should have called Maria, but that wasn't going to help his case now; he was going to need a miracle to get out of this one.

It was past lunchtime when, finally, Sammy was released from the hospital. She was clingy, disagreeable and generally hard work and Andy was exhausted just trying to keep her amused. In the end, Andy carried Sammy to the car; the nurses had tried to get her into a wheelchair, but she wasn't having any of it. "There you go, sweetheart," Andy reassured his daughter as he settled her into her seat at the back of the car.

"Not too tight," Sammy exclaimed as Andy tightened her seat belt.

"Sorry," he said as he ruffled her hair. He thought he was being careful, obviously not careful enough.

Half an hour later with Sammy in his arms Andy rang the doorbell, but there was no answer so gently settling Sammy on the doorstep he searched his pockets for the key.

"Hello," he called as he opened the door.

"Mummy, Mummy," Sammy called out. "I'm home, I've had an operation, Mummy, Mummy." Sammy looked at her daddy. "I don't think Mummy is here." She looked heartbroken and Andy's heart went out to her.

"It doesn't look like it, darling," he answered. "Don't worry, she's probably just popped out," he tried to reassure her. "Now where do you want to settle down, the sofa or your bed?"

"Can I have a bed made up on the sofa, please," she asked in a sorrowful little voice.

"Of course, just let me put you in this chair for a minute and I'll go fetch your duvet and pillow. You ok there for a second?" he asked as he carefully placed her in the armchair.

"There you go, is that nice and comfy?" Andy checked as Sammy snuggled under her duvet. "Shall I put Cinderella on for you? Or do you fancy something else."

"Cinderella please." Sammy smiled up at her daddy.

With Sammy settled for a while he had a quick look around. He really couldn't tell whether Sharon had just popped out or was out for the duration; the house was always a complete mess. He was really miffed. She knew Sammy was coming home today. She also knew he'd stay until she decided to return home; what option did he have? He couldn't leave. He sat for a while on the edge of the chair; everything was such a mess.

It was gone 6.00pm when Sharon breezed in with the baby fast asleep in her arms. Having already fed Sammy and got her ready for bed, Andy was anxious to get away but as with everything now it wasn't that easy, and it was nearly 7.30pm when he climbed into his car.

Throughout the day he'd been adamant, as soon as Sharon returned, he'd head home, change and just drive straight to the hotel. He knew initially the reception would be frosty, but he could cope with that. Realistically now though, as he sat in his car, he had to admit he was absolutely shattered and knew he would never survive the journey to the hotel without falling asleep. He put the car in gear and drove home to an empty flat and an empty life. The only consolation, he thought to himself, was that he wouldn't be in too much trouble at work. He'd left a detailed message and even offered to take the day as part of his holiday entitlement.

Andy walked into his flat, picked up the mail and headed straight for the kitchen. He didn't bother with lights; the darkness suited his mood. He opened the fridge and took out a couple of bottles of beer and drank them straight down, desperate to find absolute oblivion.

***

Kim's initial reaction to the hotel reminded Maria how she felt the first time she came here with her parents; it was indeed an impressive building. From the back of the car Maria instructed David to drive straight to the main entrance.

"Are you sure? There's a sign that says carpark to the left," David said as he slowed the car.

"I'm positive," she assured him, "the porters will take our luggage. When we came before, Dad just gave them his keys and they parked the car for him."

"Yes, that's all very well," Kim began, "but Dad has a much better car than us; they might not offer the same service for a ford escort as they do a flashy Mercedes."

"It's fine, I'll drop you off and then I'll go and park," David said, smiling at Kim who was uncharacteristically showing signs of stress.

Their journey down hadn't been without delays; they'd experienced an unusual amount of roadworks and got lost a few times, so it was no surprise to learn they were the last of their parents' guests to arrive. The afternoon tea party, which had been arranged for everyone to meet before the festivities began, was well under way, so it was a very quick change and straight down to the main lounge.

Later that evening back in her room, Maria stood back from the mirror. This was a striking dress, she had to admit, and she felt confident. She picked up the glass of bubbly her mother had sent along with the accompanying handwritten card.

"Enjoy, my darling and remember we love you very much. X"

Feeling reasonably calm, Maria smiled. She knew this was her mother's way of acknowledging what she could probably only imagine her daughter was experiencing. Determined that Andy wasn't going to ruin this evening, Maria made her way down to join the party.

The banqueting suite looked spectacular; fresh flowers were in abundance and circular tables dressed in brilliant white linen with elaborate candelabras were carefully placed leaving just the right amount of space for dancing.

With the dinner and speeches over the lights were dimmed and the live band made their way onto the stage. Within minutes the dance floor was full of eager participants ready to dance the night away.

The three sisters were among the first to hit the dance floor; they were all having great fun. Maria, though, was dreading the moment they slowed it all down; she'd already made up her mind that would be the time to make a quick exit to the "ladies". There was no way she wanted to be sitting on her own at their table, although she expected her parents would sit with her; they were so thoughtful, but she didn't want that: they loved to dance.

All too quickly the moment she'd dreaded arrived and the tempo slowed. Both her sisters beckoned their partners to join them on the dance floor. Hastily, Maria made her way back to their table to collect her clutch bag; as predicted her parents were hovering.

"Please, go and have a dance." Maria gestured to the floor. "Don't worry about me, I'm fine. I need the 'ladies' anyway."

"Are you sure, darling?" Delia looked anxiously at her daughter.

Maria nodded. "Honestly, Mum, I'm fine."

"Well, I'll be back soon to dance with my beautiful daughter," her dad said. "So make sure you're back in time for that." He gave Maria a little squeeze as he took his wife's hand and led her onto the dancefloor.

Maria managed to idle away just over ten minutes and making her way back to the party was dismayed to hear the slow music still playing.

On her way back to the table Maria sensed she was being followed. Inquisitively she turned and came face to face with the Italian waiter from the restaurant. She remembered him from her weekend stay with her parents earlier in the year; noting his very casual attire Maria guessed he wasn't on duty, so what exactly was he doing here?

"Hello, Lorenzo." Suddenly her father appeared at the table. "So glad you were able to join us."

"Thank you for the invite; it was very kind of you." He spoke softly although his accent was far stronger than Maria remembered.

"May I interest you in this dance?" Lorenzo turned to look directly at Maria and caught her completely off guard with his request.

"Maria," her mother said, embarrassed at her daughter's prolonged silence.

"Oh, sorry," Maria said quickly, and guessing by her mother's expression she had no option but to accept. "I'd love to." She managed to smile as she answered.

Lorenzo took her hand and led her to the dancefloor, he held her gently but not unreasonably close and as the music was too loud to talk over, Maria actually felt reasonably comfortable.

One song later and the band declared it was time for a break and Lorenzo walked Maria back to her table. Both her sisters were already back at the table and Maria had trouble keeping a straight face as she watched their expressions. She could imagine exactly what they were thinking; he was after all a very handsome man, not really her type though, a bit too smooth looking, but she knew both her sisters would be swooning, especially when he spoke; they would adore his accent.

Realising they had no idea who he was and vice versa, Maria thought it only polite to introduce him. She only hoped he wouldn't take that as an invitation to remain at their table. She needn't have worried, once the introductions were complete, Lorenzo excused himself and made his way to the bar to join another couple of staff from the restaurant that were enjoying their drinks.

"Well, he's very handsome, isn't he?" Clare said to no one in particular. "I'm not complaining, but how come Mum and Dad invited him?"

Maria shrugged her shoulders and grinned. "I've no idea."

"I think your parents are just being friendly," David answered, personally he couldn't see what all the fuss was about. So the guy was Italian… so what?

For the rest of the evening Maria made sure her vision didn't stray to the bar area, the last thing she needed was any more complications in her life right now.

Before long the band resumed their places on stage and the music played until 1.00am when they announced the last dance.

"You did promise me a dance," her father said holding out his hand.

"It will be my honour." Maria laughed, following her father back to the floor.

Minutes later she saw Lorenzo lead her mother onto the floor, and Maria found it extremely difficult to steer her father away from the handsome Italian dancing with his wife. As the music finished her father was quick to escort his wife back to their table leaving Maria with Lorenzo. Smiling in acknowledgement that the dancing was over, Maria went to walk away when Lorenzo spoke, "Would you like to join me for a drink?" Maria was startled at his question and for a minute she couldn't think of what to say.

"That's very kind," she began, "but I still have my champagne to finish." He looked embarrassed and suddenly Maria felt sorry for her abrupt reply. "You're very welcome to join us at our table," she offered, trying to soften the blow. Not for one minute did she consider that he would accept; she was only being polite.

"Thank you, I'd love to," he replied, smiling. "I'll just go and fetch my beer."

Instantly regretting her invitation, Maria made her way back to her family at their table. This was going to be very interesting, she thought.

***

Nothing was really working for Andy; he'd finished all the beers in the fridge and was now on neat spirits, but still total oblivion evaded him. All he could see was Maria in her new dress. Maria had insisted that she didn't want him to see her outfit until the night of the party. She'd given him a few teasers, telling him it was black and silver, and when one morning she left her wardrobe door open, he couldn't help himself and he quickly had a sneak peek. It was stunning, and he just knew she would look a million dollars. Visions of her dancing, laughing and enjoying herself were driving him insane. One phone call and he might still have had a chance, but there weren't going to be any chances now and, in all honesty, he couldn't blame her.

Staggering from the living room to his bedroom he took his new suit from the wardrobe and slowly painfully ripped it into tiny pieces. Finally exhausted he collapsed onto his bed. The way he felt right now, he never wanted to see the light of day again.

***

Gradually over the next hour the rest of the family retired, and Maria and Lorenzo were eventually the only ones left chatting at the table. He was easy to talk with, and on a one-to-one basis was nowhere near as brash and confident as he came across in the restaurant. Their conversation remained general, and Maria was astounded when she glanced around the room and realised all the other tables had been cleared away, and the staff were obviously waiting patiently for them to leave.

"Goodness me, I hadn't realised the time," she said, quickly jumping up from her chair. "It's 2.30am, I think the staff are waiting for us to leave," she explained to Lorenzo who looked a little puzzled at her sudden actions.

"I'll see you at breakfast then," Lorenzo said noting Maria's sudden wish to leave.

"Breakfast," Maria said, obviously confused.

"I work in the restaurant where we serve breakfast to the residents." He was teasing her, and she couldn't help but laugh.

"Of course," she said shaking her head. "At breakfast then." She nodded and before Lorenzo had a chance to reply she was gone.

Later back in her room she climbed into her king-sized bed and for the first time that evening she allowed herself to think of Andy.

***

With the weekend celebrations over, reality kicked in quickly on Sunday afternoon when David pulled up on her drive.

"Honestly, you don't need to get out of the car," Maria explained. "I'll be fine. I want to get unpacked and sorted ready for work tomorrow."

"Are you sure?" Kim said as she climbed back into the car.

"Yes, definitely," Maria confirmed as she waved them goodbye.

Closing the door, Maria stood for a while. The silence was deafening. She checked her phone, no messages; he hadn't even bothered to leave her a message of apology. Well perhaps it was for the best, she decided, taking her case upstairs to unpack. She'd had quite a frank conversation with her parents before they left the hotel and they'd made it clear he wouldn't be welcome back into the family unit as far as they were concerned. Her father had been particularly firm when he acknowledged that it would be far from easy, but he sincerely hoped she would now make a clean break. Deep down she knew he was right; she didn't want a life full of unfulfilled promises, constantly worrying and forever anxious.

CHAPTER SEVEN

Maria – The Present.

Andy checked the email; he'd listed all the outstanding work in detail. He'd also asked Kim to confirm that someone would be around to unlock and then lock when the work was complete. He estimated the work would take between four and five hours. Satisfied he hadn't forgotten anything he pressed send.

Maria had set her alarm for 7.00am on Saturday morning. In the end it wasn't required; she'd been awake since 6.00am. Tossing and turning she gave up the hope of any further sleep and made her way downstairs for a cup of tea before jumping in the shower. Andy plus one other was due this morning to complete all the outstanding work. Despite the fact Maria had reassured Kim she would be ok to hand over the keys, she wasn't looking forward to it at all. Instead, she thought it would be a total relief when all the work was complete and there would be no need for any further disruption.

Andy and Joe arrived just before 8.00am. Hearing them pull up outside, Maria grabbed her keys. Feeling surprisingly calm, she went outside to meet them. Andy greeted her with the warmest smile. Not able to judge whether she wanted to engage in conversation, he decided to keep it brief and to the point.

"Morning, Maria," he said as he took the keys she offered.

"Morning," she replied, acknowledging them both before turning to head back indoors.

"Oh, Maria," Andy suddenly said before she disappeared, "would you prefer it if I popped the keys through the letter box when we've finished, or would you prefer to check everything before we leave?"

Having just assumed he would knock when it was all finished, this threw her off guard.

"Just pop them through the letterbox, that will be fine," she said not able to tell whether he was disappointed or relieved at her reply.

Maria closed the door and took a deep breath; her hands were shaking slightly but she couldn't really define how she felt. What puzzled her the most was her inability to hold a normal conversation with him. Back in the day, she remembered they would spend hours just talking. They'd been able to talk about anything and everything; now she could hardly string together a couple of words, let alone a complete sentence.

Trying not to dwell on the situation, Maria set about making her breakfast. It wasn't something she'd set out to do, but absent-mindedly she cooked the whole extra-large packet of bacon and buttered enough bread to feed an army. Gingerly she opened the door to the conversion and placed a tray containing a huge plate of bacon sandwiches, a pot of steaming fresh coffee and two mugs on the nearest available worktop.

"Wow, is that for us?" Joe asked, beaming with absolute delight as he spotted the sandwiches.

Maria nodded and smiled. Obviously Joe hadn't had time for breakfast this morning, judging by the way he quickly tucked in. "Mm these are so good," he mumbled in between mouthfuls.

Andy stood up from replacing some broken floor tiles. "Gosh," he said in amazement. "They look good, thanks, Maria."

"You're very welcome," she said looking everywhere apart from directly at him. "I hope you drink coffee, Joe; I should have checked."

"Oh yes, I most certainly do," he confirmed while devouring more of his sandwich.

"Well, enjoy," Maria said as she turned to leave, suddenly feeling extremely awkward.

As Maria closed the door behind her, Joe turned to look at Andy. "Something going on between you two?" he asked helping himself to some coffee.

"No, why do you say that?" Andy tried to look astonished by his question.

"Because she never asked you if you drank coffee; in my book that means she already knew."

"I've been here before don't forget," Andy replied shaking his head in mock horror.

"Well something's going on. I may not be the brightest star in the sky, but I know a spark when I see it." He nudged Andy and winked.

"Well, I'm sorry to disappoint you, but there's absolutely nothing going on."

"Not yet maybe." Joe laughed. "Not yet."

"Come on, eat up we've got work to do," Andy said, keen to end this topic of conversation and get the work finished.

***

David folded his newspaper and placed it on the table. He studied his wife for a moment.

"You've been on edge all morning, what's wrong?" he asked.

"I'm not on edge," Kim replied bluntly.

"You most definitely are." David took her by the hand. "Come on, sit down for five minutes, tell me, what's wrong?"

"I'm sorry," Kim said sitting down next to her husband. She loved her husband dearly; he was always there for her and knew instinctively when something was wrong. It took just a few minutes to explain her concerns.

"Come on then," David said jumping to his feet. "If you're that concerned Maria might be struggling with Andy working on site, we'll go over. I haven't seen it all finished yet; we can say we were passing so called in for a cup of tea."

"But you said you wanted to get some work done in the garden this weekend."

"I know, but this is obviously important to you, so it's important to me; come on let's go."

"Thank you," Kim said squeezing his hand affectionately.

It was nearly lunchtime before Maria finished her housework. Making her way downstairs with the vacuum cleaner she thought she could hear familiar voices. Checking the front window she was surprised to see Kim and David walking up the drive.

"I wasn't expecting to see you today," she said opening the front door.

"Sorry, that's my fault," David began. "We were passing, and I was keen to see the finished conversion. I didn't realise you had anyone working today, but it doesn't matter; I'm sure I can still take a peek."

"Of course, come in," Maria said as she hastily packed the vacuum cleaner away. "Would you like a cup of tea, or do you want to take a look first?" Maria asked, extremely pleased of their company.

"What time are they due to finish?" David checked his watch.

"Not until later this afternoon, I think, but I don't know for sure," Maria confessed.

"Do you mind if I go and take a look now?" David asked politely.

"Not at all," Maria said. "We'll all go. I have a tray to collect, and I can leave Kim to show you around."

"You remember David?" Kim said to Andy as all three of them ventured carefully inside the new kitchen.

"Of course." Andy walked over to shake David by the hand.

"How's it all coming along?" David enquired in his normal friendly manner.

"Not so bad thank you, all going to plan I'm pleased to say." Andy glanced at both sisters.

"I'll take this tray back," Maria said, feeling quite claustrophobic. "Then you can show David around." She smiled at her sister and left them to it. Andy had already returned to work and left Kim and David to explore.

"You must be very pleased," David declared as they walked back into the house after his grand tour.

"I really am," Maria agreed. "It's been the best decision; we were desperate for more space and it's all working out really well."

"That's good to hear…" Before David had a chance to finish his sentence Kim interrupted.

"What was on the tray you collected?" she asked, keen to find out what had been going on.

"Oh, I made them some bacon sandwiches and a pot of coffee," Maria answered, before clearly changing the subject. "Do you guys want to stay for lunch?"

"What are you offering?" David asked cheekily with a big grin.

Maria shrugged. "Fish and chips from the takeaway!"

Kim nodded in agreement.

"Sounds great, phone the order through and I'll go and collect it," David said suddenly feeling very hungry.

A couple of hours later, having enjoyed their lunch, Kim and David were relaxing in the living room with Maria when David spotted Andy packing his truck.

"Looks like they're about done," he said pointing to the window. "Have you got to go and check it all before they leave?"

"No." Maria shook her head. "Andy said to check it all tomorrow when it was all dry."

"What about the keys?" Kim asked thoughtfully.

"Andy said he would just pop them through the letter box." Maria tried her best to appear completely uninterested.

"Maria," her sister gushed. "You've got to say thank you and goodbye surely?"

Sensing that Maria was feeling slightly uncomfortable with this situation, and feeling guilty he'd mentioned Andy looked like he was packing up, David had a plan. "Well, to be honest, Kim, we need to leave now anyway," he said pulling himself up out of the comfy armchair. "We can collect the keys from Andy, that's not a problem." He smiled at Maria. "Thank you, for a lovely afternoon."

"You're welcome," Maria answered as she busied herself clearing away their teacups. She'd played out this scene in her mind involving Andy with various scenarios many times over the last few days and this hadn't been one of them. Before she knew it David and Kim had said their goodbyes and were outside. Maria watched from the window as Andy approached them with the keys. She moved slightly back from the window; she didn't want him to know she was watching, but it was now or never. This was her last chance; she could either go outside and at least say goodbye or she could just let him go without saying a word.

Finally, she decided, and taking a deep breath she walked to the front door and opened it just in time to see Andy drive away. David and Kim walked back towards the door where she stood.

"I've just got to email him on Monday confirming completion and that everything is ok," Kim explained, handing her the keys. "Then he said he'd forward the final invoice, which he assured me would be the same as Tim's original quote."

"That's simple enough," Maria replied, just wanting to be left alone now.

"Are you ok?" Kim said, thinking her sister looked incredibly sad.

"Yes absolutely," she said unconvincingly.

"Do you want to come back with us?" David asked, not wanting to leave her if she was upset.

"I'm fine, honestly, it's been great spending this afternoon with you both, but I've taken up enough of your time, now go and enjoy the rest of your weekend." She stood waving until they were out of sight.

Finally alone, Maria walked back into the living room to collect the remaining mugs and glasses. She'd enjoyed the afternoon but now she felt cheated. If she'd been alone, she would never have let Andy put the keys through the letterbox without saying something. When David and Kim first arrived, she imagined that if they were still around when Andy left, it would be easier to strike up a conversation with all of them involved, so why had she acted so churlish? Sitting back in the living room, she put her head in her hands. She had no one to blame other than herself.

As Andy drove away, he immediately remembered he'd forgotten to mention Tim had been released from hospital. He considered turning back; he was sure Maria would want to know, or was he just desperate for another chance to speak to her? He'd played out several different endings in his mind. He'd even let his imagination run really wild and imagined being invited in her house for a drink; now he knew that was never going to happen. Perhaps the best idea would be to continue his journey home and just mention it on Monday in his email. He approached the roundabout slowly, this was his last chance to turn around. Automatically he indicated left and 25 minutes later arrived home.

***

Life was so much easier now "The Bakery", as it had been officially named, was fully functional. Apart from the spare room that had now become Kim's permanent office, Maria had the rest of her house back to herself. Julie was practically working full time and between them they'd contributed some great ideas to propel the business forward. Kim was also busy and had been the driving force behind some great visuals for their website which was proving to be hugely successful.

With the good news that Tim had now returned to work, Maria invited him over for a cup of tea. For Tim it provided the ideal excuse to check everything was ok at "The Bakery". He knew it would be, Andy was an absolute professional, but he just couldn't help himself.

"You're not checking up on me then?" Andy teased his partner as Tim explained his meeting with Maria.

"The trouble with you," Tim laughed, "is you know me too well."

Andy gave him a friendly slap on the back as he packed the last parts he needed for the day's work.

"Got time to come with me this afternoon?" Tim questioned him carefully, not wanting to pry. Ever since he'd been well enough to return to work, he sensed there was something wrong. It wasn't work related, he felt sure of that; they were busy, and everything was going well in that direction, so, it had to be something to do with either Sammy or Maria and he had all bets on the latter.

"No mate," Andy answered all too quickly. "It would be a complete waste of time anyway." He mumbled as he left.

Tim shook his head as he watched Andy walk with sloped shoulders back to his van and eventually drive away. This was such a sad story and although he would never do anything to interfere, after all it wasn't his place, he wished there was something he could do for his partner. Andy wasn't a bad guy and he'd well and truly paid the ultimate price for becoming involved with the wrong girl, at far too early an age.

***

Maria sat with Kim in the kitchen enjoying a cup of tea and a sandwich, they didn't meet for lunch every day, but tried to meet at least a couple of times a week. Today Maria was excited, she wanted to run through a few ideas before Tim arrived in the afternoon.

"What exactly have you got in mind now then?" Kim asked, interested to hear exactly what Maria had planned. Kim had been dreaming of a completely new kitchen herself for a while now, but having seen some of the prices, she reckoned if she saved some of her own money before broaching the subject with David, it might help sway the idea in her favour. David, however, was far from silly, and he'd quickly cottoned on that Kim wasn't spending any of the money she earned; what he hadn't fathomed yet was what she was saving for.

"Well," Maria began, "I need a new floor that's for sure. Since I moved things around in here it's left unsightly indentations. The cabinets are ok, I think, after all they're only three years old, but the wall tiles are already looking dated." She pulled out a magazine and turned to the page folded over. "I noticed in this magazine they're using panels now in between the cabinets and the work surface, and I really think that looks so much better." Maria passed the magazine to her sister. "Anyway, as Tim was coming over, I thought I'd use the opportunity to see what he could advise."

"Sounds really good." Kim acknowledged as she briefly glanced through the magazine. "I've seen these wall panels before. I agree, they definitely look much better than tiles." She grinned and passed the magazine back to her sister.

Maria studied her sister for a minute. "Why were you looking at kitchen magazines? Are you thinking of having a new kitchen?"

Kim smiled. "Honestly, Maria, I haven't even mentioned it to David yet, but it would be my dream to have the wall between the kitchen and the dining room taken down and have a large open plan kitchencum-family room, a bit like yours really."

"Well, why don't you ask Tim to have a look? He'd be able to give you some ideas and prices." Maria was surprised, she had no idea Kim was even considering anything so drastic.

"I can't speak to Tim before I've spoken to David," Kim explained. "It wouldn't be right."

"Well, speak to David tonight, you can always just mention it to Tim while he's here, he's extremely discreet, he wouldn't let you down."

Kim was tempted. "I could I suppose," she said thoughtfully.

Tim was incredibly impressed with Maria's business set up in "The Bakery". She'd made well defined areas and it seemed to be running like clockwork as far as he could see. Andy had done an excellent job finishing the whole project. He couldn't fault his work, and finally Tim could now relax. He'd seen for himself the finished article and he was pleased.

"It looks great, Maria, it really does, you pleased with it all?"

"Definitely." Maria nodded. "It was the right decision for the business, plus it's enabled me to have my own kitchen back, which brings me onto my next project."

Tim gave her an enquiring, puzzled look, he'd originally come here today thinking this would be his last visit, but maybe not.

"Would you mind, if you have the time, looking at my kitchen? I've a few ideas and I would appreciate your professional opinion."

"Let's go take a look," he said, eager to hear what she had in mind.

Nearly two hours later Tim climbed back into his truck, he had a good idea of what Maria was looking for and was keen to get back to the office to put pen to paper and recreate some of the ideas they'd discussed.

He'd also spent a short time listening to Kim's ideas, but like he explained, it was difficult to make any suggestions without having seen her property. Kim promised to speak to David then she would be able to arrange a proper meeting.

As they said their goodbyes to Tim, both sisters were left with a lot to think about.

"What do you think of his suggestions?" Kim said, breaking into her sister's thoughts.

"I like the sound of it all," she admitted. "Although it's a lot more than I originally planned, so it does depend on the cost. What about you?"

"Well, as he said, he hasn't seen our house, but once he mentioned an 'island' I was sold." Kim laughed. "It's not just up to me though, it must be agreeable to David as well." Kim paused for a minute; she had a guilty conscience. "I must admit I do feel bad now discussing it with Tim first. David would be really hurt if he found out. Anyway I'm going to broach the subject with him tonight."

"Don't worry, Tim wouldn't let you down," Maria assured her sister. "Not that they're likely to meet anywhere before the meeting."

"No, that's true," Kim agreed, relieved for that, at least.

Maria was just as excited about the prospect of Kim's new kitchen as she was her own, although in case she couldn't afford it she was trying to contain herself until Tim had time to send through the quote.

"Goodness look at the time," Maria said, suddenly realising exactly how long they'd been chatting with Tim. "I must get back to work. Julie will be wondering what on earth has happened to me."

Kim had other plans. "Do you think it would be ok for me to finish up now?"

"You never have to ask, you know that," Maria assured her. "But you're not going anywhere until you tell me why," she added, teasing her sister.

"I thought I'd get the supper ready early, that way we'll have more time to talk." She was worried how David may react; he never appeared to notice anything around the house. "I have absolutely no idea what he'll have to say. I'm guessing he'll say it's a waste of money."

"You never know, he may surprise you," Maria said giving her sister a big hug. "I've got my fingers crossed for you. Now go home and get your supper ready." She passed Kim her coat and ushered her out the door.

***

Back at the office Tim immediately began work on Maria's quote. He'd been given the impression there was a definite ceiling point to the budget; with that in mind, he was going to have to engage Andy's help. He was by far the best at haggling and practically always managed to get excellent discounts. Whilst Tim was busy transferring his ideas onto his laptop, it crossed his mind whether he should tell Andy who the quotes were for. At the end of the day, knowing Andy as he did, it wouldn't make any difference, he would always do his utmost for anyone. Tim looked up and gazed into mid-air; his mind had temporarily drifted away from his kitchen design. It would be so much easier for everyone, he thought, if these two would sort themselves out. A couple of hours later, completely satisfied with his work so far, Tim closed his laptop for the day. He was going to be late home tonight, but Lisa wouldn't mind once she knew who the work was for. She was desperate to make amends to Maria. They hadn't spoken since Lisa had practically blamed Maria for Tim's accident. It had been purely out of shock and worry that she'd lashed out. It was just a shame, he thought to himself, she chose Maria as her victim. Tim switched off the lights and locked the office. All he needed now was some good deals courtesy of Andy and he could send off the quote, but that was a job for tomorrow.

***

Kim prepared one of David's favourites for their supper: Shepherd's pie with lashings of grated cheese melted over the mashed potato. It smelt delicious as she carefully placed it in the centre of the table. It was just the two of them tonight, the "Kids" were both away at university and although they missed them both, they were also enjoying the peace and quiet.

"What are we celebrating?" David said as he sat down to enjoy his meal.

"Is it that obvious?" Kim asked as she poured the wine.

"It's not your birthday," he said frowning. "It's definitely not my birthday. I'm pretty sure it's not our wedding anniversary." He looked at his wife for confirmation.

"No, it's not our wedding anniversary." She laughed. "We're not really celebrating anything as such," she admitted.

"If we're not celebrating, what have you done, Kim?" David asked quite obviously troubled. "Please tell me it's not the car."

"Don't worry I haven't damaged the car," she confirmed. "Let's just eat then I'll tell you." Kim was beginning to lose her confidence; already it wasn't going quite as she'd planned.

"You'll have to give me a clue, otherwise I'm not going to enjoy this wonderful meal you've prepared," David said uneasily.

Kim placed a rather large helping of Shepherd's pie in front of her husband and sat down opposite.

"I've had an idea for a while now," she began, "and I've been saving all my wages."

"I've noticed that." David was quick to acknowledge.

"Well, I haven't got enough to pay for it all yet, but I was rather hoping if you like my idea, you will help me pay for it."

"What on earth is it that you want to do?" David asked as he took a rather large sip of wine.

"I'd like a new kitchen," Kim said very quickly.

David couldn't conceal his utter relief, for one moment he'd been worried.

"What did you think I was going to say?" Kim asked witnessing his sigh of pure relief.

"I have no idea." He was telling a little white lie, but he didn't want to give her any ideas, she had enough of her own.

"Well," Kim said waiting for his response.

"Let's eat first," David said. He needed a little time to mull this over, he honestly couldn't see the reasoning behind this; their kitchen was perfectly functionable as it was, surely the money would be better spent on a new car or a couple of luxury holidays.

"I know what you're doing," Kim said looking directly at her husband, "you're playing for time."

"As if." He laughed. How was it Kim always knew what he was thinking, it was most infuriating, he clearly, never had a clue what was going on in her mind.

***

Lisa could never really settle until she heard Tim's truck pull up outside, then it was all systems go to prepare their evening meal.

"Something smells good," Tim said as he walked into the kitchen.

"It'll be about another ten minutes." Lisa turned from the hob to look at her husband, who she noted was looking extremely pleased with himself. "What's happened?" she asked. "You look very smug."

"We haven't won the lottery, so don't get too excited," he began as he retrieved an ice-cold beer from the fridge. "But

I think I'm probably about to get another commission from Maria and maybe even one from her sister."

Lisa had been fully aware that Tim was due to meet with Maria today, but she'd made up her mind not to enquire how it went. Last time Maria's name had come up in conversation they'd ended up arguing; she wasn't going down that road again.

"How come?" she answered, trying not to sound too interested.

"Maria is interested in a few changes to her kitchen," Tim began to explain as he perched on a kitchen stool. "To be honest some parts of it took a real bashing when she used it for her business. Anyway I came up with a few ideas and she asked for a quote." He flicked through the post that Lisa had left out for him. "I'm hopeful we'll get the job if the price is right."

"And for Kim?" she asked as she placed their plates in the oven to warm before serving.

"She hasn't actually spoken to David yet, but she wants walls taken down. She wants the whole package, but we'll have to wait and see on that one."

Lisa smiled to herself. She hoped Maria would respond kindly to her message that she'd sent earlier. Lisa knew she had been unfairly "offhand" with Maria, practically insinuating it was her fault Tim had been involved in an accident. Originally, she'd thought Maria had put too much pressure on Tim during the conversion work, and he hadn't been concentrating, but as the details unfolded and Tim was exonerated of all blame, she realised she'd been wrong. Now was the time to apologise and hopefully move on.

**

Andy checked his phone and messages before he left home the next morning. There was only one message and that was from Tim. He listened intently.

"Andy mate, can you pop into the office first thing? I just need your expertise on a few matters."

Andy couldn't help grinning, he knew exactly what that meant; he needed a couple of good discounts for someone. He wondered who it was for this time.

Tim looked up from his laptop as Andy walked through the door. "Thanks, mate, for coming in, I appreciate it."

"That's ok, we're all on track up at Orchard House, and Joe has enough work to be getting on with until I arrive, so how can I help?" He sat down at his desk directly opposite Tim.

"I've got a new quote. This is the list of the expensive stuff that I'd like to use, but only if you can get me a good price."

"Another kitchen?" Andy asked looking at the list Tim had written out. "When did this come in." He couldn't remember seeing any emails relating to a new kitchen.

Recalling Lisa's words encouraging him to be totally honest with Andy, he decided for once, to take her advice. "It's for Maria." Tim watched for a reaction, but Andy was difficult to read on this subject, and he had no idea what was going through his mind.

If the truth be told, Andy wasn't thinking anything much, he knew without any doubt he wouldn't be asked to complete the work, so it wasn't going to make any difference to him. None of that would prevent him from trying his best to get some good deals though, and he picked up the phone ready to haggle.

***

Kim arrived early to work the next day; she was eager to see Maria and tell her the news. Excitedly she made her way straight into "The Bakery" to find her sister.

"Are you ok?" Maria asked as she looked up. She had been deep in conversation with Julie discussing their plan of action for the day. She was surprised; it was unusual for Kim to be in this early.

"Have you got a minute?" Kim sounded anxious.

"I won't be a minute, Julie," Maria excused herself. "Come on then, spill the beans," Maria encouraged her sister as she led

189

her back into the house. "What's going on? You've obviously got something exciting to tell me."

"David has agreed that Tim can come round and give us some ideas and quotes." She was beaming and could no longer conceal her delight. "I can't actually believe it myself yet."

"That's fantastic, how did you swing that?" Maria knew that Kim would have had her work cut out; David liked a clean house, but he wasn't bothered if it was up to date. As far as he was concerned all a kitchen needed to do was fulfil a purpose.

"Well, it took a while and a couple of bottles of wine." Kim laughed. "I have everything pinned on Tim's art of persuasion to seal the deal. I'm going to send him an email straight away and get a time arranged. I need to strike while the iron's hot; if I leave it too long David will talk himself out of it and change his mind."

"I'll be interested to see what ideas he comes up with for you," Maria said, excited for her sister. "He's got a very good imagination."

"I'll let you know when he's coming. It would be great if you came over as well, I'll need all the support I can get." She laughed as she literally skipped up the stairs to her office.

A few hours later, Tim emailed a few dates when he would be able to look at Kim's kitchen layout and have a chat about plans going forward. He also enclosed a quote for the proposed work on Maria's kitchen, which Kim printed off anxious to show her sister.

For the second time that morning Kim burst into "The Bakery" and whisked Maria away. Louise, naturally a very inquisitive person, looked over at her sister who was busy measuring ingredients. "What do you think is going on now?"

Julie just laughed and shrugged her shoulders.

"You know something don't you? Why can't you just tell me?" Louise asked her sister with a hint of annoyance.

"I don't know for certain; I'm literally putting two and two together," Julie answered, as she packed away some of the ingredients she'd finished with.

"Please feel free to expand on your last comment," Louise said as she waited patiently for her sister to continue.

"Maria mentioned that she was thinking about having her kitchen redecorated and maybe renewing a few things; I'm just assuming it could be about that, but I could well be wrong," Julie admitted as she added all the remaining ingredients to her mixing bowl.

"Oh, I was hoping for something a little juicier than redecorating the kitchen," Louise mumbled. "It seems an awful lot of secrecy for something so mundane. You sure that's all you know?"

"Positive," Julie answered as she started the mixer.

Realising she wasn't going to get any more information from her sister, Louise returned her attention back to her order book. Over the last few months, she had taken over reordering all the basic ingredients. Well, she would write the order in the book and send it upstairs to Kim who would place the order and return the book with the date the order was due; it all seemed to be working perfectly well and Louise enjoyed a little bit of extra responsibility.

Kim ushered her sister back inside the main house before beginning to explain.

"I've got your quote." She handed the printout to Maria. "I've also got some dates that Tim can come over to look at our kitchen. I'd really like you to be there as well, so we'll have to work out between the three of us when would be the best time."

Maria took the paper from her sister and read the figures that Tim had submitted. "This can't be right," Maria said shaking her head in disbelief.

"I know, that's exactly what I thought," Kim agreed "Do you think he's made a mistake?"

"I think he must have," Maria said as she read through the quote for the second time. "Can you email Tim and just get him to clarify this is correct?"

"I can, but wouldn't it be quicker to give him a quick ring?"

"I suppose," Maria said already excited. If this was in fact the real price, it was well within her budget and would literally transform her kitchen.

"Before you ring him," Kim said, breaking her train of thought, "look at these dates, would you be able to make any of these?"

Tim had suggested three dates all in the evening; one was for tomorrow, the others were next week.

"I can do any of those," Maria said. "Just let me know what you decide."

"If that's the case, I'll speak to him after you and tell him tomorrow night."

Tim put the phone down after speaking with both Maria and Kim and sighed with relief. Andy had secured some excellent prices for Maria's kitchen but there'd been a clause; they would have to place the order straight away. So after a very quick discussion they'd agreed to take a gamble and, luckily, it had worked in their favour. Maria had been more than happy and had instantly accepted the quote. He'd also arranged with Kim to visit her and David tomorrow evening. Making a mental note of Kim's earlier requirements Tim realised that with all the structural work she'd mentioned, it would be beneficial to them all to have Andy on site for their meeting. He was by far more experienced in this area; all Tim had to do was ask him.

"Sorry, mate, I know you're busy," Tim began as Andy answered his phone. "I thought I'd let you know; we got the job. Maria has just confirmed."

"That's great," Andy said balancing his phone between his neck and chin as he tried to continue mixing up the next batch of cement.

"Also," Tim continued, "Kim has requested a meeting tomorrow night, to discuss possibilities for her new kitchen, but as she's talking about taking walls down etc., I was wondering if you'd come along as well."

"That's fine," Andy agreed. "Let me know the time and her address and I'll meet you there."

It wasn't until Tim pulled up outside Kim's house the following evening and saw Maria's car parked outside that he began to panic. At no time had it even entered his head that it would be a problem bringing Andy along. Admittedly he hadn't mentioned it to Kim, but then why would he? As far as he was concerned this meeting had absolutely nothing to do with Maria.

Tim was still sitting in his truck deciding the best course of action when Andy pulled up behind Maria's car. He'd been a million miles away and it made him jump when Andy knocked on his window.

"Are you ok, Tim?" Andy said peering through the window.

"Yes, mate, I'm fine," Tim said as he got out of his truck, now wasn't the time for explaining, he'd take his chances and brave it out.

David spotted them both walking up the drive. This was going to be interesting, he thought as he walked towards the front door.

"Kim," David called out, "Tim and Andy are here." He emphasised their names, keen to give both Kim and Maria plenty of warning before he let them in.

Immediately the sisters stopped chatting and stared at one another. "I didn't know, honestly. Tim never mentioned anything about bringing Andy along; truly I had absolutely no idea," Kim said, keen to dispel any ideas Maria may have that this was some sort of set up.

"It's ok," Maria began. "I'll leave through the back door; they won't even realise I was here." Maria grabbed her handbag from the table just as David showed both the men into the kitchen.

Trying not to appear too awkward, Kim welcomed them both and Maria decided to continue with her exit and make it brief.

"Nice to see you both," she managed to say quite charmingly, "but I'm just leaving, so it's hello and goodbye." Before she could say another word David interrupted.

"Don't go yet, Maria. I was banking on you for support; I have a feeling I'm going to need an ally." He smiled and raised his eyebrows, hoping she would take the hint. He'd noticed Andy had parked right behind Maria, effectively blocking her exit, and realising the potential issues decided to take matters into his own hands.

Maria gave David one of her looks, what was he playing at? She couldn't read him, but she had a feeling he was trying to tell her something. "Well, if you put it like that, how can I refuse?" She smiled in acknowledgement and David returned her smile, relieved she'd taken the hint. "Looks like I'm staying." She laughed as she pulled out a kitchen stool and made herself comfortable. Tim, who was keen to get down to business, had already laid out some plans, and Andy was already busy inspecting the wall he presumed was to be taken down. This gave David the opportunity to whisper to Maria.

"Sorry but you wouldn't be able to get out; Andy has blocked you in. I thought it might save a lot of hassle if you just stayed put."

Maria smiled at her brother-in-law, realising now that he might have saved her from an embarrassing close encounter.

It wasn't too long before they were all fully engrossed listening to Tim and Andy, whose ideas were flowing in abundance. Maria had to admit, they made a great team, and she was surprisingly impressed with Andy; he was just as good as Tim and obviously far more knowledgeable when it came to structural matters. She couldn't help wondering how this had all come about. D.I.Y. had never been his strongest attribute; she couldn't help a sly smile escaping as she remembered some of the antics in getting a picture hung on the wall. He'd absolutely hated anything to do with tools. She wondered what had changed in his life to go from selling cars to becoming an equal partner in a very successful refurbishment business. There was so much she didn't know.

Eventually Kim and David whittled down all the ideas to one they were both happy with. Kim had secured her dream of an "island" with an open plan kitchen diner, and David, who was anxious for it to remain in keeping with the rest of the house, he wasn't interested in any highly polished shiny surfaces, was happy with Tim's idea of wooden cabinets in a soft cream colourway, and wooden flooring throughout.

As the two men worked quickly, packing away all their plans and samples, Kim realised she hadn't even offered them a drink.

"I'm so sorry, I haven't offered you a drink, can I get you something before you leave?"

"That's really kind," Tim was the first to reply, "but I really must make a move."

"Another time," Andy added.

"Definitely." Kim smiled, acknowledging they both probably wanted to get home for their supper.

"I'll show you out," David offered as they finished collecting the last bits and pieces.

"I'll get a quote out to you by end of play tomorrow," Tim explained as he said his goodbyes.

"That's great, thank you so much for your time this evening and for yours as well Andy," Kim said, genuinely grateful. "I really appreciate you both coming over; it's been very informative and extremely entertaining," she added, laughing as David walked them both to the front door.

"I'm really sorry about that," Tim said as he turned to look at Andy who had already reached his truck. "It wasn't a setup, or anything like that, I genuinely had no idea Maria was going to be here."

Andy opened his truck ready to climb in. "Don't worry about it," he said shrugging. "I recognised her car, that's why I blocked her in."

Tim frowned. "So, she couldn't leave, or am I missing something?"

"I was rather hoping she would leave, then I'd have to come out at the same time to move my truck."

"What would that achieve?"

"I have absolutely no idea," Andy confessed. "It was a bit irrational I suppose, anyway, I'll see you in the morning," he said as he climbed into his truck and drove away.

"That wasn't too bad, was it?" Kim turned her attention to her sister who she noted had sat very quietly listening and watching.

"Not at all," Mara admitted. "I think you're going to have a kitchen out of this world; they both have some incredible ideas."

David walked back into the kitchen and put his arm gently around his sister-in-law.

"Are you ok? I'm sorry about all that, it just seemed the easiest option."

"Yes, I'm fine, honestly no problem at all," Maria assured her brother-in- law.

"Why, what happened?" Kim asked, realising she had no idea what they were talking about.

Maria quickly explained why she'd decided to stay. "But now I'm definitely going to make a move," she declared.

"Oh, don't go yet," Kim pleaded. "I was going to order a takeaway, I don't feel like cooking, stay and eat with us. Please."

"If, you're sure." Maria said looking from one to the other.

"Definitely," Kim confirmed. "It's the least we can do, after you had to sit through all that."

"It really doesn't matter; it was just one of those things," Maria professed. "I can see why Tim brought Andy along though, can't you?"

"Definitely," David said as he reached for his coat and car keys, ready to collect their takeaway. "I think he was far more knowledgeable than Tim in all the structural issues."

"I think so as well," Maria replied as both her sister and brother-in-law looked at one another and smiled.

***

Lisa had eventually received a light-hearted reply from Maria, who had completely ignored her suggestion to meet. Not being one to give up easily, Lisa decided, as Tim was going to be late home, she'd try one more time to arrange a lunch or evening meeting between the three of them. First though, she thought to herself, she really should just check some dates with Karen.

"To be honest, Lisa, I don't know if I can be bothered," Karen admitted to her friend. "Don't get me wrong I've always got on ok with Maria, but this Andy saga, I really don't have the time for it all. It's pathetic, what happened between them was a long time ago; it's about time she moved on. Well, that's how I see it," Karen concluded.

"I can see where you're coming from, I really can, I just don't want any bad feeling. She's just given Tim another big job and potentially another one from her sister as well."

"Meeting up with us isn't going to make any difference to any of that is it?" Karen was surprised at this change of heart from Lisa. It wasn't that long ago she was blaming her for Tim's accident, and now she wanted to arrange a lunch or dinner. "What if she's just not interested?" Karen asked her friend.

"Well then I've tried," Lisa answered, "but if she agrees can I count you in?"

"Ok, if you want," Karen finally agreed, she had more important family issues of her own to deal with and didn't have the energy to continue this conversation.

Lisa wasted no time and immediately sent an email to Maria suggesting a lunch or dinner and even went as far as suggesting a couple of dates.

It wasn't until much later that evening when Maria put her phone on charge, she noticed she had a couple of messages. The first message was from Clare, she was just confirming Jon's birthday dinner that she'd been planning and wanted to make sure Maria hadn't forgotten. Instantly Maria felt guilty; she hadn't forgotten, and she should have made the time to speak with her sister. Currently though time just seemed to fly by, but that was no excuse, and she made a mental note to call her back tomorrow.

The second message was from Lisa. Maria was surprised; she'd only heard from her about a week ago. Maria shook her head as she read the message. Lisa didn't change at all, once she had an idea she kept on and on. Deliberately Maria had ignored her previous request to meet and here she was again, keen to get a date in the diary for either a lunch or dinner. It was strange really, the three of them had been such good friends when they were younger, but now she wasn't sure if she could be that bothered with either of them. Reprimanding herself immediately for her lack of compassion, she put her phone down. She would reply, but not tonight. She was tired, and tomorrow was another day.

With everything ready for Maria's refurbishment, a date had been set giving her just over a week to get herself organised. It wasn't a huge project, but it was still going to incur a lot of dust, and aware of how lovely she kept the rest of her house, Tim had been quick to reassure her that he would contain the working area as best as possible. Although Maria hadn't made any stipulations this time, Tim had been quick to make it very clear it would be himself and Joe that would complete the work. Anyway, as far as he was concerned, Andy would be starting the work at Kim's at a similar time, pending the arrival of all the equipment.

***

Maria had gladly accepted Clare's offer to stay over for the evening of Jon's birthday meal. Kim and David, though, had decided to drive home as they still had a lot of work: clearing their kitchen and making a temporary set up in the study with a portable electric oven and the microwave.

Maria had offered to bring a selection of desserts and a birthday cake and Clare had gratefully accepted. She wanted the evening to be special for Jon; he always made so much effort for her birthday and now it was her turn. By the time Maria arrived, late-afternoon, Clare wished she'd just booked a nice restaurant. She'd been busy for the most part of the day and was still knee deep in vegetable preparation.

"Where's Jon?" Maria asked as Clare opened the door looking very flustered.

"I've sent him for a game of golf with a couple of his friends," she said welcoming her sister.

"Ok, well just let me fetch my overnight bag from the car and I'll help you."

"You did bring a cake and the desserts?" Clare asked panicking that Maria hadn't mentioned either.

"Of course," Maria reassured her sister. "Don't panic, all will be revealed in a minute."

Maria took her overnight bag straight up to the guest bedroom. Clare had a beautiful house, completely different to Maria's. Clare loved "Olde Worlde" with chintzy fabrics and thick piled carpets. Her fetish with lamps was evident; she had them everywhere. Maria opened the door to the bedroom and giggled when she saw the vase of fresh flowers. Clare always made sure she had fresh flowers in her room when she came to stay. Quickly she hung her dress for the evening and returned downstairs to rescue her sister in the kitchen.

"I'm desperate to see what you've brought," Clare said, looking up as her sister came to join her in the kitchen.

"I tried to incorporate everything you told me Jon really liked," Maria explained. "Are you ready for the big reveal?" she teased her sister.

"I most certainly am," Clare answered cheerfully.

"Ok, well here we go." She smiled and taking the first box she carefully removed dessert number one. "Here we have individual lemon and champagne posset, especially for those who prefer something light."

"Gosh, Maria, they look amazing," Clare said while taking a closer look.

"Thank you," Maria said as she carefully unpacked box number two. "Here we have 'old-fashioned trifle', it's bursting with fresh fruit, and I used cream in the custard to make it extra indulgent."

"Goodness, Maria, I could eat a dish of that now. It looks delicious, and so deep. How many layers?" Clare asked trying to count.

"Quite a few," Maria agreed as she carefully revealed dessert number three. "Here we have a chocolate and coconut banoffee pie. I've used bourbon biscuits for the base. I know those are Jon's favourite. Finally," she continued, "we have the classic birthday cake, as requested, with Genoese sponge, a buttercream and raspberry jam filling and completely covered in soft icing."

"Wow, honestly, Maria, you've included everything I suggested. Jon isn't going to know what to try first, nor will the rest of us." Clare was amazed, she'd tried Maria's desserts and cakes before, but these showstoppers were a whole different league. Now she could see why her business was going from strength to strength.

"I need to get the desserts into the fridge," Maria mentioned, slightly embarrassed with her sister's obvious gratitude. "Is there room?"

"I think you should be ok, although you will have to move the shelves to get that trifle in."

Maria placed the desserts carefully in the fridge and decorated the cake with candles ready for later. Between the two of them they quickly finished the food preparation and transferred their efforts to the dining room, where they set about laying the table using Clare's best crockery and her finest cut glasses.

"It all looks very grand," Maria said admiring the room.

"Too much?" Clare asked anxiously, as she placed the red wine next to the decanters she had chosen to use for tonight.

"Not at all, it looks wonderful," Maria assured her sister. "Come on let's have a well-earned drink before we get ready."

"Good idea, what do you fancy?" Clare asked as the two of them made their way into the living room.

"I could murder a gin," Maria admitted, flopping herself into a chair.

"Gin it is then." Clare smiled.

Kim was beyond excited and was busy packing all the samples she'd requested from Tim into a large holdall.

"Surely, you're not taking all that to Clare's, are you?" David enquired while watching his wife tick off each item from her list.

"Clare wants to see them," she explained, looking over to her husband who was still deciding what colour shirt to wear. "The blue one," Kim suggested as she took her holdall and left him to it.

***

"I don't think I can actually move," Jon said as he pushed his plate to one side to make room for his coffee.

"I'm not surprised," Clare quickly responded. "You've had three desserts and a piece of birthday cake."

"I only had a small piece of banoffee pie," Jon explained in his own defence.

They all laughed, it had been a fun evening with extraordinary amounts of food and wine but now feeling very tired, David was keen to leave. It wasn't the alcohol, he was the designated driver and would never drink and drive, but he had overindulged with all the delicious food and was feeling tired and uncomfortably hot.

"I'm sorry to break up the party," he said regrettably, "but I think we should be making a move soon." He looked directly at Kim and smiled.

"Are you ok?" Kim was quick to ask, as she noticed how tired her husband suddenly looked.

"I'm fine, just begun to feel a bit tired that's all," he reassured her.

"You're both very welcome to stay over," Clare offered, feeling sorry for David having to drive home.

"Thank you," David said politely as he stood, pushing his chair back from the table. "I'll be fine once I get going."

"It's been a wonderful evening," Kim said giving her sister a big hug. "Thank you so much."

"You're very welcome, and I just love all your choices for the new kitchen, it's going to look amazing when it's complete."

"Oh, that reminds me, I've left my bag of samples in the sitting room," Kim said hurrying off to find them.

"Please send a quick message when you get home," Clare insisted as they said their goodbyes.

"Will do," Kim called from the car as they drove away.

"Give them 45 minutes and they should be home," Maria said, checking her watch as the three of them made their way back to the dining room to finish their coffee and brandy. She couldn't help feeling concerned; David didn't look too good when they left. She'd be glad when they were safely home.

Exactly 48 minutes later Clare's phone bleeped with notification of a message.

"They're home," she announced as she read the message.

"Thank goodness for that," Maria exclaimed, sighing with relief. "David had me worried for a while, I thought he might be feeling unwell."

"He's very careful though isn't he?" Clare remarked as they all carried plates and dishes back to the kitchen. "He wouldn't take any unnecessary chances; I don't think he would have driven if he wasn't well," Clare said as she carefully stacked the dishes.

Maria packed the dishwasher for the second time that evening, while Clare handwashed all her crystal glasses and Jon polished each one until it gleamed. Eventually, the kitchen was clean and tidy and feeling very full and tired Maria was grateful to fall straight into the big comfy bed waiting for her upstairs.

As Kim finished sending a message to Clare, she heard David call her from upstairs.

"What is it?" she called from the bottom of the stairs.

"Can you come here a minute? I seem to have a weird rash coming up on my arms and legs."

Kim rushed up the stairs two at a time. "Oh, my goodness, David, what on earth is it?" Kim was horrified; she could literally see the rash spreading from the wrist upwards covering the whole arm.

"I have no idea, but it's really itchy and my lips have begun to tingle, and they feel like they're swelling." David looked panicked as he continued to examine his face in the mirror.

"How do you feel?" Kim asked feeling extremely concerned.

"I don't know, a bit weird I think."

202

Kim rushed into the bedroom and carried a chair back into the bathroom. "Sit here a minute, I'm going to ring 111."

"It sounds like your husband is experiencing an allergic reaction," the N.H.S. advisor kindly explained, having listened carefully to Kim's explanation of David's ailments. "I'm going to send an ambulance immediately. Please stay on the line; I'll come straight back to you."

Kim waited nervously for her to return.

"The ambulance is on its way," the advisor spoke calmly and directly. "How is your husband now?"

"About the same, I think."

"Can you just confirm that his tongue is still not swollen?" the advisor asked.

"Hang on a minute," Kim said turning her attention back to her husband. "David are you sure your tongue is not swollen?" she asked worriedly.

"I don't think so," David managed to say through his swollen lips.

"He doesn't think so," Kim relayed, "although his lips are now very swollen."

"Please don't worry, the ambulance will be with you very soon; can you make sure the front door is open when they arrive?"

"I'll go and open it straight away," Kim said, hurrying down the stairs. She opened the front door just as the ambulance pulled onto the drive.

"It's my husband; he's upstairs in the bathroom," Kim explained as two paramedics made their way into the house and straight up the stairs.

Less than two hours later, David was sat upright in the emergency department having already received one dose of epinephrine (adrenaline).

"You have definitely had what looks like an allergic reaction. Have you eaten any shellfish within the last eight hours?" the young doctor asked, busily writing up his notes.

"Yes, I've eaten lobster salad this evening."

"Have you had any reactions to shellfish before?"

"No, never," David answered honestly.

"Ok, well we need to see how this medication reacts for you." The doctor hung the clip board back on the end of the bed.

"Can I go home now?" David asked the doctor as he was about to leave.

"I'm afraid not, we need to see a significant reduction in the swelling before we would even consider sending you home." He smiled at David. "Are you comfortable?"

"Yes." David nodded, unable to hide his disappointment that he was now going to have to wait a considerable time, judging by the size of his lips.

Kim pulled her chair closer to the bed as the doctor left. "Go home and get some rest, I'll be fine," David said as he acknowledged how tired his wife looked. "It could take a while for any significant reduction. Look at me, I could possibly be here all night."

"I'm not leaving you." Kim was defiant. "The nurse said I was welcome to stay, anyway, she's given me this form to fill in. I've got to list everything you've eaten in the last 12 hours." She looked at her husband and smiled. "This isn't going to be enough paper; I'll need twice this amount listing everything you've consumed."

"Cheeky." David tried to smile, but instead just laid his head back onto the pillows.

It was nearly Sunday lunchtime before Kim was allowed to take her husband home. The first thing she did was let both the kids know they were home, and their dad was going to be fine. The second call was to Maria; there was no way David was going to work in the morning and she wanted to stay home with him, just in case.

"Do you know," Maria began, "I just knew there was something not quite right, but once you'd sent the message saying you were home, I presumed everything was ok. I can't believe you both spent the night in the hospital."

"I know, but there wasn't anything you could have done, so I didn't see the point of disturbing you," Kim explained to her sister.

"Don't even think of coming into work until David is a hundred per cent better, however long it takes," Maria insisted.

"Thanks," Kim said feeling extremely tired.

"Did they give you any indication exactly what it was that caused the allergic reaction?" Maria was concerned that she hadn't given David anything that had caused so much distress.

"Yes. It was the lobster, but please don't tell Clare; she'll take it personally."

"I won't say anything, but she will find out; she always does."

"I know, but I'd just rather wait until we've got more definite answers. I mean David has always eaten shellfish; he's never had a reaction like this before."

"I understand, now remember I don't want to see you back to work until David is better."

"Thank you I really appreciate that," Kim said, now desperate to join her husband who was tucked up on the sofa relaxing.

***

After some careful consideration, Maria decided that she really didn't want any bad feeling between her old friends. With recent events uppermost in her mind, she realised you never knew what was around the corner, so she messaged Lisa suggesting that if they were interested in seeing her new "Bakery" and her new kitchen they were very welcome to come to hers for lunch. It would, however, mean they would have to wait until Tim had finished the work, but that only meant postponing by a few weeks. She couldn't see that being a real problem. Maria wrote a friendly message and pressed send; now it was up to the two of them, they could decide between them if they were interested or not.

Although she would never say, Maria missed Kim considerably. She was always so organised; every morning, like clockwork, she would print off any orders that had come in overnight, discuss enquiries, pay suppliers, confirm orders, and continually update their social media platforms. But Maria recognised this episode had taken its toll on them both and had absolutely insisted Kim take the whole week off. Tim had also been extremely considerate and had agreed to put back the start of their refurbishment by a week. That at least took the pressure off that particular issue.

Maria made herself comfortable at Kim's desk and scrolled through the emails. There were a few enquiries requiring prices, a few she decided were a waste of time and then one that caught her eye. The bride to be that had previously requested the four-tier sponge cake and the cake of cheese, was now enquiring if they would be prepared to supply, additionally, the favours that she would like for each guest. Maria sat transfixed looking at the email. She hadn't met this woman. She remembered now she'd had her last appointment at the hospital the same time the bride had requested her first meeting. She stared at the name at the bottom of the email. "Kind Regards Samantha Porter." It had to be the same person. Obviously Kim hadn't registered the name, and she wouldn't have recognised her. Maria didn't think Kim had ever met her, not that she looked the same now obviously. Maria printed off the email. She'd speak to Julie, she was always full of exciting new ideas, and then they'd get some prices off to her. She folded the email and popped it into her pocket. She couldn't wait to see Kim's reaction to this.

By mid-week Julie could see Maria was really feeling the pressure. They were up against it with a big order and spending time in the office sorting out paperwork wasn't really in the plan. Julie, however, thought she might have the answer. "You should offer to help Maria with all the office side of things," she encouraged her sister. "You always put yourself down," she continued as she saw her sister frown. "Before you had the kids you worked in an office, you know the score."

"I know, but I don't have any actual qualifications to prove my worth."

"I know but you have experience. Anyway, Maria's not the sort to dismiss you just because you don't have a paper certificate." Julie raised her eyes to meet her sister's. "Why don't you go and speak with her now? I could really do with her back in here with me, rather than spending time in the office."

"Shall I?" Louise sounded nervous.

"Definitely, now go," Julie said waving her arms in the direction of the door.

Maria was pleasantly surprised to see how proficient Louise appeared to be; she was incredibly fast at typing, and it didn't take her very long to decipher and work her way around Kim's systems.

"You're a dark horse," Maria said, absolutely delighted to be leaving the office to someone else. "I had no idea you were so talented. What on earth are you doing working here? You're overqualified for the job."

Louise was suddenly worried. "I love my job here; the hours are just right for me with young children."

"Oh, don't worry," Maria quickly reassured her. "I wouldn't want to lose you." She touched her shoulder affectionately. "I'll leave you to it, call me if you need anything."

"I'll do these four enquiries that you've priced up first, then if you check them, I'll get them off," Louise confirmed as Maria turned to leave.

"Great." Maria smiled and made her way back to "The Bakery".

It had been an exceptionally busy week and by Friday evening Maria couldn't believe they'd managed to complete all their orders on time. All that was left to do on Saturday morning was complete some icing decoration for a birthday cake that was due for collection later that afternoon. This would leave Sunday free to clear her kitchen ready for Tim on Monday morning. Louise had been amazing and had managed to keep up to date with all the enquiries. She'd entered all the purchase invoices and kept the diary updated, making sure they didn't overlap on big orders. Maria knew Kim would be surprised to find that she didn't have too much to catch up with on her return, and Maria would be pleased to have Louise back; she was an integral part of the operation in "The Bakery" and they missed her being around.

By nine o'clock on Monday morning, Maria's kitchen was completely out of bounds to everyone apart from Tim and Joe. Thick plastic sheeting secured each integral doorway to prevent the spread of dust; it was a good effort but a thin film of the pesty stuff still managed to filter through daily. Luckily, Maria had the foresight to move some of her general bits and pieces into "The Bakery," so she would at least be able to use these facilities to prepare her food. It was far from ideal, but it was better than not, and the inconvenience would all be worth it when her new kitchen was finally complete.

Realising Maria's kitchen would now be out of bounds, Kim stopped off on her way to work to pick up a couple of cappuccinos; at least this way, she thought to herself, she had an excuse to get Maria to sit and go through all the events of the past week.

"Do you want to borrow my headphones?" Maria joked as she sat down opposite her sister in the office. "Are you going to be able to concentrate with all this noise?"

"I'll be fine, Tim did say it might be a bit noisy for the first couple of days, I am prepared." Kim pulled open her handbag and held up her earplugs. "I was a girl guide don't forget." Both sisters burst out laughing, Maria in utter relief to have Kim back to work and Kim in relief that all was well, and David had returned to work.

Maria unfolded the email she had printed off last week and handed it to her sister.

"What's this?" Kim said taking the crumpled paper.

"It's from the bride that has requested the four-tier sponge cake and the cake of cheese."

"She's not cancelling, is she?" Kim said grabbing her glasses.

"Far from it," Maria said waiting for Kim to finish reading the email.

"Favours, we haven't been asked for those before." Kim looked up, not quite sure why her sister was looking so amused. "Are you interested?" Kim asked, watching Maria's reaction intently.

"How did you find her?"

"Ok," Kim said realising she was definitely missing something. "She's the teacher, that's why she came so late one afternoon, weren't you at the hospital?"

"Yes," Maria confirmed and not being able to keep her sister guessing any longer continued, "What's her name?"

"Samantha Porter," Kim read out loud immediately registering what she was reading. "How do you know it's the same person?" she exclaimed wide eyed.

"It is, I just know it, how many Samantha Porters do you think there are in this area? And also when Chloe met her in the waiting room, she mentioned that she was busy planning her wedding."

"I'm just trying to remember what she was like," Kim said rereading the email. "She was very polite. I think she had long hair, but I seem to remember it was tied back, not very much make-up, very slim, quite tall. I can't picture her facial features clearly; I was so busy taking notes, gosh I can't believe it."

"That does sound like her, from what I remember when I saw her at the hospital," Maria confirmed.

"Do you think she knows this is your business?" Kim said wondering if this was going to make a difference once she knew.

"I honestly don't know, but I think we should make her aware before we go any further, for both our sakes. If you look further down your list, you'll see we've put together a few ideas and prices, but she hasn't replied to that yet, maybe give her a couple more days and then send her a reminder and sign it off from me; that way she won't be left in any doubt."

"That's fine, I'll do that," Kim said, still stunned at this latest turn of events.

It took another hour to cover all the correspondence and Kim had to admit her head was spinning.

"Thanks for the coffee, good idea to bring one in," Maria said as she stood to leave. "I think I've covered everything; I hope Louise has left it all in order."

"It all seems fine, just hang on a minute and I'll print off today's orders."

Maria took the orders and headed off, pleased to get away from the noise.

Kim sat back in her chair; she hadn't expected to find all her work up to date. Flicking through the emails Louise had sent she couldn't fault them. Clearly she had plenty of experience. She was being silly, she knew that, but she'd been relieved to hear Louise was no longer interested in office work, preferring instead to continue in her work downstairs. Kim opened the diary; business was good. She made a mental note to speak with Maria; she really should pencil in a holiday, although this was going to be easier said than done, but she was adamant. Maria would need a break in the not-too-distant future, they all would. Kim entered a note for herself for the end of the week, not that she thought she'd forget, but still she wrote, "send reminder to S. Porter."

Maria couldn't help herself, every evening when she returned to the house, she took a crafty peek at the work completed so far; she was so excited it was already looking so much better. Tim had great vision, there was no doubt about that. The wall tiles had already been replaced by glass panelling in a deep blue which coordinated with the light grey units, the work surfaces hadn't been fitted yet, and nor had the floor, but Maria could see it was going to look spectacular when complete. She switched off the light and resealed the plastic sheeting. One more week, she thought to herself, and it would probably be finished.

***

Relieved it was finally Friday, Andy emptied his truck for the weekend. He'd just completed a bathroom refurbishment where the couple had been one of the most demanding he'd ever encountered. Eventually he'd had to draw the line and explained as far as he was concerned all the work he had originally quoted for was complete, and from this point on it would involve further charges. From then on, miraculously, all further demands stopped. Andy was nobody's fool; he'd been in this game for too many years, and these two weren't the first to pull a stunt like this. Andy finished off and was just about to lock up when Tim pulled up.

"Do you fancy a quick pint?" Tim asked as he climbed out of his truck.

"Just a quick one then," Andy said checking his watch.

"Have you got a date or something?" Tim asked nosily.

"No." Andy laughed. "I'm having dinner with Sammy later; it's her birthday tomorrow and she's going away, so we're doing birthday celebrations tonight."

"Ok, just a quick one it is then," Tim confirmed jumping back into his truck. "See you there."

The pub was literally about half a mile down the road, so it wasn't too long before the two partners were sat at the bar enjoying their pints. It was a good way to communicate the events of their working week and generally just catch up with one another.

"You can definitely have Joe from first thing Monday," Tim confirmed. "I'll be able to finish off on my own now."

"How's it going?" Andy had given up trying to find a reasonable excuse to call in and see for himself, and maybe even catch a glimpse of Maria. He couldn't help it, he thought about her so much, for him there was unfinished business, and it would be good to be able to sit down and clear the air. Obviously, though, Maria didn't feel the same and maybe he couldn't blame her.

"It's looking really good," Tim answered, aware that for a minute Andy had been completely lost in his own thoughts; he could guess where his mind had wandered. "She certainly knows exactly what she likes, there's no doubt about that," Tim added trying to bring Andy back into the conversation.

Andy smiled but the smile didn't quite reach his eyes and, after a quick general chat, Andy downed his pint and made his way back home; he needed a shower and change of clothes before he met Sammy.

Tim left soon after. He was sorry he'd mentioned Maria's kitchen; he liked Maria, but he would be pleased when the work was finished, and there would be no further reason to mention her name. Hopefully that would be easier for Andy. At first, he'd thought there might be a chance for the two of them. He guessed that's what Andy would like, but as far as he could tell Maria showed no interest at all. Shame, he thought to himself, life was too short to harbour any resentment for this long and he knew he was biased, but Andy really was a genuinely nice guy.

CHAPTER EIGHT

Maria – The Late 1980s – Early 1990s

Andy arrived at work early on Monday morning; he knew he had a couple of deliveries later that afternoon and had allowed plenty of time to catch up before his clients arrived. As Andy stepped inside the building, Ian Kendrick stepped outside his office.

"Morning, boss," Andy said cheerily.

"I'd like a word in my office if you don't mind," his boss replied in a very solemn manner.

"Now?" Andy asked.

Ian Kendrick nodded and held the door open for Andy. It was common knowledge within this company; you were only called into the office for two reasons: one, to discuss salaries, the other a reprimand. Andy guessed he wasn't in line for a pay increase, so braced himself and entered the office.

"Take a seat, Andy, please," Ian Kendrick instructed as he made his way around his desk to his own chair. "Now would you care to enlighten me as to the exact reason you failed to turn up for work on Friday, and more importantly why you obviously felt it completely unnecessary to let me know?" Ian Kendrick looked inquisitively at this young man who appeared to be on a one-man collision course with himself.

Andy looked surprised, but Ian Kendrick took it as a look of disdain and immediately saw red.

"That's if it's not too much trouble," he stated looking directly at Andy.

Honestly, Andy had never seen his boss look so angry. Focusing his attention away from the extremely untidy desk his boss sat behind, he quickly began to explain the course of events, beginning from where he'd finished his message.

"It would be most helpful, Andy," his boss interrupted, "if you started at the beginning, as currently, I have absolutely no idea what you're talking about."

Andy thought his boss was being particularly pedantic, but with no other choice he began with the trip to A&E and continued from there.

"At no time during this period did you feel it necessary to let me know about any of this?" Ian Kendrick asked as he listened to what he thought might be an exaggerated version of events. He watched Andy fidget uncomfortably in the chair. It was a shame, he actually liked this young man, but this wasn't the first time Andy had let him down. Previously he'd always given him the benefit of the doubt, feeling sorry for him and his situation, but this time he felt betrayed and disappointed.

"Like I said," Andy continued realising for whatever reason, Ian Kendrick had not been informed of his message. "As soon as I had the opportunity I rang in. It was early and I knew there wouldn't be any one here, but as we had discussed in the past, when you made it perfectly clear you would prefer I left a message rather than nothing at all, I left a message."

"We never received any such message." Ian Kendrick leant back in his chair and folded his arms. He suspected Andy wasn't being completely truthful; he'd checked and double checked with Jenni, and she had confirmed there'd been no message or call from him at all.

"I'm not lying, I definitely left a message," Andy repeated apprehensively, realising he was probably heading for a final warning.

"Well, someone is not being truthful. I checked with Jenni numerous times during Friday and again before I left for the day."

"I don't understand." Andy shrugged his shoulders. "I know I've let you down in the past, but I assure you, I most certainly left a message."

Andy was persistent, Ian had to give him that, so he leant forward to his phone and with his chubby little finger pressed the button marked "secretary".

"Good morning, Mr. Kendrick." Jenni had heard raised voices coming from her boss's office and guessed it was probably Andy behind the closed door.

"Jenni, would you be so kind to join me in my office straight away please?"

"Of course," Jenni replied, already feeling nervous.

Ian Kendrick released the button and in complete silence they waited. Jenni straightened her skirt and quickly searched her handbag for a tissue, her hands were already clammy. She'd had the worst possible weekend; every moment of the day and night, all she could think about was those two messages she'd accidentally erased, and even now as she gingerly entered her boss's office, she had no idea if she should own up and probably lose her job or carry on with this charade.

***

Fresh challenges awaited Maria who returned to the office on Monday morning, to find the whole office in disarray. A power cut on Friday evening had completely wiped out all the data the girls had entered that day. Maria couldn't understand it, the end of day procedure she had carefully devised for each operative automatically saved all the work entered.

"How long do you think it will take to catch up?" her boss enquired as he walked into her office.

"A couple of days, but that isn't really my main worry," she began to explain as her boss pulled up the chair opposite her desk. "I just don't understand why all Friday's data has been wiped, with the end of day procedure I have in place, it's automatically saved." She was seriously concerned, there was no way this should have happened.

"I don't suppose it's just a case of human error?" her boss enquired. "If the end of day procedure wasn't completed correctly, would that have caused this? Could it just be pure coincidence that we had a power cut?"

"That could be the case," Maria agreed. "But all the girls know that this procedure must be followed before shutting down for the night. They even have to sign off in their diary to prove they've completed the procedure," she explained shaking her head in utter disbelief.

"I suggest you check their diaries then," her boss said as he got up to leave, convinced this was a case of human error rather than, as Maria had initially thought, a computer blip.

Maria decided to give each of her girls the opportunity to be honest and own up, rather than try and catch them out. Inevitably, it meant someone would end up feeling awful, but it would be a relief to know there wasn't a fault in the system.

Maria spoke with each of her girls individually in a separate office, not wanting to embarrass or belittle any of them, and it wasn't long before her boss was proved correct in his assumption and the culprit was identified. Lyndsey was the youngest of the team at just 19 and was completely mortified to learn of her error, offering to work late and full of remorse. Maria couldn't help feeling sorry for her. This could have happened to anyone of them, but at least now they all knew the consequences of not following the end of day procedure, and it could have been so much worse if it hadn't been picked up immediately. By mid-week the office was back on track and on Wednesday evening Maria managed to arrive home before 8pm. In truth she'd been pleased of the distraction, evenings were unquestionably the worst part of the day, but tonight she was so tired that the idea of being alone didn't worry her at all. Armed with a quick T.V. dinner, a glass of wine and a blanket, Maria snuggled down on the sofa. Less than halfway through her meal, Maria reached for the T.V. zapper and reduced the volume slightly. It was as she thought, the phone was ringing in the hallway, goosebumps appeared over her arms, and she felt a shiver run through her body.

Having already spoken to both her sisters and her mum earlier, Maria sat frozen listening to the phone ring and ring.

It could be Lisa, she suddenly thought, but she had a sneaky feeling it wasn't. She'd always known Andy would eventually ring and if it was him, she wasn't strong enough to deal with him yet. So she waited and eventually the answer phone clicked on.

***

After what seemed to Andy an interminable wait, Jenni eventually stood awkwardly in front of her boss. "Can you please confirm," Ian Kendrick spoke with authority, "there were no messages from Andy on Friday morning, or at any other time throughout that day?"

"I can confirm," she said swallowing hard, "there were no messages."

"Thank you, you can return to the switchboard now." Ian Kendrick dismissed her.

Straight away Andy could tell Jenni wasn't answering her boss truthfully. It was as plain as day she was covering for one of her own errors. He knew full well she'd struggled with the switchboard; he'd even helped her out on numerous occasions, now he wished he hadn't bothered.

Flustered, Jenni turned to leave avoiding any eye contact with Andy. She'd had no option; she couldn't afford to lose this job.

The following conversation between the two men left Andy with a lot to think about. By Wednesday, even though it would leave him out of work, Andy recognised he had no choice other than to resign. It was mainly his pride; he sensed his boss had lost confidence in his abilities and if nothing else he knew he was a good salesperson. On Wednesday evening just before his boss left for the evening Andy knocked on his door and waited patiently for him to answer.

"Sorry to disturb you. I wanted you to have this before you left today," Andy said handing his resignation letter directly to his boss before he hurriedly left for the day.

Ian Kendrick reluctantly accepted the letter and guessing its content ripped it open. He read the letter a few times before carefully placing it back in its envelope. The tone of the letter was remorseful and, although Andy didn't accuse Jenni of lying, he continued to maintain that he had most certainly left a message on the Friday in question. Ian Kendrick tucked the letter in his briefcase. He had a lot to consider this evening; he was a father of three himself, so he knew only too well how the unexpected could quite easily happen when you had kids. All he had to do now, was to find out who was telling him the truth. He closed his office door behind him. He noted Andy had already left. He wasn't surprised; he'd had a good day with three confirmed sales before 4pm. There was no denying it, he was by far the best salesperson he had, and he couldn't let him go without finding out a little more about this situation, and there was no time like the present.

"Had a good day, John?" Ian asked casually, as he walked by a young salesman, he'd employed about a year ago.

"Not too bad, a few possible ones lined up," John confirmed, anxious for his boss to move on. He had the greatest respect for Andy who had helped him meet his targets on more than one occasion, so he had no desire to aid any decision Ian Kendrick was about to make and was gutted when Ian Kendrick pulled up a chair in front of his desk.

"I'm looking for a little feedback, and I would welcome your input," Ian said, watching John's response interestedly. "The allocated time of Jenni's trial period is close to ending and I have to decide whether she stays or goes or whether she needs more training, you know the sort of thing."

Relieved the conversation wasn't concerning Andy, John was happy to offer his opinion. "To be totally honest, boss, I don't know if you've noticed, but personally I don't think she's mastered that switchboard yet. Twice today she's cut me off while I've been talking with a customer, and it's hit or miss if you ask her to transfer the call."

"Definitely needs more training then." Ian laughed, not wanting this little chat to appear too serious. He'd learnt enough to warrant another conversation with Jenni, but in the meantime, he had a small experiment of his own to conduct.

This probably wasn't the most sensible idea, Andy acknowledged as he parked his car outside the pub. Now wasn't the time to be wasting money on beer, but with the week he'd just had, he needed the distraction the pub offered, and a pint sounded like a very good idea. Finding a quiet table in the corner Andy settled down with a copy of the local paper and immediately turned to the situations vacant; he had to find another job and fast.

Minutes later, Tim pulled up outside the same pub. He'd had a busy couple of days and needed a little downtime before he headed home. Having ordered a pint of best bitter Tim surveyed the pub; it wasn't that busy yet so there were a few tables to choose from. Looking closer he spotted Andy sat in the corner, head down reading the paper.

"Situations vacant," Tim teased, as he peered over the top of the paper Andy was reading. "Are you thinking of changing your job?"

Andy looked up and smiled. "It's a case of having to I'm afraid." Andy took a sip of his pint before he continued, "I've just handed in my notice."

"Why?" Tim was shocked. Andy appeared to love his job, well, that was the impression he gave when he sold him his truck.

"It's a long story, and there's nothing suitable in here that's for sure," Andy said as he neatly folded the paper and placed it on the table in front of him.

Witnessing Andy's desperation, Tim didn't hesitate. "Look," Tim began as he pulled up a stool and sat himself opposite Andy. "I'm getting very busy, and I'll be looking for another person to work alongside me soon, so if you're interested." Tim took a large gulp of his beer. "Even if it's just to keep you going until something better comes along."

"But I only know how to sell," Andy answered honestly, watching Tim's response.

"I'll be happy to teach you all I know as we go along. Look, take my phone number, if nothing comes up in the next week or so, give me a call." Tim watched carefully for Andy's reaction, clearly this offer would provide a little respite from the immediate worry of having no job.

"Thank you, and I most certainly will be in touch." Andy took his pint and raised it to Tim. "Cheers to you, Tim and thanks again."

"Cheers." Tim downed the remaining beer, he would have to make a move now otherwise Lisa would wonder why he was later than expected, and he didn't need all the grief that would bring, not tonight anyway.

With no one waiting at home, Andy ordered another pint and this time stood confidently at the bar enjoying his pint, relieved he would have some work, even if it was only a temporary job until something else came along.

***

Maria shivered as she listened intently to the answer phone as it clicked off and watched as the light began to flash. Her finger hovered for a while over the "play" button, then without really thinking she pressed delete. She returned to her comfy sofa; she couldn't face any more food so pushed her plate away. She did, however, manage a few more glasses of wine before stumbling into her bed.

With the problems of the beginning of the week behind them, Maria was pleased that on Friday afternoon they were fully up to date and ready for the following week which, as the last week of the month, was always going to be busy. She filed the last few invoices as the girls finished off their work chatting excitedly. It was Friday night, and now their main concern was where they were going tonight, and with whom.

Already regretting her decision not to join Lisa and Karen tonight, Maria felt flat. She was even wondering if this job was going to be enough for her. Initially she'd enjoyed the challenge, but now with her original challenge complete, she was beginning to feel bored. She checked her watch for the hundredth time in the last few hours.

"Time we weren't here anymore," she exclaimed, watching with envy the excitement on their faces as the prospect of the weekend beckoned.

Maria switched off the lights and closed the door behind her. She couldn't face the idea of going home and eating another T.V. dinner, so instead of turning left at the top of the road and heading home she turned right and made her way over to see her parents.

Much later the same evening, having enjoyed a superb meal with her mum and dad, Maria drew up outside her own house. It was a particularly dark evening with no visible moonlight and fumbling around in her handbag in search of her house keys Maria heard her neighbour, Kate, calling her name.

"Are you ok, Kate?" Maria answered, peering down the driveway.

"Yes, I'm fine, I didn't want to walk up and startle you," Kate explained as she walked up the drive towards Maria.

"Hang on a minute," Maria said as she scrambled to quickly open the door and switch on the lights. "That's better," she said as she turned to face her neighbour. "Gosh, who are they for?" Maria could hardly see her neighbour behind this enormous bouquet of beautiful flowers.

"These came for you this afternoon. I offered to take them in for you. I didn't want the florist to just leave them on the doorstep."

"Thank you, that's very kind," Maria said taking the flowers from Kate. "How are you? Not too long to go now."

"Just another three weeks approximately." Kate smiled, rubbing her baby bump. "I'll be so glad when it's all over now, it's just incredibly uncomfortable. In fact, why don't you pop in for a drink one evening next week? Once the baby comes, I doubt I'll have time to entertain."

"I'd love that," Maria agreed watching Kate walk carefully back down the drive.

Once inside, Maria ripped off the card that was attached to

the cellophane covering this huge bouquet. They just had to be from Andy, she thought, eager to see what he'd written. She stood in the hall reading the words over and over.

"Thank you for a wonderful evening last Saturday, I hope we will have the opportunity to do it again sometime."

She was so disappointed, why hadn't these gorgeous flowers been from Andy? She'd wanted them to be from him. It would have given her the reassurance he was at least sorry for last weekend if nothing else. But they weren't from him, and they probably wouldn't be, ever again.

Carefully she unwrapped the flowers; they were beautiful, but they meant nothing to her. There was no doubt in her mind they had to be from the waiter at the hotel, and she wasn't the slightest bit interested in him, of that she was completely sure. Searching for a couple of vases large enough, Maria suddenly had a thought: where had he got her address from? She most certainly hadn't given it to him. Surely reception didn't give out personal information to their staff. She began to display the flowers. Anyway, it didn't really matter very much, he'd been a welcome distraction on Saturday night, but he wasn't really her type. He was a handsome guy, there was no denying that, but he knew it and undeniably used it to his advantage. No, she decided, definitely not my cup of tea.

***

Ian Kendrick waited until Sunday afternoon before he rang and left a message.

"Jenni, as soon as you get this message, pop into the office for a minute please. Thank you." Ian Kendrick hung up, convinced this was the only way to the truth.

By the time Andy walked back into work on Monday morning, his future was decided. He'd spent Sunday afternoon with Tim, sitting in his garden enjoying the sunshine discussing all the points of concern for both parties. Eventually, over a couple of beers, the two men shook hands and agreed that Andy would start work the

Monday after he finished working his notice from the garage.

For the first time in a very long while Andy felt he had a worthwhile future. He was a good salesman, he knew that, and it was always something he could fall back on if it didn't work out with Tim, but this was a chance to learn a completely new trade. He was excited just thinking about it. It wasn't going to be easy; it was going to be hard physical work, but he was young and strong, so why not give a go?

It was midday when Ian Kendrick decided he'd given Jenni enough time to retrieve his message and asked her to join him in his office. Jenni picked up her notebook, as far as she was concerned the saga of last week was over. She'd seen Andy busy at his desk, so presuming everything was ok she happily joined her boss in his office.

"Come in and close the door." Ian instructed the young girl. "Take a seat." He gestured towards the chair opposite his desk. "Jenni, I'm sorry to go over all this again but are you absolutely sure there were no messages on Friday from Andy."

"There weren't any messages on Friday from anyone," she answered, playing nervously with her cardigan buttons.

"What about today? Have there been any messages at all, anything from the weekend maybe?" Ian Kendrick waited patiently for her answer.

"I don't think so," Jenni answered quietly, instantly remembering that she had seen a message, but had completely forgotten all about it let alone try and retrieve it.

"Do you mind very much if we go and check?" Ian said, already on his feet.

Jenni stood and walked slowly back to her desk.

"Ahh," Ian exclaimed, "it appears we do have a message today; could you play it back to me?"

Trying to look effortlessly in control, Jenni sat at her desk miserably trying to remember what she'd been taught, but it was useless, she had no idea. She hung her head in shame as tears trickled down her cheeks.

"When you've composed yourself, I think we need another

little chat," Ian Kendrick explained in a relatively soft manner, before he returned to his office. Realising he owed Andy a huge apology, he hoped it wasn't too late to make amends.

Feeling hungry, Andy checked his watch for the first time that morning and was amazed to see it was already gone midday. Since first thing when he'd followed up a few outstanding queries with a few potential customers, he'd been busy sorting a few ideas for the next stage of his life. Unusually, he hadn't noticed any other activities; in truth he had no time for any of them anymore. He'd worked hard for Ian Kendrick and now that he'd accepted the word of a young girl, who had literally worked in the job for a matter of weeks, over his, well, it said a lot, he realised. He picked up the phone, just one more call to make before lunch; he'd found a brick laying course that offered evening classes, which would be ideal. With fingers crossed he waited for his call to be answered.

Smiling broadly, Andy pushed his chair back, having just secured the last place on the course, it was time to eat. He was starving and was just about to leave the showroom for an hour, when Ian Kendrick appeared.

"Can I have a quick word, Andy, please."

Without saying a word Andy followed his boss into his office.

"Take a seat," Ian instructed as he made himself comfortable in his big leather chair. "I'll get straight to it," he said smiling. Producing Andy's letter of resignation he continued, "I would like you to reconsider this decision. I owe you an apology." He paused for a moment watching Andy's reaction, but he couldn't read him today. "It seems that Jenni made a mistake and there is every chance you could well have left a message, as unfortunately a couple of messages were accidently erased on Friday morning."

"I see," Andy said as he sat further back in his chair. He was going to enjoy this meeting after all.

"I see no reason to continue with this resignation, and I'm very happy to destroy this letter and we'll say no more about it." Ian Kendrick went to remove the letter from its envelope.

"Hold on a minute, boss." Andy held up his hand to prevent his boss continuing and watched the expression on his face change to one of concern. "I'm sorry, but I wish for my resignation to remain. I think my time here is done."

Completely shocked, Ian Kendrick placed the letter back on his desk; this was one scenario he hadn't planned for. "I'm sure we can sort out any issues you may have, and as I've already said, I apologise for the whole unfortunate situation."

"I don't have any issues," Andy interrupted, "other than my resignation still stands." Andy watched as his boss shuffled a few papers around on his desk, before he took a tissue from his pocket and wiped his brow.

"If it's money," Ian Kendrick began, "I'm sure we can look at that, you're due a review in a few months and I'd be happy to bring that forward."

"That's kind of you, but I'll be honest." Andy was hungry and couldn't see the point of dragging this out any longer. "I've already made plans for my future, and I will be leaving in one month's time."

"What plans are these then?" his boss asked indignantly, suddenly realising he was about to lose his best salesperson and had no one to blame but himself.

"I'm not really in a position to discuss them at the moment," Andy explained, enjoying every moment. "Suffice to say, I'm not going to work for another garage, so there's no need to worry about the fact I might take any customers with me."

"And there's nothing I can do to change your mind?" Ian Kendrick asked, almost apologetically.

Andy shook his head. "Afraid not," he replied as he stood to leave.

"Well, if that's the case, I'll set the relevant wheels in motion with regard to holiday that you're due etc., and I'll confirm your exact leaving date; leave it with me." Ian Kendrick was beat, and he knew it.

"Thank you." Andy nodded at his boss as he turned to leave

and, closing the door quietly behind him, headed off for lunch.

***

"You can't just ignore the fact he sent you the most beautiful bouquet of flowers," Kim exclaimed as she made herself comfortable while Maria made some tea. "How come you never mentioned you'd received them?"

"Because I don't want them," Maria said indignantly. "I'm trying to forget who sent them, I'm not in the slightest bit interested in him," she quickly added, before her sister embarked on any more questions.

"You don't have to be interested to just say 'thank you' it's just being polite," Kim said, surprised at her sister's reaction.

"I don't want to give him any ideas," Maria continued as she poured the tea. "You're making me feel uncomfortable," she added as she looked up to see the noticeable disappointment in her sister's eyes.

"Does Mum know?" Kim asked gingerly.

"Why would I tell her?"

"Well, she'd be very interested." Kim couldn't help teasing her sister.

"I'm not going down that road, thank you very much." Maria offered her sister one of her favourite chocolate biscuits. "That's the last thing I need, Mum and Dad on my case, anyway I don't suppose any of us will ever go to that hotel again, there's no more big celebrations on the horizon, that I know of." Maria sat opposite her sister and helped herself to a biscuit.

"That's where you're wrong," Kim said with a huge grin on her face.

"Why, what do you mean?" She wasn't sure if her sister was serious or still teasing her.

"Mum and Dad have been invited back for a weekend on a heavily discounted rate as a thank you for all their business."

"When?"

"Whenever they want."

"No, I mean when did this all happen?" Maria asked impatiently.

"The other day, anyway that's why I think you should mention the flowers."

"Oh great, this is all I need." Maria sighed, her expression leaving her sister in no doubt this conversation wasn't at all what she wanted to hear.

"I'll leave it with you." Kim smiled as she finished her tea. "Don't forget we're home at the weekend if you want to come over."

"Thanks." Maria gave her sister a big hug as they said their goodbyes.

***

Sammy had recovered well and, as it wasn't Andy's turn to see his daughter this weekend, the thought of two lonely, empty days ahead loomed over him like a black hole in outer space. Apart from Sammy his private life was a crumbling mess. He tried to keep himself busy and, in all honesty, it wasn't too bad during the day. Even though he was on count down until his last day, he could still manage to remain occupied while he was at work. It was the evenings and the weekends he found the worst; the silence the night brought was unbearable. What he wouldn't give to speak to Maria. If he could just hear her voice, feel her touch, look into her beautiful eyes. He'd given up any hope of her returning his call. She probably hated him with real vengeance, and he didn't blame her. It was the very thought of witnessing the hurt he'd caused, etched upon her face that kept him away, but it couldn't be any worse than the pain he'd caused himself, and the thought of living the rest of his life without her was unthinkable. He dreamt of her regularly and at first went to great lengths to be in the same places he thought she might be. He walked around her favourite shopping centre on his Saturday off in the hope of bumping into her, he walked by the hairdressers she used in the hope she might be inside, he went far too many times to collect fish and chips in the hope she might be there, but it never worked out for him, and he never bumped into her.

***

Maria wasn't too surprised to receive a call from her mother later that day, in fact she'd expected it.

"Maria, why didn't you tell me you've received flowers from Lorenzo?" her mother asked excitedly.

"I didn't realise you'd be that interested," Maria replied dismissively.

"Did he suggest the two of you meet anywhere, or anything like that?" her mother continued, oblivious to Maria's tone.

"No, Mum, he did not."

"Well, I hope you've sent a thank you note; your Dad and I are going back next month for the weekend. We don't want any bad feeling."

"It's all in hand, Mum, don't worry."

"I hope so, Maria." Her mother was disappointed; she'd had high hopes for Lorenzo. He would have made an ideal distraction for her daughter, then suddenly from nowhere she had an idea. "Why don't you come with us when we go back? We'd love to have you with us; you really enjoyed it last time and so did we."

"That's really kind of you, Mum, but I don't think so, not this time."

"There's no need to decide yet, we're not going back until next month." Her mother was on a mission and defeat wasn't an option.

By the time her parents were due back to the hotel, Maria had received, unbeknown to anyone, two more bouquets from Lorenzo. She'd never bothered to send a thank you note, although she led everyone to believe she had, and by the time the third bouquet arrived Maria was finding the whole situation irritating. She wasn't interested and was now regretting having ever met him.

In actual fact, Maria was wrestling with her own conscience.

Regretting her decision to erase Andy's message without ever listening to it; all she wanted was to see him. He was like a drug to her. She knew he wasn't right for her, but still she craved to see him, or even just hear his voice, anything would do, but there was nothing: just complete silence. It was completely out of character; he'd never normally give up after just one unanswered call, and she was beginning to worry. She hoped he wasn't ill, or maybe it just meant he wasn't interested any more. The thought was sobering and compounded her feelings of loneliness.

It wasn't until the following week when Maria had time to catch up with Lisa over the phone that she'd been brave enough to admit to her friend how concerned she was about Andy.

"It's just so out of character," she explained. "I suppose I thought he would put up more of a fight to see me, how arrogant am I?"

"You're not arrogant," Lisa assured her friend. "It's natural to feel hurt, but you're doing really well, and please don't worry about him. I saw him in the pub the other day, he's absolutely fine." Immediately Lisa realised she shouldn't have mentioned this, but it was too late now, and she was relieved when Maria hung up without asking any more questions.

Maria walked slowly back into the kitchen. She turned off the oven and took out the chicken pie she was cooking for her supper, the crust had burnt, and it looked as bad as she felt. In temper she scraped the whole pie directly into the bin. With a packet of crisps and a large glass of wine Maria made her way into the living room and switched on the T.V. She was looking, but not really watching, and at the end of the evening had no idea what had been showing. Her mind was elsewhere. Lisa's admission that she'd seen Andy in the pub had completely thrown her off track; so much so she'd hung up without asking Lisa any further questions. She tormented herself for the rest of the evening with one unanswered question after another and by the following day, she couldn't stand it any longer and that evening she rang her friend back.

"Hi, Lisa, it's only me," Maria began.

"Hi, Maria, are you ok?" Lisa was concerned, they'd only spoken yesterday. Suddenly she had an uneasy feeling, was this going to be an uncomfortable conversation?

"I'm fine, but I've been thinking about something you said last night."

"What did I say?" Lisa asked, praying it didn't concern Andy.

"You mentioned you'd seen Andy in the pub, so I was wondering if he was with anyone?" There was an uncomfortable silence before Lisa answered.

"Why do you want to know, Maria?" Lisa was extremely sympathetic towards her friend, and now wished, more than ever, that she'd never mentioned she'd seen him. "You told me that it was definitely all over between the two of you and you didn't want anything more to do with him."

"Oh, so he wasn't on his own then?" Maria's voice was tense as she waited for Lisa to reply.

"I didn't say that."

"Was he, or wasn't he?" Maria didn't understand, why was Lisa being so prickly, unless she had something to hide.

Eventually Lisa answered. "He was most certainly on his own."

"Was he ok?" Maria asked uneasily. "How did he seem? Did he mention me?"

"He appeared to be fine. I honestly don't know if he asked about you." Lisa's tone mellowed, she had no one to blame but herself for this conversation.

"What is it you're not telling me, Lisa?" Maria asked her friend desperate for some answers.

"I didn't speak to him; Tim had a quick chat with him at the bar. I was already sitting at a table, so I couldn't hear the conversation for myself. I do know, though, why he didn't turn up on that Friday, if you would like to know?" Lisa offered this information hoping Maria wouldn't pursue why Tim alone had spoken to Andy. Tim had warned her several times, it wasn't any of her business who he employed, and it wasn't for her to inform Maria. That was for Andy if he so chose.

"No, not really," Maria answered. It wasn't any good, this conversation hadn't helped her at all, and it never would, she realised that now. "I'm sorry, Lisa, I shouldn't have called. You're right, knowing, not knowing, it's not going to make any difference. I've got to make the break; it's just proving to be much harder than I expected. Time is not healing fast enough." She laughed, trying to sound light-hearted.

"It's ok, Maria," Lisa replied feeling desperately sorry for her friend. "If it helps, he hasn't got anyone else; in a way I wish he had, at least that way it would be final."

"Don't worry, I'm not going to ring him or jump in the car and go visit him, I'll be fine."

"Promise?"

"I promise," Maria assured her friend as they said their goodbyes.

Despite the sound of the T.V. and the washing machine, the only sound Maria could hear was the unmistakable sound of her breaking heart. Her phone call to Lisa had been a mistake and one she would regret for a long time.

For the rest of the evening Lisa couldn't settle, she was in two minds whether to drive over and make sure Maria was ok. In the end after dithering she decided it would be best to leave it for tonight, but first thing she would give her a ring, just to make sure she was ok.

The following days ran into weeks and Maria fell deeper into her own world of despair and heart break. Both her sisters took it in turns to visit, and ring, but it was her parents who were most concerned. At first, they'd thought Maria was coping well, and hoped it wouldn't be too long before she met someone else. She was an attractive girl, everyone said so, but the last few weeks had seen her fall into a massive depression, and they were both very concerned.

"Why don't you come with us next weekend?" her mother asked her daughter over lunch on Saturday.

"Honestly, Mum, I'm not up to it," Maria replied as she pushed her lunch around the plate. "I'd ruin your whole weekend, I don't feel like enjoying myself, I'm better off at home on my own."

"I don't think you are, dear," her mother continued. "I'm worried about you and, to be honest, I really don't feel comfortable going away and leaving you behind."

Maria tried hard to smile and offer her mother some reassurance. "Mum, I'm an adult. I'll be fine, honestly, I will."

"I'm not so sure," her mother said as she moved her chair closer and put a comforting arm around her daughter.

It was the comfort of her mother that brought tears to Maria's eyes and, snuggling like a child deep in her mother's arms, she could no longer stem the flow and she cried until eventually there were no more tears left to cry. By the end of the day, Maria had finally agreed to accompany her parents next weekend, on the proviso her father would have a word with the amorous Lorenzo if he appeared too friendly.

***

For a couple of months now, Maria's boss had been concerned. He couldn't fault her work, that wasn't the issue; she was always the ultimate professional. No, it was just her overall demeanour, she always looked so terribly sad. She'd always been extremely private about her life away from the office, and he respected that, but even he could tell the signs of a broken heart, after all he could still remember how that felt even now. He grimaced shamefully as he remembered some of the antics he'd subjected himself to, as he'd desperately tried to win the heart of the college sweetheart. He'd never stood a chance, but that hadn't prevented him having a good try. He wondered what she was doing now.

The following Monday, when Maria requested the Friday afternoon off, Peter made up his mind to make sure she got away on time. He'd never been one to pry, but he sincerely hoped she had something nice planned and come Friday kept a watchful eye on the time.

"I thought you'd booked this afternoon off?" he asked Maria when she looked up, as he approached her desk.

"I have, but I've still got another hour to go," Maria

answered wondering where this was going.

"How come? I always thought the afternoon began at noon." He smiled, checking his watch.

"I will be finished by one o'clock," she assured him.

"I'm sure you will," he replied, "but I'd like you to pack up and leave now, go and enjoy your weekend, there's nothing here that can't wait until Monday."

Maria could tell by the look on his face, this wasn't up for discussion. "Thank you, I'll pack up and get going then." She smiled, acknowledging her boss as he turned to leave.

"See you Monday," he called as he left, smiling to himself.

As it turned out, the fact they'd been able to leave for the hotel an hour earlier than originally planned, meant they missed the inevitable heavy traffic of a Friday evening and arrived in time to enjoy another afternoon tea by the fireside.

Absolutely determined to erase Andy from her mind and enjoy the weekend, Maria sat back in one of the comfortable lounge chairs and thoroughly enjoyed the freshly made finger sandwiches, followed by warm scones with lashings of clotted cream and jam complemented with a perfectly chilled glass of champagne.

"I've got déjà vu." Maria laughed. "This is becoming a habit, enjoying afternoon tea here at this hotel, in this very lounge."

"It's a habit I thoroughly enjoy. Cheers." Her father held up his glass.

"Cheers," Maria replied clinking her glass with each parent.

"This is just delightful," her mother agreed as she relaxed, relieved Maria had finally agreed to join them for the weekend.

Finishing her champagne, Maria checked her watch.

"Have you got a train to catch?" her father joked as he kept a watchful eye on his daughter.

"No." She laughed in response. "But I've just realised time is getting on and I booked a sauna, so I'd better get a move on." Maria wiped her fingers on her napkin and carefully placed her empty plate on the table.

"Oh yes you mentioned that earlier," her mother said.

"Enjoy and we'll see you later."

***

Tim left his accountant's office with a spring in his step. He'd always known that eventually it would pay off branching out on his own, and if he carried on as busy as this, which he should, he had good healthy forecasts, they'd make a good profit this year. Andy had been a huge asset; he had a good work ethic and could even teach Tim a thing or two after he'd completed several building courses. Despite that, there'd been a few hiccups at the beginning when Andy first started working for him, when Tim witnessed for himself how awkward and generally useless Sammy's mother Sharon appeared to be. On Andy's first day she must have rung a dozen times or more, before lunch, and Tim wasn't happy.

To begin with Tim had been impressed that Andy had one of these new "mobile phones" it was a brick like contraption that he carried everywhere. Tim just had the old-fashioned car phone, which was a permanent fixture in his truck, but once he'd observed the chaos Andy's phone seemed to cause, he made a mental note not to bother to hurry out and buy one.

"Andy, mate," Tim began as they took a break to eat their sandwiches, "this isn't going to work if these calls are going to continue. If your little girl is unwell and you need to go to her, you must say, other than that I'm not interested in listening to your domestic issues every time your phone rings."

At first Andy was shocked at Tim's blunt approach, but he couldn't afford to blow this opportunity. "I'm sorry about that, I guess I'm just used to it, it's not a problem. I'll leave it in the van from now on and just check it during my lunch break."

"Great," Tim said as he shared his thermos of tea with his new work mate. "I don't want to come on all heavy handed."

"Please," Andy jumped in, "it's fine, I understand."

He did totally understand, although he knew Sharon wouldn't, and instead of her consistent calls all day, he had the pleasure of them every evening, unless of course she managed to get a babysitter and went out.

With his new job came a new lifestyle. There were no definite hours of work; it depended on the job in hand. Sometimes they finished late, other times, but not very often, they finished early. All this frustrated Sharon and she did her utmost to spoil what little free time he had, calling up late at night, changing Sammy's visiting time without very much notice, anything to be awkward and cause Andy as much inconvenience as possible. Amid this chaos Andy found himself delaying any plans he may have had to secure any sort of future with Maria. His current lifestyle wasn't conducive to any relationship, let alone trying to repair one, and although there wasn't a day that went by that he didn't think of her, he knew that, unfortunately, at present it could never work.

***

Feeling relaxed after her sauna and massage, Maria strolled carefree along the wood panelled hallway leading to the reception area, where the grand staircase led to the beautifully appointed bedrooms. Turning into the main hallway her senses were alerted as she heard the distinctive tones of the Italian waiter. She froze for a second; should she turn back or just carry on? Listening to his conversation he was clearly discussing the numbers booked into the restaurant. She couldn't quite make out who he was talking to, but as it didn't sound like the conversation was about to end any time soon, Maria decided to hurriedly continue, and pass as quietly as possible. Breathlessly she unlocked the door to her room and immediately collapsed onto the huge comfy bed. That was a close call she didn't want to repeat.

Just over an hour later, Maria followed her parents into the restaurant where they were seated at a round table by the fireside and left to peruse the menu. The restaurant was busy, and the ambience relaxed as everyone enjoyed their evening and as Maria hadn't seen or heard any more from Lorenzo, she was hopeful he'd got the message. As usual the food was superb and, feeling extremely full, it was a unanimous decision to take coffee in the lounge. There was already a large party occupying the table by the fire, so the three of them settled for the table in the corner.

"I don't remember that party in the restaurant tonight," Maria commented as they took their seats.

"They were in the private dining room adjacent to the restaurant; they're celebrating a 60th birthday."

Maria looked at her mother in amazement. "How on earth do you know all that?"

"Lorenzo told us earlier," she proudly announced. "He popped in to say hello when you were enjoying your sauna and massage. He told us then that he was looking after them."

For a split second Maria felt uncomfortable; she wondered what else they'd discussed, but now wasn't the time for questions. She was just grateful he'd been busy elsewhere.

"He's going to try and join us for a drink later," her mother suddenly added.

Maria nearly choked on her coffee as she heard her mother's last comment, and without giving them too much warning, Maria decided to call it a night.

"I'm sorry I can't wait," Maria said as she stood up ready to leave. "I'm really tired; I've had such a lovely evening, thank you both." She leant down to kiss her mother then her father. "Goodnight, and I'll see you for breakfast about 9.00?" she added.

Her father smiled and stood as Maria left. "I did tell you that wouldn't go down too well," her father said as he sat back down. "But you wouldn't listen." He offered his wife some more coffee before pouring his own.

From a secluded area behind reception, Lorenzo watched as Maria left the lounge and made her way up the stairs. He'd had plenty of encouragement from her mother earlier when he'd popped in to say hello, but he would have to be very careful, the last thing he needed was another complaint against him at work. He wasn't on duty for breakfast or lunch tomorrow, so he would have to wait and see how she was on Saturday night. This was a first for him and nowhere near how things usually went; one bouquet or even a phone call normally did the trick, but this was different, and he had to admit, he was actually enjoying the challenge. He knew she liked him, well that was the impression she gave at her father's party, but if she didn't, she was a good actress, he concluded, as he collected his coat. If Maria wasn't around, her parents, he decided, would have to wait until another day for that drink and he left for home.

Not wanting to hang around the hotel all day and anxious for some exercise and fresh air, Maria suggested to her parents over breakfast that they meet for lunch in the pub on the village green.

"Darling," her mother said, "we can have a light lunch here."

"I know that, Mum, but I just thought it would be good to try somewhere else and, as I would like to go for a walk, I thought I could meet you there." Maria didn't think her mother was too convinced, so was pleased when her father added.

"I think that's a really good idea, shall we say about 1.30pm?" He smiled at his wife, hoping for once she would admit defeat.

"That's great," Maria said as she finished her breakfast.

Quite a few hours later and completely invigorated by her walk and the fresh air, Maria made her way back to the hotel to change out of her muddy boots before heading off for lunch. Crossing the car park, she noticed that her parents' car was nowhere to be seen. Checking her watch, it was later than she'd thought. She had just half an hour to change and return to the pub. Not wanting to keep them waiting, she asked reception to order her a cab back to the village in fifteen minutes.

Maria paid the cab driver and headed straight into the pub. It was a quaint building with a thatched roof. It reminded Maria of a typical chocolate box picture. Coming in from the brilliant sunshine it took a while for her to focus; she stood inside looking for her parents. She expected to see her mother frantically trying to attract her attention, but they were nowhere to be seen. Back outside she checked the carpark to the rear; there was no sign of their car. Guessing they wouldn't be very long, they were never late, she made her way back inside and headed for the bar where she pulled out a stool and ordered herself a glass of white wine. Minutes later she heard someone call her name, instantly recognising that accent, she checked her watch, 1.33pm, hurry up Mum and Dad please, she prayed as Lorenzo pulled up the stool next to her.

It was difficult to ignore his impeccable appearance; with his dark hair, chiselled features and perfectly matching casual wear, he cut a fine figure, she had to admit.

"Hi, how are you? You look amazing, what are you doing in here?" he asked as though they were old friends.

"Hi back," she answered slowly. "I'm waiting for Mum and Dad; we're supposed to be meeting at 1.30 for lunch."

Lorenzo checked his watch. "They're running a little late then, do you mind if I keep you company until they arrive?"

He was only trying to be friendly, Maria conceded, and even his company was better than sitting here on her own, so she smiled sweetly and agreed. Lorenzo ordered her another glass of white wine and himself a glass of orange juice. The next thirty minutes flew by, he always had so much conversation, and Maria was now feeling slightly guilty for not mentioning the flowers. Checking her watch, she realised it was already 2pm.

"I'm sorry, Lorenzo," she said as she climbed off her stool. "But Mum and Dad are never this late and now I'm really worried, so I'm going to head back to the hotel."

"Why don't you just ring the hotel and see if they're there?" he asked, anxious for her to stay.

"I would, but I only have a car phone and that's in my car back home." She laughed, immediately regretting her sarcastic reply. "Anyway, I don't have the hotel number on me," she added thoughtfully.

"There's a payphone around the corner in the other bar." Lorenzo pointed in the direction of the payphone. "Obviously I know the number, then you can check to see if they're still there."

Not really knowing what else to do, Maria finally agreed, and they both made their way to the payphone. Lorenzo got through to the hotel and asked the receptionist to confirm whether her parents were at the hotel. Maria watched his expression intently and when he began to smile, she presumed they were there and ok. Finishing his conversation, he hung up.

"What's happened?" Maria asked anxiously.

"Well, your parents aren't at the hotel, but they did ring through a message, so you wouldn't worry."

"What's happened to them?" Maria's hands were shaking, something must be wrong, if they'd had to ring into the hotel.

"Please don't worry, they're fine," Lorenzo quickly added as he witnessed her concerned expression. "They went into town to have a look around, parked in the multi-storey carpark where your dad inadvertently left his lights on. When they came back, they had a flat battery, so they are currently waiting for the A.A. Apparently, they said to tell you they've grabbed a sandwich for lunch, so they'll see you back at the hotel later this afternoon."

"Oh, thank goodness for that," Maria said sighing with relief.

"As your parents won't make it for lunch, can I buy you a sandwich?" he asked hopefully. "They serve their sandwiches on homemade bread accompanied by homemade chips, they're very good." Behind his back Lorenzo held his fingers tightly crossed.

"Why not?" Maria answered, surprising herself at her lack of hesitation. "You're not paying for my lunch though, I'll pay."

"No, no, no." Lorenzo held up his hand in a light-hearted manner. "I insist."

"Can we eat, then fight it out?" Maria asked, unable to prevent herself from smiling. "Otherwise, I think we may be too late to order anything."

"Don't worry, they serve food here all day." He smiled, leading her back to the bar.

"Do you mind if we sit at the table over there?" Maria suggested as she quickly scanned the cosy room. "I'm not really that comfortable sitting on the bar stools."

"Certainly, you grab the table and I'll get a couple of menus."

The next time Maria checked her watch it was 3.45pm;

Lorenzo had been very entertaining, and sometimes in his hurry to speak his translation was quite funny, and on numerous occasions Maria had to explain why suddenly, for no apparent reason, she couldn't stop laughing.

"Look at the time," Maria said checking her watch. "I should get back to the hotel. Mum and Dad will wonder where on earth I am." She folded her napkin and finished her drink.

"No problem, I'll drive you back," Lorenzo declared as he quickly finished his orange juice. "Please don't worry though, I'm pretty sure if they're back, Gill on reception would have mentioned that I was with you in the pub."

Maria frowned, that would most certainly please her mother. She could already imagine the conversation at dinner tonight.

"Thank you for lunch and a very entertaining couple of hours," Maria said as she watched Lorenzo confidently reverse out of his parking space.

"It was my pleasure," Lorenzo replied, turning briefly to look directly at her before returning his gaze to the road ahead. The lanes back to the hotel were narrow and Maria was pleased she wasn't driving, and for the first time that afternoon, Lorenzo fell silent as he concentrated and manoeuvred his car through the road ahead.

As they entered the beautiful grounds of the hotel, Maria began to wonder how this was all going to end. He'd been very kind; she just hoped he hadn't read too much into their lunch. While Maria was busy planning a quick exit, Lorenzo suddenly pulled the car into a little slip road off the main driveway.

"Would you think it terribly rude of me to drop you here?" He looked apologetically in her direction. "It's just management frown on staff fraternising with customers."

"Not at all, I completely understand," Maria assured him as she quickly climbed out of the car. "Thanks for the lift."

"No problem." He smiled. "I'll see you tonight, in the restaurant," Lorenzo called out as he drove away.

Maria made her way up the drive heading straight for the hotel. That was a nice relaxed easy end to the afternoon, no need to have worried after all.

Lorenzo parked his car at the rear of the hotel and made his way back to his accommodation. As a manager he had a small sitting room, a kitchen, a bedroom and bathroom; it was pure luxury compared to some of the accommodation he'd been offered at other hotels, plus it was all his, he didn't have to share with anyone. With just over an hour before he was due in to work, Lorenzo kicked off his shoes and made himself a pot of Italian coffee. He'd long since given up drinking coffee in a pub or café since he'd lived in the U.K., he had no idea what they used, or how they made it, but it wasn't for him.

Armed with his fresh coffee, Lorenzo settled down to watch the last hour of the football replay. He switched on the T.V. and tried his best to follow exactly what was going on, but all he could really think of was the last few hours he'd spent having lunch with Maria. He'd hoped that he might get a chance to speak with her, but lunch with just the two of them, that had been beyond his wildest dreams, and he still couldn't quite believe his luck. He stretched out in his chair and sipped his coffee, still a little bit concerned at the way he'd dropped her off at the bottom of the drive. She'd been pretty relaxed over lunch once she knew her parents' whereabouts, but in the car, he noticed she became a little edgy; she constantly fiddled with either her handbag or the buttons on her jacket, so he'd decided to play it really cool, and without giving it too much thought concocted the story that she seemed to accept and dropped her at the bottom of the drive. He just hoped he'd read the situation correctly.

Noticing her parents' car in the car park, Maria headed straight to their room but after the excitement of the day, they were resting, and they all agreed to meet in the lounge for a drink at about 7pm. Maria was left feeling restless so, with a few hours to kill, she settled for a vigorous swim to burn off a few calories and clear her head.

At exactly 7pm Maria headed down to the lounge to meet her parents. For no other reason than she'd had plenty of time, or so she told herself, she'd taken extra care with her hair and make-up, and her mother was quick to notice. Remembering her husband's advice, however, she refrained from commenting and even kept the questions about lunch to an absolute minimum, instead choosing to regale the events of their morning, which she had to admit were nowhere near as interesting.

Maria, however, wasn't completely engaged in her mother's conversation. She hadn't really known how this evening would pan out and was dreading Lorenzo spending too much time at their table. On the other hand, what she hadn't considered was the fact that he would be too busy elsewhere, concentrating all his efforts looking after a large group of people at the other end of the restaurant, some of which were annoyingly hidden from her view by a pillar. Not that it really bothered her, she told herself, as once again she tried to concentrate on her parents' conversation.

Climbing back into her own car on Sunday afternoon, Maria had to admit, she most certainly felt so much better than she had for a very long time. She'd even managed to put Andy out of her mind for a while thanks to Lorenzo. He'd been a great distraction and she'd enjoyed the fact that he'd flirted with her throughout their lunch; it was the ego boost she'd needed, but in truth he didn't make her heartbeat faster and there were no butterflies in her tummy when he looked deep into her eyes.

"Damn you, Andy Porter," she said out loud as she drove herself home from her parents' house.

During the weeks that followed, Maria often found herself wondering what could possibly have happened to Andy on that fateful weekend. Many a time she considered asking Lisa who, after all, had offered to tell her at one time, but then common sense would kick in and she'd change her mind. She'd even been tempted on more than one occasion to just drive by his flat, but then what good would that do? And if by chance she was to see him with another woman, well that just didn't bear thinking about.

Eventually, after wallowing in her own self-pity for a few more weeks, Maria decided for own self-respect, enough was enough and instead of constantly refusing her friends when they invited her out, she'd make a real effort to join in, so when an invitation arrived in the post, it was a true test of her promise to herself.

"You should definitely go," Kim said excitedly as she read the letter Maria handed her. "What have you got to lose?"

The letter had been a complete surprise to Maria. Lorenzo was the last person she expected to hear from, especially as he'd shown no interest in even saying goodbye when they'd left the hotel.

"Did you know he was looking for a new job?" her sister continued as she reread the letter.

"No, he never mentioned anything to me," Maria explained. "But then why would he? To be honest I don't know him do I? I've had one lunch with him and seen him at the hotel a few times. That's not conducive for a heart-to-heart about his career, is it?"

"I know what you mean." Kim handed the letter back to her sister. "Well, he's got an interview in a top London hotel, so he must be good. Whichever way you look at it, he's offering dinner in London, that must be worth a trip surely?"

Maria couldn't help smiling at her sister's reasoning.

"And like you said yourself," Kim continued, "he makes you laugh, which is more than any of us can manage at the moment. I say go, have some fun…" Kim folded her arms and grinned at her sister.

"I am seriously considering it," Maria almost whispered, as though she still wasn't sure.

Kim clapped her hands together rejoicing. "Well go then." She laughed. "Go and have some fun, Maria, it will do you the world of good."

The following Sunday evening Maria caught the train, destination Victoria. Arriving at 6.55pm exactly, she quickly made her way to the taxi rank where she'd arranged to meet Lorenzo. She spotted him immediately; he struck a very handsome figure in his sharp grey suit.

She'd guessed correctly that he'd be dressed formally,

especially after an interview, so she was pleased that yesterday she'd spent the whole day trawling the shops and found herself an outfit in a beautiful cobalt blue; she knew it looked good and was grateful for the confidence it provided.

Lorenzo greeted her with an air kiss to each side of her face, and she couldn't help noticing that he smelt divine.

"Thank you so much for accepting my offer." He smiled as he looked deep into her eyes. "I really hoped you would, but I wasn't completely sure," he admitted as he tucked his arm through hers. "I really hope you like Italian food; I've taken the liberty of pre-booking without checking with you first."

"You're in luck," Maria joked. "I eat absolutely anything and everything."

"Let's go then, it's just a short walk," he said as he led the way.

Realising that perhaps she shouldn't have been surprised they would be eating Italian, it soon became apparent it was a little more upmarket than the pizzeria in the local shopping mall. There wasn't a pizza or lasagne in sight and most definitely no gingham tablecloths, no, the décor was modern, and a complete contrast to the restaurant at the hotel.

The food was divine, the individual dishes were simple but expertly cooked and Maria sampled pasta dishes with accompanying wines until she could literally eat no more.

"That was just amazing," she exclaimed. "I've honestly never had pasta like that before; it puts my T.V. pasta dinners to shame." She laughed, enjoying the last of the wine.

"I'm so glad you enjoyed it; I'd hoped you would." Feeling quietly confident that his interview had gone well, Lorenzo felt relaxed and comfortable as he wined and dined Maria and was sorry that the evening was coming to an end all too soon. She looked amazing tonight; her dress was beautifully tailored, and the colour suited her complexion and hair colour. It was all part of the package as far as he was concerned, appearance, personality, and he had to admit, she had both.

Back at Victoria station, they quickly swopped telephone numbers and Lorenzo promised to let her know if he'd been successful with the new job.

Slightly breathless from her short sprint to catch the train, Maria sat back in her seat. Lorenzo had been on top form tonight, entertaining and extremely funny and in his absolute element when ordering the food in his native tongue. Maria couldn't help smiling to herself as she remembered watching his actions and listening to his voice as he ordered their food. It was all part of his charm offensive, she thought as she took his business card from her pocket. She genuinely hoped he'd ring; she'd like to keep in touch.

***

Over the last month or so, Andy had noticed a steady decline in panic and nuisance phone calls from Sharon. It had become almost a ritual, as soon as he arrived home, he would check his mobile and his landline and always answered if she'd left any sort of message. At first, he'd found it a little unnerving; it felt weird when she didn't call, but after spending a weekend with Sammy, it soon became apparent why.

Throughout the weekend, Sammy continuously mentioned someone she referred to as "Uncle Paul" and Andy soon realised Uncle Paul must be Sharon's new boyfriend.

It didn't bother him, he was pleased for her, although he felt sorry for whoever he was, but at the end of the day if he was spending time with his daughter, and clearly, he was, Andy wanted to meet him, hopefully he'd be around when he took Sammy home on Sunday.

"Mummy, Mummy," Sammy said jumping up and down as Sharon opened the door. "Daddy bought me new trainers." She pointed to her feet. "Look, Mummy they're all sparkly."

"You're a very lucky girl," Sharon said encouraging her little girl inside. "Say goodbye to Daddy, we need to get you bathed and ready for bed."

Normally Andy would be keen to leave, but tonight he wasn't going anywhere until he'd found out a bit more about this chap named Paul.

"Bye then," Sharon said dismissively.

"Hang on a minute." Andy put his foot in the door preventing her from shutting it in his face. "Sammy has been talking quite a lot about someone called 'Uncle Paul'." He looked directly at his ex who was giving nothing away voluntarily, so he continued. "If you have a new man in your life, that's fine. I don't have a problem with that, but if he's involved in the day-to-day life of our daughter, I think I have the right to meet him."

Before Sharon had a chance to reply, Andy spotted a small-framed thin man a lot shorter than himself with scraggy blond hair, emerge from the living room and walk towards them both.

"Hi, I'm Paul," he said as he held out his hand.

"Hi," Andy replied shaking his hand. "I'm Andy, Sammy's dad."

"Pleased to meet you. She's a lovely little girl; you must be very proud."

"Yes, she is," Andy agreed while still trying to decide whether he liked this guy or not. He wasn't her usual type that was for sure.

Sharon, who'd been side lined during their introduction, suddenly spoke out. "Paul, I just need a quick word with Andy, if you don't mind." She gave Paul one of her looks that Andy had experienced many a time.

"No problem," he said, immediately retreating like a naughty schoolboy.

"Happy now?" Sharon said indignantly.

"Not really," Andy answered. "I'm not entirely sure I know enough about Paul yet, I have a few more questions."

"Go on." Sharon leant against the front door with her arms folded.

"Is he living here full time?" he asked, watching her reaction. "And what does he do for a living? I take it he has a job," he added as he waited for her response.

"No, he's not living here full time, as you put it, and he's in between jobs. Satisfied?" She raised her eyebrows.

Ignoring her sarcastic remark Andy continued. "Where does he live then?"

"He rents a room somewhere in town. I haven't been there yet."

"So, no wife then?"

"No," Sharon replied impatiently. "Look, if you're that worried why don't you have Sammy live with you? That would solve all our problems." She stood waiting for Andy to compute exactly what she'd just said.

"You've changed your tune," Andy said, stunned by her comment. "It's never been an option you'd even discuss before."

"If you want custody, I'll not fight you." She surprised herself, she'd never actually voiced any of these thoughts before.

This was an awful lot for Andy to consider, especially standing on her doorstep. His head was reeling, finally he found his tongue. "We need to sit down and discuss this properly. You can't say this to me today, then tomorrow change your mind," he said trying to gauge how serious she might be. "Once we start down this road there's no going back, you do understand that don't you?"

Sharon nodded, she didn't want to lose her little girl, but she needed more freedom, and she was sure Sammy would have a good happy life with Andy. She'd played about with this idea for weeks now; Paul had big plans and she liked the sound of the life he had in mind and wanted to be part of it. She'd realised it would probably be too much to expect Paul to take on two kids, but one, she might just get away with.

Recognising she wouldn't be able to offload the baby, Sammy was the only other option. Initially she'd tried her utmost to convince Andy her second baby was his, after all it could have been, but with his auburn freckled complexion even she had to admit he wasn't Andy's.

Unfortunately, he was the result of a one-night stand. She couldn't even remember the chap's name and she'd never seen him since. But Sammy, however, was his; she was a female version of him through and through. Suddenly registering that Andy was still firing questions, she tried to pick up the conversation.

"When can we sit down and discuss this?" Andy repeated in a slightly raised voice. He wanted to get this sorted, if this was her decision it wasn't something that would happen overnight.

"If you can have Sammy next weekend, bring her back about the same time as today and we'll sit down and talk next Sunday evening."

"Fine," Andy agreed. "Make sure she's ready, I'll pick her up about 6pm on Friday." He turned to leave, acknowledging that in the last ten minutes his whole life had turned completely on its head.

Arriving home, Andy opened the front door and collapsed in the nearest chair. He had no recollection of the drive back; all he could think of was his daughter. How on earth would Sammy deal with all these changes? Hadn't they put her through enough in her young life? Then there was the question of how he would manage this situation, there was so much to consider and so much to discuss.

The rest of the evening passed in a haze. Settling for something simple for his tea, Andy prepared himself a couple of slices of cheese on toast and sat at the kitchen table writing notes. By the end of the evening, he had two lists: one to be discussed with Sharon and the other a comprehensive list of everything he was going to need for the future.

Luckily money wasn't something he needed to worry about, he earned a good salary, and Tim had hinted that if business continued in the same way a bonus was on the cards for the end of the year, but he worked long hours in order to earn his money and high on his list was hiring a professional Nanny. How much was that going to cost? He had no idea.

After a restless night, it was a huge relief for Andy to get to work. He needed to concentrate on something other than being totally responsible for a toddler. It had always been purely a dream of his, that one day Sammy would want to live with him, but he'd imagined her to be a lot older and able to make her own decisions. It never crossed his mind that Sharon would give her up voluntarily at such a young age. The idea that work would somehow take his mind off his immediate troubles didn't work out; by the time Tim decided it was time to stop for their breakfast break, Andy had already told him the whole story.

Tim was incredibly supportive. To begin with Andy had been concerned that Tim's main concern would be the effect it might have on his work, but if it was, he kept it to himself. "If you want my honest opinion," Tim offered as he sipped his coffee. "I think in the long run it will be for the best. You worry now about what's going on when you're not there, and let's be honest, it's never going to get any better; Sharon was always going to be a complete pain. Now you'll call the shots, it's a win, win situation." He smiled at his partner and shrugged, absolutely convinced he was right.

By the time they'd finished their break, together they'd thrashed out loads of ideas, and Tim even had some news that might eventually help Andy in his quest to find a Nanny.

"I can't remember if I've ever mentioned it," Tim began. "But my sister is a paediatric nurse. One of her best friends is a full-time professional Nanny and you never know she might know of someone that could help, even if it's just temporary until you find someone else. I can give her a ring if you want."

"That would be brilliant," Andy said gratefully. "I have no idea how to go about hiring a Nanny. I'll see how it goes next Sunday and if she's still serious and we're really going to do this, I'd appreciate the help, I really would."

"That's fine, just say the word and I'll give her a call," Tim assured him as they both made their way back to work.

It wasn't until much later that day that Tim broached the subject that he'd initially considered when Andy first broke the news. "How does Maria fit into all of this, or doesn't she?" Not long ago he'd overheard Lisa chatting with Maria, and although he never asked and Lisa never said, he'd guessed from her response that Maria was interested in someone else.

"I'm still thinking that one through," Andy replied

unconvincingly.

***

The minute Lorenzo received the good news he had been anxiously waiting for, he formally accepted the position and handed in his notice. He needed to get out of this place, village life wasn't for him; he needed a lot more space to live the sort of life he enjoyed. That same evening, he rang Maria.

"That's amazing, congratulations." Maria was genuinely pleased for him. Several weeks had passed since they'd met in London and Maria often wondered if he'd heard anything yet. He'd seemed very confident when they last met that the interview had gone well. In the end she presumed he'd either forgotten, or just hadn't bothered to let her know, so she was pleasantly surprised when he rang. "You must be over the moon, when do you start?" she asked out of curiosity.

"I have to work a month's notice unfortunately, so in about five weeks." There was a short silence before Lorenzo continued. "I'd love to meet up once I get to London." Another short silence followed.

"Yes, I'm sure we'll be able to work something out," Maria answered, instantly regretting her non-committal answer. Why, she reprimanded herself, do I always do that…?

Lorenzo took the hint as he interpreted her reply; the call was over. Slowly he put the phone down. He couldn't quite make her out, and miserably he realised he'd lost the connection that had been there when they met. He took out his pen from his jacket pocket and marked the calendar; in just five weeks he would be a fifty-minute train ride away from her. In the meantime, he had a lot of work to do.

***

Every so often, since the day all three sisters had been working, they arranged a day out and this Saturday it was their special day at the spa. They'd opted to try the new spa everyone was raving about. It wasn't cheap, so they were expecting complete luxury, and they weren't disappointed.

They'd all agreed on "The indulgent" spa package, to include a deep tissue back massage, facial, manicure and a champagne lunch. The treatments were proving a huge success and by the time they'd finished eating their lunch they were all feeling extremely relaxed and refreshed.

"I feel absolutely wonderful," Kim said as she raised her glass to her sisters for a toast.

"So do I," Clare agreed. "But I think that's more the after-effects of the champagne rather than any of the treatments, although I have to say I enjoyed them all."

"I agree," Maria said before ordering another bottle of champagne. "So, I think we'll have more of what works best for us." Her laugh was contagious and before long they were all in fits of laughter.

In their extremely happy, giggly state, relaxing in their big fluffy white towelling dressing gowns, they discussed everything under the sun, including their partners.

"Come on Maria." Kim giggled. "Tell us more about the Italian, what's happening with him?" She leant in closer, keen to hear her sister's reply.

"Nothing's happening with the Italian," Maria answered, deliberately teasing them.

"Why ever not?" Clare taunted her sister. "He's gorgeous, and that accent," she said dreamily.

"Does he always speak with that accent?" Kim asked sceptically. "Or does he exaggerate it when he's in company?"

"I have no idea," Maria said, trying to stifle more laughter as she looked at her sisters who were desperate for some gossip. "It's always the same I think."

"When's he starting his new job?" Kim wasn't giving up; she had a strong feeling Maria was holding back and there was definitely more of this story to tell.

"In two weeks," Maria answered quite innocently.

"Ahh." Clare wagged her finger in a friendly gesture. "So,

if you know it's exactly two weeks, I reckon you've been in touch with him." She sat back in her chair as though she'd just solved one of the world's biggest mysterys. "Am I right?" she asked cheerfully.

Maria was finding it difficult to keep a straight face. "He phones occasionally," she admitted, hoping this would be enough information for her inquisitive sisters.

"Define occasionally," Clare said as she folded her arms in anticipation for a long wait.

"Oh, I don't know, it depends," Maria mused, slightly embarrassed by all the attention.

"Once a month, once a week, every day?" Clare wasn't giving up, so Maria thought she'd give them something to think about.

"Well, it started as every other week, then it was once a week, now it's a couple of times a week." She tried not to burst out laughing as her two sisters looked at one another in amazement.

"A couple of times a week, and you don't know when you're going to see him again." Kim raised her eyebrows in disbelief. "I think, dear sister, you've been holding out on us." Kim tried not to slur her words as she picked up her glass. "Let's have a toast, to our dear sister Maria and the Italian waiter."

"Cheers," they said, all clinking their glasses, as once again they burst into fits of laughter.

***

The following Sunday evening Andy pulled up outside Sharon's and, before he'd had a chance to get Sammy out of the car, Paul walked down the path heading for his car. He waved and Andy half-heartedly waved back, he couldn't quite make this guy out.

Not knowing what to expect of today's meeting, Andy was pleasantly surprised when Sharon produced a detailed plan of how she imagined they would gradually introduce Sammy into her new life with her daddy.

"I'm impressed," Andy said as he read through a typed

schedule of dates. "Looks like you've given it all a lot of thought, and you're quite sure this is definitely what you want?" he asked as he looked up after digesting its contents.

Sharon swallowed hard before she answered, "Yes."

Andy waited for her to continue; when she didn't, he watched her carefully. He'd never seen her emotional side before; he'd only ever experienced her anger and frustration. "I was half expecting to come here today, and you'd changed your mind," he said in a light-hearted manner. Sharon managed a smile. "I'm grateful for the gradual transition," he continued. "Obviously I've got an awful lot to sort out but looking at this plan you've taken all that into consideration, so that's a huge relief." He smiled as he considered that maybe Sharon wasn't as tough as she let everyone believe and wondered how much of this was actually her idea.

"I don't want her to know anything just yet," Sharon whispered. "Let's wait a while until we have more of it all sorted."

"That's fine, but I would like to be here when you tell her. I really think we must be very careful how we explain what's going to happen."

Sharon looked apprehensive. "I thought you'd want to tell her," she said as though it was the most obvious conclusion.

"Don't you think we should both explain?" Andy said, completely flabbergasted at her last remark.

Sharon shrugged her shoulders. "You can keep that plan; I have a copy. Will it be the same time on Friday evening?"

Guessing that was as far as their discussion was going for today Andy folded his copy neatly and placed it carefully in his pocket. "Right," he said as he stood. "I'll just say goodbye to Sammy, and I'll be off."

He gave his little girl a big hug and kissed the top of her head. "I'll pick you up next Friday, for another fun weekend, sweetheart." He smiled as her cute little face lit up and watched her dance off as her mother called her for her bath.

***

Tim hung up after his conversation with his sister and smiled; he'd spotted Lisa's reflection in the mirror as she'd hovered outside his study. She'd always been incredibly nosey, she just couldn't help herself and normally he would keep her guessing, but he knew it wouldn't be too long before she heard the news from somewhere, so it was probably for the best she heard from him.

"You'll never guess what's happened to Andy, even I couldn't believe it at first," Tim said as he leant against the door frame watching Lisa prepare their supper. "Now I've had the time to digest it all, I'm convinced it will be for the best in the long run."

Lisa hastily finished washing her hands and turned to face her husband. "What exactly has happened then?" she asked impatiently.

"Basically, Sharon the infamous ex, has decided to offload her daughter in order to follow her dream with this new boyfriend of hers. She's told Andy he can have full custody."

"How's that going to work out then?" Lisa asked as she lowered the temperature of the oven, keen to hear more of this story and not wanting to burn their casserole.

"That's why I've been on the phone to Liz. I know one of her best friends is a professional Nanny, so I was just putting out the feelers, on Andy's behalf, looking for any possible recommendations of Nannies that may be available in the not-too-distant future."

"That's a bit of a long shot, isn't it?" Lisa sounded sceptical; she couldn't understand why Tim was getting so involved.

Sensing her disdain, Tim realised that, clearly, Lisa was still holding a grudge against Andy for the way she perceived he'd treated Maria. "Look, Lisa, it's fine by me that you have no time for Andy anymore," he said adamantly. "But I work with the guy every day and apart from the fact he works extremely hard, I really like him. As I see it, unfortunately he's just a victim of circumstance, he's single handily trying the best way he knows how to sort out his life, and more importantly secure a good future for his daughter..."

"Well," Lisa interrupted. "He can put any ideas of reconciling with Maria out of his head. From what she was saying the other week, it sounds very much like she's found someone else. A handsome Italian by all accounts." She couldn't help it, she didn't trust Andy and couldn't understand Tim's obvious admiration for the guy; it really needled her.

"That's not any concern of mine or yours," Tim pointed out. "I'm just trying to help a mate, and I most certainly do not want to learn you've accidently or otherwise passed on any of this information to Maria. This is not your story to tell." He opened the fridge and grabbed a beer. "I hope I've made myself clear." He turned just in time to miss her grimace.

"Perfectly," she sneered as she turned off the oven and stormed upstairs.

Tim settled himself in front of the T.V. He loved his wife dearly but hated the way once she'd taken a dislike to someone, there was no room for manoeuvre. Why didn't I make that call from work? he reprimanded himself as he picked up the T.V. zapper and flicked through the channels, making a mental note to speak to Andy tomorrow. His sister had sounded optimistic that her friend would probably know of someone who could help, even if it was on a temporary basis for the time being, it was better than nothing. He made himself comfortable in the chair and opened his can of beer, it could be a long wait until there was any sign of food tonight.

CHAPTER NINE

MARIA – THE PRESENT

"It's fantastic, Tim, it really is," Maria exclaimed happily as Tim proudly presented her finished kitchen. "I absolutely love it, I really do."

"I'm glad you like it," he said watching her glide around her newly refurbished kitchen/family room. "I'll come back in a couple of weeks to check for snagging, but other than that, I can't see that there will be any other problems."

"Thank you so much, honestly, it's just a dream." Maria couldn't stop smiling. The flashback panels had replaced wall tiles and complemented the new work surfaces in shiny granite perfectly; the slate tiled flooring, that initially Maria hadn't been that keen on, finished the look magnificently. "Lisa is going to be so jealous," she added, teasing him. "I've promised her lunch once it was finished."

"Well at least give me the heads up on that one," he joked. "I'll book the golf course for the whole weekend in the hope she'll be over it when I get home." He packed up the last of his tools and quickly checked he hadn't left anything behind. "Thanks again for the daily cake treats, that was very much appreciated."

"Oh, you're very welcome, I'm sure Kim will have some for you next week. I take it you're joining Andy at Kim's next week?" she added.

"I will be at some stage," he confirmed as he made his way towards the door. "Take care and I'll see you in a couple of weeks." Climbing into his truck, he checked his watch, the working day wasn't quite over for him yet; he still had to call into the office before heading home.

As soon as Tim left, Maria wasted no time. She'd already invited both Clare, Jon, Kim and David for lunch on Sunday, so time was of the essence. Unfortunately, it took longer than Maria imagined wiping down all the cupboards and work surfaces, but with all that complete and shiny clean, next she was keen to reassemble all her kitchen utensils that were spread between the main house and "The Bakery". Realising Julie was still working she decided to concentrate on retrieving everything that she'd placed in the spare room upstairs.

By Friday evening, Andy had practically completed all the structural changes to the layout of Kim's kitchen. He swept up the remnants of the wall and packed away his tools, he would need them next week so they could stay here over the weekend. He surveyed the wide open area; Kim was going to be pleasantly surprised when she realised how much extra space she'd gained by removing the dividing wall. Andy secured the area, locked the house and headed home.

Saturday morning and Andy was up early; he was keen to make inroads into some changes he wanted to make to his back garden. By his own admission his own garden was purely functional. He had a few raised veg beds at the bottom of the garden, a path down the middle, lawn to each side, and the patio area with its BBQ and kitchen space, which was the only positive, if he had to describe it. He'd often thought about making some changes, but never really had that much enthusiasm, until that is, he saw Kim's back garden.

Overall, it wasn't that much larger than his, but it had far more character with defined planting areas, separate patios: one in the far corner to capture the sun and one by the French doors, and the grass areas were divided by gravel pathways. All in all, the layout really appealed to him, and he was eager to do something similar with his own garden.

However, come Saturday morning it didn't look like any of that was going to happen this weekend. It was raining heavily, and according to the forecast was due to continue for most of the day.

Andy sat at the breakfast bar in his kitchen with a cup of tea and a piece of toast, watching the rain literally fall from the sky. It was only 8.30 in the morning, and he felt the emptiness of the weekend loom before him. He needed the distraction more than ever this weekend. Relying on his gardening ideas to keep himself occupied: he hadn't made any other plans.

His thoughts drifted to Maria; he knew exactly what she was going to be doing this weekend. David had returned home early on Wednesday evening and had used the time to catch up with his "kids" at university. Kim wasn't home so there was no music or T.V. to blur the sound of his conversation and, although Andy wasn't one for listening, he could hear quite clearly David's conversation.

At first, he wasn't paying that much attention until he heard David mention Maria's name, then quite unashamedly he stopped work and listened intently. They were obviously discussing plans for the weekend and David was busy explaining how they'd all been invited to Maria's for Sunday lunch to christen her new kitchen. What he wouldn't give to be invited to that lunch party…

Andy finished his breakfast; it was going to be a very long day if he was going to mope about all day so as the garden idea wasn't going to happen this weekend, he could use the time by attacking the attic. It was a job he'd been putting off for far too long, but it was time now and he felt ready to deal with the memories he would undoubtedly recover.

***

Completely soaked, Maria closed the back door. She'd managed a few trips from "The Bakery" collecting some of her essentials, at least she had enough to crack on with and could start preparing the desserts for tomorrow's lunch.

It was 3.30pm when Maria begun to tidy up after making a gorgeous apple strudel, a chocolate and hazelnut torte and individual raspberry panna cotta pots. The weather outside hadn't improved and with a sudden crack of thunder and lightning the electric went off.

At first, she wasn't too concerned, assuming it would probably come back on very soon. After an hour, Maria realised it wouldn't be long before she would need to light some candles and at the same time decided to give the electric company a call. It was a recorded message that activated as soon as Maria dialled the number. It listed the postcodes that were affected by the storm and explained that engineers were already on site and power would be restored as soon as possible.

Kim and David were watching the early evening local news which opened with the lead story of the power cut, which was affecting huge parts of the county. The affected postcodes were continuously listed at the bottom of the screen.

"That's Maria's postcode," Kim said jumping up from her chair. "I'm just going to give her a quick ring."

"Tell her to make her way over here," David called after her. "She can have a Chinese with us, she won't be able to cook without power."

"Will do," Kim answered as she waited for Maria to pick up.

Disillusioned with the whole situation, Maria had curled up on the sofa with a torch and was trying to read a book which she'd bought ages ago and hadn't had time to read.

"Hi Kim, what's up?" She wondered if they were without power as well.

"I've just seen your postcode come up on the T.V. as one of the areas without power."

"Yes, it went off about 3.30pm, I keep checking for an update but there's no time scale for how long it's all going to take. Are you ok, you still have power then?"

"Yes, we're ok here," Kim confirmed. "Look, David is going to order a Chinese later, why don't you come over and eat with us, otherwise you might not be able to have a hot meal tonight?"

"Well, I keep thinking it's going to come on any minute," Maria answered honestly.

"I wouldn't count on that Maria, otherwise it wouldn't have been the lead story on the news, would it?"

"No probably not," Maria agreed. "Well, if it's alright with you I will pop over. I'm going to go mad here all evening if it doesn't come back on until much later."

"Bring an overnight bag, just in case it's the worst-case scenario and it doesn't come back on tonight," Kim quickly added before Maria hung up.

"It won't take that long surely." This was most inconvenient. It was ruining all her plans and meant she'd have a lot more to do in the morning.

"Just bring one anyway," Kim insisted. "That way you can have a few drinks."

Maria laughed at her sister's logic. "Ok, I'll see you in a while."

Concerned about her newly baked desserts and the beef that she'd bought for tomorrow's lunch, Maria decided to take them all with her. She knew Kim had transferred her fridge into the garage while all the work was going on, so she knew she'd be able to store them safely until she returned home.

After too many servings of Chinese and far too many glasses of sauvignon, Maria was grateful she'd bought an overnight bag and as soon as her head hit the pillow in Kim's spare room she immediately fell into a deep sleep.

The next morning as soon as Kim heard her sister patting about upstairs, she took her a very welcome cup of tea.

"Ahh thank you." Maria smiled at her thoughtful sister.

"Maria, David's just checked with the electric company and your power still isn't on and isn't expected to be restored until later today, at the earliest."

"Oh, you're kidding." Maria sat on the edge of the bed as she listened to her sister, registering exactly what this meant for her plans. "I'm supposed to be cooking you all lunch."

Having already given this some thought, Kim explained her idea. "Look, obviously we can't do it here, but how about we collect all your food and take it down to Clare's? You can still cook everything; it will be the same, just a different venue." She waited for some sort of response and when it didn't come, she continued. "Clare won't mind, I can give her a call if you want."

Maria was incredibly disappointed and realising her sister was trying her best to at least make an alternative arrangement, she put her cup of tea down and gave her sister a hug. "If you think she won't mind, give her a call."

"We're on," Kim called out five minutes later. "She didn't mind at all."

"Ok, I'll just have a quick shower then I'll be down," Maria answered as she closed the bathroom door.

***

Maria eventually served Sunday lunch in Clare's dining room at 5.30pm.

"I'm sorry, guys, this isn't at all how I'd planned today," Maria explained as she carried the roast beef resplendent on a beautiful serving dish that she'd found in one of Clare's cupboards.

"It looks and smells divine," Clare happily declared. "I'm starving, who's going to carve?"

"I'll carve." David moved swiftly round to the top of the table. "Pass your plates," he said, carving knife at the ready.

Despite the obstacles and the inconvenience caused by the storm, everyone appeared to enjoy their lunch. "That was a superb meal, Maria, it really was," Jon said as he scraped his dish clean. "That beef was cooked to perfection and that strudel, that was pure heaven."

"Can't tempt you to anything else then, you don't fancy some chocolate torte?" Maria teased.

"Not at the moment thank you, but feel free to leave behind anything you don't want." Jon laughed.

"Honestly, Jon," Clare began. "Anyone would think I never fed you."

"You don't feed me desserts," he answered defensively.

Maria couldn't help laughing, it was refreshing to see them bicker like a normal couple. Clare had always been the same, desperate to portray an idyllic lifestyle, even to her own family.

"It's exactly the same in our house," David assured Jon as he helped himself to a raspberry panna cotta pot. "It's worse really," he continued. "I have to listen to Kim explain, in detail I might add, all the delicious recipes Maria and her team have made each day, then I get offered a piece of fruit for dessert."

They all burst out laughing and the three sisters decided it was time to leave them to discuss their hardships, while they made a start on the clearing up.

"Do you know if your electric is back on yet?" Clare asked as they loaded the dishwasher for the second time.

"Actually, you've read my mind; I was just going to check," Maria said, reaching for her phone that she'd previously left on one of the kitchen stools.

She dialled the number and as instructed entered her postcode.

"This is ridiculous." Maria placed her phone in her handbag. "My postcode still hasn't been repaired and is not expected to be fully restored until Monday afternoon."

"You'll have to come back to ours tonight," Kim said as she wiped down all the work surfaces.

"Thanks," Maria said gratefully. "I'll have to message Julie and Louise and tell them not to come in tomorrow until I let them know I have power. This is just so inconvenient. I have a lot of work to do tomorrow; this is going to put me so behind."

"Good job you hadn't made any ice-cream cakes," Kim added trying to lighten the mood. "They would have melted." She just managed to duck as Maria threw a very wet tea towel in her direction.

"Nearly got you." Maria laughed as Kim checked she was no longer armed before standing.

Later that evening Maria made a detour to her own house before heading back to Kim's. She needed fresh clothes for Monday and was anxious to check everything was ok. Using the torch light from her phone, Maria checked each room. Kim had also given her a list of bits and pieces she needed from the office; they were going to use the morning to discuss some new ideas.

Maria was interested in venturing into the bread market, but they needed to do their homework and look seriously at their catchment area; bread needed to be sold on a daily basis.

Collecting up everything on the list, Maria added generator to the list of things to discuss. It might be a good idea to invest in one of those; it might save a lot of hassle in the future. Satisfied her house was ok for the night, Maria locked up and headed back to Kim's.

***

Andy pulled up outside Kim's at 8.00am on Monday morning. He wasn't surprised to see Kim's car, she left for work at all different times, but he was surprised to see Maria's car. Assuming there must be something wrong, instead of going straight round to the back door where he normally let himself in, he thought it only polite to check first that it was ok to continue with his work. He climbed out of his truck, ran his hand through his hair and smoothed out his jumper before casually walking up the driveway to the front door. He walked carefully past Maria's car checking out the interior as he went; just as he expected, spotlessly clean. You wouldn't find any old sweet wrappers in there, he guessed.

Then he spotted it, he wondered if she knew, or was that the reason her car was still here? Her rear tyre was completely flat.

"Sorry to disturb you," Andy said politely as Kim opened the front door. "I noticed Maria's car on the drive, so thought I'd better check if it was ok to continue with the work today."

"Oh yes, it's absolutely fine," Kim reassured him. "Maria's had a power cut since Saturday afternoon, so she's been staying here. Apparently, it's not going to be restored until later today, fingers crossed." She held up her hand showing her fingers crossed and laughed.

"I heard about all the postcodes affected on the news on Saturday, that's tough," he said, genuinely concerned. "I don't know if Maria is aware," Andy continued, "but one of her rear tyres is completely flat."

Anxious to know why Andy had knocked at the front door, when Kim had already mentioned he would just let himself in through the back door, Maria was trying to listen to their conversation from the living room.

Once she heard the mention of her car, without giving it a second thought, she joined her sister at the front door.

"Oh Maria." Kim was startled for a moment. "Andy was just saying you've got a flat tyre."

Completely forgetting the pleasantries of saying "Good morning", Maria pushed past her sister. "This is all I need," she mumbled walking towards her car.

It was a natural reaction on Andy's behalf to follow Maria, which left Kim standing alone at the front door. Feeling like the original spare part, Kim decided to leave them to it and made her way upstairs to watch discreetly from the window.

"I can't believe this," Maria exclaimed as she bent down to examine the tyre. "It was fine yesterday when I drove back." She looked up to where Andy was standing watching her. For the first time in a very long time, with no one else around, their eyes met. His eyes were still as clear and bright but there was also a certain sadness about them, and she wondered what could have happened to cause a lingering pain seen by only those who really knew him.

Andy felt his face blush like a schoolboy with a crush, as her eyes met his and his heartbeat so fast, he thought his chest would explode.

Maria was the first to break the gaze, keeping her eyes fixed firmly on the tyre she stood and kicked it furiously. "This is so inconvenient." She sighed heavily. "But thanks for letting me know," she quickly added, keen to return indoors.

"I know the guy who owns the tyre shop in town," Andy said, keen to keep her talking. "I can give him a call if you want." His tone was gentle and just as she remembered; he could be so caring, when he wanted.

"But the car needs to be picked up surely." She couldn't look directly at him; her legs couldn't cope.

"Oh yes, definitely," Andy agreed. "He'd have to come and pick it up. Let me give him a ring; I'll just make a note of what size tyre you need, and I'll call him."

"Thank you, that's very kind. I'll wait inside." She gestured to the door, not sure if he expected her to stay while he rang or not.

"Yes, of course. Don't worry I'll come back to you once I've spoken to him." He smiled, watching her quickly disappear.

Maria walked back indoors and shutting the front door she leant against it for a second as she regained her composure.

"What's happening?" Kim said as she hurried back down the stairs.

"Andy has a friend in town who owns the tyre shop, he's going to give him a ring." She stood up straight and brushed a small amount of gravel from the knees of her jeans.

"That's nice of him," Kim said, prompting for a little bit more information.

"I can't believe it, the one year I didn't insure my tyres," Maria spoke quietly, deep in thought. "I always insure them; the one year I didn't bother, and this happens."

"It looks like he's on the phone to him already," Kim called from the living room, as she carefully peered through the window, keen not to be seen. "He's talking to someone, and he's looking directly at the flat tyre. How much do you think it's all going to cost?"

"Don't know," Maria said joining her sister in the living room. "The last time I had reason to check they were about £175 each, but I have no idea how much he'll charge to pick up as well."

"Well, looks like you're just about to find out." Kim turned to her sister. "Andy is walking back up the drive; you'd better go and open the door," she gently instructed her sister while smiling sweetly.

Maria opened the door just as he was about to knock.

Appearing startled by the sudden opening of the door, Andy was left standing for a couple of seconds with his hand mid-air. "I've spoken to Steve," he finally managed to say. "He has a tyre in stock and can get your car done by lunchtime for a total price of £205."

"Does that include transporting the car to the garage?" Maria enquired, desperately trying to look everywhere but directly into his eyes.

"Yes, everything including wheel balancing, the whole caboodle."

Maria hadn't heard that word for ages, caboodle. She remembered it had been one of Andy's favourites back in the day. Registering he was still waiting for her agreement, Maria continued, "That's a very good price, and he's a reputable guy?" she asked cautiously.

Andy frowned. "Of course, he's a mate."

For the first time that morning Maria smiled. "That's settled then. I'll go with that and thank you for sorting it all out for me; I really appreciate it."

"I'll call him back and he'll come and collect your car. If you let me have your keys, I won't need to disturb you again."

Maria grabbed her keys from her handbag and passed them carefully to Andy trying to avoid any actual contact, but Andy had other ideas as he took the keys, and for a brief second their hands touched, and their eyes met. Maria stood staring as Andy tilted his head to one side and smiled, and for a second Maria was transported back to a time when they were much younger.

The sound of Andy's mobile broke the spell, and in a flash, Maria was gone with the door closed firmly behind her.

Kim had been craning her neck from the living room window. This was like watching a love story unfold, she thought, as she walked back upstairs, anxious that Maria didn't know she'd been watching.

A couple of hours later Andy knocked on the front door. "That'll be for you," Kim said peering out the window.

"How do you know?" Maria said looking up from her laptop. "It's Andy."

"It might be for you; it might be about your kitchen."

"I doubt it. I don't think he's done much work today." Kim laughed. "It's been very quiet down there today."

Reluctantly, feeling extremely vulnerable, Maria answered the door.

"Steve has rung, your car is ready," Andy informed her. "Unfortunately, though, his pickup is out for the rest of the day, so you will need to collect it."

"That's fine, Kim will drop me off," Maria began to explain, before Kim, who had joined her, interrupted.

"Don't forget, Maria, I have the dentist, but I can run you there as soon as I get back," she said almost apologetically.

"You never said anything about the dentist." Maria looked at her sister in utter disbelief.

"Oh, I thought I told you."

"It doesn't matter," Maria said, turning her attention back to Andy. "I'll get a cab; tell Steve I'll be there in half an hour."

"I'll be going right past the garage in about ten minutes, I've got supplies to collect. I can drop you off if you don't mind travelling in my truck," Andy offered hopefully.

"That's very kind, but I couldn't put you out anymore, you've already done so much for me today."

As a bystander Kim was losing her patience with these two. "Maria, you'll wait ages for a cab, let Andy drop you off. I'm sure he doesn't mind, at least he can make sure everything is ok with your car before you drive away."

"I don't need anyone to check my car," Maria said, embarrassed by her sister's last comment.

Not wanting to miss out on this opportunity, Andy was keen to interrupt.

"Honestly," he began in earnest. "I'm going right past the door, it's absolutely no trouble at all."

Feeling trapped, with no way out, Maria gritted her teeth before replying, "If, you're sure."

"Absolutely," Andy replied before hurrying away to clear the front seat of his truck.

"Thanks for that," Maria said sarcastically as she changed her shoes and collected her bag.

"I'm sure I told you I had the dentist," Kim said unconvincingly. "Anyway, it doesn't matter; you've got a lift." She shrugged her shoulders and smiled. "Are you going straight home to check your electric?"

"I will actually," Maria said as she stood up from fixing her shoes. "According to their latest updates all power has now been fully restored. The thing is, I really don't want to take all my overnight stuff in the truck, will you bring it with you in the morning?"

Suddenly Kim felt guilty for her part in this. "Of course, and don't forget you can always come back if you want to."

"Why would I want to do that?" Maria teased. "Don't think for one moment, I don't know what you're up to here." She hugged her sister. "You do know about things said in jest, don't you? And you're off to the dentist supposedly."

"See you in the morning," Kim said ushering her out of the door.

Having hastily cleared the front seat, Andy picked up his phone and quickly dialled Tim, but unfortunately it went straight to answer phone. "Tim, I'm going off site for about half an hour. Joe has just arrived, he was held up at the suppliers; he knows what he's doing, speak later." Andy put his phone on vibrate. Tim would pick that message up when he went for lunch by which time he'd probably be back.

He started up his truck and turned down the volume of the radio. Nervously he tapped the edge of the steering wheel; his mouth was dry, his palms sweaty, and his brain a complete mush. What on earth would he find to talk about that Maria would find remotely interesting?

Climbing into the truck, Maria secured her seat belt and sat back, her handbag perched on her lap. She felt ridiculously nervous and prayed this wasn't going to be a long journey.

"Right, hopefully we won't meet too much traffic at this time of day," Andy began, echoing her sentiments exactly. "It should only take us about 15 to 20 minutes." He turned to look at her, but her gaze was fixed directly forward, and he put the truck in gear and set off.

By the time Andy pulled up on the forecourt of the tyre shop, Maria was amazed at just how much she'd learnt. She'd opened the conversation by asking him about Sammy's wedding; initially she wondered if he was aware she was making the wedding cake, but he seemed to know everything, and once he got going there was no stopping him.

"I can't believe you ended up with sole custody of Sammy," Maria said as she slowly digested everything Andy had told her. "That wasn't part of the original plan, was it?"

"No, it wasn't," he said, remembering the early days when he never thought he would survive the challenge.

Absent-mindedly, Maria continually twisted the handles of her handbag as she imagined how difficult his life must have been. "And Sharon never made any effort to see her daughter again. What on earth happened to her?"

"I've no idea." He paused briefly as he negotiated a busy roundabout. "She was moving to Scotland, so she said, with this new boyfriend, Paul." He paused again as he slowed waiting to overtake a cyclist. "She gave me her address and a phone number, and initially she called Sammy once a week, always promising to visit soon. Gradually the phone calls stopped and when I rang her, the number was disconnected. I wrote to her and asked her to contact me, but she never replied, and I never heard from her again."

"What about birthdays and Christmas, did she send Sammy cards and presents?"

"No never. But Sammy never knew that, because I bought cards and presents from her, for Sammy."

"Wow." Maria was struggling to take all this information on board. "And Sammy never found out?"

"I don't believe so," he answered honestly.

"Surely Sammy asked to see her mummy, didn't she? What did you tell her?" Maria stopped suddenly. "I'm sorry, I'm asking too many personal questions."

"No, it's fine." Andy took a deep breath and continued. "It was a gradual process; there was a lot going on and as she got older, she stopped asking about her. One year I completely forgot to send a present and card from her mother, Sammy never mentioned it and nor did I."

"How old was she when that happened?"

"Twenty-one."

"Oh," Maria answered looking directly at him.

Andy burst out laughing. "No, I was kidding, she was 11."

Maria smiled; he still knew how to catch her out. "Did you start working for Tim before or after Sammy came to live with you?" she asked. It wasn't the question she really wanted to ask, but she hoped he might elaborate. She'd noticed ages ago that he wore a wedding ring, although he always had it covered by a plaster when he was working, obviously to protect it.

"Before Sammy, but only just. It all seemed to happen about the same time." He frowned as he remembered those chaotic early days. "Well, here we are then." Andy switched off the engine and immediately climbed out of his truck.

A tall lanky man, wearing a baseball cup and a pair of ill-fitting dungarees, appeared from the office.

"It's all ready," he explained. "If you would like to pay in the office, I'll bring the car round."

"Thanks, Steve," Andy said as he held open the office door for Maria. A rather elderly lady stood in disbelief as Andy approached her desk. "Hello, Jackie, long time no see, how are you?"

"Well, I never, Andy, how are you?" Andy walked over and gave her a big hug. "Where have you been hiding?" she asked as he released her. "We haven't seen you in ages."

"I've been busy at work, Jackie." He laughed before turning towards Maria. "Jackie, this is Maria. Steve's just replaced one of her rear tyres so there should be an invoice."

It was clear from the look on Jackie's face that she remembered the name. Maria could only imagine what she was thinking and feeling slightly uncomfortable offered her credit card for payment without saying a word.

"That's all gone through. Thank you." Jackie handed the card back. "Don't be a stranger." She smiled warmly at Andy.

"I won't, I promise."

The tall lanky man called Steve appeared at the door. "Here's your keys," he said offering them to Maria. "It's just over there." He pointed to the far end of the car park.

"Thanks," Maria said as she took them from his greasy hands.

In the end Maria had to make a quick exit as her car was blocking an incoming car and she had no option but to leave the two men busy chatting.

It was like completing a jigsaw puzzle trying to piece together all the information she'd just learnt. Andy had mentioned that

Sammy was three years old when she had come to live with him, so she had to assume all this had happened not too long after that infamous weekend, when he hadn't turned up for her parents' party. But she was still none the wiser if there was still a wife on the scene, or even if he'd had any more children. Obviously, it wasn't Sharon he'd married. She wondered who she might be; was it the woman she'd seen Andy with all those years ago?

There was a meeting planned with Sammy re her wedding cake sometime soon she remembered, somehow, they'd have to try and find out more.

It was a huge relief when Maria arrived home and switched on the light. Thank goodness for that, she thought, as she closed the door behind her. Her mind was in overdrive and seeking solitude she headed for The Bakery, she would work on her own for the rest of the day.

Five minutes after Maria left with Andy, a truck pulled up and Kim watched as Tim made his way towards the house.

"Morning, Tim," she called out. "Everything ok? Didn't know you were due here today."

"Not supposed to be, but I had a strange message from Andy and as I can't get hold of him, I thought, as I was passing, I'd pop in and make sure everything is ok." He smiled, suddenly realising it was strange for Kim to be home at this time of day.

"Don't suppose you have time for a quick cup of tea?" Kim enquired while deciding exactly what she was going to say.

"Is something wrong?" he asked looking very concerned. "You're not normally home and Andy's truck isn't here."

"No, no there's nothing wrong, please don't worry. But I would like a word, if you have the time."

"A cup of tea it is then," Tim said, taking off his boots at the front door.

Tim was extremely easy to talk to and before she knew it Kim found herself explaining the whole story. Including the power cut on Saturday, through Sunday's events, finishing with the whole saga of the flat tyre.

"I really hope none of this will get Andy into trouble, because I most certainly encouraged the whole thing."

"Kim, please don't worry," Tim immediately assured her. "Andy is my partner and, in all honesty, works a lot harder than me. I'm not here to check up on him; only to make sure he's ok."

"I wouldn't normally interfere," Kim began. "But I feel there's a lot of unfinished business." Before she could continue Tim interrupted.

"I know exactly what you mean, Kim, I really do, and, in a way, I agree they need a little push in the right direction." Tim put his mug of tea down on the little side table as he considered how much he should divulge. "Over the years I've witnessed Andy suffer more than his fair share of painful experiences, including the breakup with Maria all those years ago." He studied Kim's reaction before he decided to continue. "His life has been anything but plain sailing and, through everything, he's always kept his daughter his main priority and I have the utmost respect for the guy."

"Thank you for your honesty," Kim said. "But I know my sister and I've always believed Andy to be her one true love. Don't get me wrong she's not sat back and wasted her life in the hope they would meet again. She was involved with someone else for several years and before "The Bakery" she ran a very successful business." She paused taking a sip of tea and decided there and then to fill in all the details Tim probably had no idea about. When she'd finished, she could tell Tim was deep in thought. "The only thing is, neither of them give too much away on their social media accounts and Andy less than Maria, so the last thing I want to do is encourage the two of them if Andy is happily married."

Deciding to trust Kim implicitly, Tim sat back in his chair and slowly he told her the whole story as far as he knew it.

Kim was completely transfixed, hardly believing what she was hearing as the whole story unravelled.

"And there you have it." Tim, who had fidgeted continually the whole time, finally sat leaning slightly forward, with his hands clasped in front of him.

"I don't know what to say," Kim admitted wiping a tear from the corner of her eye. "It takes a while to take it all on board. I truly believe though that Maria should know all of this, would you mind if I told her?"

"I'll leave that for you to decide," Tim said before adding, "I would ask though that she doesn't let on it that it originally came from me." He felt uneasy, but deep down, was convinced he'd done the right thing.

"Maria is the height of discretion, Tim; you don't have to worry about that. I really believe this is something she needs to know."

"As I said, I'll leave that all up to you. Anyway, I need to get back to work. I'm sure Joe has seen my truck, he'll wonder what on earth I'm doing…"

"And here comes Andy," Kim said pointing to the window as she watched Andy make his way straight round the back.

"Definitely time to leave then." They both smiled and Kim showed Tim to the door.

For the rest of the afternoon Kim found it difficult to settle, her mind was wandering all over the place; she was anxious to know how the journey to pick up the car went and equally concerned about how and when she would tell Maria everything she had just learnt. In the end she made the decision to just give Maria a quick ring.

Maria's phone went straight to answer phone.

"Hi it's only me," Kim began. "Just wondering how it all went with your car, obviously your power is back on, anyway give me a call back."

Maria worked until after 8pm, and by the time she cooked her supper and checked her phone it was nearly 10pm.

"Hi, sorry I've been working and only just seen that I missed your call," Maria explained as Kim's phone clicked onto answer phone. "Don't worry I'll see you in the morning. We'll have coffee together, I have quite a lot to tell you."

Not as much as I you. Kim thought to herself as she listened to Maria's message. Tomorrow was going to be a very interesting day, she thought to herself as she climbed into bed.

CHAPTER TEN

Maria – The Past Meets the Present

During the last few months Andy had continually experienced highs and lows. There had been so much to learn and prepare, but the one shining light through it all had been his daughter. Sammy had adapted well and seemed to enjoy every moment she spent with her daddy, and now with everything in place he was looking forward to the day he had sole responsibility.

With the help of Tim's sister, Andy had found an ideal applicant for the position of Nanny. It was all arranged, she would be working 7.30am until 6pm Monday to Friday, until Sammy began full-time schooling, then she'd been more than happy to leave the situation open for further discussion later.

Her name was Lynne. She was a year older than Andy and looked every inch the professional Nanny, with her long blond hair swept into a bun and a fresh clean complexion. She was probably quite attractive when dressed for a more social activity, he decided, as he watched her sign her contract, although she was a little short and stumpy for his taste, but ideal for this job.

Lynne had insisted on meeting Sammy as many times as possible before her official position began. She gave the impression she was as anxious as Andy to ensure Sammy felt happy and comfortable with her new Nanny, and from what Andy could see after a few weeks, Sammy was already forming a strong bond with Lynne. The only hitch was explaining Lynne's position. Sammy couldn't quite grasp the concept of having a Nanny. In her little mind Lynne must be Daddy's new girlfriend therefore she should call her Aunty Lynne. It took a while, but eventually Sammy got the idea and the two of them were practically inseparable.

***

With the encouragement of her family, Maria continued to accept Lorenzo's invitations to join him in London on his days off. She couldn't deny, she enjoyed his company; he was funny, interesting, very lively, always jovial and treated her with the utmost respect and kindness. But there was something missing and the last thing she wanted to do, was just use him to fill a gap in her broken heart.

"Don't get me wrong, I like him, I really do," Maria explained over coffee with her sister Kim. "He's great fun, but I continually feel guilty because I just don't feel the same connection to him as I did with Andy. To be honest I sometimes wonder if I'm just using him and I don't want to do that. I'd hate it if someone did that to me." She stirred her coffee and peeled back the paper case of her blueberry muffin. "I don't know what it is really; it's just me being really silly and I know I shouldn't compare, they're very different individuals, but it does feel like there's something missing." She paused briefly to enjoy a bite of muffin. "When I was with Andy, if he held my hand my heart would race, if he touched my face, my knees would go weak. We could go out for dinner, or just sit and watch T.V., it didn't matter so long as we were together." She sighed, just remembering was still so painful.

Kim sat listening to her sister; she understood, it had been very much the same with David. He'd been her soul mate from the very beginning, but she couldn't help wondering if Maria was expecting too much too soon.

"He obviously really likes you," Kim said sympathetically. "Why don't you just enjoy it for what it is, give it a little more time? You never know, he might be the best thing ever, in time."

Maria smiled and finished her muffin. Nobody really understood.

Lorenzo was in a very happy place; he was having the time of his life working and living in London and as far as he was concerned everything was going extremely well between Maria and himself. He'd been happy to let her set the pace but was now keen for her to meet his family. This he thought might help her realise he was in this for the long haul; it suited his situation to have a steady girlfriend and he got the impression she thought he was a "non-committal" sort of guy.

If she agreed, it would be an experience she wouldn't forget. They were completely different to her own family. They were extremely vocal and believed vehemently in freedom of speech, and provided everyone agreed with their views, there wasn't an issue. He laughed to himself, as he imagined such a meeting.

Maria decided to take Kim's advice. Who knew what the future would hold? But for now she wouldn't worry; it was time to enjoy life and have some fun. So, when Lorenzo asked if she would like to join him for Sunday lunch with his family she accepted without any hesitation. "I'd love to, after all you've met all my family." She laughed.

"Fantastic," he said giving her a big hug. "I warn you though, my family are not sophisticated, they are very loud, and it most certainly won't be a quiet relaxing lunch."

"They can't be that bad," she mocked.

"Don't you believe it. To begin with they'll be on their best behaviour, but that'll only last for ten to fifteen minutes at the most. The one thing I can promise though, is the food. My mum and sister are exceptional cooks, and the food will be amazing."

"It sounds wonderful, it really does, and I can't wait," she said excitedly.

"So…" He stood a little way apart from her watching her reaction. "I was thinking, if you come up on Saturday morning, we could have lunch somewhere nice, then instead of going all the way home and then back again on Sunday, you could stay over. I don't need to be in work on Saturday until 6pm and I'll be home by 11.30pm at the latest." He watched her intently, but as usual she was so difficult to read.

"Can I confirm that later?" Disappointment was written all over his face, so she felt she should explain. "It's just that I don't normally see you on a Saturday night and I've promised to babysit for a friend." She squeezed his hand gently. "I'll see if I can get out of it," she promised. She'd been expecting this suggestion and previously she thought she was ready, but now she wasn't so sure. She needed to think about it in her own space and time.

Lorenzo wasn't convinced Maria was being entirely truthful. It was true, they didn't normally see one another on a Saturday night, but he most certainly couldn't ever remember her mentioning a friend with a baby.

She'd always given him the impression she wasn't that interested in babies.

"Are you ok? You were miles away," Maria asked.

"Sorry." Lorenzo smiled. "I was just thinking, shall I confirm with my family for next Sunday, even if it turns out you can't make it on Saturday?"

"Yes please, I'm really looking forward to it." Sensing a certain despondency, she took her handbag and handed Lorenzo his jacket.

"What are we going to do today? Sundays are my favourite day of the week, and we have all day to ourselves."

Within the hour they were huddled together on a busy train heading for Covent Garden, one of their favourite haunts.

***

Although there was plenty of room for the two of them in Andy's flat, he wanted a house with a garden for his little girl to grow up in. He openly discussed his plans with Tim and between the two of them they drew up a financial forecast, but it wasn't a viable proposition. Lynne's salary took a substantial amount from his salary, and he wouldn't be able to afford a larger mortgage just yet.

"It's not always going to be like this, mate," Tim explained. "The business is getting busier year on year."

"I know that," Andy interrupted. "You've been extremely generous; I wouldn't have been able to afford to pay for a full-time Nanny if I'd still been at the garage. No, I'm more than happy, and like you say, I'll get there eventually."

Andy didn't begrudge Lynne's salary; from day one she'd gone over and above her duties, the flat had never been cleaner, she kept all Sammy's clothes washed and ironed, changed Sammy's bed once a week and very often prepared supper for Andy, so all he had to do was heat it through when he was ready to eat. He had complete confidence in her abilities to look after his daughter, and for the first time in a very long time he felt like his life had a purpose.

Previous to this position Lynne had worked abroad; her charges had been children from extremely privileged backgrounds, so this was a refreshing change. Initially she was just back in the U.K. for a holiday, but a dear friend had asked her if she knew of anyone that may be interested and for some reason, she'd gone along to the interview herself. She'd immediately taken to Sammy and had accepted the position willingly.

Within weeks, Lynne realised that Sammy was used to spending large amounts of her time watching T.V. Keen to break this habit she decided to approach Andy with one of her ideas.

"Everything ok?" Andy said as he realised one evening that Lynne was making no effort to leave.

"Yes, absolutely," she said cheerfully. "I was just waiting for you to say hello to Sammy, then I was hoping I might have a word."

"What is it?" he said as he settled Sammy.

"Nothing to worry about," she assured him. "It's just that I have noticed that Sammy is content to sit and watch T.V. for too long and I would like to try and break the habit. For this reason, I was wondering if you'd mind if I enrolled her in nursery school for a couple of mornings each week?"

Immediately Andy felt embarrassed, he should have picked up on this himself, and already have a nursery school sorted for his daughter.

Lynne took the silence as disapproval. "If you're not keen on the idea, it's not a problem."

"I think it's a great idea." He smiled. "I just feel this is something I should have already thought about."

Appreciating his total honesty, and sensing his embarrassment, Lynne decided to keep some of her other ideas to herself for the time being.

"Not at all, you can't think of everything, anyway." She smiled, trying her best to ease the situation. "It's my job to organise these things for Sammy. That's what you pay me for." She collected her coat and bag, said goodnight to Sammy and left them to their evening. He was such a nice man, she reflected as she made her way to the bus stop: very handsome, kind and very considerate, well out of her league, she conceded as she caught a glimpse of her reflection in a shop window.

The next day, Lynne took Sammy to visit two nurseries that were within walking distance from the flat, and by the time Andy came home from work Sammy was enrolled and due to start the following Monday. Once Sammy became used to her new routine of nursery school three mornings a week, Lynne introduced playtime in the park for the remaining two mornings, where Sammy learnt to climb, and thoroughly enjoyed playing on the swings and the roundabout. The afternoons were spent colouring, painting or learning to read. T.V. was a treat reserved for the end of the day.

Not usually one to interfere, Tim considered his options carefully. He'd heard via his sister Liz that the new Nanny was completely smitten with her new boss, and according to Liz, Lynne was a lovely person. She'd lost both her parents at an early age and her childhood had suffered unnecessary disruption as she was moved from one family member to another. It was probably because of her childhood experiences, that she'd been drawn into a career working with young children.

It was time, Tim concluded, that Andy was made aware that Maria had already moved on and was seeing someone else. He sincerely hoped once Andy knew the situation, he would be able to release any notions he harboured of a reconciliation and move forward himself. It was all too obvious to anyone who knew him that Andy didn't notice any other women, or if he did, it was always as a poor comparison to Maria. Left to his own devices he'd never notice that Lynne liked him; he probably couldn't even remember the colour of her hair if questioned. Once the decision was made all Tim had to do was choose the right time.

A little while after settling Sammy into nursery, Lynne decided it was time to broach another one of her ideas with Andy. In her view it was imperative every child was taught to swim.

"I think it's a great idea, I really do," Andy said as he took off his boots and hung up his jacket. "Have you spoken to Sammy? I don't think she's had much experience with water, apart from the bath obviously," he continued as he made his way into the living room to check on Sammy.

"I have, because some of the other kids at nursery go and Sammy was asking lots of questions," Lynne confirmed as she followed him into the living room.

"Daddy." Sammy jumped up and ran towards her daddy who bent down to cuddle and tickle her until she could laugh no more.

Guessing this was probably the end of the conversation, Lynne returned to the kitchen where she quickly finished clearing the kitchen. She'd hoped they would have had the chance this evening to discuss this in more detail. In the mornings Andy was always in so much of a rush and normally just left her a pile of notes he'd made the night before.

A little later that evening with Sammy safely tucked up in bed, Andy settled himself at the table to enjoy his supper. Lynne had left him a lasagne with extra grated cheese, one of his favourites. He took his notepad to write a few notes; he didn't know if he should write an apology or make time in the morning. As normal these days, Sammy demanded his whole attention when he got in from work and he remembered that Lynne had tried to discuss the prospect of taking Sammy for swimming lessons. He'd agreed but clearly, they hadn't covered all the necessary issues. For a start Sammy didn't have a swimsuit that was suitable, and there was transport to and from the pool to sort out. He scribbled a few notes just in case he didn't have time in the morning.

From the very first day, Sammy enjoyed her swimming lessons, and it was hard to believe she'd never had a lesson before. She appeared to be fearless in the water and progressed quickly and by the end of term she no longer needed her water wings. "She's definitely ready and more than capable," the teacher confirmed as she asked Lynne if Sammy could join the rest of the class in the end of term gala. "She will need to come in for a few extra lessons this week, but that's just so she knows what's expected. She has worked so hard I think it would be a shame to leave her out."

"I'm sure it will be ok, but I do need to check with her father; obviously he has the final word," Lynne explained to the teacher.

"I understand, and I'm sorry to press you, but I really need to know by tomorrow morning."

"I'll definitely let you know by tomorrow," Lynne confirmed as she cuddled Sammy in her drying towel.

Andy had hardly stepped inside the door when Sammy suddenly appeared jumping up and down.

"Please say yes, Daddy, please," Sammy pleaded with such concern.

"Say yes to what exactly?" Andy asked as he swept her up into his arms.

"My swimming, please say yes."

Carrying Sammy into the kitchen, they found Lynne busy clearing the dishes.

"Can you please explain to me what this over-excited little girl is actually talking about?" He laughed as he gave Sammy a big squeeze.

Lynne continued clearing the kitchen as she began to explain. "Mrs Jenkins, the swimming teacher, would like to enter Sammy in the end of term gala next Saturday." She packed away the last few plates and turned to face him as she continued to explain. "She assures me Sammy is ready, but she'll need a few extra lessons this week with the other beginners, so basically, they're all in sync with each other. I told her I would speak to you, but I do have to confirm either way by tomorrow morning."

"My little mermaid." Andy looked adoringly at his daughter.

"Please, Daddy, please can I go."

"Well, I guess it's a yes from me then," Andy said as Sammy threw her arms around his neck.

"Thank you, Daddy, thank you so much." She wriggled to escape his hold.

"I'll let Mrs Jenkins know in the morning then," Lynne said as she put Andy's supper in the oven. "That will be ready in 40 minutes."

"Thank you." he smiled. "You don't have to cook for me every day, but I do appreciate it. Oh, by the way," he continued. "What time will I have to get Sammy to the pool?"

"I'm not entirely sure," Lynne replied. "But I'll get all the details for you tomorrow."

Sammy stopped in her tracks and turned to look at her Nanny. "Are you not coming to watch me?" she asked, already looking terribly sad.

"No darling." Andy crouched down to her level as he tried to explain. "Lynne doesn't work on a Saturday does she, you know that don't you?"

Sammy stood biting her bottom lip and looked close to tears as she listened to her daddy.

"Don't get upset, sweetheart," Lynne said affectionately. "I can come along to watch you if you want me to." She ruffled the little girl's hair as she walked past to collect her coat.

"Yes, yes." Sammy jumped up and down excitedly.

Andy felt slightly uncomfortable; he couldn't help feeling sorry for Lynne. He understood why she felt compelled to promise Sammy that she would be there on Saturday, but he didn't want it to ruin any plans she might have already made. He was all too aware of the damage that could cause.

"Are you sure?" he asked her anxiously as she popped her head around the door to say goodbye.

"Absolutely," she answered probably a little too quickly. "I didn't have any plans that were set in stone," she answered honestly before saying goodnight to Sammy.

She walked slowly to the bus stop digesting the events of the last few minutes. For once she had something to look forward to at the weekend.

***

Maria had thought of nothing else, but finally resolved she would stick to her original story. Having gone to great pains to explain how she didn't like to let her friend down, they finally arranged to meet at midday just outside Victoria station on Sunday.

Apart from his initial warning about his family, Lorenzo had been short on any further information and with no photos to hand, she'd been left to imagine what they might look like and where they lived.

"Don't worry," Lorenzo reassured her as they walked hand in hand down a tree-lined avenue. "They'll love you, why wouldn't they?"

Maria managed an apprehensive smile as they continued their journey past rows of Victorian terraced houses.

Lorenzo opened the lopsided wrought iron gate and stood aside as Maria made her way steadily along the uneven cracked pathway. Before they'd even reached the front door Lorenzo's mother appeared and greeted them excitedly with open arms. Maria had imagined her to be of similar age to her own mother, but at just five feet tall, with scraped back silver hair and a weathered complexion she looked a lot older.

Sensing her hesitation at this overwhelming welcome, Lorenzo, while speaking to his mother in Italian, guided Maria gently inside the house. "Are you sure you're ok with this? I did warn you they'd be full on."

Maria felt a little bewildered but not wanting to spoil the day she smiled reassuringly. "It's fine, honestly."

Lorenzo led her down a narrow dark hallway to a large living/dining room that then led onto the small compact kitchen.

Previously he'd explained that although he had two elder brothers, one would still be away visiting family in Italy. The remaining brother and his heavily pregnant wife were the first to be introduced, followed by his younger sister Isabella, who quickly disappeared back to the kitchen where she continued helping her mother with the lunch.

"Now come and meet my dad," Lorenzo said as he took her by the hand and led her into another room which everyone referred to as "the front room". His dad, who again appeared to be much older than her own father, sat in an oversized armchair in the corner of the room surrounded by several small tables adorned with a brandy glass, a small cup of black coffee, a few newspapers, a paperback and a packet of very thin cigars. He remained sitting but smiled broadly and offered his hand as Lorenzo completed the introductions. He had an air about him, Maria noted, with his slicked back hair and abundance of gold jewellery, he instantly reminded her of The Godfather.

Obviously a man of few words, after the initial introduction he seemed to turn his attention back to his paper and Lorenzo led her back to join the others.

"I bet that was an unexpected experience for you, meeting Papa." Lorenzo's brother Pepe laughed as Maria sat uneasily in one of the various chairs. "Don't worry," he continued, noticing Maria's concerned expression. "He's a man of very few words is Papa. Unlike the rest of the family." He gestured to the others who were already deeply involved in a conversation that went from English to Italian at regular intervals.

Isabella proudly announced lunch at exactly 2pm. It was a typical Italian affair, beginning with Antipasti, followed by two huge bowls of delicious smelling pasta: one meat, one cheese, endless amounts of homemade garlic bread and the best Tiramisu Maria had ever tasted.

"Isabella that was incredible," Maria said as she finished her second helping of pasta. "You should definitely have your own restaurant."

Isabella smiled but before she could say a word Pepe answered, "Don't give her ideas, she has enough of those as it is." He smirked. "Anyway, her repertoire is limited; we have the same thing every weekend." Everyone except Maria laughed heartily, and still laughing the three men retired to "the front room" for more brandy, leaving the women to clear the dishes.

Maria couldn't imagine how her mother and sisters would react if her father was to retire for brandy leaving them to clear the dishes. This was an incredibly old-fashioned way to behave, and Maria quickly realised there was no way this family could ever meet hers; it would be a complete disaster.

It wasn't too long after the women finished clearing that Lorenzo reappeared. "Do you want to make a move now?" he whispered in her ear.

"I really don't mind," Maria said honestly.

"I'm ready to go," he said before declaring in Italian they had to make a move.

They said their goodbyes in record time and as they turned out of the gate and out of sight Lorenzo pulled her to one side.

"If I'd explained their antiquated ways, I was afraid you wouldn't have come, and I wanted my family to meet you." He looked worried as he spoke.

Maria burst out laughing and for a while couldn't speak, eventually she managed to reply, "Honestly, Lorenzo, don't worry, it was an experience and, at the end of the day, they're your family and I'm pleased that I've meet them."

"But never again…" he finished the sentence for her, and they both burst into floods of laughter.

***

Lynne checked her appearance for the umpteenth time that morning. Originally, she'd planned to wear her hair down today, but she'd changed her mind at the last minute and, instead, settled for wearing a little mascara and lip gloss. Not that it would make any difference, Andy never noticed anything where she was concerned.

She locked her front door and headed for the bus stop. She'd arranged to meet Andy and Sammy at the swimming pool at 11.00am. The gala was due to begin at 11.30am and the youngest group, of which Sammy was one, were due to swim first.

Sammy insisted they wait outside for Lynne to arrive and watched excitedly every time a bus pulled up and one by one the passengers disembarked. Andy was just beginning to wish they'd arranged to pick her up from her home, when quite unexpectedly Sammy squealed with delight and ran towards Lynne. Her bus had been late, and now with not very much time before the start, Lynne took Sammy straight off to the changing rooms.

Lynne crouched down to secure Sammy's hair under her swim hat, when surprisingly Sammy threw her arms around her neck and nestled her head into her shoulder.

"Are you ok, honey?" Lynne asked as she held the little girl firmly to her.

"I feel funny," Sammy whispered into her ear.

"Are you in any pain, sweetheart?" Lynne moved back slightly so she could watch Sammy's expression.

Sammy shook her head. "No."

"Tummy doesn't hurt at all?" Lynne asked.

"No, it doesn't hurt, but it feels funny."

Smiling at this adorable little girl she gave her a big cuddle. "That's ok, sweetheart," she reassured Sammy. "That's just what we call 'butterflies'. It's sometimes how we feel when we do something we've never done before, or if we do something like today in front of a lot of people." Sammy looked directly into her eyes, taking strength from her words of encouragement.

"Do you still want to do this, Sammy? You don't have to do anything you don't want to; you know that don't you?"

"I want to show Daddy my swimming," she answered very quietly.

"Ok, well Daddy is sitting in the front row." Lynne pointed in Andy's direction. "He'll definitely be able to see you, so don't worry."

"Will you wait by the side of the pool for me, please?" Sammy asked thoughtfully.

"Yes of course I will, I'll be there with your towel ready as soon as you get out of the water." She took the little girl's face between her hands and kissed her forehead. "Are you ok now?"

"Yes." Sammy smiled. She looked a lot happier now and taking her hand they followed the other little ones towards the pool.

Watching as the little ones approached the pool side, Andy leant over the safety screen searching for his little girl. It was Lynne he spotted first as she walked slowly beside Sammy holding her hand, clearly offering words of encouragement. He could see the anxiety Sammy was feeling in her face and watched intently as Lynne crouched down and gave Sammy the biggest cuddle.

Witnessing the compassion and tenderness between the two of them was something very special and he could see for himself how much Sammy needed and relied on her Nanny. He really hoped Lynne had no plans to move on any time soon, it would break Sammy's heart.

Sammy looked up into the crowd searching for her Daddy. She was anxious to make sure he was watching and, just before she climbed down into the water, she saw him and frantically waved; in return Andy blew her a kiss and gave her the thumbs up sign.

The little ones swam well, and Andy was impressed with the speed Sammy could move around the pool, her little arms and legs giving it their all. As they finished their routine and climbed back out of the pool, Lynne was there ready with a big towel which she quickly wrapped around Sammy, cuddling her tenderly.

"Well done, you were brilliant. Daddy is going to be so impressed," Lynne assured her as Sammy looked up and waved frantically.

As the little ones made their way back to the changing rooms, Andy made his way down to the foyer where they'd arranged to meet after the event. It wasn't long before Sammy came running out.

"My little mermaid," Andy said as he picked her up and swirled her round. "You were amazing, I'm so proud of you, you make me so happy." He kissed her cheek and held her tight.

"Daddy I'm starving," she said pulling away from Andy's tight hold.

"I bet you are, after all that exercise." He laughed. "Do you want to go to 'The Diner' for some fried chicken?"

"Yes please," she said happily.

Lynne watched them both and feeling surplus to requirements decided now was probably time for her to head home. "I'm going to say goodbye now, Sammy," she explained watching Sammy's face drop unexpectedly.

"Don't you want to come and have some chicken with us?" Sammy asked innocently.

"Darling, it's Lynne's day off," Andy tried to explain. "She may have plans for the rest of the day. It was very kind of her to give up most of her morning," he explained while hopelessly trying to pacify his daughter.

"I'll see you on Monday morning as normal," Lynne confirmed as she touched Sammy's cheek affectionately.

"But why can't you come and have chicken with us?" Sammy said not understanding why anyone wouldn't want to go to the Diner for chicken.

"Because today is your day with your daddy," Lynne desperately tried to explain, while in truth she would have given anything to join them.

"Look," Andy began suddenly. "You're more than welcome to join us if you're not doing anything else. But please don't feel pressured, Sammy must learn the boundaries at some time."

This was music to Lynne's ears; this was her chance, and she wasn't going to miss it. "Well, I love chicken." She laughed.

"Great, come with us then," Andy replied, keen to get going.

"Goody, goody," Sammy said jumping up and down. "We're all going for chicken," she sang repeatedly.

To any outsider they looked like any normal family, chatting and laughing while enjoying fried chicken, French fries and cola on a Saturday lunch time. They were all very much at ease with one another. So much so that after a very enjoyable lunch, it seemed a natural progression to take a walk across to the park to allow Sammy some time to play on the swings.

Andy was pleasantly surprised to discover how comfortable and relaxed he felt over lunch. At first, he thought Lynne might feel outnumbered and he wondered what on earth they might find to talk about, but he needn't have worried, the conversation flowed continuously between the three of them.

Initially, Andy presumed Lynne would be keen to leave once they'd eaten. He'd noticed she was wearing a little make-up today and guessed there must be someone waiting for her somewhere. In the end it was gone 10pm when, finally, Andy called a cab to take her home.

They'd returned to the flat much later that afternoon and Sammy had insisted that Lynne stay for bath time, then story time, and finally fell asleep holding her hand.

Emerging from Sammy's bedroom Lynne felt a little awkward, should she just collect her coat and say goodbye? She wasn't sure how to play this; the last thing she wanted was to outstay her welcome. She could hear Andy in the kitchen, so she popped her head around the door. "She's finally gone to sleep," she whispered.

Andy held up a bottle of wine and an empty glass. "Fancy a glass, I'm having one."

"Definitely." She smiled. "I make it a rule, never pass on the offer of wine."

Are you hungry?" Andy asked casually as he placed two glasses of wine on the kitchen table.

"Mm, don't know," she answered honestly.

"I'm a dab hand at cheese on toast; it's one of my specialities." He laughed. "Do you fancy that?"

"Ok, why not," she replied, watching him move confidently around the kitchen.

"Take a seat then." He offered her a chair. "It won't be long."

***

It was a gradual process, Tim acknowledged, but there was most certainly a different air to Andy's conversation. Invariably, he noted, there appeared to be the three of them at weekends as well as weekdays, and without realising it Andy didn't seem to be able to hold a conversation without mentioning her name. It was with a little sadness, though, that he learnt through his sister, Lynne thought Andy only looked upon her as a friend.

This might be the time, Tim considered, to clear the path for Andy, he suspected he knew exactly what might be holding him back.

Later that day over their tea break, Tim had the ideal opportunity. "Have you got any plans for this weekend?" Tim enquired as he poured them both a hot drink from his thermos flask.

"Lynne managed to get tickets for the new Disney film for Saturday afternoon." He laughed.

"She appears to be around a lot more these days," he began tentatively. "Anything I should know?" He laughed, while trying to keep the conversation very light-hearted.

"No mate," Andy declared adamantly. "She's just so good with Sammy, and Sammy adores her."

"And you think she spends all this extra time with you, for Sammy's sake." Andy didn't look up from his paper, but Tim could see him grinning. "If you like her, which you obviously do, as you talk about her a lot, and she likes you, what's the problem?" Tim paused for a moment before he added his last few words of wisdom. "You should move on you know."

Andy looked up. "Where's this going, Tim?" he asked, noticing a concerned look on Tim's face.

"I just don't want you to waste your life waiting for Maria."

"I'm not," he answered reflectively. "I know that's a no-go area now." Tim watched trying to gauge how much he might know.

Sensing this, Andy continued, "It's ok, Tim, I know she's with someone else. I bumped into her sister Clare in town, and she couldn't wait to tell me Maria was dating some Italian guy."

"How long have you known?" Tim asked.

"A while," he replied. "I've known for a while."

***

It was quite normal now for Maria to spend every weekend in London with Lorenzo. She would rush home from work on Friday evening, quickly change, grab her overnight bag and jump on a train, London bound. She normally arrived about 8.30ish and headed straight for Lorenzo's rooms, and together they would enjoy a late meal together when he finished work about 10.30pm.

Saturday mornings were always very relaxed and when Lorenzo went into work on Saturday evening, Maria would settle down with a video or a book. Occasionally on a Sunday they would head to hers for a relaxing day, but more often they preferred to remain in London. Lorenzo loved London and enjoyed exploring every inch of it, and Maria was totally enjoying her life with him.

She'd long since given up any idea of trying to recreate the same feelings she'd experienced with Andy. She did have feelings for Lorenzo, but they were nowhere near as intense or passionate, and maybe they never would be, but Lorenzo made her feel very special and that was reassuring.

Her work life, however, wasn't proving to be as fulfilling as she had originally hoped. Having successfully transferred all the office procedures from manual to computerization, the day-today running of the office was now a little boring, but with such a busy social life, she didn't really have a lot of time to actively search for something a little more challenging. As it was, she was already feeling the pressure to spend more time with her friends and family. Her priority had to be her parents who had expressed a wish to see her regularly during the week, so between them, they'd agreed on Thursday evenings. They alternated between each other's houses and occasionally they met in the pub. This week it was her turn to cook, and she'd decided on one of her father's favourites of steak, chips, mushrooms and peas.

"Wow, Maria, something smells absolutely delicious," her father said as he took off his coat.

"Thanks, Dad." Maria smiled as she welcomed them in and took their coats.

"Do you need any help, darling?" her mother said as she made her way straight to the kitchen anyway.

"I'm ok thanks, Mum." Maria followed her mother, shrugging her shoulders as she looked at her father, who was busy carefully removing a bottle of red from a carrier bag.

"Where's your corkscrew, Maria?" her father called, holding up the bottle.

"It's on the table, ready and waiting."

Her father laughed and made his way into the dining room.

Maria carefully placed their plates on the table. "Please help yourself, before it gets cold," she said as she uncovered the dishes of mushrooms, peas and chips. "Cheers, Mum and Dad." Maria held up her glass of red wine.

"Cheers," her father replied.

"Yes cheers." Her mother clinked her glass with them both, before tucking into her meal.

"How's work going?" her father enquired casually as he cut into his steak.

Maria frowned. "About the same," she answered truthfully.

"Where do you see the job leading?" her father asked. "Are there any further promotional avenues for you to explore within this company?"

"Why?" Maria looked at her father. "What do you mean?"

"I'm just asking, that's all." He paused for a second before deciding to carry on. "Before you started to see Lorenzo on a regular basis, you mentioned that you were finding it boring, and you were going to look for something else. I was just wondering how that was going."

"Well, I'm already the office manager; there isn't anyone above me. I report directly to the boss." She shrugged dismissively and took a sip of wine. "Anyway, it's ok for the time being. I really don't have that much time to actively search for something else at the moment."

"Surely Lorenzo would understand if you explained that you needed to spend some time looking around for a new job?" her mother asked.

"He's not stopping me," Maria said, sensing her parents weren't too pleased with her answer.

"I'm sure he's not, darling," her mother continued. "It's just that you've always been very strong willed and made your own path in life…" Noticing her husband's look of concern, she left the sentence in mid-air.

"I don't understand, what exactly do you mean, Mum?" Maria said trying to maintain a civil tone.

"I think," her father began. "We're just concerned that you keep your own identity in this relationship. Previously, you'd never waste time in a job that didn't fulfil your full potential."

Maria pushed her unfinished plate to one side. "Lorenzo doesn't know I find my job boring, so how can he be stopping me?" she explained defensively.

"That's my point," her father replied. "Does he even know what you do for a living?"

"Of course he does," Maria protested.

"That's ok then, darling," her mother interrupted before her husband had a chance to reply. "It's just we worry about you. It does come across that it's always about what Lorenzo wants…"

"I thought you liked him." Maria looked from one to the other desperately searching for their reply. "I don't get it; you were the ones that encouraged me to go out with him in the first place." She refilled her own glass with more wine, before immediately drinking half of it.

"We do like him." Her mother sounded cautious. "What we know of him, but we don't really know any more about him now, than when we first met him."

Her father took her hand in his. "Keep your own identity and remain your own person with your own definite ideas. That's all we ask."

Accepting his advice graciously, Maria squeezed her father's hand and tried to hide her feelings of despair, while at the same time anxious to lighten the mood. "I am thoroughly enjoying my life. Lorenzo treats me very well; he makes me laugh and we have lots of fun." She looked from one to the other.

"As long as you're happy, we can't ask for any more than that," her father concluded, content that at least he'd had the opportunity to express his concerns.

Maria collected the plates and made her way to the kitchen, grateful for an excuse to escape, even if it was just for a few minutes. "Anyone for dessert?" she called after composing herself.

"What are you offering?" her father was the first to reply.

"I have trifle from your favourite shop, or cheese and biscuits," Maria answered popping her head around the door.

"Trifle for me please."

"And me," her mother agreed.

Eventually, and completely exhausted, Maria closed the door behind her parents. That was the first time she'd ever been pleased to see them leave. She had no idea what had brought on that conversation, but she sensed their attitude towards Lorenzo had taken a turn for the worse, and she wasn't quite sure why. Maria busied herself clearing the dishes but for the rest of the evening she couldn't shake off this uneasy feeling. It was too late this evening, but first thing in the morning she'd speak to Kim; if anyone knew what was going on, she would.

Up and about early the next morning, Maria was anxious to catch Kim before she left for work, but either she'd already left or didn't hear the phone, leaving Maria with no option but to try again later this evening, before she left for London.

It was gone 6pm when Maria finally arrived home. Keen to speak with Kim she picked up the mail from the mat and sitting on the stairs picked up the phone.

"Hello," Kim answered after just a few rings.

"Hi, Kim, it's only me."

"Oh, are you ok?" Kim answered brusquely.

Immediately sensing her off hand manner, Maria remembered that her sister had left a couple of messages last week, and she'd completely forgotten to reply.

"Yes, I'm fine. I just wanted to apologise for not replying to your messages last week. Life has been a bit hectic." She laughed hoping this would be enough to pacify her sister.

"So, I understand," Kim replied indignantly.

This was going to be hard work, Maria realised. "Anyway, are you and David ok?" Maria asked politely.

"Yeah, we're fine. Is everything still going strong with Lorenzo?"

"Yes, everything is really good, but aside from that there is something I want to talk to you about." Maria sensed her sister was warming and hoped this conversation wasn't a waste of time.

"Gosh, Maria." Kim laughed. "I'm not a great one to ask for relationship advice. David has been my one and only." Both sisters laughed and this helped to break the ice.

"No, it's more to do with Mum and Dad. They came for dinner last night, and I distinctly got the impression there is something bothering them." Maria paused for a moment; she would need to choose her words carefully. "They started off enquiring about my work and it was obvious they didn't want to upset me, so it all got very confusing. I was wondering if they'd spoken to you about any of this." There was a prolonged silence and Maria was just about to check Kim was still on the other end of the phone when she finally answered.

"Maria, can I call you back in about half an hour? I've literally just got in from work and I need a bit of time to at least get our evening meal in the oven."

"Ok, sorry I didn't think. Yes, that's fine; call me back in about half an hour." Maria hung up. She collected her mail and headed towards the kitchen. She was parched and in need of a nice hot cup of tea. While she waited for the kettle to boil, she sorted her mail: one pile for the junk mail and one for items needing attention.

Forty minutes later, still waiting for her sister to return her call, Maria carried her weekend bag down the stairs and left it by the front door. She was going to have to catch a later train tonight, but it didn't matter, she'd still be there before Lorenzo finished work.

Maria watched the minutes tick by. She wasn't sure what to do, should she ring Kim back, or should she wait for her to call? Kim wouldn't forget and remembering the frosty reception when they first spoke, Maria decided it was probably best to wait.

It was one hour and five minutes later when the phone rang. Maria grabbed the phone. "Hi."

"I'm so sorry," Kim began. "Everything has gone wrong this evening. Do you still want to talk, or are you just about to leave for London?"

"Don't worry," Maria said reassuringly. "I was just interested to know if you knew what was bothering Mum and Dad. I was thinking they may have said something to you."

"They've not actually spoken to me directly," she answered her sister honestly. "But as none of us get to spend very much time with you." She waited a second expecting Maria to interrupt. When she didn't, Kim continued. "I know you see Mum and Dad in the week, but that's only just started and, well, I know they miss you. You're never around at weekends and I think they get the impression Lorenzo makes all the decisions. I could be wrong; I mean does Lorenzo ever ask you what you'd like to do?" Kim's voice was soft and compassionate, and Maria realised her sister was trying her best to be as subtle as possible, but she couldn't help feeling perturbed. They finished their conversation on a friendly note and Maria promised to go over straight from work next Tuesday evening for dinner.

Preoccupied, Maria sat on the stairs. Did they have a point or were they just being overprotective? She hadn't realised it until Kim pointed it out, Lorenzo did always arrange and plan the weekends, but Maria thought he was just trying to keep her entertained, and why wouldn't he?

Maria arrived at the station in time to catch the later train to find all trains to London were now cancelled. Disappointed and completely exasperated, Maria made her way back home again. It would have to be a bowl of soup tonight, there wasn't much else in the cupboards.

The living room was in complete darkness when Maria was woken from a deep sleep by the sound of the phone ringing. Stumbling, still half asleep, to the hall, Maria grabbed the phone anxious to pick up before whoever it was hung up.

"Hello," she said croakily.

"Maria, what's going on? Why are you still at home?" Lorenzo said sounding more like he was angry, instead of concerned.

"I had something I needed to sort out before I caught the train," she said trying to wake up. "Then, when I finally got to the train station all the trains to London were cancelled." At first, she'd intended to apologise but she didn't appreciate his tone tonight, so she didn't bother.

Lorenzo continued to speak at his usual fast pace and for the first time Maria found herself not in the slightest bit interested.

"Lorenzo," she butted in. "I've had a hell of a day, I'll see you tomorrow; I'll try and get there for lunch." The phone fell silent. "Bye then," she continued, but Lorenzo had already hung up. Dazed, she walked back into the living room. She collected her supper tray and left it in the kitchen. This could all wait until the morning; she'd had enough for one day.

***

Although no actual words had ever been spoken to confirm his suspicions, Andy was convinced by her actions and general manner that Lynne really liked him. Frankly over the last few months he'd become very fond of her; they got on well and shared many common values, but he had to admit there wasn't the same passion or desire he'd experienced with Maria. If the truth be told he knew he still had strong feelings for Maria. He'd tried to bury them and forget all about her, and for most of the time he could keep them relatively dormant, but from time to time they surfaced, and he wondered where she was, what she was doing and if she was happy.

It was comforting though, he couldn't deny, to receive the sincere friendship and support of such a kind-hearted woman. He knew Lynne was happy, but he also knew eventually she would probably want more, and that idea still concerned him slightly. For the time being, he hoped things would just tick over, although, he was seriously considering asking her to come along on a short holiday he was planning, but that was more for Sammy's benefit than his own.

Lynne was counting down the weeks with absolute dread. Andy had rented a log cabin on the grounds of a working farm, where the amenities for children were apparently exceptional. There were special lessons for those who wanted to ride the ponies, animal feeding sessions and so much more, and Sammy was truly excited. For Lynne it was the complete opposite, she would miss them both and would be glad when it was all over, and they were back home.

As the weeks went by and the holiday got closer and closer, Lynne sensed that Sammy had automatically assumed she would be joining them on their holiday. For the most part she managed to dodge any direct questions Sammy would suddenly ask, but when they became more direct, Lynne decided it would probably be for the best to explain the situation. Sammy would understand, she was a bright little girl far older than her actual years.

"Don't you want to come away with us then?" Sammy asked, tears filling her eyes.

"It's not that," Lynne tried to explain, wiping Sammy's eyes. "This holiday is for you and your daddy to enjoy together; it's going to be such great fun, but it's only for the two of you. I'll be here waiting as soon as you get back and you can tell me all about it."

"No, it won't be fun if you're not with us." She buried her face in Lynne's arms and Lynne stroked her hair tenderly.

"You'll have a great time, just think of all those animals waiting to see you," she said, wishing she hadn't started this conversation.

In the end, as Sammy was unable to change the situation, she decided to sit by the front door in protest, waiting for her daddy to return from work. For once Lynne was unable to talk her round.

As soon as she heard a key inserted in the lock, Sammy was on her feet. "Daddy, Daddy." She couldn't get the rest of her words out quick enough, and Andy couldn't understand a word she was saying.

He picked her up and held her high so she could put her legs around his waist. "What's up with you, my little mermaid?" he spoke gently hoping to calm her down.

"Lynne said she's not coming on holiday with us. Why isn't she coming, Daddy?" Her sad little face melted his heart.

"Maybe she needs a rest from us. Maybe she wants to go on holiday with her own friends, or her own family, have you thought of that?" But Sammy wasn't interested, and tears fell down her cheeks as she continued to plead her case. Unable to console his daughter, Andy walked into the kitchen where Lynne was busy with supper and with Sammy still in his arms he spoke quite sternly.

"Lynne." She looked up, instantly worried he was angry but when she saw him smiling, she relaxed. "Sammy and I would like it very much if you would be able to join us on our holiday. Please, if you've made other arrangements or would prefer not to, there's no obligation, you certainly don't have to." He'd hardly finished his sentence when Lynne interrupted.

"I'd absolutely love to," she said radiating happiness.

Sammy wriggled down from Andy's arms and ran to Lynne who cuddled her tight.

***

Lynne arrived on Saturday morning with her suitcase packed, she was probably just as excited as Sammy and couldn't wait for the holiday to begin.

Driving slowly along the approach road, Lynne counted eight log cabins nestled in the woodland adjacent to the farm.

"Daddy, which is our cabin?" Sammy enquired excitedly from her seat in the back of the car.

"Don't know yet, darling." Andy caught the look of excitement on her face as he glanced in his rear-view mirror. "We have to check in first then they'll tell us, but they all look very nice, don't they?"

Check in was quick and efficient and it wasn't long before they all stood admiring the cabin which would be their home for the next week. There was plenty of room: two large bedrooms, with two single beds in each, so Sammy could decide who she wanted to share with. There was a bathroom with a shower and bath, a well-equipped kitchen with a welcome hamper perched on the worktop, and a cosy living room with a comfy sofa and two armchairs all placed neatly around the log burner and T.V.

"Oh my, look at this place," Lynne said unable to believe how spacious it was inside. "This is just fantastic; I had no idea it would be so luxurious."

"You've been watching too many westerns." Andy laughed. Lynne, who'd never watched a western in her entire life, had no idea what was so funny, but laughed anyway.

While Andy checked out the contents of the hamper, Lynne began to unpack her case.

"Lynne, where's my wellingtons?" Sammy asked as she tried to unpack her own little case.

"Hang on a minute, I know where they are," Lynne answered as she closed her empty case, pleased that at least she'd managed to get that done before Sammy decided she wanted to go and see some of the animals.

"There's loads of nice things to eat in this hamper," Andy called from the kitchen, as he opened a packet of chocolate biscuits. "There's tea, coffee, biscuits, fruitcake, biscuits for cheese…" guessing no one was really paying any attention, he grabbed the bar of chocolate and went to find them. "Oh, and there's this bar of chocolate," he teased as he reached their bedroom door.

"What sort?" Sammy asked jumping up.

"Ahh, I knew the mention of chocolate would get your attention." Andy laughed, as he began to tickle Sammy until she screamed with laughter.

Lynne watched them both with a warm heart as she quickly tried to locate Sammy's wellingtons. How lucky was she? A whole week with this gorgeous man and his daughter, who she absolutely adored.

For the first couple of days Sammy was the first one to wake, and once she was awake so was everyone else. Lynne was surprised how quickly they all settled into a well-established routine. Andy would cook them all a delicious breakfast, while Lynne and Sammy got ready for the day ahead.

Each day was full of action and adventure and, with a little help, Sammy had her first ride on a pony, she also fed practically every animal on the farm, several times, and trekked through the forest to find the children's park with climbing frames, swings, slides and a bouncy castle. Every day they found a different pub to enjoy lunch and after a busy day they made their way back to their cabin about 5pm, so Sammy could relax for a while before her tea. After tea it was time for a bath and then Andy would read her a story, although by the time he got to the end of the first page, she was normally fast asleep.

The holiday was working out far better than he'd imagined and between them they'd catered for all of Sammy's needs. It was important to Andy that she enjoyed her first holiday. She'd had a lot of upheaval to deal with, and all things considered she'd adapted well to her new life. It had helped enormously, of course, that Sammy quite clearly adored Lynne and from what he could see, the feeling between the two of them was entirely mutual.

The evenings were Lynne's favourite time of day. At the beginning of the holiday Lynne felt obliged and offered to "babysit" so Andy could go to the pub for the evening, but he'd looked most indignant at her suggestion and flatly refused. Their routine was relatively simple, as soon as Sammy was asleep, they usually enjoyed some wine and nibbles. Andy loved peanuts and Lynne couldn't believe how many he could consume in one evening. At the beginning of the holiday the plan was that they'd take it in turns to prepare supper, but it wasn't long before it became more of a joint venture.

"What's it to be tonight then?" Andy asked casually as he walked back into the living room once Sammy was fast asleep.

Lynne was curled up in one of the comfy armchairs flicking through a magazine and looked up as Andy perched on the arm of her chair.

"Well?" he asked looking into her big eyes. "What's it to be for supper, what do you fancy?"

The proximity between them caused Lynne to blush. She could feel her face turning a very unattractive shade of crimson and hoped that Andy couldn't hear her heart pounding against her rib cage. She dropped her gaze and quickly returned her attention back to her magazine. "I really don't mind," she managed to reply after a short delay.

Andy continued to sit on the arm of her chair watching her for what felt like forever but was probably just a few seconds. "Are you ok?" he asked gently. "Not that hungry tonight?" He leant over and, with genuine concern, gently tilted her head to face his.

Her heart melted as his touch sent shock waves through her entire body, and from somewhere deep within she managed to answer. "I'm fine." But still Andy didn't move. "Come on then," she murmured before she suffocated from his sheer presence. "Let's go and see what's in the fridge."

Andy stood and held out his hand. "You look like you need help getting out of that chair." He smiled. She took his hand as he pulled her up. It was surprisingly smooth, she noted, considering he was a manual worker.

Lynne's hand was hot and clammy to touch, and she was looking flushed, Andy realised as he pulled her from the chair. Concerned that she might not be feeling too well, he insisted upon cooking the supper himself while Lynne relaxed and enjoyed her wine. Troubled by her general demeanour, Andy watched as Lynne made her way back to the living room. Maybe, he considered, he'd taken her for granted during this holiday; he hadn't even thought to offer her any time for herself. Up until now it hadn't even crossed his mind, they'd laughed so much, and he thought she was enjoying herself. But what did he know?

Admittedly Lynne was feeling tired, it was all the fresh air and with the added excitement of earlier, her head began to pound. She laid her head back as she sat in the chair and unconsciously untied her long blond hair from her trademark bun. That felt so much better and, slowly relaxing, she closed her eyes.

Andy placed their bowls of spaghetti Bolognese on two trays. It would be easier and more relaxed to have supper on a tray tonight, rather than sitting at the table as they'd chosen too previously, especially if Lynne wasn't feeling too well. "You've not gone to sleep on me, have you?" Andy said quietly as he approached Lynne's chair.

Hearing his voice quite close, Lynne opened her eyes. "No, I'm just resting my eyes," she answered as he passed her a tray. "This looks very good, thank you." She quickly tried to tie her hair back while carefully resting the tray on her lap.

"Leave it," Andy said as he turned to collect his own supper from the kitchen. "It looks good loose; you should wear it like that more often."

Slightly embarrassed, Lynne removed the band she'd just used to tie her ponytail.

"Sorry," Andy said returning to the living room. "It's not for me to tell you how to wear your hair."

Lynne only managed an awkward smile before Andy sat himself on the floor by the side of her chair. Balancing his tray on his outstretched legs and absolutely starving, he wasted no time and began to enjoy his supper. The top of his head was level with Lynne's knees and the temptation to run her fingers through his thick dark hair, tested her self-control to its limits.

"It tastes ok," Andy said as he turned to see if she was enjoying hers.

"It's great, really tasty." She nodded looking down at him.

Andy was the first to finish his food and pushing his tray to one side, he turned slightly so he could look directly at her.

"Lynne." He paused waiting for her to meet his gaze before he continued. "Tomorrow, would you like to take the day to enjoy some time alone, maybe there's something you would like to do without us in tow?"

"Sorry," she said, clearly confused. "I'm not sure I understand." This was the last thing she wanted to do, spend a whole day alone.

"It's only just entered my head," Andy continued. "That we haven't given you five minutes to yourself so far this week. I've just gone ahead and planned the day, totally absorbed with Sammy and what she would enjoy. I'm sure there must be so much you'd love to do without us." He watched her face expecting to see relief that she could spend the day doing exactly as she pleased, but instead, all he saw was disappointment.

Not really knowing how to answer, Lynne shrugged her shoulders. "I can if you want," she eventually replied, as she turned her attention back towards her tray and fiddled unnecessarily with her cutlery.

Recognising that he'd got this all wrong and realising that it wasn't something he would relish, spending a day without her, he reached for her hand. "Hey," he spoke gently. "I was concerned that you might think we were taking you for granted, and not really taking into consideration the fact you might want some time alone."

"I don't want any time alone," she answered honestly. Unable to meet his gaze she kept her eyes fixed upon his hand, which held hers gently.

"I'm glad to hear it," he tried to joke before he continued in a more serious tone. "I'm sorry if I've upset you, that wasn't my intention, far from it."

"You haven't," she replied quickly, discreetly wiping a watery eye hoping he wouldn't notice. But he had noticed and, pushing himself up, he sat on the arm of her chair and kissed the top of her head and whispered, "Sorry", into her ear.

For Lynne it was the best feeling in the world to be so close to him, and if she could have one wish, it would be for time to stand still so she could enjoy this moment forever.

Releasing her hand, Andy put his arm around her shoulders. "Are we ok?" he asked her tenderly.

She nodded her head and smiled happily. "We're ok."

Andy stood up and took her tray from her lap. "Well then, at least have an early night; you look tired, and we have another busy day ahead tomorrow. I'll do the dishes tonight."

"Thank you, an early night is probably a good idea." She stood up from her chair and stretched. "Good night then, and thanks again for supper."

"Night, night," he answered as he watched her leave the room. She wasn't Maria, in fact the two women were worlds apart, but he liked her; he liked her a lot.

The rest of their holiday passed in a flash, and before they knew it their last evening was upon them. Earlier over lunch they'd discussed their options for their last evening; neither of them were keen to keep Sammy up late in order to go out, so in the end, they'd settled on watching a movie. After supper Lynne settled herself on the sofa where she thought she would have the best view of the T.V. screen.

"I see you've got the best seat in the house." Andy laughed as he brought two coffees and two brandies into the living room.

"I have haven't I," she agreed smiling widely as Andy placed the tray on the low table directly in front of her.

"Well budge up a bit." He gestured for her to move over, as he sat himself beside her.

It was something Lynne had dreamt of, just to sit next to him. Immediately she could feel the heat radiate from his body and when he put his arm around her shoulders without hesitation, she snuggled into his body. This was the perfect end to a perfect week.

The journey home was a lot more subdued than their journey last week when they had the whole holiday in front of them, and Lynne was dreading the moment she would have to leave them and return home.

They arrived back at the flat by mid-afternoon and uncharacteristically Sammy was extremely hard work. She was demanding of their attention and was grumpy and tearful in equal measure. Leaving Lynne to unpack Sammy's case and put a wash on, Andy went off to the supermarket for supplies and immediately on his return began preparing Sammy's tea. It wasn't very long after her tea that Lynne had her bathed and ready for bed.

Andy quietly closed Sammy's bedroom door; he never thought she was going to fall asleep. He crept into the kitchen where Lynne was clearing the last of Sammy's tea things.

She turned to look at him and smiled. "That was a marathon, wasn't it?"

Andy raised his eyebrows and shook his head. "I have no idea what was wrong with her today, I really hope she wakes up in a better mood." He stood uncomfortably in the doorway.

"Well, I guess I should make a move and head home." She placed the last few bowls in the cupboard and turned to find Andy standing directly in front of her.

"Don't go." He took both her hands in his. "Please don't go," he repeated looking directly into the depths of her soul.

Lynne could hardly breathe, she couldn't answer so she just squeezed his hand and he pulled her so close she could feel his heartbeat through his shirt.

From that day onwards, the only time Lynne returned to her own flat was to pack her remaining bits and pieces and move out.

***

Maria woke early, she was suffering with one of her "heads"; it was bordering on a migraine and she searched desperately for her migraine tablets finally finding them in the kitchen. They would have it sorted in no time.

Two hours later she was still sitting in the same place. Her head was bad; she couldn't even open the curtains. The light was too painful.

Unfortunately, she knew the signs and this migraine was here for the day. There was no way she would be able to travel to London. She couldn't even make it back up the stairs; every step thundered through her head like a landslide on a ski slope.

Eventually, mustering the energy from somewhere, Maria made it to the hall and picked up the phone.

"Hello," Lorenzo answered groggily. He'd had a very late night and at 10.30am had still been sleeping when the phone woke him from a deep contented slumber.

"Lorenzo, it's me," Maria said quite quietly.

It didn't sound like Maria, and still muzzy from sleep, Lorenzo wasn't sure; he didn't want to make any mistakes. "Who?" he asked casually.

"It's me, Maria, who do you think it is," she said raising her voice.

"I'm just joking." He laughed. "I knew it was you, who else would it be?" He shook his head trying to wake up. "Are you ok? You don't sound too good."

"No, I've got a migraine," Maria moaned.

"That's a shame; have you taken anything?" He surprised himself at how concerned he sounded. "I wish I was there to take care of you."

"Oh no," Maria was quick to reply. "I'm better on my own with a head like this." That was the last thing she needed, Lorenzo arriving on her doorstep.

"Would you like me to call you later?" he asked. "I'll be worried if I can't find out how you are. I'm going to miss you tonight."

"If I'm feeling better," Maria said. "I'll give you a call later, but if not, I'll give you a call in the morning."

"Won't you be coming up tomorrow either?" Lorenzo asked, wondering exactly how long a migraine lasted.

"Sometimes they last a few days; there's no way of telling. I'm going to say goodbye for now. I feel bad."

"Ok, look after yourself and try and ring me later."

"I'll try," she agreed.

Relieved that call was over, Maria made her way back to her armchair. She couldn't go to bed; laying down made her feel nauseous. It wasn't really a huge surprise she'd woken with a migraine; she was disturbed to realise her family thought she didn't have time for them, and even more disturbing, they thought Lorenzo controlled her. She would never let that happen. She covered herself with a blanket and laid her head back; it would be so good if she could sleep, even for just a short while.

On Sunday morning, still feeling bad, Maria waited for what she considered to be a reasonable hour before she rang Lorenzo. She let the phone ring for quite some time before she hung up, he'd always been a devil for remembering to switch his answer machine on. She checked her watch; it wasn't that early, and for one awful moment she couldn't dismiss the idea that he might have taken it upon himself to come down and see her anyway. With all her might she hoped he hadn't. She couldn't cope with that. She knew how bad she looked and Lorenzo was the last person she wanted to see today.

By lunchtime it was obvious he hadn't been on his way, so Maria rang again. Still there was no answer, but at least this time the answer machine came on and she left a message and apologised for not seeing him this weekend.

As the hours slowly ticked by, and feeling depressed and completely fed up, Maria decided to ring her parents. "Hi, Dad, it's only me," she said as her father answered the phone.

"Maria, are you ok? You don't sound too good, is everything alright?" Maria couldn't help herself and immediately burst into tears.

"Hey, hey, what's wrong, sweetheart?" her father asked her anxiously while trying to attract the attention of his wife who was busy in the kitchen.

"I've got a terrible migraine; I've had it since yesterday morning," she sobbed into the phone.

"Where are you?"

"I'm at home."

"Have you been there all alone the whole weekend?" her father said shaking his head in disbelief. "Why on earth didn't you ring yesterday?"

Maria couldn't answer without sobbing and wasn't surprised when her mum came on the phone.

"Maria, your dad and I are on our way over; we'll be there in about half an hour."

"You don't have to do that, Mum. I'll be ok in a minute."

"Your dad is already in the car; we're on our way."

Maria relaxed in her chair, surprised at how relieved she felt that today she wouldn't be all alone again.

It was gone 11pm that night when Maria finally got to speak with Lorenzo. Apparently, not wanting to disturb her, he'd decided to spend the day with his family. Grateful that he hadn't decided to visit her, she was pleased to hear he'd taken the opportunity to see his family and thought no more of it. Enjoying his obvious concern, it still took her by surprise when Lorenzo suggested that next weekend maybe they could go away somewhere, just the two of them.

"I'll take Saturday off, we'll go early and come back Monday," he said excitedly. "Do you think you'd be able to get Monday off?"

"That won't be a problem," she assured him. "Let me know what sort of clothes I need to pack."

Lorenzo laughed, typical female question. "Let me know for definite tomorrow night re Monday, and I'll let you know what sort of clothes you'll need to pack."

"Deal," Maria replied cheerfully.

Climbing into bed, Maria snuggled down under the covers; she was feeling so much better. Her parents had brought over lunch they'd already cooked and, although she'd struggled at first, it had been good to get some food inside her, and it had done them all the power of good to spend the rest of the day together.

The following weekend Lorenzo hired a sporty little number, and it wasn't long before Maria guessed they were heading towards the Welsh borders. Their destination was a surprise, Lorenzo had insisted, but Maria wasn't worried. He'd always taken her to very nice places and she didn't consider for one minute this would be any different.

Having stopped for a sandwich in a tiny country pub, Maria was surprised that only thirty minutes later they pulled into a narrow driveway leading to their weekend retreat.

Lorenzo parked the car outside a somewhat tired looking red brick Edwardian house. "Here we are then," he declared smiling. "Come on, let's check in and explore."

At first Maria thought he was teasing her and any minute he'd call her bluff and they'd drive off to their real destination. As she watched him unpack the car and wheel the cases into the hotel, she realised this was no joke, this was for real.

The rather large wooden porch entrance housed a beautiful display of fresh flowers which were replicated in smaller displays around the hotel. Although this was a promising start, Maria was quick to notice the carpet in the foyer was well worn, and on further inspection the lounges were all of a similar standard. Once upon a time they'd probably looked very luxurious, but not anymore.

Unfortunately, when they went to check in there didn't appear to be anyone around. Lorenzo was surprisingly patient, ringing the bell as requested by the note pinned to the desk, several times, before an elderly woman appeared. Without any apparent introduction, Lorenzo instantly began a conversation in Italian and Maria could only assume that this hotel was owned by someone he knew, or maybe even a family member.

After a rather long conversation, Lorenzo grabbed their cases and called for her to follow him to their room.

"Where's the porter?" Maria asked innocently.

"They don't have such luxuries here; the owner normally carries the cases but he's on a break apparently," Lorenzo explained without any great concern.

The hall to the bedrooms was more a corridor; it was narrow and dingy with squeaky floorboards. Eventually, right at the very end, they found their room.

"How many bedrooms do they have here?" Maria enquired as they passed several numbered doors.

"Not many, about 14 I believe," Lorenzo said as he held open the door for her.

Not really knowing what to expect, Maria was astonished to see this room had recently been refurbished. The colour scheme of orange and yellow wasn't exactly her cup of tea, but the carpet was a lovely thick pile, and her feet sank right in. The bathroom was dated, but extremely clean and for that Maria was grateful.

"Well, this is lovely." Lorenzo wheeled the cases in and walked straight over to the window. "Look at this view, Maria, it's so peaceful out there." He suddenly pointed to something that had caught his eye. "Look, they've got Deer in the woodland, can you see them?"

"Where, I can't see them," Maria said as she joined him by the window, unable to see anything in the direction he was pointing. Lorenzo put his arm around her as he pointed to the Deer roaming freely.

"Do you know the owners of this place?" Maria asked as she searched to see the elusive Deer.

"No." He looked at her seemingly puzzled. "Why do you ask?"

"You knew the lady on reception was Italian, so I wondered."

"I guessed." He laughed. "I know the owners are Italians and she looked very Italian, so I took a chance."

"How do you know the owners are Italian?" she asked, anxious to find out why he'd chosen this hotel for their first weekend away together.

"I was reading about them."

"Are they famous for something then?" Maria asked as she began to unpack her case.

"No not really."

Realising this conversation was going nowhere, Maria changed the subject.

"Do you fancy a walk? I think we could probably walk into the village from here. We could find somewhere for a cup of tea," she said, not relishing the thought of using the tea set in the room.

"Or coffee," Lorenzo said as he quickly unpacked.

"Or coffee." Maria laughed, and arm in arm they headed off to find the village.

It was early evening by the time they returned to the hotel and the car park was practically full. Inside the hotel had come to life and was like a completely different place. Members of staff were bustling around, drinks were being mixed and served from a well-stocked bar, the restaurant was softly lit, and the tables were dressed ready for the diners.

"Good evening, sir, madam, can I get you anything?" A smartly dressed gentleman, probably in his early sixties with a distinctive Italian accent, stood behind the bar.

Deciding on two glasses of champagne before they went to change, it wasn't too long before Lorenzo and the gentleman behind the bar were enjoying a conversation in Italian. Maria hated the fact that she had no idea what they were talking about and decided there and then to enrol in some lessons. She tried her best to look interested, but it wasn't until much later that suddenly the Italian gentleman turned to her. "I'm so sorry, I just assumed you spoke Italian and could understand our conversation."

"Please don't worry," Maria said reassuringly. "It's not a problem."

"No, I'm sorry that was rude." He smiled warmly. "Well, I won't keep you any longer, but maybe you would both like to join my wife and I for a drink later, after your meal that is."

"That would be lovely," Maria answered, smiling as the Italian gentleman nodded and left them to enjoy their drinks.

Unfortunately, dinner wasn't a great success. Even Lorenzo, who had enthused about the hotel most of the afternoon, had to admit the food was awful and as each course became progressively worse, it got to the stage where it was so bad it was funny. By the time they left the restaurant they were both very giggly, a few pre-dinner drinks, a bottle of wine and a lack of substantial food had left them both light-headed and carefree.

"Let's hope, being Italian, they make a decent coffee." Lorenzo laughed as they found two cosy chairs in the corner of the main lounge.

"I wouldn't bank on it; they can't cook pasta that's for sure," Maria said before they both burst out laughing and, between them, they opted to play it safe and order another cocktail instead of coffee.

Maria sat back and relaxed into her chair; despite the strange choice of venue Maria was enjoying the fuss and attention Lorenzo displayed towards her. She had to admit he had the most engaging personality and Maria knew that together they presented an enviable couple.

Just before they finished their cocktails a waiter presented two more of the same, plus a couple of brandies. "These are courtesy of Carlo and his wife Yvette, who will join you in a few minutes." He smiled and returned to the bar.

"I'd forgotten about that." Maria finished her first cocktail and moved the empty glass out of the way.

"Well, at least we know their names now," Lorenzo said as sipped his drink.

Carlo and his English wife Yvette were an extremely friendly couple. They'd had an action-packed life together, starting out with a small café, they'd quickly progressed to a restaurant and then onto a hotel. Making a success of the hotel meant a lot of hard work and juggling between work and their family of four boys had been exhausting. Unfortunately, none of their children were interested in hospitality; their eldest was a Lawyer, their second son had returned to Italy and now ran a successful vineyard and the youngest two were both in medicine.

"So that is why," Carlo began. "We've now decided to sell up and take some time for ourselves. I don't need to tell you," Carlo continued looking directly at Lorenzo, "this is a seven day a week occupation, for 52 weeks of the year."

"And each year," Yvette interrupted. "It gets tougher and tougher, and the days get longer and longer. But for you youngsters, it's more of a challenge than a chore." She smiled at them both.

Suddenly the penny dropped, and Maria was left in no doubt, they thought Lorenzo and herself were in the market to buy their hotel. She now began to wonder exactly what Lorenzo and Carlo had discussed so intently earlier.

In the end it was well past midnight when they finally said goodnight to Carlo and Yvette, and Maria couldn't wait to get back to the privacy of their room. "You do realise don't you," she began in earnest. "That both Carlo and Yvette think you, or we, are in the market to buy this hotel." She paused expecting Lorenzo to reassure her this wasn't the case. When he didn't, she continued, "That's why they've just spent the last few hours of their precious time with us."

Lorenzo flopped onto the bed and propped himself up with one arm so he could watch Maria as she sat at the dressing table removing her jewellery.

"It's always been my dream to own my own hotel. Just imagine how good it would be to be your own boss, and what you could do with a place like this, it's got great untapped potential."

"It sounds like a lot of very hard work to me," Maria answered flippantly. Not for one moment did she think Lorenzo was being serious or, more importantly, realistic.

"You'd be surprised what a reasonable price a place like this is actually on the market for," Lorenzo said thoughtfully. "I guess the price reflects its location, plus over the years they've obviously let trade slip. Let's face it they've not really kept up with the standards required to acquire a top rating."

Maria turned around to look at him. "Are you kidding? A place like this would cost a fortune; it must be set in at least two acres of ground." But Lorenzo wasn't really listening. "You're serious, aren't you?" Maria raised her voice slightly, trying to attract his attention.

"I think I am," Lorenzo said, instantly confirming her suspicions. This was no coincidence; this was the very reason they were here.

***

Lynne had never been more content; she loved and adored both Andy and Sammy, they were her whole life. Not that long ago, she'd dreamt of a life just like this, but never for one moment had she imagined it would ever materialise and now she was in her element and radiated pure happiness. There was probably only one issue that bugged her, if she had to be totally honest, and that was Andy's past. He was very open concerning Sammy's mother; Lynne knew all there was to know with respect to her, but apart from that the subject was taboo.

Unbeknown to Andy, Lynne had always been aware of his previous serious relationship, she even knew her name; it was one of the first questions she'd asked her friend Liz not long after she'd accepted the position. Liz originally heard about the position from her brother, Tim, and consequently didn't know too much, other than Andy had recently split with his girlfriend and was now fully committed to securing a good life for his daughter. Andy always refused to discuss the matter, and Lynne often wondered what had happened and what she looked like.

It was purely by chance one morning during a major spring clean in the living room, that quite unexpectedly Lynne came across some photos.

She'd decided to tackle a couple of drawers that always drove her mad; they appeared to be full of either junk mail, or sweet wrappers and as she pulled them out and emptied their contents on the carpet some loose photos nestled on the top of the pile. She sifted through a few of beautiful beaches and sunsets and then froze as she examined the last few photos of two people obviously very much in love. One of them was Andy and presumably the woman was Maria. She studied the photos in detail. They were obviously holiday snaps; the location looked idyllic.

Tears stung her eyes as the realisation dawned, never had she witnessed Andy look at her with the same total adoration and obvious passion that he clearly had for this woman, even in the photos it was as plain as day. Lynne sat cross-legged on the carpet, mesmerized by pictures of a woman she hoped she would never meet until, finally, she realised that it really didn't matter. If this woman was Maria, or even someone else, she wasn't here now and that's what she needed to focus on. It wasn't like she wasn't happy; Andy had always treated her with the utmost respect. He was kind, loving, considerate, generous and totally faithful, she had no worries there. She pulled herself up from the floor and carefully replaced the photos in the drawer, but before she'd even left the room she could feel the pull. This was useless, now she knew they were there, she was drawn to them like a magnet. She opened the drawer, took out the photos and sorted together the scenic ones, which she replaced; the others she tore into tiny pieces and put the images completely out of her mind.

***

Tim literally skipped out of the meeting with his accountants. After a couple of tough years where both Tim and Andy had worked late nights and sometimes all weekend, it had finally all paid off, and the bonus he was now able to offer Andy would be far more than either of them had expected. He'd also instructed his accountants that he was keen to offer Andy a share of the business; it was only fair, Andy had been instrumental in securing many of their most lucrative jobs.

Tim was excited, he couldn't wait to see Andy's face tomorrow when he presented him with his bonus cheque, but first he needed to make sure he was going into the office first thing. He picked up his phone. "Andy, mate, it's only me."

"Hi, Tim, everything ok?" It was unusual for Tim to call him at home in the evening, so Andy was concerned.

"Yes, don't worry, everything's fine. I just wanted to make sure you were coming into the office first thing."

"I wasn't going to, but it's no problem; I can. Why?"

"There are a few quotes I'd like you to check over for me before I send them off," Tim explained, trying not to give too much away.

"That's fine, see you about 7.30 is that ok?" It wasn't unusual for them to check each other's work, so Andy thought no more about it.

"Great, see you in the morning." Tim replaced the phone. Now he would show Lisa their cheque, he knew exactly what she would do first. After their wedding they'd only been able to afford a few nights away. Lisa had never complained but he knew she'd always dreamt of a proper honeymoon, maybe now they would even manage a honeymoon abroad, somewhere in the sun.

Andy was the first to arrive in the office and was busy rummaging around looking for the quotes that needed checking when Tim arrived.

"Morning," Tim said as he breezed in.

"Where are these quotes then?" Andy asked anxiously, he had a deadline to meet and didn't want to hang around too long.

Tim pulled out a cheque from his top pocket. "That wasn't the real reason I asked you here," he said as he handed Andy the cheque made out to Mr. A Porter.

Andy pulled out his chair and sat down as he registered the amount written on the cheque. "What's this for?" he asked looking surprised and confused all at the same time.

Tim was smiling from ear to ear. "It's your well-deserved bonus."

"No way," Andy said shocked. "Are you sure? Can you afford this? Is this for real?" He wasn't making much sense and his hands were shaking as he held the cheque in disbelief.

"You've earned every penny of that, you deserve it and yes I can afford it and if I was you, I'd head over to the bank this morning and get it safely deposited."

"This is going to make a huge difference; this is going straight towards our deposit fund," Andy said as he carefully placed the cheque in his top pocket. He pushed his chair to one side and held out his hand to Tim in thanks.

"You're welcome, as I said you've earned that."

Andy sat in his truck for a while before he felt able to drive off. He knew he didn't really have the time, but he was desperate to share the news with Lynne. She would be so excited, and he knew that by the time he came home tonight she would already have all the properties in their area, within their price range, ready for him to peruse. A house of their own with a garden and a garage, it would all be just perfect.

Lynne turned into the grounds of their flat; she'd just walked Sammy to school and was heading home to tidy up when she spotted Andy's truck in the car park. Worried there might be something wrong, she hurried to their flat.

"Andy," she called before she'd even got through the door.

Andy appeared from the kitchen with the biggest smile and held out his hand. "You better come in and sit down."

Lynne followed him into the kitchen and immediately spotted the bottle of champagne on the table. She looked at Andy who was beaming. "What on earth is going on?"

Andy handed her the cheque.

"You're kidding, what's this for?" Lynne spoke quietly as she stared at the cheque.

"It's my bonus," Andy said, unable to stop smiling. "With the rest of our savings we have enough for a deposit now." Andy pulled her up and into his arms. "Our own house, our own proper home, can you believe it?" his voice trembled as he spoke.

Lynne snuggled into his arms; it was the best feeling. His words echoed in her head. "Our house, our home." There was only one more thing to make her life complete, but they'd never even discussed it, so it would have to wait for now.

The next few weekends were given to house hunting, but it wasn't as easy as either of them had imagined. They'd viewed just about every property in their area and price range, but neither of them felt at home in any of them and were feeling quite despondent when by pure chance they passed a development of new houses.

Andy slowed the truck. "How do you feel about a new build?" He pulled over to read the huge notice board. "Look, they've got four, three and two bed houses for sale, and they've got show homes ready to view. What do you think? Do you want to have a look?"

"Why not." Lynne shrugged as Andy pulled into the car park.

Originally focusing on the plans of the two-bedroom house, they were both astounded to learn that they could easily afford the three-bedroom semi-detached. Hardly able to contain their excitement, they headed off to the show house.

Andy opened the front door and for a few minutes they were speechless.

"Andy, can we really afford a house like this?" Lynne whispered, hardly able to believe her eyes.

He smiled as he ushered them inside. "It's roughly the same price as some of the other houses we've been looking at, so I don't see why not," he said as they walked from room to room.

"This is a dream home," Lynne said as she took Sammy upstairs to look at the bedrooms.

An hour later they drove home armed with brochures, site plans and loads of ideas.

***

Over the next few months Maria noticed that Lorenzo was becoming increasingly unsettled. At first, she wondered if he was becoming bored, maybe their routine wasn't exciting anymore; she wasn't sure what it was but there was certainly something wrong.

"You must be joking," he declared one Sunday when once again he appeared to be completely preoccupied. "You are my world," he continued. "I live for our weekends together, why do you ask me this?"

"Sometimes, like just now," Maria tried to explain. "You seem a million miles away, so I was wondering if you were bored."

"Not with you," he answered immediately without any hesitation.

"With what then?"

"I'm frustrated with work. I think I need more; I need a real challenge."

"Like what?" Maria asked, genuinely interested.

"Maybe something of my own," he said with reflection.

Since their weekend away on the Welsh borders when Lorenzo had indicated he would like his own place one day, they'd never really discussed it seriously. Maria had no idea how financially secure he was, if at all. She had no idea how much he earned, or how much he saved.

Money was just something she preferred not to discuss.

"What are you thinking of?" she asked. "A restaurant, Italian of course?" she quickly added laughing.

"No, a restaurant wouldn't provide enough profit as I'd have to employ a chef, and to tempt a reasonably good one would cost. I'm thinking it would have to be a small hotel; the profit from the rooms would help offset a chef's salary."

"Well, that would cost, wouldn't it?" Maria was worried he might be setting his sights a little too high, especially to begin with.

"I know, I'd definitely need a financial backer, my parents have offered to help, and I could probably get the rest on a mortgage." He trailed off, concentrating for a minute or two on stirring his coffee. "I don't know, Maria; I haven't thought that through properly yet."

"So how do you know how much you can afford?"

"I have a rough idea, of course I do." He sounded irritable and agitated so Maria decided not to push it any further. Obviously, if he was looking to buy a small hotel it wouldn't be around the London area; he'd have to look much further afield to find something remotely affordable. One thing was for sure though, he wasn't planning on sticking around.

***

Eventually, after months of waiting, their new home was ready and Andy, Lynne and Sammy moved into their very first house.

Built in red brick with a flint stone frontage, it looked a good solid house. Inside there was a separate living room and study to the front and a huge kitchen/diner spread right across the rear. Upstairs they had two good-sized bedrooms and one a bit smaller, reserved for Sammy's playroom. Andy had left the interior colour choices to Lynne, and she'd gone for a neutral palette throughout.

"We can add colour with our furnishings," she'd explained reassuringly. "We'll probably need a few new bits and pieces; we definitely haven't got enough furniture."

"You mean we haven't got enough furniture that you like." Andy laughed.

They'd both worked nonstop all weekend unpacking, hanging curtains, putting up blinds and generally sorting out their new home. Sammy loved her new bedroom and playroom and had happily spent hours unpacking her toys.

By Sunday evening they were both exhausted. "Another takeaway?" Andy asked as he finished putting up the last curtain rail.

"I can cook something if you prefer." Lynne felt bad, they'd lived on takeaways for the last few days.

"I fancy a Chinese; we haven't tried that one yet." Andy laughed. "We've tried all the others in the village."

"I'm ok with that, but I'm going to cook some fresh pasta for Sammy, and I'll quickly make her a little fresh fruit salad for her pudding."

Andy gave her a big hug. "You're the best, you know that."

"I do," she said, snuggling into his arms. Just one cuddle could melt her heart, she loved this man so very much.

"I think we're ready for that champagne tonight now, don't you?" Andy declared as he released her from his hold.

"That's a great idea, especially now I've found the glasses." She smiled as she began to prepare Sammy's tea.

"I'll just put all my tools away and once you've given Sammy her tea, I'll get her bathed and ready for bed."

Lynne checked her watch. "Andy it's only five o'clock, if she goes to bed before six, she'll be up at four thirty… Are you that hungry?"

Andy shrugged his shoulders, it wasn't anything to do with being hungry, he'd been planning something all weekend, but it just hadn't been the right moment.

"What time do you want to eat then?" he asked as he sorted out the takeaway menu from a pile of junk mail that had been delivered over the weekend.

So, he was hungry then, Lynne surmised as she watched Andy tick off all the dishes he thought they might enjoy.

Finally, with Sammy tucked up for the night, the Chinese unpacked, and the champagne poured they sat down at their new table.

Andy appeared nervous and a bit on edge. Lynne watched him from the corner of her eye as she finished unwrapping the foil dishes. He hadn't stopped fiddling, and she was just about to ask him if he was ok when he suddenly took a huge gulp of champagne before he pushed his chair out of the way and stood awkwardly by her side. Seconds later he took her hand and knelt beside her; he smiled nervously before he opened a small navy-blue velvet box to reveal the most beautiful diamond solitaire ring.

His voice was full of emotion as he spoke and, although he'd planned over and over exactly what he would say, his mind went completely blank and all he could manage was "Will you marry me?"

Lynne didn't care how he worded it, she'd yearned to hear those four words; it was a dream come true for her. "Yes, yes I most certainly will." She laughed and cried all at the same time she was so incredibly happy.

***

Maria was restless and unsettled, all she could think of was that once Lorenzo had found a place to buy, he'd be gone. It had been a bitter pill to swallow as she came to terms with the fact that obviously what they had together wasn't enough for him. With all this uppermost in her mind, it was time to reevaluate her own life. Without Lorenzo in her life there was no way she could remain in this house. It was full of memories of her life with Andy; everything in it had some sort of link to the life they'd shared. It was bearable now, she was hardly ever here, but to remain here alone at weekends it would drive her mad.

Then there was her job which was slowly driving her insane. The same old thing day in day out, but the money was good, and it did mean she would easily be able to afford a larger mortgage. In fact, just the other day, she'd noticed an advert in the local paper of a new development the other side of town. The first phase of the development was completely sold out, the young woman on the other end of the phone explained, but they were now able to sell the plots on the second phase and Maria, keen to view the show homes, made an appointment.

A couple of days later Maria pulled up outside the makeshift sales office. She'd originally planned to view the houses with her father, but he'd lost a filling and needed to see his dentist urgently, so she was on her own.

"Hello, welcome. My name is Nicola how can I help?" the young sales agent smiled warmly.

"Hello, I'm Maria, I have an appointment at 3.30." Before she finished her sentence Nicola had pulled up a chair for her.

"Can I get you a tea or coffee?" Nicola asked as she gathered plans, brochures and a few sample products.

"No, I'm fine thank you," Maria answered keen to get on.

It took well over an hour to go through all the information on house types, plots available, estimated finish dates, interior finishes, the list went on. In the end Maria was feeling completely baffled, and it was a relief when, finally, Nicola suggested that Maria make her way over to the show homes.

"They're all open, so feel free to have a good look round, but please be aware all the surrounding houses are now privately occupied so please appreciate their privacy." Nicola noted Maria's expression. "We have had instances of people trying to peer through windows and all sorts," she explained.

"I can assure you I will confine my attentions to the show houses." They both laughed and Maria set off down the path.

The first house was a two bedroomed semi-detached, it was very nice but quite a lot smaller than her own house. Closing the door behind her she was just about to make her way over to the three bedroomed house next door when the occupants of the house opposite pulled up on their drive.

Aware of Nicola's previous warning, Maria kept her head down and quickly made her way inside the next show house. Watching discreetly from the living room window, Maria had a very clear view of the house opposite.

The woman in the front passenger seat was the first out and immediately began to release a child from the back seat. The driver was next out of the car and made his way straight around to pick up the child. Maria felt faint and nauseous and steadied herself by leaning on the armchair.

She'd thought the little girl with the curly hair was familiar: someone she'd only ever seen in a photo, but the driver, she knew him very well. She watched completely dumbstruck. The little girl must be Sammy, Andy's daughter, the woman must be Sharon his ex. Maria had never seen her before, not even in a photograph, she was clearly the child's mother, even from this distance you could see their closeness.

Maria continued to watch as Andy held the little girl with one arm and casually put his other arm around the woman until they reached the front door, where he took a key from his pocket and opened the door and one by one, they went inside, and he closed the door.

She moved away from the window. This was his house, it had to be, he had a key. She was impressed, she'd heard he'd left the garage, but she had no idea where he'd gone or what he was doing.

Realising that she couldn't live anywhere near here, she made her way back to the sales office and politely made her excuses and left.

Her hands were shaking uncontrollably as she put the key in her own front door. She'd managed to hold back the tears while she was driving, but now she was home she couldn't stop the flow and climbing onto her bed she buried her head into her pillow and sobbed.

Andy had taken the afternoon off to meet with the head teacher at a potential school they were interested in for Sammy. The meeting had gone well, and he'd been incredibly proud of his little girl; she had conducted herself well, thanks to Lynne's patience and teaching.

He glanced out of the window as he walked through the living room back to the kitchen. It never ceased to amaze him how many people continued to view the show homes. He stood for a while as he watched a visitor hurry back to the sales office. In the kitchen he opened the fridge and grabbed a beer. He could feel his heart race and he felt hot; he was almost sure he recognised that woman. He'd only seen her from the back view, but it was the way she walked. He drank his beer; angrily he crushed the can. What was he doing thinking of other women? He was due to be married very soon.

**

Tim was over the moon when Andy asked him to be his Best Man.

"I'd be honoured; I really would," Tim said as the two men shook hands.

"It's not going to be a huge wedding, Lynne only wants a small affair, she's not even that keen on having an evening

'Do'. I think the plan is that we have a nice wedding breakfast somewhere and then that would be it. To be honest she's more interested in the honeymoon." He paused for a minute. "She's never been abroad; I think she's looking at Malta."

"Sounds sensible to me," Tim answered as he watched his friend anxiously.

"What about Sammy?" he asked wondering if it was her Andy was worried about.

"She's so excited to be a bridesmaid." Andy laughed. "She'll be coming with us on the honeymoon. I couldn't leave her." Andy fell silent for a minute before he continued. "She's been left so much in her young life."

Tim patted his friend on the back. "You're a great dad, you know that don't you?"

"I try," Andy replied looking pensive.

"Is everything else, ok? You look troubled."

"I did a really silly thing the other day," Andy admitted to his friend.

"What do you mean 'silly thing'?" Tim had known there was something else bothering Andy, but now he was worried.

"I drove by Maria's house and there was a big sold sign in her front garden."

"What did you do that for?" Tim didn't like where this was going.

"I thought I saw her a while back coming out of one of the show homes. I couldn't get her out of my mind, so I thought I'd go and see if her house was for sale, if it was, I'd know it was probably her." He frowned as he saw the disappointment in Tim's face.

"Honestly, I doubt if it was her." He tried to reassure his friend. "Lisa told me that Maria was moving to the Welsh Borders with the Italian guy."

"Oh, I see." Andy was gutted and couldn't manage to say anything else for fear of showing Tim the true depth of his feelings.

"They say we all have a double," Tim added sympathetically.

"I guess," Andy said as he packed up his tools for the day.

Tim watched as Andy drove off. He'd always known that information would have a profound effect, but he hadn't realised it would still hurt so much. The raw pain Andy was experiencing had been etched right across his face, Tim only hoped that now he knew, he'd forget about her once and for all.

**

"Are you sure you've thought this through?" Maria's father looked worried and quite upset.

"Dad, I need a fresh start, away from my house and my job." She looked at her father and smiled reassuringly. "You've known that for ages and now this opportunity has come along, I really want to give it a go. It's a huge challenge and it's what I need." Maria looked at both her parents, eager for their support.

"But you're going to be so far away." Her mother sounded beside herself.

"Mum, it's four and a half hours away by car. Honestly, it's not like I'm going to Australia."

"But, Maria," her father began, desperately trying to get his daughter to see some sense. "It's all of your house money and all of your savings, everything you possess." He stopped for a breather. "May I ask exactly what Lorenzo is risking in all this?" he added brusquely.

"Mum, Dad, please." Maria had known this was going to be difficult, she'd been prepared for a lecture, but this was now an extremely uncomfortable situation. "I know what I'm doing, I've given it a lot of thought; I really have."

"You still haven't answered my question," her father declared as he became increasingly concerned.

"I've already explained that Lorenzo's parents let him down; they'd always led him to believe they had the money and were prepared to help him. None of this is his fault." Maria sighed heavily.

"Do you know for sure that's why he can't raise any money?" There was no way her father was going to let this go. "I want you to use my solicitor please, to oversee and finalise this purchase. I want this all finalised legal and proper and please, Maria, whatever you do, do not sign any part of this purchase over to anyone. This must remain in your name and your name only."

She'd never heard her father use this tone of voice with her before, she totally understood their concern, she just wished they'd give her a little more credit.

Lorenzo was over the moon when she'd first broached the subject of financing this deal. He had been incredibly down and despondent since realising his parents, for whatever reason, could not help him and was incredibly grateful for her trust and belief in him.

They'd talked and talked of nothing else for weeks discussing all their plans and Lorenzo assured her wholeheartedly that, having worked in hospitality all his working life, he was fully aware of how to run a hotel successfully. He certainly wasn't deterred that Maria knew nothing when it came to hospitality.

"Don't worry about any of that," Lorenzo quickly assured her. "I will teach you all about front of house, and I will take full responsibility of everything food and drink related. I've already got my eye on a very good chef." He was so excited she didn't like to point out some of the more pressing details. That could all come later, she decided innocently.

Every weekend for months and months they travelled the country in search of a relatively small hotel where they could begin their journey. It was purely by chance that they heard the hotel they'd visited ages ago for their first weekend break together had now been significantly reduced in price.

"You know what this means," Lorenzo said excitedly. "It's now well within our budget. It's got to be fate." He smiled as he handed her the commercial paper where he'd found the sale notice.

Maria read the article carefully. "Well, it's worth another look, and the price is good. We just need to look at their financial records, after all it must be reasonably viable from the beginning. We won't have the funds to continue without a substantial income from the start."

Lorenzo didn't answer, he was too busy dreaming of running his own business.

It took months and months of checking documents, signing documents, applying for licences and interviewing staff before, finally, Maria was handed the keys to her very own business.

Lorenzo seemed quite surprised when it became evident that Maria hadn't given him any financial part of this business. "I would prefer if everyone, staff, suppliers and customers alike believed that this hotel was ours as a couple, rather than solely belonging to you," he said after making it very clear he expected to have full control over the kitchen, bar and restaurant, leaving Maria to concentrate on bedrooms and reception.

"Honestly, Maria, that's more than enough for you to be going along with," he explained. "You won't know if you're coming or going at first. I'll try and help you as much as possible, but my time is going to be tight."

She smiled sweetly; he was clearly still a bit "hacked off". He'd been visibly shocked and annoyed when Maria explained that she alone would be responsible for signing the cheques, paying the wages and controlling the accounts. Not for the first time she remembered the words of warning from her father.

The following days, weeks and months passed in a flurry of activity. Each new day brought new challenges and the whole experience was a very steep learning curve for Maria and left very little time for the two of them as a couple.

Initially, Maria was impressed as she watched Lorenzo introduce new practices to improve the service they provided. She listened intently as he discussed in detail the new menus with their chef, and the new wine list he proposed gave a comprehensive and varied choice for the most discerning guest.

"This looks very expensive," was her first comment when Lorenzo showed her the first proofs of his new wine list. "I take it this is all within the budget that we discussed together." She emphasised the word "together".

"Well, if it's not, I expect you'll soon tell me," Lorenzo snapped as he snatched the proofs and stormed out of the office.

Maria let him go, this wasn't the time to discuss exactly what he meant by his last comment. They were both tired and she had to admit Lorenzo had worked incredibly hard and achieved so much in such a short space of time. Even so, maybe it was time to ask him for all the invoices that he'd been promising to pass on.

The promotional campaign Maria had put in place had certainly increased their occupancy at weekends, and Friday and Saturday evenings were fast becoming extremely busy in the restaurant, but they couldn't survive on just being busy at the weekend; they needed to encourage extra weekday business, and Maria had a plan.

Her idea would involve marketing the hotel as a destination place, renowned for its food and wine experience. She would capitalize on Lorenzo's talent and ability to engage with every individual customer. His love of food and wine was contagious; he could sell bottles of wine as though they were bottles of water, and their wine trade was proving to be extremely profitable, which was a great relief to Maria who very quickly realised Lorenzo had no conception of the word "budget". It had been a very expensive lesson to learn and one she couldn't afford to repeat, but she had to give him his due, he was doing his very best to sell it, although she expected his main aim was to prove her wrong and that it had all been a worthwhile purchase.

The kitchen, however, wasn't producing anywhere near the gross profit her accountant had advised her to aim for. Lorenzo had insisted it would all settle down in time, but Maria wasn't so sure and decided to investigate.

Armed with food receipts and invoices Maria made herself comfortable in the office. An hour or so later she made a phone call to the local butcher.

"Good afternoon," she began politely. "Do you have an accounts department please, or can I speak to whoever produces the invoices?" She paused briefly. "Sorry it's Maria here from Yew Tree Hotel, I should have introduced myself first."

"Oh hello," the butcher answered. "I'm actually in the office with my wife, so I'm sure between us we'll be able to help."

"Ok well," Maria began. "I've noticed on all your invoices it states line by line each product, weight and total price until at the end of each invoice there's a sundries item which just gives a total price which appears to be increasing regularly."

"Oh, I can answer that," the butcher said. "I was instructed by your chef to combine all the breakfast products, for example bacon, sausage and eggs together under sundries. A couple of weeks ago he started to order lamb chops and pork chops in packs of three and asked me to include those items in with the sundries."

Maria was silent for a minute; they didn't have lamb chops or pork chops on the menu. "Oh, ok, that's explained that," she replied. "In future can I please have everything listed individually and the invoices addressed to me personally, would that be ok?"

"Of course," the butcher said, relieved she wasn't complaining about any quality issues. "That's no problem at all."

"Thank you so much and I'll pop in and introduce myself in person as soon as I get a minute." She put the phone down. The next delivery from the butcher was due the day after tomorrow; she needed to be around when that arrived.

***

The wedding went without a hitch and the honeymoon in Malta had been just what they all needed. They arrived home happy and relaxed, and Lynne secretly had everything crossed that soon they'd have even more news to celebrate.

Before the wedding, Lynne decided it was time she had a conversation with Andy about increasing their family. It would be a blessing to have a baby of their own and would complete their happy little family unit. She had no idea how he would respond and mulled over the best way to broach the subject for several weeks before, finally, she felt ready to voice her innermost wishes. Andy's positive response surprised her. "Are you really sure?" she asked wondering why she'd been so worried.

"Of course I am," Andy reassured her as he reached across the table and took her hand. "It would be perfect. What do you want, boy or girl?" he teased, watching her face come alive with anticipation.

"I really don't mind." She laughed happily. "As long as it's healthy."

"And it sleeps all night," Andy added, grinning from ear to ear. It would be perfect and make their family complete, and now he couldn't wait.

***

Maria waited patiently all morning for the butcher's van to arrive. From the window in the office, she had the perfect view of the drive to the rear of the kitchen. She hadn't mentioned any of this to Lorenzo; he would dismiss a few chops with the shrug of his shoulders. She'd long since given up discussing anything to do with money, he just didn't seem interested. Anyway, it was true this wasn't the total answer to the lack of profit in the kitchen, but it was a start. Finally, the delivery van pulled up outside the kitchen.

Maria decided to watch and see how it all panned out. As it happened, she didn't have too long to wait.

As soon as the lunch service was over and the kitchen cleaned down, the chef sent his team off for their break. Maria had already let it be known she was heading home for a break, when in truth she was still in her office. She waited patiently for the chef to leave and once he'd checked the coast was clear, the chef left, carrying a plastic bag of fresh meat. She watched as he climbed into his car and drove home.

Immediately Maria began to check the rest of the delivery against the invoice that had been left unopened on the worktop.

"What are you doing?" Lorenzo asked as he found her rummaging around in the kitchen.

"Something is going on here, I've just witnessed the chef walk off with a bag of fresh meat. So, I'm just checking to make sure we have everything that is stated on this invoice and clearly, we do not." She hadn't expected any support from Lorenzo so was completely surprised when he sounded truly concerned.

"So, you're saying he's stolen some food."

"Yes, I am," she said confidently. "Along with goodness knows what else, the profit margin in the kitchen is practically non-existent."

"Why on earth didn't you say something to me?" Lorenzo asked her. He'd chosen this chef personally and now, quite clearly, felt responsible. "How are you going to play this?"

"I don't know yet, but I don't want him back in this kitchen. I wouldn't trust him with the rubbish."

"Just give me a minute. I'll go and speak with Pierre. I'll see if he feels comfortable about managing the kitchen until we sort something else." Lorenzo was concerned, they had a lot of diners to feed tonight. He was sure that Pierre their sous chef would be able to cope, but it was only good manners to check.

Maria waited in her office for Lorenzo to return. This was all so very unpleasant and not something she had ever imagined she would have to deal with. All the staff received generous salaries, the live in staff were well fed and had more than adequate facilities. She'd thought, incorrectly as it turned out, that a generous package would eradicate the temptation of stealing, it was a tough lesson to learn.

"Pierre is absolutely fine," Lorenzo exclaimed as he bound into the office. "He seems very confident; I was surprised. He did ask why, I just said there's been an unfortunate incident. He didn't say anymore so nor did I."

"Great," Maria said relieved. "I now have to make a very unpleasant call to the chef and ask him to return with the food immediately."

"I'll do it," Lorenzo said quickly.

"Ok, but if he starts to make excuses or actually refuses, tell him we will be calling the police."

The chef returned full of excuses and apologies, but Maria wasn't interested and in the end they all agreed if he left with immediate effect, he would leave with a clean slate and be free to go and cheat on someone else.

By 6pm that same evening Pierre had found himself a temporary sous chef and was confidently preparing for the evening service.

It was clear from the very first evening that Pierre was more than capable of running his own kitchen. He was extremely knowledgeable, and talented, his ideas were innovative to the extreme, and within months word had spread; they'd even had several visits from food critics and the results were always very favourable.

At last, they'd started to make some money and Maria was excited to begin her long awaited refurbishment programme, along with another exciting project she was interested in. The internet was fast becoming a useful tool for business and the amount of people that enquired if she had a website was growing at an incredible pace. Even Lorenzo had shown a keen interest in having a website, so Maria had arranged a meeting for them both to attend.

Increasingly they'd become like ships that pass in the night. Maria was fully aware this had, initially, been more down to her than Lorenzo. In the beginning, Lorenzo always made time for them to have at least one meal of the day and some time in the afternoon together, but bit by bit that all changed. There was always so much Maria wanted to do, she couldn't see the point of going for a walk, or to the movies, when she could spend that time working on her new ideas.

Eventually Lorenzo stopped asking and began to staff himself out for a day, or sometimes a day and a half, a week. He was most certainly entitled, and even bought himself a new mobile phone so that Maria could always get hold of him.

The first time he went away Maria had to admit she felt alone and vulnerable. Lorenzo's team in the restaurant were more than capable, they were all very efficient and professional, but they didn't quite have his flair and Maria worried in case the restaurant lacked the ambience Lorenzo created.

Pierre sensed Maria's concern, her smile wasn't as genuine, and she was in and out of the kitchen all evening. As soon as service was over, he changed into clean whites and for the first time made his way out to the front of house.

"Is everything ok, chef?" Maria asked as she watched Pierre walk towards the lounges.

"Absolutely," he replied, smiling. "I just thought I'd come out and get some feedback on tonight's menu. You don't mind, do you?" he asked.

Completely taken by surprise, Maria welcomed his idea. "I don't mind at all. I'm sure the guests will love it."

She wasn't wrong, the guests seemed to relish the idea of offering their opinions and before long Pierre was happily chatting to the guests while they enjoyed their coffee and liqueurs.

As the last guest eventually said goodnight, Maria could finally relax. "Thank you so much, chef," Maria said as she helped the waiters to clear the tables in the lounge.

"I enjoyed it," Pierre answered honestly. "I only came out to see if you were alright, you looked really concerned about something. I was worried it might have been the food, but from the feedback I've had tonight, I don't think it could be that."

"I don't know what it was," she confessed. "It's the first evening without Lorenzo, I guess it was that."

"Well, I think it's all gone very well," The chef said. "I have to be honest, as far as service went, I didn't miss him at all." He smiled and left Maria with that thought.

As the weeks went past, Lorenzo's days off became a regular event, and every evening he was away the chef would venture out of the kitchen and spend time with every guest, and they absolutely loved it.

***

Lynne was preparing a special meal for their first wedding anniversary. Their first year of marriage had literally flown by and Lynne had never been happier. As a family they enjoyed a good life together. Andy and Lynne had made new friends on the estate, and the three of them had thoroughly enjoyed a second holiday when they visited The South of France.

Sammy was doing well at school and absolutely loved it. To begin with, Lynne hadn't given much thought as to how she would occupy her time once Sammy went to school. Initially, she'd just presumed she would either be expecting a baby, or even have had one by now, but as of yet nothing had happened.

Andy kicked off his boots before he opened the front door. He knew from experience as soon as his key went in the door Sammy would be there to greet him.

"Oh, Daddy, they're lovely flowers," Sammy exclaimed excitedly.

"Can you take these for me, sweetheart." Andy passed a box of Lynne's favourite chocolates to Sammy.

"What else have you got?" Sammy asked, noticing another carrier bag.

"I've got these flowers, those chocolates and a bottle of champagne." He smiled.

"Wow," Sammy said. "Nothing for me?" She looked at her daddy adoringly.

Andy laughed. "Not this time, sweetheart, it's Lynne's day today." Sammy skipped in front of him into the kitchen.

"Happy anniversary, my beautiful wife." Andy put down his presents and gave his wife a big hug.

Lynne was sure he hadn't forgotten, but she hadn't expected all these presents. She'd bought him a new wallet; it was a bit of a standing joke between the two of them, as Andy continuingly complained his wallet was always empty. She'd put a little note inside wishing him more luck with this one.

In truth he was a very generous man, he always had been, and now Sammy was at school Lynne had made up her mind to return to work. She no longer wanted to be a Nanny, so was thinking of retraining, she just hadn't discussed it with Andy yet.

Later that evening, snuggled up on the sofa enjoying the last of their champagne and chocolates, Lynne decided now would be a good time to discuss her thoughts about returning to work.

"I've been thinking," she began. "I'd like to retrain so I can return to work. I'm not interested in returning to be a Nanny; it wouldn't work anyway. I'm looking at something that would fit in with Sammy's school hours."

Andy had been expecting this and was relieved to hear that she wouldn't return to her previous profession. "You do know, don't you, that you don't have to return to work, if you don't want to?" he said as he stroked her hair. "But I understand if you feel you need more than just being a housewife, that's perfectly understandable."

"I would like to do something," she confirmed. "I have no idea what though." She sighed with relief more than anything else, at least now he knew how she felt.

"Why don't you investigate doing something at the school? What credentials do these new teaching assistants need?" he asked. "You'd be excellent at something like that."

Lynne hadn't given anything like that a thought, but it was actually a good idea. She looked up at her husband; he always came up with the right answers, she was so lucky and very happy. "It's certainly worth looking into," she agreed. "I'd really enjoy that sort of work."

"I know you would." He smiled affectionately. "Knowing your luck, you'd just get settled in and realise you were having a baby of your own." Andy crossed his fingers as he spoke, fully aware this would make her life complete.

"I hope so, I really do," she answered truthfully.

"How long do you want to leave it before we get everything checked out?" Andy suddenly asked.

"Let's give it another six months," she spoke quietly, she had no idea Andy was even thinking along these lines. "Anyway, it has to be me doesn't it, you already have Sammy," she practically whispered.

"Not necessarily," he answered squeezing her hand. "Anyway, it's not a blame game, is it?" He turned her face towards his. "Whatever it is, we face it together, yes?"

She smiled and kissed the tip of his nose. "Together, always," she answered confidently.

***

The years flew by, and the kitchen, under the direction of Pierre, continued to acquire more accolades for the restaurant. The hotel was flourishing and slowly Maria fulfilled her dreams of a total refurbishment. Admittedly they'd had to close for a couple of weeks in order to complete the lounge areas, but it had been worth it. The dingy walls of the corridors were long gone, and the bedrooms were now sumptuous retreats for guests to enjoy.

None of this had been achieved without sacrifice. Her relationship with Lorenzo had unfortunately become its main victim, and eventually, with nothing left to retrieve, Lorenzo moved out of the converted barn they called home and took rooms within the staff block at the rear of the hotel.

To all the guests they continued to present the happy couple image. It seemed to be what people liked to see, but privately Maria was convinced Lorenzo had someone else in his life, and in truth she had to admit, the thought of him with someone else didn't bother her in the slightest.

At first when he moved out, she'd felt relief, and enjoyed the peace and quiet. But gradually that turned to guilt; this hadn't been part of their original plan, and she often thought that maybe she should have made more of an effort. In fact, now she wondered why he'd stuck around at all, and she found it amusing when one day she overheard some of the staff chatting during their mealtime.

"They have a very strange relationship don't you think?" Franco was one of the newest members of the restaurant team. "All the guests seem to think they're a couple and they're not. I've seen a photo in Lorenzo's wallet of him and another woman."

"What were you doing in his wallet?" Pierre enquired.

"The other day he asked me to get one of his business cards from his wallet."

"Well, we don't know any more than you," Pierre said quite abruptly, not wishing to continue this conversation. He had his own ideas as to what occupied Lorenzo on his days off.

"Well," Franco continued, not at all perturbed by Pierre. "I asked him who she was, he said she was an old friend that lived in London. Which is interesting as there's a girl in the village who he's taken out a few times." He stopped for a drink before continuing. "Anyway, this girl is bragging that she's going out with the handsome Italian from Yew Tree Hotel."

"That's enough gossip," Pierre declared as he took his plate back to the kitchen.

Maria crept away; she didn't want to be found listening to their conversations. She was surprised though, she had to admit, she'd never thought Lorenzo would two time someone, obviously she'd been wrong, and not for the first time, she admitted sadly.

When they first set out on this journey, she'd believed wholeheartedly that Lorenzo would be an astute businessman with a great vision, but it hadn't taken very long to realise he had no idea. He was a master in his own area, but that was as far as his contribution went. It had been a steep learning curve, and for the most part she'd enjoyed the experience.

She'd met some fantastic people and equally some not so nice, she'd learnt to read her guests and could tell instantly whether to expect any problems and could tell a food critic or hotel inspector a mile off.

Between them all, they'd earned the highest accolades for the hotel, and Pierre had continued to excel and earned himself the highest regard from far and wide. Unfortunately, he was ready for another challenge now though, and Maria was the first to understand. Pierre wanted his own restaurant, and it wouldn't be too long before he would be off to pastures new.

One of the biggest surprises of her career, though, was unexpected. It was a Sunday afternoon; lunch had been exceptionally busy, and Maria was helping Wendy the receptionist to prepare some of the bills, ready for payment. Maria picked up a bill that didn't appear to show any bar or wine and immediately checked the handwritten dockets attached to the back. They were all written in Lorenzo's distinctive writing, each course they'd ordered but nothing else.

"Ahh here you are," Maria said as she found Lorenzo clearing the last few tables in the restaurant. "Lorenzo, I'm almost sure table six had wine with their meal, but it's not on their docket." She handed the docket to him.

He looked at it briefly and handed it back. "I don't think they did," he said abruptly, without looking at her.

"I thought I saw a bottle on their table." She hadn't quite finished her sentence when he threw down the tablecloth and, mumbling something incomprehensible, stormed out of the restaurant. Maria let him go. She had no idea what was wrong; he'd been a bit weird for a few days now. She'd let him calm down and then have a chat. She just hoped table six would be honest and realise they'd not been charged for their drinks.

It was gone 5pm when the last lunch guest left, and Maria went in search of Lorenzo. She could hear his angry voice before she entered the building and making her way straight to his room was nearly knocked over as he came stumbling out carrying a large suitcase.

"Moving out?" she joked.

"You got it in one," he answered in a voice she hardly recognised.

"What's going on, Lorenzo?" she asked trying to block his way, but he pushed right past.

"What does it look like, I'm off. I've had enough." Not wanting to have this conversation where all the staff could hear, she followed him to his car.

"Lorenzo, please, I don't understand."

"There's nothing to understand, Maria, I'm leaving." Lorenzo threw his case in the back of his car along with some other bits and pieces he must have packed earlier.

Maria stood by the side of his car. "Don't you think you owe me some sort of explanation? This is ridiculous, surely this isn't all over the docket at lunch time." She looked directly at him. He looked like a stranger; he was extremely angry.

"Maria please, get out of the way, and for your information I owe you nothing." He slammed the car door shut and unwound the window. "Just in case it's still not abundantly clear, I'm leaving, and I will never return."

Maria stood watching in complete shock as his car sped off down the drive.

Pierre had witnessed the whole episode. He'd guessed a few weeks back that Lorenzo was in some sort of trouble, probably with a disgruntled husband. He wasn't sure how much Maria knew, or wanted to know, but Lorenzo had managed to get a bit of a name for himself with the women in the village and, he knew for a fact, this was the same reason he'd had to leave London.

Maria turned and saw Pierre watching from the doorway. "I don't know what on earth is the matter with him, and what's just happened is beyond me," she said as walked towards him.

"I've just checked his room; he's taken everything that belonged to him. It doesn't look like he's coming back."

Maria shrugged her shoulders; suddenly she felt extremely alone. It wouldn't take long for the word to spread. Would the guests still want to come without the infamous Lorenzo running his restaurant and bar? She had no idea.

"Don't worry Maria, we'll all be fine," Pierre said reassuringly. It was obvious how she was feeling, but he wasn't worried. Jean Paul could easily run the restaurant, if the truth be known he did most of the work anyway. Then there was Franco and Pepe, they were competent hard-working waiters, plus they always had a couple of the locals they could call on for help.

"Would you like me to give Jean Paul a call?" Pierre offered. "I think it would be a good idea if we all sat down and got a plan of action underway."

Maria, still in shock, sat in the chair behind her desk. "I can't ask you to do that, chef, it's your rest time." She tried unsuccessfully to sound positive.

"I want to, anyway I was thinking we could open a bottle of something, you look like you could do with it." He laughed as he picked up the phone.

A couple of hours later, their plan was complete. Jean Paul was anxious to prove himself and Maria had agreed he could take the position of restaurant manager on a six-month trial basis.

The next few months didn't go without a few issues, nothing to do with the hotel, but all concerning the sudden departure of Lorenzo. It seemed he'd completely disappeared and, much to Maria's amusement, it appeared he'd left a wake of broken hearts behind him. Some even turned up at the hotel demanding to know where he'd gone, but they got short sharp thrift from Maria, who was now fast losing patience with the whole saga of events.

As far as the hotel went, Lorenzo's sudden departure hadn't made any difference to business. Jean Paul had introduced several new procedures all of which were working well, even the chef seemed a lot happier, although Maria knew his own departure was still imminent.

Her parents and sisters had been particularly supportive, and Maria got the impression they were relieved to see Lorenzo out of her life for good.

***

After a short period of training, Lynne settled into her new career as a teaching assistant. She'd managed to get a position at the same school Sammy attended, but a different year group which was ideal.

With her mind fully occupied and always busy, it was another year before Lynne decided to make the first tentative steps towards trying to find out why she couldn't conceive.

The doctor was very understanding and immediately organised for the relevant tests and took the time to explain the new procedure everyone was talking about: I.V.F. Andy wasn't at all convinced, but Lynne wasn't worried; all that was a long way off yet.

It was less than a week after Lynne went for some preliminary tests that she received a call; she needed to go back as further investigation was required. She was assured there was nothing to worry about, sometimes it just happened that way.

"What exactly did the receptionist say?" Andy couldn't help feeling anxious.

"They need to do some more tests, but it's absolutely nothing to worry about." She smiled encouragingly, she knew full well Andy would be worried, and had even considered not telling him.

"So, when have you got to go back?"

"I've already arranged the morning off tomorrow so I can go and get them all done."

"That's good." Andy had an uneasy feeling and would be glad when this part was all over, and Lynne finally held the baby she craved.

It was exactly two weeks later that the doctor requested another appointment, but this time with them both.

They sat in the waiting room unable to talk for what seemed to Andy a lifetime. He couldn't imagine what the doctor had to say, although he guessed they'd found the reason Lynne couldn't conceive. Lynne sat upright; she was shivering even though it was a very hot day.

Finally, the doctor called their names. "Please take a seat." He pointed to the chairs opposite his desk. The room felt claustrophobic with this huge desk dominating most of the space.

The doctor sat back in his chair; he was an older man with a weathered complexion and a very gentle voice. "Now," he began. "There's no reason to worry at this stage, but we've found a few anomalies resulting in a few areas that may be of concern." He smiled at them both before he continued. "I'm going to refer you to a consultant for further investigation. But like I said there's no need to worry or panic at this stage."

"Do you know what the areas of concern may be?" Andy was the first to speak.

"At this stage it's too early for me to confirm anything. Once you've been referred, more in depth tests can be carried out and then we'll know more."

"Are these areas of concern the reason I can't conceive?" Lynne asked, her voice shaking as she spoke.

"At this stage I couldn't say for sure," he spoke slowly and quietly. "I'm going to get the letter off today and you will hear directly. Any questions you may have at any time in the future, I'm always available and please don't hesitate to ask."

"Thank you, doctor," they said in unison.

They left in silence but once in the car Lynne couldn't hold back the tears.

"Hey, don't get upset, please don't cry." Andy leant over and held her tight. She sobbed into his shoulder for the next few minutes, unable to believe what she'd just heard.

The next few weeks passed amidst a flurry of appointments and tests. Lynne was visibly shaken by the series of events and Andy became increasingly worried. He'd noticed how unusually tired Lynne had become, she nearly always fell asleep in the chair after their evening meal, and at the weekend she'd taken to sleeping in, whereas before she'd always been the first up and about. At first, he put it down to work and looking after Sammy, but now he wasn't so sure.

For the second time in less than a month on a wet and windy day they both hurried into the hospital to see Lynne's consultant. Less than an hour later, with their worst fears confirmed, they didn't notice that the sun was shining and the wind had dropped as they made their way in silence back to the car.

Within minutes their whole world had turned on its axle and neither of them really knew how they were going to get through it.

For Lynne it was a case of wishing the earth would stop spinning so she could get off and take stock. Andy didn't know how he felt, he only knew he wished this was happening to himself and not his wife, who was now going to experience horrendous treatments and literally fight to save her place on this planet.

On the way home they made only one plan and that was to save Sammy from as much worry as they could. She'd realise Lynne was ill soon enough, but there wasn't any need for her to know the severity, she was still far too young.

***

It was a sad day when Maria said goodbye to her chef. They had the utmost respect for each other, so much so Pierre had even found a suitable replacement and settled him in before he left.

Henri had a completely different style to Pierre, but Maria liked him and felt he would make an ideal replacement. Jean Paul had proved himself beyond Maria's wildest expectations and it seemed her guests approved. Impressively he made it a priority to keep pace with the ever-changing world of the food and wine industry. He'd made some excellent changes to their wine list and introduced a larger variety of "New World" wines that were increasingly becoming extremely popular.

The hotel business was also facing changes. The internet was proving a good tool for advertising, but Maria found it was taking up more and more time. It was like running two hotels, one actual and one virtual. In general, the demands of running the hotel were now far greater. Guests were looking for "experiences" to make their stay extra special. Jean Paul had mentioned a master class of wine as one idea, and Maria had some additional ideas, but they were all in their infancy and would involve changes all round. Once again Maria had some difficult decisions to make.

***

Life in the Porter household was never quite the same after the day Lynne received her cancer diagnosis.

Lynne fought a hard battle for many years, with determination and dignity, she even managed several years in remission, when for a brief period, life returned to some sort of normality. But the cancer returned with a vengeance and Lynne struggled with the treatment.

"I need to speak to you both," Lynne said out of the blue one morning after an extremely bad night, which had left her feeling too weak to leave her bed.

"Do you want me to call Sammy now? She's only in her bedroom," Andy asked tenderly.

"Please," Lynne answered quietly.

Sammy sat on the edge of the bed next to Lynne, and Andy pulled up a chair as close as he could get it.

It took all of Lynne's strength to finally say the words that she'd only ever thought about before. Initially she'd believed it the hardest decision to make but looking at the faces of the two people that she loved more than anything else, she realised that making the decision was relatively easy, compared to explaining her wishes vocally.

They both sat in stunned silence while slowly, painfully, they listened as Lynne spoke. "I hope you understand, and I hope you can forgive me," she said with tears filling her eyes. "I just can't do this anymore; I don't have anything left to fight with. I'm done." She could hardly bear to look at their faces as they digested her words.

Andy was struggling to comprehend what Lynne had just said and sat frozen in time. Sammy who was now in her very early teens, couldn't stand the silence anymore and leaning over she took Lynne's hand gently in her own. Her voice shaking with emotion she gave the woman that had been like a mother to her, who she loved very much, her total blessing.

"Whatever you decide, we'll support you with all our love always."

With tears cascading uncontrollably down his face, Andy climbed onto the bed next to his wife. He held her tenderly, her thin fragile body rested against his as she savoured his love.

In their early years together, Lynne had always known in her heart that she loved Andy far more than he did her, but over time that feeling faded and now right at this very moment she could feel the strength of his love as he held her weakened broken body.

Lynne closed her eyes, clearly, she could see the two of them together as they were years ago, and even now through the pain she could easily remember the feelings she experienced when she first met Andy, she smiled as she slept wearily.

It was less than a month later, in the arms of the man she loved and holding Sammy by the hand, Lynne passed peacefully away. For a long time neither of them could move as they realised the finality of the moment. Eventually, as their tears subsided, they kissed her goodbye for the final time, and clung to each other for strength as they watched her taken away. They were all alone once more.

***

With the incredible support of the staff, and in particular Jean Paul, Maria devised a programme of specific events designed to enhance and delight her guests that were available to book prior to arrival.

The reaction was incredible, from the moment they introduced them on their website, their guests were keen to book. The most popular was the champagne tasting classes, they were good fun and extremely informative and they received high praise for their professionalism. But it was a fast-paced world now and, after devoting nearly eighteen years to the hotel, Maria couldn't help feeling it was time to consider her future.

She'd seriously considered employing a full-time manager, if only to alleviate some of the pressure and the number of hours she worked, but deep down she knew she wouldn't be able to stand aside and let someone else run the show; that simply wasn't her style.

That only left her with one other option as far as she could see and she was pleasantly surprised at the speed an agent arrived to provide a valuation.

Not wanting to alarm any of her staff at this very early stage, Maria decided to spread the word that her accountant would be visiting and would probably expect a tour of the hotel.

"Will they be wanting lunch, or dinner?" the chef enquired as the senior members of her team sat listening to her explain the appearance of this stranger.

"I'm not sure." Maria was already feeling uncomfortable, without getting into more detail. "I think probably not, probably just coffee or tea and a sandwich will suffice." She smiled as she swiftly moved onto the next subject she wanted to discuss.

A few days later the agent arrived and seemed genuinely impressed as Maria presented her hotel. The valuation Maria received in the post a week later was far higher than she dared hope, and the prospect of this money would enable her to purchase a nice home for herself and secure a decent future. It was all very tempting.

A couple of weeks later, after giving it a lot of serious consideration, Maria decided to go ahead with a very low-key promotion to sell her precious hotel. The agents had been keen to explain that selling a hotel was not like selling a house. It was a very long drawn-out process, and it could take anything from a year to five years just to reach the right sort of client. She signed the relevant paperwork the agent required before they could market the hotel and immediately made the decision to keep this information to herself. If it was going to take years, the last thing she wanted was to lose any of her staff prematurely. She posted the signed documents and wondered where she would be in five years' time.

***

It was no good, Andy couldn't settle in this house that he'd shared happily with Lynne. It was full of memories; everywhere he looked all he could see was the image of his wife and although everyone told him that he shouldn't rush into anything, he knew he couldn't stay here. He needed a project, something to keep him occupied, especially at weekends; he absolutely hated the weekend. Everywhere he went all he could see were happy couples, happy families and people having fun and everything he saw compounded his grief and loneliness.

Sammy was a busy teenager; she was a fun-loving girl with lots of friends and her weekends were action-packed adventures. At such a young age she'd been a pillar of strength for Andy, but she needed her own space and he openly encouraged her to join her friends at weekends, wherever that may be.

In the end, after searching for many months, it was Tim that found a house that he thought might interest Andy. It was owned by one of his friend's parents, who were now needing 24-hour care, so it was no surprise that it was all in need of a thorough overhaul, but it was in a good size plot in a secluded avenue, not too far from where they lived now.

"Dad, it's absolutely awful," Sammy said as Andy walked her around the house.

"It is at the moment, but I've got loads of ideas."

"What, like knocking it all down?" Sammy said as she made her way out of the house. "Please tell me you're not serious about this." She looked at him intently, desperately seeking an answer. Andy just smiled; he still had a lot of work to do to impress her but decided for now, it was probably enough for one day.

It was about a week later during an overnight stay with her best friend Caroline, that Sammy had the opportunity to discuss the prospect of moving with another adult and understand her dad's logic. "I hope you don't mind," Caroline's mum began as she pulled up a chair to join the two girls eating their breakfast. "I couldn't help overhearing your conversation about this house your dad's found. I know it's absolutely nothing to do with me, but I know that when I lost my mum, I was a little older than you, Sammy, but I remember my dad explaining to me how difficult he found it just keeping himself occupied. Maybe your dad is just trying to keep himself busy; maybe this is just something he needs to do in order to keep his own sanity." She touched Sammy's hand before she put her chair back and left the two girls to finish their breakfast.

Later that night when Sammy returned home, instead of retiring to her bedroom, she curled up next to her dad on the sofa.

"What have I done to deserve this?" Andy said as he stroked her hair.

"I was just wondering if you still have all those plans that you were going to show me."

"I do," he replied.

"Shall we have a look at them now?" Sammy asked gingerly.

"Absolutely." Andy laughed as he pulled her up and dragged her into his study where he spent the next hour going through all his plans and ideas.

Unbeknown to Sammy, Andy managed to gain access to the property before they officially collected the keys. In quite a short space of time he had removed a wall downstairs and completely redecorated Sammy's room. As part of their deal, Andy had agreed that Sammy's room would be his first project. She'd been clear and concise of what she expected, and Andy had gone over and above her original requirements anxious to impress. He stood and admired the finished room, it was a lot bigger than her current bedroom; she had a designated area for her desk with built in shelves and cupboards and room for a comfy chair to relax and watch T.V. if she wished. He closed the door and smiled.

A week or so later, after officially collecting the keys, Andy drove Sammy to their new home and arrived minutes before the removal van.

"I'm not unpacking any of my things in that room until it's redecorated," Sammy declared as Andy opened the front door.

"Well, all your furniture will have to go in there, and you've got to sleep somewhere," Andy answered as the removal men brought in the first pieces of their furniture.

"Do me a favour, Sammy, just take your clothes up to your room, they can't stay down here," he said quite sternly.

"I'm not unpacking anything though," she repeated cheekily as she stormed up the stairs.

Andy waited at the bottom of the stairs. Suddenly her head appeared over the banister.

"Dad," she screamed with excitement. "It's amazing. My room is fantastic. When did you get all this done? I can't believe it; I love it so much." She ran down the stairs straight into his arms. "Thank you, Dad, thank you so much."

"I'm so glad it meets with your approval," he teased as she pulled a face.

"No slacking though, Dad," she said as she looked around downstairs. "This place is practically uninhabitable."

"Just wait," he said looking around. "It'll be amazing before you know it."

"I hope so, Dad, I really do," she said as she made her way back to her room eager to unpack.

Andy said goodbye to the removal men and walked slowly from room to room. For the first time he began to doubt himself. This was a huge project and maybe he shouldn't have been quite so ambitious. Anyway, it was too late now, he had no choice. He missed his wife; she would have put her arms around him now and given him all the encouragement he needed. For a split second he felt her presence and suddenly he knew she approved and would be with him all the way.

In the end the house took a lot longer to complete than Andy had originally planned, but now it was finished he was extremely pleased; it was everything they could ever need and was now their forever home.

It wasn't huge and he'd changed the layout considerably. Upstairs the two main bedrooms were now ensuite and the fourth smaller room was now Sammy's dressing room.

Downstairs there was a separate study/office, a good size living room and the main feature was the huge kitchen/diner that led straight onto the patio that was divided into two areas, one undercover and one open to the elements. Sammy's favourite area apart from her bedroom was the undercover patio which also housed the built in BBQ and sink area and often on a warm sunny evening Sammy would invite friends over for one of her dad's famous BBQs.

Andy enjoyed these evenings, he would cook all their food then disappear and leave them to it, happy just to know where she was and that she was safe. It wouldn't be long now before she would be off to university and he accepted that he was used to his own company anyway and wasn't interested in becoming involved with anyone else. He'd had the privilege of loving two exceptional women and that was enough for him.

***

It was a further two very long years before the day dawned that Maria would finally hand over the keys of her beloved hotel. She'd poured her heart and soul into this place and was surprised now, how much she was looking forward to passing the responsibility over to someone else.

She was heading back to her home county, far enough away not to be tempted to return. It was time for a clean break and a good long rest.

Her priority once the sale price was agreed was to make sure all her staff would be kept in employment for at least the next 12 months. They'd nearly all decided to stay on, which made everything so much easier, and last week they'd surprised her with a small leaving party.

She'd been fine until they presented her with a framed photo of them all outside the hotel with the caption "From your hotel family". This had brought tears to her eyes, and she rewarded them all with a cash bonus she thought they would all appreciate.

Handover day was awkward, with the new owners anxious to take over, Maria waited patiently for her solicitor to confirm completion before eventually she handed full ownership to this eager young couple. They were full of energy and new ideas and Maria wished them well as she said her final goodbyes.

She took one last look at the hotel before she climbed into her car and drove for the last time down the driveway. She smiled to herself as she remembered some of the huge life experiences that had passed her way.

She pulled out onto the road, she had a four-and-a-half-hour journey ahead of her and a whole new episode of life to begin.

CHAPTER ELEVEN

The Present...

Andy was miles away when he pulled up outside Kim's. It didn't even register that he'd parked behind Tim's truck. His head was all over the place, dissecting the events of the journey he'd just experienced with Maria, and he really couldn't concentrate on anything else.

"Everything ok?" Tim asked as he walked towards Andy who didn't even appear to notice him.

"Oh hi," Andy said glumly. "I didn't realise you were coming here today."

"I hadn't planned to but, as I was in the area, I thought I'd stop off and see how it was all going and Kim offered me a cup of tea, so it seemed rude to refuse…" Tim didn't bother finishing his sentence; it was clear Andy wasn't listening. "Hey, earth to planet Andy," he said waving his hands.

"Sorry, what did you say?" Andy asked, suddenly realising Tim had just spoken.

Tim raised his eyebrows and shook his head. "Have you had lunch yet?"

"No, I haven't had time, anyway I'm not that hungry." Andy sighed and attempted to smile.

"Well, there's definitely something wrong if you're not hungry," Tim said thoughtfully. "Come on, let's treat ourselves to a pie and a pint somewhere and you can tell me exactly what's happened."

"I'd love to, but Joe's been working on his own most of the morning, I need to get back."

"Well, tonight then, I'll see you in the pub at 6pm."

Andy nodded and smiled. "I'll see you later."

After a long laborious afternoon, Andy was glad when at 5.30pm they came to a natural end with their work for the day, which meant first thing in the morning they could start assembling the new kitchen units.

He climbed into his truck and was tempted to go straight home, but thought better of it and drove towards the pub. He had no idea if Tim was aware of what had been going on today, but as he'd mentioned something about tea with Kim, he assumed Kim had told him that he'd taken Maria over to collect her car.

Tim already had two pints on the table when Andy walked into the pub.

"Oh, I really need this," Andy said as he sat down and took a long sip of beer.

"Do you want to talk about it?" Tim asked casually, noticing Andy's tense expression.

"Don't know if there's that much to talk about really, I take it you know about the saga of the flat tyre."

"I do, and I was told that you'd kindly sorted it all out and had taken Maria over to collect her car. I take it from your expression, that didn't go too well."

Andy laughed. "Does it ever?" He took another sip of his beer before he continued. "In all fairness it wasn't too bad. She seemed keen to find out if I was aware they were making the wedding cake for Sammy, and that sort of led onto more questions about Sammy. Apparently, Maria had absolutely no idea that I'd ended up with sole custody…" His mind wandered for a second or two. "But then why would she? I didn't go into too much detail about Lynne, it didn't seem appropriate other than to mention I had to employ a Nanny."

"So, you didn't really find out very much about Maria then?" Tim enquired.

"No, nothing at all," he mumbled. "We ran out of time really."

"How was it all left? What happened when you got to the garage?"

"Before I even got a chance to say goodbye she rushed off as her car was blocking the way for someone else. That was it, she was gone."

After a moment's thought, Tim leant forward. "Look, mate, I'm going to tell you exactly what I know. Please don't ask me how, or why I know any of this, because I can never answer that question. Once I've told you, it will be entirely up to you what you do with the information. I just hope it helps and makes life easier for you."

Andy sat back in his chair and folded his arms. He had no idea what Tim was about to tell him, but he was certainly keen to find out.

Well over an hour later, Tim shrugged his shoulders and sat back in his chair. "There you have it, her whole life story, as I know it."

Andy shook his head in amazement. "Blimey, I would never have imagined any of that. I guess neither one of us had it that easy."

"Well, now you know, what are your plans?"

"Do you need to ask?" Andy said, smiling widely for the first time in a very long while, as memories of a trip to the fairground many years ago, sprang to mind. So, the fortune teller had been correct in her predictions after all, he acknowledged as he finished his pint. "I won't be in work tomorrow; I have a few things that need sorting."

"I understand." Tim smiled and nodded. "And good luck."

***

Kim hadn't found it easy to switch off, all night she'd been tossing and turning and still, this morning, had absolutely no idea how Maria would react to any of this information, or more importantly where would she even begin this story?

"I take it you've still not decided how you're going to tell Maria?" David asked, handing his wife a cup of tea as she sat on the edge of the bed.

"Thank you, I need this." Kim smiled at her husband. "No, I haven't really, it's just so intense. Just thinking about it all, I feel as though I'm intruding into Andy's private life."

David sat down beside his wife. "I understand. Are you sure it's something Maria needs to know, after all, it was all a very long time ago?"

Kim turned and looked at her husband. "Yes definitely, without question." She watched his response. "You don't agree?"

David shrugged his shoulders. "What do I know?"

"Well, I would want to know, so I think it only fair to tell Maria. Then it's up to her what she does next, if anything." Kim drank her tea. "Thanks for that." She handed him back her empty teacup. "I'm just going to grab a shower then I'll be down."

"I'm going to head off soon, so I'll see you tonight, good luck." David kissed his wife goodbye.

Maria was determined to start work early; she knew full well Kim would want word for word detail about what happened yesterday and was anxious to at least make a start on preparing some of her work for the day ahead.

It was only 8.30am when Kim arrived. Initially she'd hoped to sit down with Maria before she'd had the opportunity to begin her baking for the day, but as she walked up the drive, she could hear the unmistakable sound of the electric mixer, so detoured round to "The Bakery" entrance.

"Morning," she called, trying to catch Maria's eye.

Maria looked up and smiled. "I knew you'd be early today, but not this early. Give me a minute, I'll just finish this, and I'll be with you."

"Shall I go ahead and make some coffee?" Kim offered while watching her sister pour her latest creation into a ring mould.

"Ok, great, but I have to warn you, I really don't have too much to tell," she answered cheerfully.

Literally, minutes after Kim left to make the coffee, Julie arrived. "Gosh," Maria exclaimed. "Everyone's early today."

"The kids wanted to go to breakfast club, apparently most of the class go, so I agreed to one day a week, and they chose today."

"Actually, that's worked out well," Maria began. "I've got to have a quick meeting with Kim this morning, do you think you could carry on here?"

"Of course, what are you working on?"

It didn't take long for Maria to hand over to Julie and make her way inside the house to join her sister for coffee. "You should have popped over last night, if you were that desperate to know what was said." Maria sat on the stool watching her sister.

Kim placed two mugs on a tray. "Shall we take these into the living room? It's more comfortable."

Maria looked puzzled. "Honestly, it's literally going to take a matter of minutes to recite word for word what was said."

"I guessed as much, but that's not the real reason I want to talk to you."

"That sounds ominous," Maria remarked as they both made themselves comfortable. "What is it?" Maria asked, noticing for the first time how tired her sister looked this morning.

"I've got some information I think you should know. I promised that I wouldn't divulge my source, so please don't ask how I know all this, but take it from me, it's all true."

Maria felt compelled to ask. "Has this got anything to do with Andy, by any chance?"

Kim nodded. "Yes."

"Ok, well come on then, let's hear it," Maria said bracing herself.

By the time Kim got to the part in the story where Lynne lost her battle with cancer, Maria had tears in her eyes.

"Do you need a minute?" Kim asked sympathetically.

Maria retrieved a crumpled tissue from the pocket in her jeans. "No, I'm fine, carry on."

Half an hour later, Kim concluded her story with a huge sigh of relief.

"I saw them all once you know, outside their house," Maria announced reflectively.

"When?"

"Years ago, before I had the hotel. I went to look at a show house on a new development. Dad was going to come with me but had to cancel, so I went on my own. I remember the sales rep made a point of telling me that, apart from the three show homes, the other properties were privately occupied. I saw them pull up on the driveway of a house opposite. I thought the woman must be Sharon, but now I realise it must have been Lynne. They didn't see me," Maria explained woefully.

"Andy saw you, well he thought it was you, he only saw you from behind as you left the show house."

"No way." Maria shook her head in disbelief.

"He even drove by to see if your house was for sale."

Maria put her head in her hands and sat completely still while she tried to make sense of everything. "I feel really bad." She looked up at Kim, searching for an answer. "I never gave him the opportunity to explain, I was so wrapped up in my own anguish…"

"I didn't tell you all this to make you feel bad," Kim interrupted. "I thought it might help you to understand. You must have been curious to know if there was still a wife on the scene, I know you've noticed he wears a wedding ring…"

"You know I was curious; who wouldn't be? It's just this is a lot to take in." Maria stood up and walked to the window. "Do you remember when you had that meeting with our first Bride, who we now know to be Sammy, she mentioned her flowers would be in memory of her stepmum?"

Kim joined her at the window. "Yes, I do, I'd forgotten all about that. Well, obviously her stepmum was Lynne, previously her Nanny."

Maria continued to stare aimlessly out of the window. "I can't help it. I feel guilty. I should have been more forgiving and understanding. I even erased his messages without listening to them."

"Don't feel bad, after all it wasn't the first time, he'd done this was it? Nobody could blame you for blanking him; in fact we all encouraged it." Kim put her arm around her sister. "What do you want to do next?"

"Apologise, for starters," Maria said frankly.

"Well, it looks like you're just about to get your chance," Kim said pointing to the driveway. "Andy has just pulled up outside."

"Oh, my goodness, I'm not ready, I've got sponge mix on my jeans and…"

Kim gave her sister a big hug. "You look fine, honestly, I promise. Now go answer the door."

Maria took a deep breath. "Wish me luck."

"Good luck," Kim said and smiled before disappearing via the back door.